A Lesson Learned

Rosie Goodwin is the four-million-copy bestselling author of more than forty novels. She is the first author in the world to be allowed to follow three of Catherine Cookson's trilogies with her own sequels. Having worked in the social services sector for many years, then fostered a number of children, she is now a full-time novelist. She is one of the top 50 most borrowed authors from UK libraries. Rosie lives in Nuneaton, the setting for many of her books, with her husband and their beloved dogs.

Rosie GOODWIN
A Lesson Learned

ZAFFRE

First published in the UK in 2023
This paperback edition was published in 2023 by
ZAFFRE
An imprint of Bonnier Books UK
4th Floor, Victoria House, Bloomsbury Square, London, England, WC1B 4DA
Owned by Bonnier Books
Sveavägen 56, Stockholm, Sweden

Copyright © Rosie Goodwin, 2023

All rights reserved.
No part of this publication may be reproduced,
stored or transmitted in any form by any means, electronic,
mechanical, photocopying or otherwise, without the
prior written permission of the publisher.

The right of Rosie Goodwin to be identified as Author of this
work has been asserted by her in accordance with the
Copyright, Designs and Patents Act, 1988.

This is a work of fiction. Names, places, events and
incidents are either the products of the author's
imagination or used fictitiously. Any resemblance to
actual persons, living or dead, or actual
events is purely coincidental.

A CIP catalogue record for this book is
available from the British Library.

ISBN: 978–1–83877–363–2

Also available as an ebook and an audiobook

1 3 5 7 9 10 8 6 4 2

Typeset by IDSUK (Data Connection) Ltd
Printed and bound in Great Britain by Clays Ltd, Elcograf S.p.A.

Zaffre is an imprint of Bonnier Books UK
www.bonnierbooks.co.uk

In loving memory of Honey and Sassy,
my beautiful fur babies.
In between hello and goodbye there was
love . . . so much love.
'Some angels have paws'

Prologue

November, 1850

The young woman raced up the drive towards her home, her heart singing and her lips still warm from her lover's kisses. But as the house came into sight, she slowed her steps and began to walk more sedately. Not that there was much chance of her being observed, she thought. She had taken every precaution to ensure that no one would ever know she had even ventured out.

Her breath hung on the air and all around the grass was covered in a thick hoar frost. Somewhere a wise old owl hooted in a tree and she stopped in her tracks, holding her breath as she listened fearfully until her heartbeat slowed to a steadier rhythm and she continued on her way, trying to be as quiet as she could on the gravel driveway.

The house was in complete darkness as she entered and only the sound of the grandfather clock ticking away the minutes broke the silence. She smiled with satisfaction and tiptoed towards the stairs.

But she'd only taken a couple of steps when suddenly the door to her father's office banged open and her mother appeared like an apparition, clad in her long nightgown and holding an oil lamp aloft.

1

'And just where have *you* been, young lady!' Clara Bishop's voice was as cold as ice and in the dim light Olivia could see her eyes flashing with anger.

Heart hammering with shock, she licked her dry lips and said cautiously, 'I . . . I couldn't sleep, Mother, so I decided to go for a walk.' Even to her own ears the excuse seemed poor.

'And you *really* expect me to believe *that*, Olivia? I wasn't born yesterday, you know!'

At that moment Olivia's father appeared on the stairs, also dressed in his nightwear, and gazing down into the hall he hissed, '*Whatever* is going on, Clara? You'll wake the whole house bellowing like that.'

'Go back to bed, Charles,' she retorted sharply, her eyes never leaving her daughter's face. 'I think this young lady has some explaining to do.'

'Oh dear.' Sensing trouble, the man walked down the stairs. 'You haven't been out to meet that awful young boatman again, have you?' he asked his daughter anxiously.

The girl's brilliant blue eyes flashed and she stuck her chin in the air. 'He isn't *awful*,' she denied hotly. 'He's the nicest, kindest person I know.'

Her mother visibly shuddered as she conjured up a vision of the dark-eyed, dark-haired youth her daughter was so clearly besotted with. Moving forward she caught Olivia's arm roughly and hauled her into her father's office.

'This has got to stop *right* now!' Hands on hips she glared at her.

'You don't understand!' Olivia wailed, outraged. 'I *love* him!'

'Love, pah!' Her mother waved her hand airily. 'What has that got to do with anything? Why, if you were patient, you could marry Marcus up at the big house. He's only five years younger, and just think of the life you could have!'

'*Marcus?* But we're more like brother and sister,' Olivia snorted in disbelief, tossing her long silky black hair across her shoulder. Her father was the farm manager of Canal Farm, a large sprawling estate siding the canal in Tuttle Hill in Nuneaton, and this had given her mother ideas above her station. She was painfully aware that her parents only wanted her to marry Marcus Berrington, the farm owner's son, for the prestige it would bring. She was also aware that her mother cared not a bit about her happiness.

'*Enough!*' Her father stepped in.

But his wife ignored him and pointed a quavering finger at her daughter. 'Go to your room! Look at the state of you, standing there with your hair loose like a common whore and not even a bonnet on. We'll deal with this in the morning.'

The girl stared back at her for a moment, her face defiant. 'Very well, I shall do as you say, Mother, but I can assure you I shall feel exactly the same in the morning.' She wondered where she had found the courage to answer her back. Her mother had always been strict and she had always obeyed her orders, but this time she was prepared to make a stand no matter what the outcome.

'*Wh-what* did you say?' Clara boomed, her hands bunching into fists. 'While you are under my roof, miss, you *will* show me some respect!'

Her mother had never shown her any affection, even as a child, so Olivia supposed there was no reason to hope she would change now. She glanced at her father, but knew he was far too mild-mannered to stand up to her.

'I have always shown you respect,' Olivia said quietly. 'But I am eighteen and old enough to choose my own path in life, so you should know I intend to marry Reuben.'

Her mother's face turned a frightening shade of purple and she loomed over Olivia menacingly. 'You wouldn't last a single week living with the boat people,' she sneered. 'They're nothing but uneducated savages. How long do you think you would stick it? And anyway, I shall refuse to give my permission.' She swiped a stray lock of black hair from her forehead. 'And now I wish to end this conversation, apart from to say that if you persist in this silly obsession, I shall disown you!'

'Then so be it.' There was a tremor in Olivia's voice as she turned towards the door.

Clara grasped her arm and swung her about. 'Do you *quite* understand what I'm saying?' she asked incredulously. 'I'm telling you that if you walk out of that door now and go to *him* you will never be allowed to return. You will be *dead* to me!'

Wrenching her arm from her mother's grasp, Olivia nodded. 'I understand perfectly, and I'm sorry it has come to this, but I must follow my heart.'

November, 1851

'Come on now, one more good push should do it. An 'ere, bite on this els'n you'll be wakin' the dead wi' yer screamin', wench.' The old woman unceremoniously pushed a piece of wood between Olivia's teeth as tears streamed down the girl's pale cheeks. She felt as if she was being rent in two and desperately wanted Reuben by her side, but the men had taken him off to the inn, leaving the women to deal with the birth.

'That's a good little wench,' old Mother Adams told her as she narrowed her eyes and peered between the girl's slim legs. 'I can see the 'ead now. Another good couple o' pushes an' yer should be a mother. Come on, gel.'

With the last of her strength, Olivia pushed with all her might and seconds later the stifling cabin echoed with the sounds of a baby's cry.

The old woman, who was clad in a shawl and the customary black bonnet, common to the boatwomen, held aloft a small bloodied body triumphantly. 'It's a little wench,' she told Olivia as she quickly cut the cord that bound the child to its mother then deftly placed the shiny penny that she had ready over the child's belly button and tied it securely. Then she wrapped the wailing baby in a towel and handed her to her mother. 'An' a bonny little wench at that.'

Olivia stared at her daughter in awe, oblivious to the sound of footsteps pounding along the towpath outside.

Suddenly the cabin door burst open and Reuben Doyle rushed in, his face pale. 'Is it all over?'

'Aye, lad, nearly,' the old woman responded. 'Have a peep at yer new daughter then make yerself scarce till I bid yer to come back in.'

Cap in hand, Reuben quietly approached the bed and at the sight of the new mother snuggling the newborn he smiled.

'She's just perfect, Reuben.' Olivia smiled up at him, her face glowing.

A glimpse at the child confirmed what she was saying: the little one had a thatch of thick black hair as dark as the night, just like her mother's, and her eyes were a beautiful bright blue, nothing like the pale blue so common in most new babies.

'Ah, Livvy, me love.' Reuben was so emotional that he was almost lost for words and, as always, Olivia's heart swelled with love at the sight of him. With his shoulder-length curly brown hair and brown eyes he was a very handsome young man.

'What do you think we should call her?' Olivia asked and his face broke into a broad grin.

'Why, it's got to be Sapphire, ain't it? Our boat's called *The Blue Sapphire* an' wi' eyes that colour what other name could we find that'd suit her as well?'

Olivia nodded in agreement. 'And we'll call her Saffie for short, eh?'

He smiled, but then Mrs Adams shooed him away so he went to rejoin his friends in the inn where he would stand them all a jug of ale to wet the baby's head.

Once she was finally alone, Olivia stared at her brand-new daughter, and reflected on the year that had passed. In some ways it seemed much longer since she had left her mother and father, and it hadn't been easy. Reuben Doyle had lived on the canals all his life and soon after Olivia had joined him, he had bought *The Blue Sapphire*, a seventy-two-foot wooden-hulled narrowboat, for them to live and work on. It had a long hold at the front for ferrying the cargo and the living quarters was a small cabin at the back of the boat. It was so small they had to make every inch count and for some time Olivia had felt claustrophobic, but she had grown used to it and now took great pride in their home. There was a tiny black-leaded range that served for cooking and heating the room and it gleamed, as did the large copper kettle that stood on top of it. A cupboard housed their bed, which folded away neatly during the day giving them more living

6

space, and next to it a bench seat also pulled out to make yet another bed. Shelves ran along the top of the cupboard on which stood pretty plates and pieces of ornamental brass, again polished to a high shine. Flowered curtains hung at the tiny windows and rag rugs, which Olivia had painstakingly made on dark winter evenings when Reuben was at the inn, were thrown across the planked floor. She had strongly objected to him going off and leaving her alone of an evening when she had first joined him but she was used to that now too.

The outside of the cabin was painted red and blue with castles and roses, and on the cabin roof were a number of buckets and watering cans that Reuben had also painted in bright coloured patterns. At the moment the hold was full of coal that gleamed in the cold moonlight and Olivia was aware that whether she had just given birth or not, tomorrow they would have to continue their journey to deliver it to a factory in Coventry. Neither births nor deaths stopped the boatmen from doing their job and as Olivia had soon learned, they worked hard for every penny they made.

But for now she snuggled down onto the thin mattress and sighed with contentment as she placed baby Saffie to her breast for the first time. As the baby suckled, just for an instant she thought of the grandparents who would never get to know the child and she felt sad. But her parents had made their feelings clear on the night she had walked out to join Reuben and she knew there could be no changing their minds, and so she would just to have to make the best of things.

Very early the next morning she was woken by a thin mewling cry and the sound of Reuben clattering about the small cabin. He had made up the fire and was toasting bread on it for their breakfast, and the kettle was singing ready to make the tea.

'Now, don't go gettin' too used to this,' he teased with a twinkle in his eye as he poured the boiling water into a big brown earthenware teapot. 'I'll give yer today off the 'ard jobs to get yer strength back, but I'll expect you to be up an' about again properly tomorrer.'

She nodded as she sat up and lifted the baby to her breast. She was already dreading having to go back to work; she couldn't imagine finding the energy after yesterday's exertions, but needs must and the other women on the boats were always up working the very next day. It was just the way it was, and this was the life she had chosen.

It was almost seven o' clock that evening before they reached their destination and while Reuben and the factory workers began to shovel the coal from the hold she hurried into the cabin with Saffie, the warmth from the little range wrapping around them like a blanket. She fed and changed the baby and after settling her in a drawer she hastily set about peeling some vegetables to make a stew. Once the hold was empty, Reuben washed as best he could in the cold canal water before leading their old horse Nellie to the nearest stables. When he came back he found his wife fast asleep with a stew gently bubbling on the range.

The next morning they took on board a load of timber that was to be delivered to Warwick, and yet another hard day started, but today it was Olivia who led the horse along the tow path and opened and closed the lock gates as she

8

fretted about her baby who she had left in the drawer in the cabin. Every three hours she insisted on stopping so she could go inside to feed her, and although Reuben grumbled, he didn't stop her. They were further delayed by the snow, which now lay inches thick on the towpath, making it dangerously slippery for Nellie. And so, it was eight o'clock at night before they finally moored the boat in Nuneaton, and Reuben went off with Nellie to the stables.

Olivia had been distracted by thoughts of Saffie throughout the day's journey and now, in the peace and quiet, she became aware of just how close they were to her former home. In fact, she could vaguely see the roof of it from the small cabin window and she wondered if she should visit her parents and introduce them to their first grandchild.

'What do you think?' she asked Reuben later as he sat shovelling the remains of last night's stew into his mouth.

He shrugged. 'Suit yersen, wench. But I doubt yer'd get a very good reception.'

She chewed on her lip and when Reuben left to join the other boatmen in the nearest inn, she still hadn't made a decision. But then Saffie woke up for a feed and as she fed her and stared down into the child's startlingly blue eyes, she made her mind up.

'We're going to dress you up in your Sunday best and take you to meet your grandmother and grandpa in a minute,' she told the baby. *And I'd better tidy myself up while I'm at it*, she thought as she looked down at her drab black skirt and tattered shawl. Her eyes settled on her red, work-worn hands and she sighed. There was nothing she could do about them but at least she could get out the dress she had arrived in and make herself look presentable.

Half an hour later, she patted her hair into place. Her best dress was desperately tight about the waist and she realised with a little shock that she looked so much older than she had a year ago. But she'd had a lot of growing up to do in that time. So after throwing some coal onto the fire to make sure the cabin stayed warm, she wrapped Saffie in a thick shawl and they set off into the fast-falling snow.

As she approached her old home, she saw the lights shining in the windows and she suffered a momentary pang of regret as she remembered the home comforts she had once taken for granted. Her steps slowed as she suddenly wondered if coming back here was the right thing to do. She could well have the door slammed in her face. But then she took a deep breath and moved on. No matter how they had parted, surely her parents deserved to know they were now grandparents?

When Olivia reached the door, she knocked tentatively and soon she heard someone padding along the tiled floor. The door inched open and Minnie, the maid, peered out into the dark night, her face instantly breaking into a bright smile when she saw who it was.

'Miss Olivia!' She was so pleased to see her that she could scarcely speak. Mrs Bishop had fetched her from the work-house to skivvy for them some years ago and while she had been grateful to have a warm home and enough to eat, her mistress had never given her one kind word, whereas Olivia had always been nice to her. 'Eeh, it's good to see yer,' the girl whispered. ''Ave you come 'ome?'

Olivia shook her head. 'No, I'm afraid not. I've come to see my mother and father. Are they in?'

Minnie nodded, her face fearful as she glanced across her shoulder.

'Minnie, is someone at the door?'

Clara Bishop's voice echoed from the drawing room and with a nod towards Minnie, Olivia clutched Saffie to her and walked towards it.

Her parents were sitting in the wing chairs on either side of a roaring fire, sipping a glass of wine each. After becoming used to the confines of the small cabin she now lived in, to Olivia the room looked utterly enormous.

'Hello, Mother . . . Father.'

Their heads snapped towards her and for a moment they stared at her as if she were an apparition.

And then her mother broke the silence when she said cuttingly, 'So you've come back with your tail between your legs, have you?'

Olivia shook her head as her father rose from his seat and tentatively took a step towards her. 'No, I haven't actually. But I have someone here who I thought you might like to meet.'

She gently unwound the shawl and held the baby towards them. Then doing her best to ignore her mother's horrified expression, she said, 'This is Sapphire, your granddaughter, but we call her Saffie for short.'

Clara's face paled and she clutched at her chest, while, as always, Olivia's father said nothing.

'Our *granddaughter*! You dare to bring your bastard here to a respectable house and expect us to *accept* it? Why, you should be *ashamed* of yourself!' she spluttered. 'And what sort of a name is *Sapphire*? Are you a complete heathen now, like that terrible thug you ran away with?'

'Reuben isn't a thug,' Olivia answered evenly, choking back tears. Too late she realised what a terrible mistake this had been. But she had so wanted Sapphire to know where

11

she had come from and to have some sort of a relationship with her grandparents. 'And as for her name, we think it suits her.'

Her mother jumped out of the chair and waved her arm towards the door. 'Get out and take your flyblow with you! And don't *ever* darken our door again. You made your bed when you left to live with your *boatman* and now you can lie in it!'

Hearing the raised voices, the infant began to whimper. Olivia glanced towards her father, but his lips were set in a grim line as he stared into the fire, almost as if he couldn't bear to even look at her, so there would be no help there.

'Very well, I shall go,' she said quietly.

Out in the hallway, she found Minnie chewing on her knuckle with tears sliding down her face. The girl hurried to open the door for her and just before Olivia stepped out into the cold night she whispered, 'I'm right sorry it's come to this, miss. An' by the way, the baby is right bonny.'

Olivia reached up to gently touch Minnie's cheek. 'Thank you, Minnie. I think so too. Take care of yourself.' And with that she set off into the snowy night, thankful that she didn't have too far to go.

She was walking along the lane that led down to the towpath when she heard the muffled sounds of horse's hooves coming up behind her and, turning, she peered into the darkness as she stepped towards the hedgerow.

The horse had almost reached her when a voice she instantly recognised said, 'Olivia, is that you?'

'Marcus!' She smiled as the boy lithely hopped down from his saddle to stand beside her, and she realised that in the year she had been away, he had grown and was now somewhat taller than her. 'My goodness, you seem to have shot up all of a sudden.'

He grinned and asked, 'And who's that you have there?'

'It's my new baby daughter.'

Marcus looked momentarily shocked but all the same he peeped into the baby's shawl and said warmly, 'She's a little beauty. Like her mum, I suppose.' Then becoming solemn he asked, 'Are you happy, Olivia? It didn't half cause a palaver when you left.'

Olivia hesitated only a moment before answering, 'Yes . . . I'm happy enough. And what about you?'

He shrugged. 'Oh, you know, still doing battle with Father. He wants to train me to run the estate and I want to teach so there's no change there. But I missed you when you went.'

Until she was sixteen, Marcus's parents had allowed Olivia to join him in his lessons with a private tutor, and so she was very well educated. Too educated, her mother had used to complain, for she believed that girls didn't need as good an education as boys.

'I missed you too,' she told him, suddenly realising the truth of this. Even though he was just fourteen, they had always got on so well.

Seeing Olivia's teeth start to chatter, he said quickly, 'Look, it's been lovely to see you but don't let me keep you and the baby out here in the cold. You get off home and hopefully I'll see you again soon.'

Olivia smiled at him, then gingerly walked along the dark towpath to her boat. On her way past the inn, she glanced through the window and saw the boatmen with jugs of ale singing a bawdy song. She was perturbed to see Reuben in

13

the company of Seth Black, another of the boatmen who was fast gaining a reputation as being somewhat of a rogue. He always seemed to have a roll of money to flash about and seeing as he rarely did many deliveries it was being said that the cash wasn't always honestly come by. She sighed. No doubt Reuben would roll in blind drunk again; he always did when he was in Seth's company. But then she was getting used to it, and as her mother had pointed out, she had made her bed and now she must lie in it.

Chapter One

'Happy birthday, sweetheart.' Olivia handed her daughter a small package wrapped in brown paper and tied with string, and the girl's face broke into a warm grin.

'You didn't have to get me anything,' she said softly, trying to ignore the look of disapproval on her father's face. She knew that he didn't agree with her mother insisting on celebrating occasions like birthdays, Christmas and Easter but it was one of the few things her mother had stood up to him about. Now she opened her gift to reveal a beautiful shawl that had been lovingly knitted by her mother. It was in a very thin wool, which made the intricate pattern appear as soft as a cobweb, and it was in a lovely shade of blue that exactly matched her eyes.

'Oh, Mammy!' Saffie was deeply touched. She knew how many painstaking hours her mother must have spent knitting it when she was out of the way, either leading Nellie along the towpath or sitting at the tiller steering the boat. 'It's beautiful. I shall keep it for best, thank you.'

Her brothers and sisters then presented her with a handmade card that they had lovingly coloured in and had each signed for her. Saffie was aware that this was another thing her father wasn't happy about.

15

'Why waste their time an' yours on learnin' to read an' write when they don't need to?' he had asked his wife on more than one occasion but Olivia had been determined that the children should be educated to the best of her ability. Sometimes, if they were moored somewhere for more than a day, she would even get them to attend a local school in the area, even if it was only for a morning, and each of them, apart from Archie, could now read and write fluently.

Archie was a year younger than Saffie and the double of his father to look at and in nature, while Saffie took after her mother, although the years spent on the canal had not been kind to Olivia and the hard life she had lived had taken its toll on her looks. She was still only thirty-seven years old, yet she looked much older. Her once raven-black hair was prematurely streaked with grey, and following the birth of her youngest child, one-year-old Danny, her health had suffered too. There were six children in all now, although Olivia had lost two children at birth and two to an influenza outbreak two years previously. She had never been quite the same since and Saffie had taken over most of her mother's work.

At eighteen years old, Saffie had a string of admirers, which was hardly surprising as she had grown into a very attractive young woman, although she seemed totally unaware of the fact. Reuben had hinted that perhaps it was time to let her wed or set up home with one of the boatmen who were interested in her, but again, on this, Olivia had stood up to him.

'She's still only young,' she had told him, her eyes flashing. 'And anyway, she wants to be a teacher one day. She's certainly bright enough.'

'That's your problem, you've allus 'ad ideas above yer station, just like yer mother did,' Reuben had scoffed. 'Saffie were born on the cut an' no doubt she'll die on the cut, so make yer mind up to it, woman! You were her age when you came to me, in case yer'd forgot!'

Olivia had clamped her mouth shut. She didn't want to upset him and risk a clout. She could still remember a time when he had shown her nothing but respect and love, but all that had changed when he got in with Seth Black. Then as the years had gone by and he'd got in deeper with him, he'd started to change and now he was too handy with his fists for her liking. His one saving grace was that he at least confined his beatings to her and, in fairness, they were few and far between. She didn't think she could have borne it if he had hit the children.

Still, today was the birthday of her firstborn and Olivia wanted it to be a happy one so she asked him, 'Will we be getting a load on today?'

They had been moored on the canal in Birmingham for three days now after delivering coal to one of the large soap factories and Olivia had taken full advantage of the fact, taking all the children to bathe at one of the public bath houses and visiting the market where she had treated herself to some cheap, rather dog-eared, second-hand books from one of the stalls. Her need to bathe regularly was another thing Reuben had always found strange. He, and most of the other boat people, had always been happy to keep clean with a strip wash or a dip in the canal when it was warm enough, but Olivia would visit the bath houses on their route whenever she could.

He scowled and avoiding her eye he answered, 'Ner, me an' Seth 'ave got a bit o' business we need to see to so I might be away tonight, an' I'll need Saffie to do a delivery fer me this mornin'.'

17

Olivia's face dropped as she shook her head. Saffie had been doing deliveries for her father and Seth for some time now and Olivia was none too pleased about it as she had a good idea what was in the small, tightly wrapped parcels.

'Why can't Seth deliver whatever it is himself?' she dared to ask. 'It is Saffie's birthday after all and I wanted her to have an easy day.'

'He can't can 'e?' Reuben snapped. 'He can't read the street names.'

'I could do it,' seventeen-year-old Archie piped up. Admittedly he was nowhere near as good at reading as Saffie, nor did he have any wish to be, but he was sure he was good enough to read road signs and his father was his hero. Unlike Saffie, Archie had no desire to ever be anything but a boatie like his father.

'Or I could,' Elsie piped up. She'd be sixteen in less than a week and she was sick of her mother treating her like a child.

Reuben ignored his daughter, as he eyed his son, then seeing the determined look in Olivia's eyes he reluctantly nodded. 'Very well. But just remember, what you'll be deliverin' is worth a lot o' money an' if yer should lose it I'll skelp yer backside fer yer.'

'I won't lose it, Dad,' Archie promised earnestly, and minutes later he and his father left.

Elsie huffed and sat back, her arms folded. 'I could 'ave done it,' she said moodily.

'Well, if you're so eager to do something, then take some of the soup Saffie made to Cissie Black, will you? And while you're there, see if she needs any help with the kids. Poor woman's expecting again and she's been sick as a dog.'

Elsie grimaced. 'Can't Saffie do it? She's better with kids than me. I could go to the market instead?'

Her mother shook her head. She loved Elsie, but she knew if she let her go to the market with money in her pocket she'd be more likely to come back with ribbon and lace than the food they needed – and she'd take all day about it as well. 'Saffie'll be going later. So go on, do as you're told.'

'It's not fair,' Elsie moaned as she poured the soup into a metal jug. 'Saffie gets all the best jobs.' Then wrapping her shawl around her head, she stomped out of the cabin.

After she'd gone, Saffie settled the twins at the table in what was known as the bed hole, when her parents' bed was put away, and gave them a slate and some chalks to draw some pictures, while Danny had a nap.

'Right then, Mam, I doubt we'll see those two again today, and what's the betting Elsie will take her sweet time before she returns, so how about a nice cuppa, eh?' She was concerned about her mother who was looking decidedly ill lately. She had been so poorly following the birth of Danny that Saffie had insisted her father call a doctor in, a rare thing for the boat people who usually looked after their own themselves. The doctor had informed them in no uncertain terms that another pregnancy could be fatal for her and Saffie had noticed that since then her parents' relationship had become strained.

'That would be nice, love,' Olivia answered as she pressed the palm of her hand into the stitch in her side. It seemed to be worse lately, not that she complained. Her cough was getting worse too.

It was as they were sitting side by side drinking the hot, sweet tea that Olivia voiced something that had been on her mind recently. 'You know,' she began tentatively, 'that when the oldest child in a boat family reaches the age of eleven or twelve, they're usually found a job, either on another boat or ashore, and I've been thinking . . .' She glanced at her daughter to see what response she was getting. 'Well, now you're eighteen I've been thinking that the next time we're in Nuneaton I might have a word with Marcus Berrington, my old friend. He's a teacher now and I wondered if he might be able to help you become one too. You're certainly bright enough.' She saw a flash of interest flare briefly in Saffie's eyes but then she shook her head.

'It's a nice thought, Mam, but how would you manage without me? You're not well enough to do all the jobs I do. For a start off you couldn't manage to lead Nellie along the towpath day after day, or manage the opening and closing of the locks anymore.'

'Admittedly I couldn't,' Olivia agreed. 'But our Elsie could. She's nearly sixteen and it's about time she took on more work, so I think we'd manage it very well and I can't hold you back forever.'

'Hmm.' Saffie thought about it and supposed she was right about Elsie managing, but even so, the thought of leaving her family filled her with dread. She had never known anything other than a life on the canals and couldn't begin to imagine what it would be like to live in a cottage or a house. The only time she had ever done that was on the occasions when they had moored close to Dove Cottage, Granny Doyle's home in Aynho, near the Banbury Canal.

Granny Doyle was her father's mother and, as often happened with the elderly relatives of the boat people, she had settled into the cottage when she became too old and frail to work the canals anymore. She was a no-nonsense sort of woman but Saffie knew that beneath her hard exterior was a kind heart. Sometimes she and her siblings had stayed in her cottage with her and although it was only small, after living in the cabin it seemed enormous to them.

'Let's not make a decision just yet,' Saffie suggested tactfully as she set about cleaning the brass, for although the cabin was tiny, she took great pride in keeping it spotlessly clean.

Olivia in the meantime sat gazing anxiously from the cabin window. She was worried about Archie because for some time she had had a terrible suspicion that the parcels Seth and Reuben were having delivered contained drugs. If she was right and any of them were to be caught, she knew they would go to prison for a very long time. Even so, she tried to keep her smile in place and as she watched her oldest daughter diligently cleaning, her heart swelled with pride. Saffie was turning into a very beautiful young woman. Her hair hung down her back as black and shiny as wet coal and her skin was flawless, but it was her eyes that were her most striking feature. They were the colour of bluebells and fringed with long black eyelashes. Her skin was the colour of peaches and cream and her cheeks dimpled when she smiled.

Like her mother, Saffie was tall and slim and, again just like her mother, her thirst for knowledge was unquenchable. She would read anything she could get her hands on cover to cover, be it a book or an old newspaper, and many a night she would sit when the little ones were tucked up in their makeshift beds and read them a bedside story.

Over the years, Olivia had adapted to life on the canals, but she couldn't help but think that Saffie was wasted here, and that was why she had determined to speak to Marcus when they next moored in Nuneaton.

After lunch, which predictably Elsie had not returned for, Saffie set off for the nearest market armed with a wicker basket and some money to get some food in. Since she'd taken on this job, she'd become an expert at getting bargains and knowing which stalls in which towns and cities to go to. Her first stop was the fruit and veg stall where she purchased a selection of vegetables for the stew she would cook later that day, and after that she went to the butcher's where she got some scrag end of beef that she knew would be tender if it was chopped and cooked slowly. Next stop was the baker's where she purchased two loaves that had been baked the day before – they were cheaper than the freshly baked ones and, judging by the speed her younger siblings gobbled them down, it didn't seem to matter. She found she had a few pennies left and eyed the sticky buns, then making a hasty decision she had four packed into a bag as a treat. They could all have half a one each.

The light was fading quickly from the afternoon by then and the temperature had plummeted making her teeth chatter as she hurried towards the canal. Already frost was forming on the grass and it crunched beneath her ill-fitting boots as she hurried her steps, keen to get out of the biting cold. At last she was on the towpath and as *The Blue Sapphire* came into view, she picked up her speed, breathing a sigh of relief as she clambered aboard, glad to be home.

Her mother was still sitting at the side of the stove sewing. Elsie had returned and was helping her brothers and sisters with their reading under Olivia's watchful eye.

'How did you get on, sweetheart?'

Saffie smiled at her mother as she put the heavy basket down and lifted her shawl from about her head. Her hair had been woven into a thick black plait that lay across her shoulder like a silken rope and with her cheeks glowing from the cold, her mother again thought how beautiful she was.

'Fine. Soon as I've thawed out a bit, I'll make a start on the stew.' Saffie frowned as she glanced around and asked, 'But is Archie still not back?'

Hiding her worry her mother shook her head. 'No, not yet, but you know what he's like. He's probably gone off exploring with a friend or something. He'll be back when he gets hungry.'

Saffie nodded and lit the oil lamps before preparing the vegetables for their evening meal.

'How much longer is dinner gonna be, Saffie?' Elsie asked at seven o'clock that evening. Elsie was as thin as a rake, despite the fact she had an endless appetite.

Saffie glanced at her mother. The stew had been ready for some time and was gently simmering on the stove but Saffie had been waiting for Archie and her father to join them before serving it up.

'I think we'd best get them fed,' Olivia said. 'But be sure to leave a good dishful for your dad and Archie for when they get in. *If* your dad comes in tonight, that is,' she said quietly. In fairness, Reuben had warned her that he might not be back that evening but there was no reason for Archie being so late.

The meal was a somewhat subdued affair with all of them constantly looking towards the door for a sign of Archie but by the time they had eaten their fill and Saffie had got the younger ones settled for the night there was still no sign of him.

'Elsie, could you wash the pots and put them away while I go to look for Archie,' Saffie asked.

For once, Elsie didn't object; she could see how worried her mother was, and in truth, she was as worried as the rest of them.

Olivia nodded – normally she didn't like the older girls venturing out after dark, but she was too concerned for her son to put up an argument today.

Saffie set off wrapped in her shawl with her mother's old coat underneath it, although she had no idea whatsoever where to start looking. Her brother was never usually out this late and as she picked her way along the towpath in the dark, a feeling of dread settled around her like a shroud.

Chapter Two

It was shortly after nine o'clock that evening when the first flakes of snow began to fall and by then Sapphire was so cold that she couldn't feel her hands and feet. It felt as if she had walked for miles along the towpath in both directions from the narrowboat, calling for her brother in vain. Eventually she turned to make her way back to the warmth of the cabin, hoping that he would have returned before she got there. The towpath was a treacherous place to be in the dark with its ruts and hollows, and the fact that the snow was now falling steadily made it dangerously slippery.

When the dim light shining from the cabin finally appeared, she breathed a sigh of relief. Not far now and she would be in the warm again. The thought lent speed to her feet, but she was only yards away from it when a shrill whistle sounded behind her and suddenly there were police everywhere, jostling her out of the way as they ran past.

Pressed back against the hedge, she watched in horror as they reached *The Blue Sapphire* and clambered aboard, shouting and brandishing their truncheons. She heard her mother's scream and the sounds of the children's terrified cries and then she was running towards the boat, heedless of the danger of slipping and hurtling into the ice-cold canal water.

'What the *hell* is going on here?' she shouted when she pushed her way breathlessly into the cabin. Her mother and Elsie were sitting with their arms wrapped protectively about the children as the policemen searched every inch of the boat. Sapphire glared at them hands on hips as she repeated loudly to make herself heard, 'Just *what* do you think you are doing?'

The most senior of the policemen turned towards her as the rest of the men continued to drag things out of cupboards and ransack the place, and ignoring her question he asked, 'Where is your father?'

'I have no idea.' She stared back at him with her nose in the air.

He ignored her then as the search continued until finally one of the young bobbies told him, 'There don't seem to be anything here, Sarge.'

'Right, then get out and search the hold.'

The men trooped outside as Sapphire informed him angrily, 'They'll find nothing out there. We don't have a load on at present and the hold is empty.'

He again chose to ignore her as he made his way outside to his men and soon after they heard them climb back onto the towpath and the sound of their receding footsteps, muffled somewhat by the snow, which was now settling.

Saffie quickly shut the door to block out the cold and shook her head as she gazed about in dismay at the chaos they had caused. The cabin looked as if a tornado had torn through it. The contents of every single cupboard were strewn over the floor, even the bedding had been tossed about. It would take hours to put everything back to rights

26

and the police hadn't even had the decency to tell them what they had been looking for. The children's frightened sobs had turned to dull whimpers now and lifting Danny from the drawer where he had been sleeping, she snuggled him into her shoulder and crooned to him softly. He was so tiny for his age and sickly too, and as Saffie cuddled him the shock set in and she had to blink back tears.

'What do you think they were looking for?' her mother asked with a catch in her voice, clutching Elsie's hand.

Saffie shook her head. 'I've no idea.' A quick glance around told her that Archie hadn't returned but now she had more pressing things on her mind as she lay Danny back down and began to collect the bedding together and remake the children's beds. Quietly and without her usual fussing, Elsie helped her.

'Let's get you tucked back in,' she said in a falsely cheery voice. 'And then I'll make you a nice hot cup of cocoa and you can settle down while me and Elsie get everything put away again. How does that sound, eh?'

Sniffing and wiping their eyes they all obediently clambered back into their sleeping places and once the blankets were tucked about them, Saffie made them cocoa, whispering to her mother, 'We'll talk when the children have dropped off again, shall we?'

Olivia nodded, grateful that Saffie was there to take charge as she huddled by the stove. The fright had brought on a coughing bout and Saffie's heart sank to her boots as she glanced up to see there were spots of blood on the rag that her mother was holding to her mouth. But she said nothing until she was quite sure the children were asleep again and once Elsie, too, had settled into a restless sleep, she went to sit at her mother's side and ask quietly, 'How long have you been coughing up blood, Mam?'

Olivia looked momentarily startled. She had hoped no one had noticed but she supposed she should have realised she couldn't hide it from Saffie for long. The girl was as bright as a button.

'Oh, it's nothing to worry about.' She gave an airy wave, although they both knew that it was very much something to worry about. 'I'm more concerned about what your dad's been up to and where he and Archie have got to at the minute.' She shook her head. 'I've been waiting for the police to turn up at our door for years – ever since he started mixing with that Seth Black,' she lamented. Then with her eyes feverishly bright she confided in a hushed voice, 'I've got a horrible feeling that Seth has been dealing in drugs and he's got your dad involved in it. I know he deals in stolen goods too, but what do we do now?'

Saffie shrugged as she stared down into her cocoa. 'There's nothing much we can do but wait for Dad and Archie to come back. Meantime I'm going to get this place tidy again. You lie down and rest.'

Olivia felt so ill that she obeyed her and minutes later she had slipped into an exhausted sleep as Saffie replaced everything in the cupboards and tidied up.

The old tin clock on the shelf showed Saffie that it was gone midnight by the time she had put everything to rights and, lifting her shawl, which had been drying by the stove, she wrapped it around herself and stepped out onto the deck with the oil lamp held aloft, hoping for a sight of her father and brother. The towpath was deserted apart from a fat old water rat who plopped into the water at the sight of her and swam hurriedly away, so with a sigh she went back into the cabin and after removing her boots she lay down fully dressed next to the twins Ginny and Lucy on the pull-out bed. She was so worried that she was sure she wouldn't sleep but within minutes sheer exhaustion claimed her and the only thing to be heard in the little cabin was the family's gentle snores.

The following morning Saffie awoke to an eerie grey light shining through the faded curtains. After sitting up and knuckling the sleep from her eyes, she drew one aside to find that the glass on the inside of the window was laced with a thick layer of ice. Shivering she hurried to throw some coal onto the stove then set the kettle on top of it to boil. There was still no sign of Archie or her father and Saffie chewed on her lip. What would they do if her father didn't come back? And what could have happened to Archie? She had never known him to stay out all night before. Her thoughts were interrupted when her mother suddenly yawned and drew herself up onto her elbow to look around.

'Still no sign of them?'

Saffie shook her head, forcing a smile as she spooned tea into the teapot.

'Not yet but I'm sure they'll be back soon.'

At that moment there was a knock on the cabin door and they both jumped, wondering who could be calling at such an early hour. Pulling her shawl more tightly about her shoulders, Saffie went to answer it to find Cissie Black standing outside.

Saffie quickly joined her on the deck, closing the door behind her to keep the warm air in the cabin.

'I take it yer dad an' young Archie ain't come 'ome?' When Saffie shook her head, the woman sighed. 'I reckon the coppers 'ave arrested 'em,' she said quietly, her face strained with worry and even more pale than usual. 'They come an' went over every single inch o' the boat last night. Did they come 'ere an' all?'

Saffie nodded.

'An' did they take anythin' away?'

Saffie looked confused. 'Not that I know of.'

'Well, they did from our boat. There were little bags o' stuff hidden under the bed, though I 'ave no idea what were in 'em. My guess is the copper's 'ave caught 'em red-'anded doin' sommat they ought not to 'ave been doin', an' if that's the case I reckon we'll not be seein' owt of any of 'em fer a very long time.'

'*What?*' Saffie's hand flew to her mouth. 'You mean . . . you think they might have been arrested?'

Cissie nodded solemnly. 'I'm afraid that's *just* what I mean, pet. An' if I'm right, Lord knows what I'm gonna do, or you an' yer ma, fer that matter.'

Saffie stared down into the sluggishly moving canal water for a moment as she thought on Cissie's words, then reaching out she squeezed Cissie's arm gently.

'You must be wrong.' She was desperately trying to put a brave face on it, although her insides had turned to water. 'They'll probably come swinging along the towpath any minute now.'

'I 'ope yer right.' Cissie turned to leave. 'But I wouldn't bank on it. Seth 'as 'ad 'is 'ands into all sorts of illegal things for a long time an' I've been tellin' 'im it's only a matter o' time till yer get caught. But anyway, I'd best get back to me

30

nippers. Let's wait an' see what the day brings, eh?' And with that she lifted her drab skirts, climbed onto the towpath and stumbled away into a bright white world.

The children were all awake and watching the door expectantly when she went back into the cabin and forcing a smile she asked them, 'Who's hungry?'

A row of hands shot up so she told them, 'Right, get dressed and put the beds away while I make you all a nice bowl of porridge.' She nodded at Elsie, indicating that she should see to little Danny.

While the children were doing as they were told, Saffie crossed to her mother and quickly told her what Cissie had said.

Olivia swallowed nervously. 'I have been telling your father that no good would come from him mixing with that Seth Black since you were a baby. He has got away with it for so long that he probably thought he would keep doing so. I have been sick with worry at times over the years and now the worst has happened,' she muttered in a shaky voice. Despite the fact she felt Reuben had let them all down, she still loved him and couldn't envision life without him. 'But would he listen? No, of course he wouldn't, and *now* look at us. What are we going to do, Saffie?'

'We're going to have breakfast and keep things as normal as possible for the children at present,' Saffie informed her with a wisdom far beyond her years. Her mother was as white as the sheet she lay on but Saffie was determined to try to keep her spirits up, for the time being at least.

After breakfast Saffie and Elsie took the twins for a walk along the towpath to let them run off some of their energy, and they collected some holly to put in jam jars in the cabin. Once they tired of that they returned and she set them to working on their alphabet while she made tea for her mother and Elsie. The snow had started to fall again, muffling all sound, and they felt as if they were trapped in a white world of their own.

And then that afternoon, as darkness fast approached, there was another tap at the door and when Saffie answered it, she found one of the young policemen who had raided the cabin the night before standing there with a blush on his face and his helmet held in his hands.

'Miss Doyle,' he gulped. He was thinking he had never seen a prettier girl, as Saffie looked steadily back at him.

'Yes?' There was a note of impatience in her voice and after glancing across his shoulder to make sure that he hadn't been followed he leaned towards her.

'I shouldn't really be here,' he confided as the snow settled on his head and shoulders. 'But I thought I ought to let you know that your father and your brother have been arrested. I'm afraid they will be up in front of the magistrates sometime next week and my sergeant is saying that he reckons they'll go away for a long spell.'

'But *why*? What have they done?' Saffie couldn't keep her calm composure any longer and as he stared into her brimming blue eyes the young constable felt as if he could have drowned in them.

'They were caught burgling a house,' he told her solemnly. 'And a lot of stolen property and some illegal drugs were recovered from Seth Black's boat.'

'But there was nothing on ours,' Saffie snapped defensively, and the young man shrugged.

'No, there wasn't, but I'm afraid they all had plenty of stolen goods on them when they were caught red-handed last night.' He shuffled uncomfortably from foot to foot as he inched towards the towpath. 'Anyway, Miss Doyle, I, er . . . thought I'd let you know.'

Saffie looked so dismayed that he wanted to comfort her but of course he knew that he couldn't so he clambered off the boat and, after brushing the snow from his hair, he rammed his helmet back on and gave her a slight bow, before setting off back the way he had come.

Saffie stood there in shock. She realised then she should have thanked him – he hadn't had to come to tell them what was happening, after all. But then, she mused, perhaps it would have been better if they hadn't known. What was it her mother sometimes said? *Ignorance is bliss!* And now she had the awful job of passing on what she had learned to her mother. Taking a deep breath to compose herself, she turned and went back into the cabin.

Chapter Three

'So, what shall we do now?' her mother whispered when they were able to discuss the situation properly once Elsie and the children were asleep that night. 'We'd never manage to load and unload the barge as your dad does but we have to earn a living somehow. We need to pay for Nellie's stabling and feed ourselves, and we'll need coal for the fire.'

'We'll think of something,' Saffie answered with a positivity she was far from feeling. 'For a start off I thought I could visit the rag market tomorrow. I know what sort of things the boat people wear and if I got some clothes that need repair we could mend them, wash and iron them and sell them for a small profit. You've always told me that I wasn't a bad cook as well, so perhaps I could make large portions and sell dishes of stew for whoever wanted them. Word would soon go round and that would probably bring in enough to keep the wolf from the door, for now at least. If we can just get through the winter, things won't be so bad, and perhaps we could manage lighter loads in the spring?'

Her mother chewed her lip before a bad bout of coughing had her doubling over. Saffie hurried away to fetch her a piece of huckaback which Olivia placed over her mouth, and when she removed it Saffie's heart sank still further as she noted the tell-tale dots of blood.

'Mam, we need to get a doctor in to see you,' the girl whispered, but her mother shook her head.

'We don't have money for doctors.' Seeing the look of dismay on her daughter's face she reached out to pat Saffie's hand. 'Stop worrying. Come the springtime when the weather warms up, I'll be as right as rain, you'll see. But now get yourself off to bed and in the morning, you can visit the rag market as you said.'

Saffie pecked her cheek before going to cuddle down on the edge of the lumpy mattress with the twins, but the sound of her mother softly crying kept her awake until well into the early hours of the morning.

She woke early, feeling almost as if she hadn't been to bed at all and quickly made porridge and a large pot of strong tea for them all before telling Elsie, 'Get yourself wrapped up warmly. We're going to the rag stall in the market.'

'What for?' Elsie looked disgruntled. She wasn't any too keen to venture out into the cold. Neither she, nor any of the other children knew what had happened to their father and brother as yet and Saffie had no intention of telling them until their fate had been decided.

'We're going to buy some old clothes and repair them then sell them,' Saffie told her in a no-nonsense sort of voice. 'You're good at sewing and I'm not bad at it either. We're also going to make some stew and sell it to anyone who wants it.'

Elsie scowled. 'But aren't we going to be taking on another load when Dad and Archie get back?'

Saffie glanced at her mother and answered cagily, 'We'll see. But come on or all the best stuff will be gone.'

Elsie reluctantly did as she was told, and soon after they set off. It was so bitterly cold that the canal had actually frozen over in places and by the time they reached the path that would lead them up from the canal, their teeth were chattering.

'The snow's come over the top of me boots and I can't feel me feet,' Elsie complained but Saffie ignored her moaning and kept going.

The market was already surprisingly busy by the time they got there and once at the rag stall, Saffie began to rifle through the clothes as Elsie stood back with a sullen expression on her face. Eventually Saffie had a pile of clothes that she felt might sell for a meagre profit when some work had been done on them, and she began to barter with the woman who ran the stall until at last they agreed on a price and, after parting with some precious coins, Saffie stuffed everything into the large bag she had brought with them. She was painfully aware that every penny would have to count from now on. Next, they visited the fruit and veg stall and the baker's, and then she and Elsie returned to the boat, carrying the heavy basket between them.

By mid-afternoon, Elsie, Saffie and their mother were all busily repairing the clothes they had bought, and once done, Saffie carried them outside to wash them before pegging them along the lines she had strung up across the deck. The water in the barrel she had filled was soon cold and by the time she was done her hands were red and chapped.

'Come and sit by the stove,' her mother encouraged when she went back inside and Saffie was only too happy to do as she was told. She knew there was no way the clothes could dry in the snow and that the best she could hope for was that most of the water would drip out of them. Once it had, she would have to bring them inside to dry by the stove, which she worried would do her mother's cough no good at all, but what choice was there?

Hours later, when a huge pan of stew was simmering on the stove, Saffie sent the twins along the towpath to inform the boaties that were moored there that there was stew for sale if anyone wanted any, and she was gratified when three people turned up with dishes for her to fill.

'That's made us a few pence,' Saffie told her mother, hoping to cheer her up a little. 'It's not much but it's better than nothing.' The clothes she had washed were now drying two at a time over the back of the chair she had placed in front of the stove and the air was thick with steam, which made her mother cough even more.

'I think till the weather improves we'll just have to settle for repairing the clothes and selling them as they are,' Saffie muttered, realising that perhaps this hadn't been such a good idea after all.

The following morning Saffie made a large batch of scones and once word went round, they sold out quickly.

'We'll give up on the clothes idea and concentrate on the food, I think,' she told her mother, who agreed. The curtains and the bedding were damp from the clothes they had tried to dry in the cabin and Saffie knew that couldn't be healthy for anyone, particularly little Danny and her mother. Only that morning she had noticed that Danny felt unnaturally hot and by the evening he was coughing and red in the face.

'We're going to have to fetch the doctor to him if he isn't any better in the morning whether we like it or not,' Saffie fretted as she sponged his forehead with a cool cloth. She was blaming herself because of the damp atmosphere he had been in but it was too late to do anything about it now.

The only good thing that had come from her first idea was the fact that she had managed to sell an old shawl and two thick skirts to the boatwoman who was moored a short way from them. The small amount of profit would pay for a doctor if need be.

The night seemed endless as Saffie sat with her little brother, tenderly mopping his head with cool water and singing lullabies to him while the rest of the family slept. But finally, as dawn was breaking, he too drifted off to sleep in Saffie's arms and soon she was softly snoring too.

'Saffie, Saffie . . . wake up. Something's wrong with Danny, look.'

Saffie's eyes snapped open to see little Ginny hanging over her with a frightened expression on her face.

'Wh-what?' She blinked to try and wake herself up properly. and as she placed a hand on his forehead, her heart skipped a beat. He had been burning up the night before but now he felt unnaturally cold.

'What's the matter?' Olivia swung her legs over the side of the bed and wobbled across to her, which set her coughing, and as she stared down at her little son, tears sprang to her eyes as she lifted his small frame from Saffie's arms. 'Oh no . . .' Her voice was so low that Elsie drew the children into her arms as they stared at her. Something was seriously wrong.

'Is he worse, Mam?' Saffie asked in a hushed voice.

Olivia dropped down onto the side of the mattress as she gently closed Danny's staring, unseeing eyes, then nodded. 'Yes, pet, I'm afraid he's gone to be an angel.'

Saffie's head wagged from side to side in denial as a cold hand closed around her heart. 'No, no he *can't* be dead! He was all right yesterday!'

38

'He hasn't really been well since the day he was born,' her mother told her in a wobbly voice. 'I think he was only lent to us. He was too good for this earth.'

Elsie and the twins were crying now as Olivia gently laid the little boy on her own bed and pulled a sheet across his face. This on top of Reuben being arrested was just too much to take in and she felt as if her heart was breaking. 'Is Mother Adams still moored nearby or have they moved on with a load?' Olivia asked dully, and without even waiting to put any shoes on Saffie went out onto the deck and shielding her eyes with her hand she peered into the softly falling snow.

'She's still there,' she told her mother when she re-entered the cabin. 'But it looks as if they're preparing to pull away. Mr Adams is getting the harness on their horse.'

'Good. Then run and tell her I need her.'

Once she'd pulled on her boots, Saffie was off like a whippet and when she stumbled into the small cabin aboard old Mother Adams's boat the woman stared at the girl's red eyes questioningly. She was the one who had brought Saffie into the world and she had always had a soft spot for her. 'So, what's to do then?'

Saffie sniffed and gulped back tears before telling her chokily, 'It's Danny. He's died and me mam asked me to fetch you.'

The old woman wasn't surprised. She'd seen Danny on a number of occasions since he'd been born and each time, she'd feared for him. The poor little chap had been so weak and frail that he had always looked as if one good puff of wind would blow him away. 'I see.' She pulled her black bonnet on and placed a thick shawl about her shoulders before following Saffie back out onto the deck where she told her husband, 'I'll not be long, Wilf. The Doyles have had a bereavement.'

'I'm right sorry to 'ear that, lass,' the old man told Saffie.

Once in Olivia's cabin the old woman looked at Danny and nodded. 'Aye, yer right, lass. He's gone, God bless his little soul.'

'So, what do I do now?' Olivia asked tearfully. 'He needs to be laid to rest but I don't have enough money to pay for the funeral.'

'Then you must give the undertaker a penny and he'll see to the rest,' the old woman advised. 'There's plenty of old folk as pass away in the winter an' the next one he buries he'll see that Danny is tucked in at the side of 'em.'

Olivia wrung her hands. 'But we won't even know where he's been laid to rest if I do that!'

'No, yer won't, but at least you'll 'ave the peace o' mind of knowin' that he's laid in hallowed ground. It's either that or a pauper's funeral. Which do you prefer?'

'The first one, I suppose.'

Olivia looked so ill herself that old Mother Adams placed a gentle hand on her shoulder. She'd heard that her man had been arrested and now with this on top it was no wonder she looked so ill. 'You'll come through this, pet. Yer may not think yer will right now but the good Lord will never 'eap more on yer shoulders than yer can bear.' She turned to Saffie, for it was more than obvious that Olivia wasn't capable of doing anything. 'Get wrapped up warm an' then go an' enquire where the nearest undertaker is, then bring 'im back with yer, there's a good girl,' she told her and Saffie nodded through her tears as she blindly began to pull her clothes on.

The man arrived at the boat late that afternoon, pulling a small handcart through the snow on the towpath. Olivia had dressed little Danny in his Sunday best and when the man lifted him to bear him away, after accepting the penny for his burial, she kissed the child and cried as if her heart would break while Saffie and Elsie tried to console the rest of the children.

It was only when they had all fallen into an exhausted sleep that night that Olivia looked at Saffie's face sadly. She was little more than a child herself but since her father's arrest she had taken on even more responsibilities of the family. For the first time Olivia questioned if she had done the right thing when she had chosen this way of life. Had she married a man of her mother's choice she had no doubt she would be living a life of luxury now. The only trouble with that was she knew she would never have loved anyone else as she had loved Reuben.

'I'll make it up to you, my sweet girl,' she whispered tenderly as she stroked a lock of silken hair from Saffie's flushed cheek, and then she returned to her lonely bed to grieve for her youngest child.

Chapter Four

December, 1869

Christmas had come and gone uncelebrated on *The Blue Sapphire*. There was little to be joyous about, and even if there had been there was not a penny to spare for festivities. As for poor Elsie, her sixteenth birthday passed unnoticed, and though she tried not to feel hurt by this, she couldn't deny that she did, even though she understood. They were living on the few pennies that Saffie managed to earn from her cooking and up until now, they had just managed to pay for Nellie's stabling, buy coal for the stove and eat.

Thankfully the snow had stopped falling a few days after Christmas but now it was hard-packed and frozen, making stepping outside treacherous. In a few days' time it would be the New Year but Saffie and her mother were not looking forward to it. Normally on New Year's Eve people would be in and out of each other's boats welcoming the New Year in and offering a toast, but word of Danny's death had spread and the rest of the boat people were keeping away and respecting their privacy.

'I think we should head for Granny Doyle's when the thaw sets in,' Olivia suggested one morning. 'There's nothing to be gained from staying here any longer and at least there, the little ones could sleep in the cottage.'

The same young policeman who had visited them to tell them of Reuben and Archie's arrest had visited again shortly before Christmas to tell them that they had both been convicted. Reuben had been sentenced to ten years hard labour, but worse still, because of his young age the judge had decided to make an example of Archie and had sentenced him to serve ten years in Australia. By the time Constable Denning told them, though, the convict ship had already sailed and taken Archie to his new life, and he had no idea which prison Reuben had been sent to. Olivia was mortified.

'But my son is only seventeen,' she had cried and the young bobby had shaken his head. There was nothing he could say to make things any better. He had often heard the boat people referred to as 'water gypsies' but having met Olivia and her family he had nothing but admiration for them. Their living quarters were admittedly cramped, but he noted they were spotlessly clean, as were the children, and they were all very well spoken.

Once he had left, Olivia had a lot to think about. Deep down she knew her days were numbered and that somehow she must ensure her children would be safe, which was why she had suggested they travelled to Granny Doyle's. Although the woman was old, she was as fit as a fiddle and she had no doubt she would look after the twins, and perhaps Elsie could find a job near the cottage. And as for Saffie . . . Olivia glanced at her daughter, and her heart ached. The girl was the one who was keeping the family together now and Olivia was ashamed that such a burden should have fallen on such young shoulders. When the young policeman had called, she had instantly recognised that he was smitten with her daughter, and it was no wonder. Saffie was very attractive and it hit Olivia that she was no longer a young girl but a young woman. Many of the other girls who worked the canals were married by her age so the last thing she wanted to do was leave Saffie with the responsibility of the twins. She was clever and bright and Olivia wanted her to have a chance to make something of her life.

Now as Saffie considered her mother's suggestion, she slowly nodded. 'I suppose it would make sense to head for Granny Doyle's,' she admitted.

Elsie pulled a face. Like her sister she was pretty, but the difference between them was that Elsie knew it. '*Why* do we have to go there?' she pouted. 'It's so quiet and there's nothing to do.'

'I think it's our best option at the moment,' her mother told her. 'We can't just stay moored here.'

'Then why don't we pick a load of coal up from Griff Colliery and drop it in Coventry on the way?' Saffie suggested.

Elsie stared at her, aghast. 'And how are we supposed to do that without Dad or Archie to help? Do you realise how long it takes to load it?'

Saffie stared calmly back at her. 'Of course I do. But I'm sure with you and me and the twins to help we could manage it, and then at least we'd have some money when we got to Granny Doyle's.'

'But we'd be filthy!' Elsie looked horrified. 'And unloading it in Coventry will be even harder. It could take us a whole day of hard slog!' She had never been keen on hard work.

Saffie shrugged, in no mood for an argument. 'So? What if it does take a while, and we'll wash, won't we?'

Elsie's heart sank as she realised her sister meant it.

A week later in January, Saffie rose early one morning to fetch Nellie from her stable and they prepared to leave.

'I'll give you a choice,' she told a disgruntled Elsie. 'Either you can stay aboard and steer or you can lead Nellie on the towpath and open and close the locks on the way.'

Elsie was clearly none too keen on either option. 'I suppose I'll stay on the tiller,' she answered sullenly. 'All that walking makes me legs ache.'

'You'd best get well wrapped up the pair of you,' Olivia told them, glancing towards the tiny cabin window from her place in the bed. She had been too ill to get up for days now and even though she was resting, her cough was getting worse.

Muttering to herself, Elsie began to pile on layers of clothing until only her face was showing before ungraciously going outside to take her place at the tiller. Saffie, meanwhile, took Nellie's reins and urged her forward, and once Elsie had steered the boat from the bank it began to glide slowly through the water as Nellie plodded along.

Each time they came to a lock, Saffie would leave Nellie waiting patiently while she took the wooden windlass to open the lock gates, and so they went on until early in the afternoon when Elsie shouted peevishly, 'Can't we have a stop now? Me hands and feet are frozen to the bone and me stomach's rumbling.'

The thaw had started and Saffie was soaked to the skin from the water that had dripped onto her from the hedgerows as they passed, so she nodded. 'All right, but just for half an hour, mind. I want to get to Napton before dark.'

Birmingham was now far behind them and above, the clouds hung low and dark making it appear as if it was later than it was. Saffie's boots were sodden through from plodding

45

through the puddles that had formed, and as Elsie steered the boat to the side Saffie quickly threw a blanket over Nellie's back and placed her nose bag on her so that she could rest too.

'Oh girls, you look frozen through,' Olivia fretted as they entered the cabin.

Saffie took her boots off and placed them by the stove then hurriedly served them all up a dish of the stew she had cooked the night before. After eating it and drinking two mugs of strong tea, she felt a little warmer and was ready for the off again.

'Those boots will be nowhere near dry yet,' Olivia told her worriedly.

'Don't worry about that. I'll line them with some old newspaper,' Saffie told her with a smile. 'And I'm going to get out of this wet skirt too and wear a pair of Archie's breeches.' Her skirts were soaked through to just below the knee and were making her legs sore.

Olivia looked mortified at the thought of her beautiful daughter wearing men's trousers but she didn't argue because she knew it made sense.

Once she was changed and ready for outside again, Saffie nodded towards Ginny and Lucy. 'Now, you two, you can wash the pots up and polish the horse brasses and the door handles this afternoon. And make sure you look after Mam as well. It will give you something to do.'

They set off again with Elsie still muttering mutinously to herself, and as they progressed into the Warwickshire countryside Saffie enjoyed the feeling of the wide-open spaces. They were surrounded by rolling fields that would be full of sheep and cows in a few months' time, and dotted here and there were pretty cottages with smoke drifting lazily from their chimneys. After the confines of being moored in the centre of Birmingham for so long it was like another world and Saffie tried not to think of her father, Archie and baby Danny as they moved along.

It was late afternoon when they arrived in Napton and, after gliding through the network of canals, Elsie steered the boat into a loop of water and drew it to a halt.

'You go in now,' Saffie told her as she took the ropes from Nellie's back. 'And heat up the rest of the stew. Get the rest of the bread buttered as well. I'll be in when I've got Nellie settled for the night.' She led the horse away, and this time Elsie was only too pleased to do as she was told and escape to the warmth of the cabin.

'I shall have to go into Napton first thing tomorrow morning and get some bread and supplies,' Saffie told them as they finished off the stew that evening.

'Can't we have a change from stew all the time,' Elsie grumbled as she mopped her dish with the last slice of bread.

'We've done well to manage to eat at all.' Saffie glared at her as she counted out the last of their money. It was just as well they had decided to pick up a load because their money was almost gone, so was the coal they had left in the hold.

When they'd finished, Ginny and Lucy obligingly washed the dishes while Saffie pulled the beds out and soon after they retired – there was nothing else to do, but at least it was warm and cosy once they were all tucked in. Even so it was a long time before Saffie could sleep as she listened to her mother's hacking cough and for the first time a little shiver

47

of dread ran up her spine. They had already lost Danny, and her father and Archie were as good as lost, and now she wondered what would happen to them all if they were to lose their mother as well. It was a daunting thought and when she finally slept her dreams were troubled and she woke the next morning feeling once more as if she hadn't been to bed.

It was gone ten o'clock the next day before they finally set off again. Saffie had sent Elsie to fetch Nellie from the stables while she popped to the nearest shop to get provisions. It was another bitterly cold and overcast day, but even so, Saffie felt at peace as she led Nellie along. There was something special about the deserted fields they passed with no one in sight and nothing but the sound of the water slapping the sides of the boat and the birds in the trees. She was painfully aware that once they reached Banbury, she should take *The Blue Sapphire* to be recaulked but she doubted they would have the money and decided she would worry about that later. First they had to get to Griff Colliery and hope that they would be able to get a load to deliver.

When they did eventually reach the colliery, Saffie made Elsie stand with Nellie while she went to find the office. Her father had always done it before and when she told the stern-looking man behind the desk what she had come for he ran a hand through his halo of thinning grey hair as he peered at her over the top of his metal-framed glasses.

'*You* want a load?' His voice was incredulous.

'Yes, I . . .' Saffie gulped before rushing on. 'My father usually deals with you. Reuben Doyle but he's . . .' When her voice trailed away, his face softened. He knew Reuben Doyle all right and he'd heard through the grapevine about his imprisonment. Personally, he'd always found Reuben a good, hardworking sort of chap. It was just a shame he'd got in with a bad one. That Seth Black who'd gone down with him would have stolen from his own grandmother. But now he was faced with a dilemma: could he trust this young slip of a girl to deliver a heavy load of coal? His expression must have betrayed his thoughts, because without him uttering a word, the girl suddenly blurted out, 'You can trust me, sir. I'm stronger than I look and I have sisters who'll help me. If you'll just let me have a load, I'll get it there on time, I promise!'

'Hm.' He scratched his chin as he stared down at the book in front of him. There was a load of coal that needed to go out today as it happened. 'Very well, steer the boat over to this side and you can start shovelling the coal into your hold. There's a pile there ready to go. But it'll be hard work, mind!'

Saffie's face lit up and even in her ugly outfit with her hair hanging in a thick braid across her slim shoulder like a velvet rope, he thought how pretty she was.

'Thank you, sir. You'll not regret it.' She quickly took the ticket he held out to her, as if she was afraid he might change his mind.

'When you reach Coventry, hand this in to the gaffer there and he'll pay you when you've unloaded. Shall I read out where it's to go?'

'Oh, no thank you. I can read it myself,' she assured him, surprising him even more and as she bounced out of the office, he scratched his head. It wasn't often he met a lass like that in this place!

Chapter Five

'This is it, Elsie, we're here!' Saffie shouted from the towpath as they arrived at their drop-off point in Coventry. 'Steer her into the side, please.'

There were already a number of boats there loading and unloading and after Elsie had managed to manoeuvre the boat into position, two men came forward to take the delivery slip from Saffie, eyeing her curiously.

They recognised her as the Doyle girl – a pretty face like hers was hard to forget. 'Dad not here, lass?' the older of the two men questioned and Saffie shook her head as she placed Nellie's nose bag on her. It had taken a long time to get here as the boat was low in the water and slow with its heavy load, and Nellie was tiring.

'No, it will be me and my sisters unloading today,' she answered.

The two men glanced at each other; clearly word of what had happened to Reuben and Archie hadn't reached this far yet.

'Are yer sure you'll manage?' The man looked doubtful. 'There's an awful lot o' coal there fer you little 'uns to unload.'

'We'll be fine.'

At that moment Lucy and Ginny came out with their shovels to join her. They had seen their father do this job dozens of times and were more than willing to help, little as they were.

'In that case, here's the barrer. Pile it over there an' I'll pay yer when it's all done.'

Saffie nodded and she and her sisters set to, Elsie muttering all the while. In no time they were black with coal dust from head to foot with only the whites of their eyes showing. At first it seemed the load wasn't getting any smaller as they shovelled away, but by the time the light was fading, they could finally see that they were winning. The smaller two were having to stop to rest frequently by then and were totally exhausted, although they didn't once complain, and Saffie was proud of them. Elsie, on the other hand, did nothing but moan, so Saffie ignored her. The way she saw it, what they were doing was as much for her benefit as theirs so she would have to pull her weight whether she liked it or not. As darkness closed in a slow drizzle began to fall, adding to their discomfort, but they worked on diligently until at last, the coal stood in a shining heap on the bank. Saffie ached so much it took all her energy to climb the bank and make for the office.

'Yer managed it then?' She found the older man who had greeted them earlier in the day sitting behind the desk, and she nodded as he counted out their wages.

Ginny, Lucy and Elsie were already in the cabin when she arrived back at the boat but she summoned Elsie, saying, 'Come on, we need to get to the next moorings now and get Nellie stabled for the night. She's worn out, poor old thing.'

Elsie groaned but did as she was told, leaving the twins to wiggle out of their filthy clothes. Once they were moored, Saffie would put all their clothes to soak overnight in a barrel on the deck, although she had no idea how she was going to get everything dry once they were washed. Still, that was the least of her worries for now. At least they had some money again so they would be able to eat. She'd also kept enough coal back to feed the stove until they got to Granny Doyle's so things were looking up.

It took another half an hour to reach the next moorings and once there Elsie went back into the warm while Saffie went to settle Nellie in the stables for the night.

'You've all done so well. I'm so proud of you,' Olivia told them as Elsie opened the door to the stove and started to toast some bread on the long brass toasting stick. It hurt her to see her girls having to work so hard and she felt guilty that she hadn't been able to help.

'I'll walk into town and get us some pies for dinner when I've got out of these dirty clothes and had a strip wash.' Saffie pressed the hard-earned money into her mother's hand and quickly went behind the curtain that stretched across the cabin separating the beds, where she could wash in privacy. Lucy and Ginny were already asleep, worn out after all their hard work. She found a bowl of canal water that had been warmed on the stove waiting for her and hurriedly made herself as clean as she could, although she would have loved nothing more than to get into a warm bath. Perhaps tomorrow there would be time before they set off to take the girls into Coventry to the public bath house? It would be lovely to be able to wash her hair and feel clean again.

Once she was respectable, Saffie visited the nearby shop and bought them hot pies for their supper, which they ate in silence before falling asleep.

At first light the next morning, she got up before anyone stirred and began the back-breaking work of scrubbing the hold out. It was lined with a thick layer of coal dust and, one after another, she hauled buckets of water from the canal to sweep it out. She was filthy by the time she had finished and the muscles in her arms felt as if they were on fire from lifting the heavy buckets. Even so, she felt a little thrill of satisfaction as she eyed the end result. Her father had had his faults but he had always taken pride in keeping his hold clean and somehow Saffie felt that she shouldn't let him down, even if he wasn't here to see it.

Ginny was stirring a dish of porridge on the stove when Saffie entered the cabin again and glancing behind her, her mother asked, 'Where is Elsie? Isn't she with you?'

Saffie frowned as she paused in the act of stepping out of the filthy trousers she had been wearing. 'No, I thought she was still in bed.'

'She went out just after you this morning. I thought she was coming to help you,' Lucy piped up.

Olivia looked worried. 'Did you notice what she was wearing?'

'Yes.' Lucy grinned as she reached for some dishes and began to set them out on the small table. 'She was all done up like a dog's dinner in her best dress and Saffie's best shawl. I thought perhaps she was going to get the shopping for you.'

'She couldn't have been. She doesn't have any money.' Olivia chewed her lip as she looked at Saffie. 'You don't think she's run away, do you?' Olivia had known for some time that Elsie wasn't happy with her life on the boat, even more so since her father and Archie had been gone.

'Where would she go?' Saffie said sensibly. 'Stop worrying, she'll be back. But now let's eat. All that cold air has given me an appetite and the porridge might warm me up.'

They ate their breakfast in silence but Saffie noticed that her mother didn't manage more than a couple of spoonfuls. She then got changed and went into the town to get some food for them all, hoping that when she returned Elsie would be home. But she wasn't, and as Saffie began to prepare some potatoes and vegetables to go with the scrag end of beef she'd bought for their dinner, she began to worry – although she was careful not to show it in front of her mother, who was staring avidly towards the tiny leaded window in the cabin. They had hoped to set off soon after lunch but if Elsie didn't return that would put paid to that idea.

The meal was almost cooked when Elsie breezed in, her face glowing. 'You'll never believe what's happened,' she gushed excitedly. 'I've got myself a position in one of the big houses.'

Olivia looked shocked. 'What do you mean *a position*? Are you going to be a maid?'

'Well . . . not exactly. At least not straightaway, but the housekeeper says if I work hard, I might soon get promoted.'

'So what will you be doing then? And why didn't you ask me about this before you went charging off?'

Seeing that her mother was none too pleased with her, Elsie sniffed haughtily. 'I didn't ask cos I knew this would be the reaction I'd get from you, and if you must know I shall be starting as a laundry maid!'

'A laundry maid!' Saffie grinned. Elsie had never been fond of hard work and she couldn't imagine her doing such a job.

'Yes, a *laundry maid*. And what's wrong with that? It's a good honest job and lots of boat girls of my age are working, so why shouldn't I?' Her blue eyes were flashing now as if she was daring Saffie or her mother to try and stop her.

'It's very hard work,' Saffie pointed out but Elsie tossed her head.

'Huh! It can't be half as hard as what you had us doing yesterday. I'm done with life on the cut and people always looking down on us, so I'm starting tomorrow, don't try and stop me.'

Olivia's eyes were brimming with tears as she stared back at her rebellious young daughter. They were still grieving for baby Danny and were missing Archie and Reuben, and the thought of Elsie leaving them too broke her heart. The family seemed to be shrinking so quickly, but Olivia was wise enough to admit that both Elsie and Saffie had stayed with her far longer than most young boat people did, and Elsie seemed so happy that she didn't want to spoil the opportunity for her.

'I won't if that's what you really want to do,' she said in a wobbly voice. It appeared that she was about to lose yet another member of her family, but then she supposed if Elsie could become independent it might not be a bad thing. 'I shan't stop you if you've set your heart on it, my love. But just remember, should you ever need us you can always find us at Granny Doyle's.'

'I shall be fine.' Elsie's eyes were dancing with excitement and Saffie didn't want to spoil her moment but she had to raise a problem she had just thought of.

'But who will steer the boat if Elsie isn't with us?' Saffie asked.

'We can,' the twins said in unison. 'We've watched Dad and Archie do it hundreds of times.'

'Hm.' Saffie chewed on her lip, but she didn't have much choice in the matter. Her mother certainly wasn't well enough to sit out there in the cold and she supposed she could always shout instructions from the towpath if she got old Nellie to go at a gentle pace. It would take them longer but as long as they got there safely it wouldn't really matter.

'We'll set off in the morning then, when you've gone. I'd better just go and pay for another night in the stables for Nellie.' She forced a smile and left them, and once outside she scrubbed away the tears on her cheeks with her knuckles.

Early the next morning, Elsie had packed her belongings and was raring to go and start her new life. 'The house I'm going to work in is ever so posh and lots of people work there,' she'd told them excitedly the evening before. 'They have a butler, a cook, a gardener, maids and all sorts. Oh, and the young groom that lives above the stables is ever so handsome.' She had flushed as she mentioned him and a little ripple of unease had coursed through Saffie. Elsie was so young, she just hoped that she wouldn't go and get herself into trouble.

And now here she was all rosy-cheeked and starry-eyed and keen to be on her way.

'Won't you at least stay and have some breakfast?' Hoping to delay her departure, Olivia pointed to the porridge simmering on the top of the stove but Elsie shook her head as she stuffed her final bits and pieces into her bag.

'No, I'll eat with the rest of the staff when I get where I'm going.'

'All right, but can you write the address of where you'll be down so that we can get in touch if need be?' her mother asked.

'Oh, er . . . I can't remember it right now but don't worry, as soon as I'm settled in, I'll forward it on to you at Granny Doyle's.'

Then one by one she bent to kiss each of them before lifting her carpet bag and heading for the door with not a care in the world.

'Bye then, take care of yourselves.' She gave them a sunny smile and seconds later she was gone.

Olivia began to cry helplessly. She loved each and every one of her children but if she had been forced to admit it, she would have had to acknowledge that Elsie could be very self-centred and vain. She was pretty and she knew it and Olivia could only hope that she would stay safe.

'Come on, Mam, we all have to fly the nest sometime. She'll be fine. It's not as if she's run away with nowhere to go,' Saffie said gently as she bent to kiss her mother's cheek. Olivia was so thin now that she looked as if the skin on her pale face had been stretched across her bones. But Saffie was hopeful that once they got to Granny Doyle's and the weather started to improve, she would start to pick up.

'Right, I suggest whoever is going first out of you two has their breakfast and gets wrapped up warmly,' she addressed the twins. 'And while you do that I'll go and fetch Nellie.' And off she went with a heavy heart. Not so very long ago there had been eight of the family on the boat and now they were down to four.

Chapter Six

As Saffie had expected, the journey to Granny Doyle's took longer than usual with Ginny and Lucy alternating at the tiller, but all in all they did a good job, although once or twice when they reached the Oxford Canal, they had steered the boat dangerously close to the edge of the towpath. They had also struggled a little steering the boat through the locks but Saffie was proud of them and they didn't complain half as much about the cold or being bored as Elsie had. And then at last, on a cold and drizzly morning, they passed Tooley's Yard where the boats went to be recaulked or repaired and they knew they had almost arrived at Granny's. Just a few more miles and they would be there.

The sky overhead was leaden when they finally reached the nearest mooring to Granny's cottage. It was situated on the outskirts of the little village of Aynho on the edge of the Cherwell Valley and stood amongst a little hamlet of cottages inhabited mainly by retired boat people. Lucy and Ginny wrapped their mother in as many layers of clothes as they could find while Saffie went off to put Nellie in the stable at the Western Arms. Then she hurried back to join the others and they helped Olivia onto the towpath and began the short walk to the house. Olivia was as weak as a kitten, although she tried to put a brave face on.

'Almost there,' she said breathlessly as she clung to their arms. Minutes later they came to a gap in the hedge and through it they could see the cottage with smoke drifting lazily from the chimney up into the dark sky.

The cottage was surrounded by a low picket fence, and in the spring and summer, Granny's garden was a blaze of colour with every flower imaginable growing in it, but now it looked sad and the grass was covered in hoar frost. As they opened the gate, a dog came bounding towards them, growling. But then seeing who it was his tail began to wag and Ginny and Lucy bent to stroke him.

'Hello, Stanley,' they greeted him. He was quite a big dog and Granny had had him since before the twins were born. She had adopted him as a stray and ever since they had been inseparable. His hair was a rusty brown colour and he had one ear that stood up straight while the other one drooped, giving him a comical appearance. His bushy tail would not have looked out of place on a fox and they had all long since given up on trying to decide what breed he might be. But even if he wasn't the prettiest of creatures, he was totally devoted to Granny Doyle and protected her fiercely, so they all loved him.

Olivia was clearly flagging by this time so while the younger girls fussed Stanley, Saffie led her down the little path to the front door and rapped on it smartly.

It was opened seconds later by Granny Doyle, who didn't look the least surprised to see them as she stood aside for them to enter.

'Get yerselves in then,' she said crossly. 'Yer lettin' all the warm air out.'

Saffie grinned. It wasn't the warmest of welcomes but then she wouldn't have expected any other sort from Granny.

She helped her mother into the kitchen, which was directly behind the door, and the twins and Stanley scooted in after them making the room seem even smaller.

'I 'ad a feelin' in me bones yer'd be comin' today, so I made a big steak an' kidney pie an' a pan o' potatoes.' Granny pointed to an old wing chair at the side of the fire, studying Olivia's face as Saffie gently lowered her mother into it.

It amazed Olivia that Granny always seemed to know when they were going to descend on her. She had asked her once how she knew and Granny had grinned, showing the gaps in her teeth as she patted the side of her nose. 'I gets these feelin's,' was all she would say and with that Olivia had to be content.

Today Granny was dressed in her customary black bonnet and a long, thick Wolseley skirt that trailed the floor when she walked. Over it she wore an old jumper and a woollen shawl. Now Saffie came to think of it she had never seen her in anything else.

'I'll get yer some tea,' Granny told Olivia as she bustled over to the large brown teapot on the small table to one side of the room, where she poured some tea then shuffled back to press a mug into her hand.

Olivia gave her a grateful smile as she began tentatively, 'I'm afraid I have some rather bad news for you, Granny.'

'If yer meanin' what's 'appened to our Reuben an' Archie, I already knows. I know about little Danny an' all. Word soon spreads down the cut. I rue the day our Reuben took up wi' that Seth Black.' She shook her head. 'Now *there's* a bad 'un if ever I knew one. Still, what's done is done. There's no turnin' back the clock. But where's our Elsie?' She looked towards the door.

'She's managed to get herself a post as a laundry maid in one of the big houses back in Coventry.'

''As she now? Well, let's 'ope she knows 'ow to conduct 'erself, eh? But now, lookin' at you I reckon a quick kip after you've eaten wouldn't do you no 'arm. Saffie, get that dinner dished out then 'elp me get yer ma up to bed fer an hour.'

Saffie did as she was told, and once they'd all had their meal she left Ginny and Lucy to wash up the dirty pots while she and Granny helped Olivia upstairs to lie down and rest on Granny's bed.

Once they were back downstairs again, Granny Doyle sighed as she packed some tobacco into her clay pipe and lit it. 'I dare say yer've realised yer mam is in a bad way, 'ave yer, girl?'

Saffie flicked her long plait across her shoulder and blinked furiously to hold back tears as she nodded. 'Yes, that's why we've come here, to be honest, Granny. I didn't know what else to do. I thought perhaps if you didn't mind us staying for a while, I could find a job to pay for our keep.'

Granny puffed on her pipe as she stared thoughtfully into the flames that were licking up the chimney. The day outside was bleak but inside it was warm, cosy and absolutely spotless. The horse brasses and the copper pans suspended on the beam above the inglenook were gleaming and every stick of furniture and every window in the room had been polished until you could see your face in them. Even the red quarry tiles on the floor were so clean that Saffie felt she could have eaten her food off it, but then she had never seen it any different. The standards that the women adhered to on their boats had remained when Granny got her cottage, and Saffie sometimes joked that the dust wouldn't dare try to settle while Granny was about. The cottage was tiny, admittedly, just two up and two down, but it was Granny's little palace and she took great pride in it.

'Yer did right bringin' 'em 'ere,' Granny told Saffie in a low voice so the twins wouldn't hear – they were sitting at the table playing with a pack of cards. 'You an' the young 'uns will 'ave to share the double bed in the back room an' yer mam can come in wi' me.' She sucked her breath in before going on, 'But yer do realise that yer mam's not long fer this world now, don't yer?'

Saffie couldn't hold the tears back any longer and they rolled down her cheeks as she wrapped her arms about her waist and nodded miserably.

'If our Reuben were 'ere I'd kick 'is arse fer 'im, so I would, fer leavin' 'er in such a fix when she's so poorly. But there, what's done is done an' we'll just 'ave to mek the best of it now, won't we, eh?'

Granny nodded towards a letter that had come addressed to Olivia on the mantelshelf. 'That come fer yer ma, it must 'ave been at least about four weeks ago now, an' I 'ave a feelin' that it don't contain good news either. Still, it'll wait till she gets up.' Any mail Olivia had had since running away with Reuben had always been delivered to Granny Doyle's. It was the nearest she could get to a permanent address, but it meant that sometimes weeks could pass before she got it.

It was actually early that evening when the curtains had been drawn against the cold night that Olivia was finally handed her mail and as she looked at the handwriting on the envelope she smiled. It was from Marcus; she recognised his neat copperplate writing immediately.

Eagerly she slit it open, but the smile slid from her face as she read the letter and she became even paler, if that was possible.

My Dear Olivia,

I hope that this letter finds you well and that you and your family had an enjoyable Christmas. Unfortunately, I am writing to you with bad news. Sadly, your father passed away just over a week before Christmas. It was a massive heart attack but thankfully the doctor assured your mother that he would not have known about it or have suffered in any way and it was over very quickly. I am so sorry to be the bearer of such bad news but I felt you should know, even though it has been many years since you and your parents were estranged. The funeral will be on Christmas Eve should you get this letter in time and wish to attend. Your mother has asked me for the first time since you left for your address but I told her I would have to ask your permission before passing it on. Do let me know if you're willing for her to have it.

Mathilda and I will be spending Christmas quietly at home with Mother. She is much changed since my own father's demise. Life can be very harsh at times, can't it?

Anyway, Olivia, my deep condolences once more. I pray you and your family stay safe.

With kind regards,
Your friend,
Marcus.

'Is something wrong, Mam?' Saffie asked tentatively as she saw the look on her mother's face.

Pulling herself together with an effort, Olivia took a deep breath. Never once had she ever spoken of her parents to any of her children, but now she realised that Saffie was growing up and it was time to be honest with her.

'Yes, actually, there is you see . . .' Olivia glanced at Granny Doyle as if for support before going on quietly, 'It seems that my father has died.'

'Your *father*?' Saffie looked shocked. She had never heard her mother talk about her own father.

Ginny and Lucy's ears had pricked up too and the three girls watched her avidly.

'We have been estranged for many years,' Olivia told her. 'Because I chose your father above the person my parents wanted me to marry. I ran away and we have never spoken from that day to this. They completely disowned me, but now it seems my mother wishes to know where I am.' She tactfully refrained from telling Saffie that she had taken her to meet her grandparents when she was just a babe and had been turned away. There was no point in hurting her.

'So, we have a *grandmother* too?' Saffie could hardly take it in. 'And where does she live?'

'Very close to my friend Marcus. You have met him many times in the mooring at Tuttle Hill in Nuneaton.' Saffie knew who Marcus was; he was a teacher and her mother had once talked of the possibility of Saffie working with him to become one too. From the very first moment it was mentioned, Saffie knew this was what she desperately wanted but couldn't ever imagine it coming to pass. She was needed here.

Her mother continued, 'His father owned the farm there until he died last year and my father was his manager and lived in a rather large house on their estate.' She shook her head as memories flooded back. 'They wanted me to marry Marcus, purely because he was the farmer's son, for the status it would bring, even though he was five years my junior. But although I have always had a kind regard for Marcus, I could never have imagined being romantically involved with him. I'm afraid once I had met your father no other man could hold a candle to him in my eyes. Marcus is married himself now, to Mathilda, and is the teacher at the school in Abbey Green.'

'But if that's the case who will run the farm for him now your father has died?' Saffie queried.

Olivia shrugged as she pulled her shawl tighter about her thin shoulders. She never seemed able to get warm nowadays.

'I have no idea. Perhaps he will appoint another manager? Marcus was never interested in running the farm. He told me that when his father died, he left the house to my parents in his will for all my father's faithful years' service, so at least I know that my mother will have a roof over her head.'

'But why do you suppose she wants to see you now, after all this time?'

'I suppose because I am all she has left. Oh, and you too, of course. And that's if she does want to see me. She hasn't actually asked for that, has she? She has merely asked Marcus if she might know where I am.'

'So will you allow him to tell her?'

Olivia bit on her lip for a moment as she stared into space before slowly nodding. Life was too short and she realised she would like to make her peace with her mother before her time came. 'Yes, I think I will.' She patted Saffie's hand affectionately. 'It can't do any harm, can it? So why don't you fetch me some paper, a pen and some ink; there's no time like the present. Then perhaps when I've written back to Marcus you could pop into the village and post the letter for me.'

'Of course.' Saffie was actually quite excited to think she had a grandmother she had never known about and wondered if she would ever get to meet her. Only time would tell.

Chapter Seven

January 1870

The letter from Olivia's mother arrived late in January. Saffie saw the postman striding up Granny Doyle's path with it and took it straight to her mother.

Olivia eyed it tentatively for a moment, almost as if she was afraid it might bite her, but then with a sigh she slit the envelope and opened it.

> *Dear Olivia,*
>
> *Marcus has informed me that he has told you of your father's death. It is unfortunate that you could not attend his funeral. Marcus has passed on the address of where you are staying and I wonder if you could possibly visit me at your earliest convenience as there are things I wish to discuss with you,*
>
> *Yours sincerely,*
> *Mother*

'That's a little cold and to the point, isn't it?' Saffie commented when her mother had passed it to her to read.

'That's my mother.' Olivia looked sad. 'She was never one for showing affection and it seems she hasn't changed.'

'But what will you do now?' Saffie looked worried. 'You're in no state to travel at the moment.'

Olivia nodded in agreement. 'You're quite right, I'm not, but perhaps you could go and see her for me?'

'Me?' Saffie looked shocked.

'Why not? It's time you met her properly, although we shall have to get you some new clothes before you go.' Olivia looked at the drab skirt and blouse Saffie was wearing. The skirt had been darned so many times it almost looked like a patchwork quilt, and her pride wouldn't allow her mother to see her daughter dressed like that. 'You could go into Banbury on the cart and get a new outfit on market day. There's a very good second-hand clothes stall there if I remember correctly, and I still have plenty of money from the coal load to see us through for the time being.'

Saffie looked uncertain. Unlike Elsie, who would happily have spent every penny she could get her hands on on herself, Saffie had never really bothered much about clothes or being in fashion.

Half of her really wanted to meet the grandmother she had never known about until recently, while the other half was reluctant to leave her mother. She seemed to be getting frailer by the day, but then, if this was what her mother wanted her to do, she could hardly refuse her.

'All right, I'll go into Banbury on Friday and while I'm there I'll book a coach to Nuneaton.'

And so, it was decided.

On Friday Saffie was up bright and early and after arriving in Banbury, she began to stroll through the market stalls until she came to the one that sold second-hand clothes. There were already a few women rifling through the wares displayed but they seemed to be after working clothes, whereas Saffie was hoping to find something a little grander.

'Can I help you, me dear? Was you lookin' for somethin' in particular?' the stallholder asked. She was a small woman, almost as far round as she was high, although Saffie realised that was probably partly due to the layers of clothes she was wearing to keep out the cold.

'Yes. I, er . . . I was looking for something a little more, er . . .'

'Grand?'

When Saffie nodded, the old woman grinned. 'Then come round the back o' the stall 'ere. I might 'ave just the thing yer lookin' for. It just so 'appens that I got a load of very posh clothes from a big house on the outskirts of town just the other day. Nothing at all that would interest the farmers' wives but they might be just the job fer a pretty little thing like you. Now, where did I put 'em?'

As Saffie joined her, she began to rummage through some bags and seconds later she smiled as she came across what she was looking for. 'How about this then?' She held up a very attractive velvet skirt in a lovely shade of deep blue. 'An' I reckon I've got the little jacket to go with it an' all somewhere . . . Yes, 'ere it is.'

Saffie fell in love with it immediately. The skirt was full while the jacket was fitted into the waist with a very flattering little peplum. However, when the woman held it against her they both quickly realised that it was rather big for her.

'Any good at sewin', are yer?'

Saffie grinned and nodded.

'Well, there yer go, then. It shouldn't be too much of a job to shorten it an' take it in a couple o' sizes. But now let's see if I can't find yer a blouse to go with it.'

Half an hour later, Saffie left the stall with not only the blue velvet suit but a white blouse with ruffles down the front and a pair of soft leather button boots. They, too, were slightly big on her but she wasn't concerned as she could stuff the toes with newspaper. She felt rather guilty for spending money on herself, but her mother had insisted she should have a nice outfit so she supposed it would be all right. Even so she made a quick visit to the baker's where she treated Lucy and Ginny to an iced bun each and then she booked a seat on the coach into Coventry for the following week. From there she could get a train to Nuneaton.

Shortly after she stood at the side of the road and waited for the carrier cart that would take her back to Aynho, feeling content with her morning's shopping. Suddenly she felt quite excited about her upcoming trip. It would be almost like embarking on an adventure.

'What did you get?' the twins asked excitedly when she arrived home. They were as excited and curious about Saffie's visit to their grandmother as she was, and they wished they could meet her too.

Saffie smiled as she handed them a bun each before unpacking her bargains to show to her mother and Granny Doyle. 'You don't think the costume is a little too grand, do you?' she asked worriedly as she held it up for them to inspect.

'It's just *perfect*,' her mother assured her. 'Or at least it will be when we've taken it in a little and given it a good press. You're going to look the bee's knees.'

'I just wish we were coming with you,' Ginny pouted, spitting crumbs everywhere, which earned her a glare from Granny.

'Perhaps she will want to meet you once she's met me.' Saffie stroked Ginny's hair, which was tied into two plaits with blue ribbon.

'Let's just take one step at a time,' Olivia said hastily, wishing that she was well enough to go and see her mother herself.

That evening she sat and carefully altered the jacket of Saffie's new outfit by the light of the oil lamp and when it was done it fitted Saffie as if it had been made for her. 'I'll do the skirt tomorrow.' She stifled a yawn, and seeing that she was tired, Saffie hurried away to make them all a cup of cocoa before they went to bed.

In no time at all it was the night before Saffie was due to get on the stage to Coventry and she was beginning to feel nervous. Olivia had written a letter to her mother, which Saffie would take with her, and it was now safely tucked away in her bag.

'What shall I say to her?' she asked her mother.

Olivia smiled and stroked her hair. 'Just tell her who you are and give her my note, which explains why I couldn't go myself. And then just take it from there and come back and tell me what she wanted to see me for.'

'Perhaps it's cos our grandfather left you a fortune in his will,' Lucy said as her fertile young imagination took hold. 'And perhaps we're all rich now!'

'I think there's about as much chance of that happening as seeing a purple pig flying past the window.' Olivia grinned.

'But whatever it is, we'll know soon enough.' And with that she shooed the twins off to bed.

Saffie followed soon after as she would have to be up early the next morning to get the carrier cart into Banbury, but sleep didn't come easily and she heard the old clock on the mantelshelf downstairs strike midnight before she finally fell asleep.

'Oh Saffie, you look beautiful,' her mother told her the next morning when Saffie was all done up in her new finery. 'Doesn't she, Granny?'

Never one to show her feelings, Granny Doyle sniffed. 'I dare say she'll do. But now come on, girl, shake a leg els'n you'll be missin' the cart an' then you'll be goin' nowhere!'

Saffie quickly gave them a peck on the cheek and after hastily checking that she had everything she needed in her carpet bag she set off at a brisk pace in the cold morning air with her breath streaming in front of her.

It was mid-afternoon when the train steamed into Trent Valley Railway Station and as Saffie stepped down onto the platform, she received more than a few appreciative glances. Once outside she set off towards Abbey Green, noting that a cattle market was in progress. She had often taken the younger children to see the animals that were for sale there when they had been moored in Nuneaton and would have liked to have a wander amongst the stalls, but thought better of it.

Best go and get this over with, she decided and set off purposefully.

Once on Tuttle Hill she cut across the fields to the canal and sure enough there was the farm cottage that her mother had told her about. It looked rather grand and Saffie gulped as she opened the gate and stepped onto the path leading to the front door. Tentatively she lifted the brass knocker and rapped on it, and seconds later it was opened by a maid who gasped at the sight of her and clapped her hand over her mouth.

'Ooh, sorry, miss,' she said when she'd composed herself. 'It's just you reminded me o' someone who used to live 'ere a long time ago. You're the spit out of 'er mouth, so you are.'

'That would be my mother.' Saffie gave her a friendly smile. 'And you must be Minnie. My mother told me all about you. But I'm here to see my grandmother.'

'Well, I'll be.' Minnie shook her head. 'This is a right turn up fer the books. Come on in, miss.' She ushered her into the hall, which Saffie thought was rather grand for a farm cottage with expensive rugs on the floor and flock wallpaper on the walls.

'I'll just go an' tell the missus yer 'ere. What did you say yer name was? I know she'd written to yer ma an' I think she were expectin' her.'

'Unfortunately, my mother isn't well enough to come, and I'm Sapphire, but everyone calls me Saffie.' She dropped her bag down on the hall floor as Minnie scooted away. Minutes later she was back to tell her, 'Come this way, she'll see yer now.'

Saffie stifled a grin – anyone would have thought she was visiting royalty, but she managed to keep a straight face as

Minnie pointed to a door. 'The missus is in there, pet. I'll just go an' make yer a nice pot o' tea, eh? I dare say yer could do wi' one after yer journey.'

Saffie took a deep breath and straightened her back before tapping gently on the door.

'Come in!'

She turned the door knob and entered the room to find a woman sitting in a wing chair to the side of a roaring fire. She looked like an older version of her mother. Her once jet-black hair, which was piled on top of her head, was peppered with grey and her face was lined, but she was still an attractive woman. She was dressed in the latest style in a needlecord gown in a lovely shade of green, and her fingers were adorned with gemstones that sparkled in the firelight.

She stared at Saffie for a moment before saying coldly, 'So you must be Sapphire, my granddaughter. What a *ridiculous* name. I dare say your father chose it!'

Saffie didn't want to get off to a bad start so she bit back the hasty retort that sprang to her lips.

'I believe both my parents agreed on my name,' she said instead with her head held high.

'And why are you here? In my letter I stated quite clearly that it was my daughter I wished to see.'

'Unfortunately, my mother is not well enough to make the journey,' Saffie answered calmly. 'So she sent me in her place.'

'Hmm.' The woman was holding an ebony-handled walking stick in both her hands and she leaned on it as she sat forward. 'And what exactly is wrong with Olivia?'

Saffie gulped. 'I . . . I fear that she has the consumption,' she answered in a small voice.

The woman sniffed unfeelingly. 'And it's hardly surprising considering the lifestyle she has led on a cold damp narrowboat.'

Once again, Saffie bit her tongue but after a moment she dared to ask, 'May I ask why you wished to see my mother?'

'I was rather hoping that she would have seen sense by now and wished to return home. I heard what happened to your brother and father. Villains, the pair of them no doubt, so they're probably in the best place.'

Now Saffie did open her mouth to object but her grandmother held her hand up to silence her. 'I wanted your mother home because . . .' For the first time she looked uncomfortable before going on, 'Things have arisen since my husband's death that were not anticipated and I need her help.'

'As I explained, she is not in a position to help, but perhaps I could?'

Clara Bishop stared at her thoughtfully. She had to admit the girl looked presentable enough. Admittedly the clothes she was wearing were not the latest fashion but they were respectable and the girl was well spoken, which was surprising seeing as she had been dragged up on the canal. But how much could she trust her? And was the girl reliable?

'That would all depend,' she said cautiously. 'For a start it would mean you had to live here. I could give you a wage – only a small one, you understand? But you would also have your board and keep.'

Saffie was so shocked that for a moment she was speechless, but then finding her tongue again, she asked, 'And what is the job you have in mind for me?' It was obvious that her grandmother wasn't offering her a home out of love for her.

'It would entail you caring for a, er . . . family member, so to speak. Would you consider it?'

'Well, I would have to discuss it with my mother,' Saffie said cautiously. 'And if she agreed to it, when would you want me to start?'

'As soon as possible.'

'Then I shall see how my mother feels about the offer and let you know. But first would it be possible for me to stay the night? I doubt I would manage to get back to Banbury today.'

'I dare say that Minnie could find you a bed. So now I suggest you join her in the kitchen and over dinner this evening I shall explain a little more to you.'

The woman turned away and Saffie knew that she was being dismissed so without another word she left the room and once out in the hallway she headed in what she hoped was the direction of the kitchen where she felt she would no doubt get a far warmer reception from Minnie than she had from her grandmother.

Chapter Eight

As Saffie had thought, Minnie was delighted to spend time with someone other than her harsh employer, and after making Saffie a hot drink and a sandwich to keep her going until dinner, she led her upstairs to the small room at the back of the cottage.

'Will yer be all right in 'ere, miss?' she asked. 'I can 'ave the bed made up an' light a fire to air the room in no time for yer.'

'That would be lovely, Minnie.' Saffie gave her a warm smile as she placed the small carpet bag she had brought with her on a chair. 'But I can make the bed up myself. I don't expect to be waited on, and please call me Saffie, everyone else does.'

Minnie waved away her offers of help as she took clean sheets from an ottoman at the end of the bed. 'No, no, it's my place to wait on any o' the mistress's guests, not that we've had many since the master passed away, mind.'

'You must have been here a very long time now; I didn't expect you to still be here,' Saffie commented and Minnie nodded in agreement.

'Aye, I 'ave that. I were ten when the mistress fetched me from the work'ouse an' your mam were the closest thing I ever got to havin' a sister. I missed her somethin' terrible when she took off wi' yer dad, an' I thought the master an' mistress would go mad. They were so angry wi' 'er.' She blushed then, realising that she might be speaking out of turn. 'Sorry, the mistress is always tellin' me me gob will get me 'ung one o' these days.'

'It's all right, Minnie.' Saffie stared at her curiously as she straightened the crisp white sheet across the mattress. 'But have you never thought of leaving or perhaps getting married?'

Minnie shrugged. 'I did 'ave a friend,' she admitted. 'He works as a farm labourer up at the big farm. We'd been walkin' out together fer some time but 'e never mentioned gettin' wed an' it slowly just fizzled out. But then, why would anybody want to marry me? I'm just a nothin' from the work'ouse, as yer grandmother is fond o' remindin' me.'

Saffie frowned. 'Where you came from shouldn't matter; it's the person you've become,' Saffie said heatedly. 'And from the little I've seen of you up to now you're hard working and kind. This friend of yours must have seen that, surely?'

'Well, Davey is very shy.' Minnie grinned as she tucked the sheet in and started to ram the pillows into the clean pillowslips. 'It took 'im ages to pluck up the courage to even ask me to go fer a walk wi' him an' we are still friendly.'

Minnie was bursting with curiosity to find out why Clara had summoned Saffie after all this time but didn't feel it was her place to ask. No doubt she would find out eventually, though.

'So will you be stayin' fer long?'

'Not immediately. Grandmother has offered me a job, although she hasn't said exactly what the job is yet. I suppose I'll find out over dinner this evening.'

Minnie had piled the blankets and a pretty eiderdown onto the bed. 'Yes, an' speakin' o' dinner I'd best get back to the kitchen. The missus don't like it if everythin' ain't ready to serve for six o'clock sharp. I've made us a nice rabbit pie fer tonight – Davey brought the rabbit over this mornin'. But I'll bring you a jug o' hot water up afore I do any more so yer can freshen up after yer journey.' With that she slipped away, and crossing to the window Saffie stared out across the garden towards the canal, which she could see through a gap in the hedge.

Would she like living here? she wondered. That was, if her mother agreed to it. And who was the family member her grandmother wanted her to care for? She wouldn't have long to wait to find out now hopefully.

At ten minutes to six she made her way downstairs and joined her grandmother in the dining room. Like the rest of the rooms she had seen, it was very elaborately furnished and after being used to the confines of the cabin on *The Blue Sapphire*, it felt absolutely enormous. A large mahogany dining table surrounded by eight ladder-back chairs stood in the centre of the room and a matching sideboard took up almost the whole of one wall. Plush velvet curtains were drawn across the window and a fire burned brightly in the grate.

She noted immediately that her grandmother had changed for dinner into yet another expensive-looking dress, although she wondered why she would have gone to so much trouble when there was only the two of them to dine.

'You may eat with me this evening,' Clara informed her regally as if she was bestowing some great gift on her. 'But should you decide to take the job I am going to offer you,

you will eat in the kitchen with Minnie in future. I can't, of course, acknowledge you as my granddaughter.'

Saffie bristled. 'Oh, and why is that?'

'You are a flyblow – a bastard, in other words,' her grandmother informed her coldly and Saffie was so shocked that she almost choked. It had never occurred to her before that her parents hadn't been married, but then lots of the boat people didn't bother to get wed.

'I-I wasn't aware of that,' she stuttered. 'I had always assumed that my parents were married.'

Clara waved her hand regally. She clearly had no more to say on the subject. 'Anyway, more importantly we will now discuss the job I have in mind for you.' She sipped at the glass of sherry wine she was holding, obviously feeling uncomfortable. 'For some time, a relative of your grandfather's has been staying at Hatter's Hall at his expense.'

Saffie gasped. She had heard of the place. 'But isn't that a mental asylum?'

Avoiding her eye, Clara shrugged. 'I believe so, although it does have people who stay there for other reasons. Anyway, now that my husband is deceased, I'm afraid I shall find it difficult to meet the fees and so as I am now legally the next of kin, the person will have to come here, for a time at least, until I can think of somewhere else for them to go.'

'I see.'

'I would expect you to care for them until alternative arrangements can be made. They would of course stay hidden from view and I would not wish to see them. There is an attic room that we can make suitable for them.'

'What? You mean to lock them away?' Saffie was horrified at the unfeeling way her grandmother was speaking of the unfortunate soul.

'Why not?' Clara snapped, her eyes flashing. 'They have been locked away up until now, haven't they, so what difference would it make to them?'

'And may I ask, are we speaking of a man or a woman? And how old are they? If it's a man, would I manage to contain them?'

'It's a child, actually.' There was colour in the woman's cheeks now. She was clearly finding it difficult to talk about. 'A girl of ten or eleven years old, I believe. Her mother died in childbirth.'

'Oh, and what relation was she to my grandfather? And why didn't the child's father look after her?'

Clara glared at her. 'She was his cousin's child, as far as I know, and I have no idea why the father didn't want her,' she said shortly. 'But now I don't wish to discuss the matter anymore. Are you interested in the job or not?'

'Well . . . er . . . yes, I think so. If my mother is happy for me to do it,' Saffie answered doubtfully.

The door opened and Minnie appeared with a large tray of food which she proceeded to put in the middle of the table. As well as the rabbit pie she had told Saffie she was making, there was a dish of creamy mashed potatoes and another of cauliflower along with a jug of thick, steaming gravy. It looked and smelled delicious and Saffie felt her stomach rumble in anticipation. She hadn't realised quite how hungry she was, despite the sandwich that Minnie had made for her earlier.

She and her grandmother took their places at the table and the meal was eaten in silence. Next Minnie breezed back in with a dish of bread-and-butter pudding and a jug of rich yellow custard, and by the time she had finished a large portion Saffie felt so full she could hardly move.

'That was lovely, thank you,' she told Clara appreciatively, but the woman clearly had no more to say to her.

'I suggest you go and rest now if you have an early start tomorrow,' she told her as she left the table. 'And if you want the job, I shall expect you back here within a week. If you haven't arrived by then I shall have to look around for someone else to do it.'

'Very well, Grandmother, good evening.' She made to leave but once again the woman held her hand up.

'Before you go, I want you to know that should you decide to come here, you will not address me as Grandmother. It will be Mrs Bishop or ma'am to you, especially if we have company, and you will dine in the kitchen with Minnie, as I believe I have already mentioned? I think it is wise to begin as we mean to go on. Is that understood?'

'Perfectly!' Saffie could not keep the note of sarcasm from her voice and she left the room, her chin in the air without looking back even once. One thing she had already discovered, Clara Bishop was not going to be an easy woman to live with.

She spent the next hour in the kitchen with Minnie helping her with the dirty pots. At least she felt comfortable and at ease with her and she could see why her mother had always spoken so fondly of her. But she didn't tell her what the job her grandmother was offering was. She didn't feel it was her place to and no doubt her grandmother would tell her when the time was right.

Despite her mixed feelings she slept well and it felt as if she had only just fallen asleep when Minnie woke her gently the next morning with a steaming mug of tea on a tray, a hard-boiled egg and some toast.

'I didn't want yer to start yer journey wi'out sommat warm inside yer,' she said pleasantly as she crossed the room and swished the curtains aside. As she looked out at the dismal landscape, she shuddered and confided, 'I can't wait fer the spring now. I 'ates the cold winter months. But there you go, it ain't that far away now, is it?'

'It certainly isn't,' Saffie agreed as she hoisted herself up onto her pillows. She wasn't used to being spoiled but she rather liked it. Minnie left her to eat her breakfast in peace and soon after, when she had washed and got dressed, Saffie carried the tray and her carpet bag down the stairs.

'Is my grandmother about?' she asked.

Minnie chuckled. 'Not likely, miss . . . I mean, Saffie. She don't usually get her arse outta bed afore ten o'clock at the earliest. I could go an' wake her, though, an' tell her yer ready fer the off, if yer like?'

'Oh no, no, Minnie, it's quite all right,' Saffie assured her hastily. 'I'll just slip away, but hopefully I'll be seeing you again very soon.'

'I 'ope so,' Minnie assured her with a cheery smile.

The return journey was very uneventful and as the light began to fade from the afternoon, she arrived back at Granny Doyle's. Stanley rushed to greet her with his tail wagging furiously and she faced a barrage of questions the second she set foot through the door. Laughing, she dropped her bag onto the floor and held her hand up to stave them off.

'Whoa, one question at a time, please. And can I get my boots off and have a nice cup of tea first?'

'I'll make it,' Ginny said obligingly as she rushed off to fill the kettle.

'And I'll get the cake tin,' Lucy added, heading to the pantry. 'Granny's made some lovely scones and we have jam to put on them.'

Now Saffie had time to have a good look at her mother, who was huddled in the chair at the side of the fire, and her heart sank. She looked even worse than she had when Saffie had left the day before, and her cough was almost incessant now.

'So, you've finally met your grandmother?' Despite looking so poorly, a grin twitched at the side of her mouth and Saffie laughed.

'Yes, and she was just as you said she was. Not the easiest woman to get along with.' She went on to tell Granny Doyle and her mother what the meeting had been about and when she was done, her mother frowned.

'But I wasn't even aware that my father had a cousin,' she said, bemused. 'He was an only child and my grandparents died before I was born. And you say this person is just a child? Then I wonder why Minnie and Mother can't look after her and why was she in Hatter's Hall? It's such a dreadful place, especially for a child.'

Saffie shrugged. She had no answer to that question.

'And how do you feel about going to live there?'

'Well, she's already told me that she won't acknowledge me as her granddaughter if I do,' Saffie told her in a low voice because she didn't want the twins to hear. 'Because, as she went to great pains to point out to me, I'm illegitimate. She called me a flyblow.'

Now Olivia's pale cheeks flooded with colour and she bowed her head in shame. 'It's true, I'm afraid, and I'm sorry about that,' she said in a small voice. 'Me and your dad always *meant* to get around to getting wed but then you children all started coming along one after the other and there seemed to be more important things to spend our hard-earned money on. I'm *so* sorry, Saffie.'

Saffie shrugged. What was done was done and there was nothing she could do about it, so she supposed she may as well get used to it. It was probably one of the reasons her grandmother didn't want to acknowledge her, although she thought that once people met her they would guess who she was anyway. The similarity was obvious.

'I think I will accept the job, if you're happy with the idea?' she told her mother. 'We're rather overcrowded here and I'll be able to send most of my wages, whatever they may be, back to you to help out with yours and the girls' keep. At least I'll feel like I'm helping then.'

Her mother nodded. 'Very well, but only so long as you're sure it's what you want to do. And don't forget that if you don't like it, you can always come back here.'

As Saffie nodded solemnly the decision was made.

Chapter Nine

'So, Granny Doyle and I have decided that we are going to sell *The Blue Sapphire*,' Olivia informed Saffie that evening when the twins were tucked up in bed. 'It wasn't an easy decision, but it makes sense. We can't work the boat without a man and the money we make from the sale will pay for mine and the girls' keep for some time to come.'

'But what about Nellie?' Saffie asked hurriedly as she fondled Stanley's silky ears.

'We've thought of that too.' Olivia looked sad. 'I suppose we could sell her as well but she's old now and she's worked hard all her life so I think we'll retire her. Granny Doyle has already spoken to a farmer who lives less than half a mile from here and he's offered to take her and promised that she'll be well cared for. He has two young daughters and he says they'll love her and will be able to ride on her in her paddock, so from now on she'll be more of a pet than a working horse.'

Saffie was happy with that decision at least but she knew that she would miss her. She had never known a time when Nellie had not been part of the family but it was nice to think that she could have the rest she deserved, rather than pulling a heavy boat along the canal every day. She sniffed back a tear as she thought again just how drastically their lives had changed in such a short time. But as her mother was fond of saying: time moved on, and there was no stopping it, so change was inevitable.

'And have you heard anything from Elsie yet?' she asked, hoping to lighten the sombre mood.

'Not a word, but then our Elsie was never keen on writing, unlike you. I'm sure she will when she settles into her new position and then we can arrange for her to come and see us when she gives us her address.'

Saffie hoped she was right but didn't feel confident. Elsie had always been a free spirit and she wondered how her sister would cope with having people telling her what to do.

Could Saffie have known it, at that very moment Elsie was in her attic room crying her eyes out as Josie, the little maid she shared a room with, looked helplessly on.

'I don't know why I ever took this *bloody* job in the first place,' Elsie moaned as she rocked to and fro with her arms crossed about her chest and her raw hands grasped under her armpits.

'The last laundry maid said she used to soak her hands in her piddle in the chamber pot. It toughens 'em up apparently, or so she reckoned,' Josie ventured.

'Urgh!' Elsie curled her lip in disgust. 'I reckon I'd rather have sore hands than do that.'

Life as a laundry maid was nothing at all as she had pictured it would be. She had thought that once she was away from her mother's watchful eyes, she would have a whale of a time, but she hadn't allowed for the strict housekeeper, Mrs Beasley, who was in charge of her and the rest of the staff. The woman seemed to have eyes in the back of her head and it would be woe betide anyone who tried to finish work even a minute before their time. Her employers, Mr and Mrs Worthington, had a son and a daughter who to Elsie's mind were spoiled rotten, especially the daughter, Emma, who looked down on Elsie every time their paths crossed. The two girls had taken an instant dislike to each other, probably because Emma realised that Elsie was so much prettier than her, Elsie thought. But the son, Silas, on the other hand, was very handsome and once or twice on her way to the laundry when she had seen him crossing the yard to the stables, Elsie had gone out of her way to give him a simpering smile. She had been flattered when her smile was returned and he'd stared at her appreciatively. Until Josie had warned her that he had a reputation for flirting with the maids, that was.

Now with a sigh, she stared towards the little skylight window in their room. It was cold up here in the winter and she had no doubt it would be uncomfortably hot in the summer. Nowhere near as warm and cosy as the little cabin on *The Blue Sapphire* had been.

'Did yer hear what I just said?' Josie's voice brought her back to the present with a jolt.

'What? No . . . sorry, I was miles away for a moment.'

'I was sayin' you'll no doubt be bogged down wi' dirty washin' next week an' we'll all be run off us feet. There're visitors comin' to stay fer Miss Emma's eighteenth birthday party so Mrs Beasley will be keepin' us all well on our toes.'

'Oh great!' Elsie groaned. That was all she needed. She had enough washing to do with all the staff's clothes and the bedding as it was. But she liked doing the family's clothes, especially Miss Emma's gowns and underwear. Her underwear was all made of satin and lace and the gowns were the latest fashion and in all the colours of the rainbow. Not that they did much for the young mistress, Elsie thought sulkily. It would take more than pretty clothes to make her look attractive with her ugly face. 'So how many people will be staying?'

'I heard Cook telling the groom that the stables will be full so I suppose at least two or three families.'

'Well, I just hope I still get me Sunday afternoon off,' Elsie griped and Josie giggled.

'I doubt it. But never mind, they'll only be here for a few days then things will soon go back to normal.' While she was talking, Josie was yanking her plain cotton nightgown over her head and once it was on, she jumped into bed, shivering. Her breath was floating on the air in front of her but she was used to it now and she snuggled down in the cold sheets and was fast asleep in minutes, leaving Elsie to sit staring desolately at the rain running down the window pane.

Over the chair the plain, drab uniform dress she was forced to wear seemed to mock her. She'd imagined that once she left home, she could indulge her love for fashion, but up to now, that hadn't happened either. Still, she thought, trying to cheer herself, she would be paid next week and then she would go and spend the whole of her wages on whatever took her fancy. It didn't occur to her that she should really send some home to her mother.

The following morning Saffie was given the job of taking Nellie to her new home and as she led her along her eyes were misted with tears, although she knew that this was the best outcome for the old horse. She had worked hard all her life and deserved to lead a quieter life now.

Farmer Younger and his two young daughters were in the farmyard when she arrived and the two little girls' giggled excitedly as they raced towards her. They had been feeding the chickens who scattered and squawked indignantly at the intrusion.

'Is this the horse yer told us about, Daddy?' the younger of the two, a little girl with hair the colour of ripe corn, asked delightedly.

'Ar, it is pet,' he told her indulgently. 'Yer can show 'er to 'er stable, if you've a mind to, an' put 'er a nose bag on. I've left one ready fer the old girl an' later when it's warmed up a bit yer can take her fer a gentle ride round 'er paddock.'

Saffie knew in that moment that Nellie was going to a good home and she sniffed back her tears as she kissed the old horse's nose for the last time. 'You enjoy your retirement and be a good girl,' she whispered and then the children were leading her away.

She quickly said her goodbyes and set off back the way she had come, and when she had gone a distance she suddenly sank down to the ground beneath a tree and began to sob. But it wasn't just for Nellie she was crying, it was for her little brother, for her dad and Archie, for Elsie who had left the family fold, and for her mother whose health was deteriorating by the day. She felt as if her whole way of life had been torn apart and worse still, she knew now that it could never go back to the way it had been.

Eventually she pulled herself together and set off again and when she arrived at the cottage she went to her room and began to pack the clothes she would take with her. She had very few possessions – there had been no room on the boat for each of them to store more than the basic necessities – but it didn't overly concern her. Her grandmother had already made it more than clear that she would have very little to do with her once she went to live there; she would be nothing more than a hired help so Saffie doubted the woman would much care what she wore.

'I was thinking I'd set off tomorrow,' she told her family over lunch. There didn't seem much sense in delaying, but before she went, she strolled to the canal and put a 'For Sale' sign in the cabin window of *The Blue Sapphire* for her mother. It was strange to be alone on the boat and already it felt as if the life had gone from it now the family were no longer there. She looked around sadly. Every inch of it was so familiar to her but now it was the end of an era. The little room would soon hopefully ring to the sounds of another family's laughter.

She gave the cabin one last clean and packed the remaining few personal possessions that the family had left behind, then with tears in her eyes she locked the door for the very last time and went to enjoy her final meal with the ones she loved.

'Promise me you won't give up on your dream of becoming a teacher one day,' her mother pleaded when they sat together by the fire that evening. Saffie didn't talk much about her hopes and dreams but Olivia saw how she came alive when teaching the other children how to read and write and she could tell it was what she wanted.

Granny Doyle and the twins had retired to bed and Saffie was enjoying having her mother all to herself. 'I know you're taking this job with my mother for now but it doesn't have to be forever. I've written to Marcus today and asked him to help you any way he can.'

Saffie nodded. When they had been moored in Tuttle Hill she had met Marcus on a number of occasions. He had usually come to see her mother in the evening when he knew her father would be in the pub, because Reuben could be insanely jealous. Not that he had any cause to be, as Olivia often pointed out. Despite his faults, and they had seemed to increase as he got older, she still adored him and Marcus was also a very happily married man.

'I shall write to you every single week,' Saffie promised. 'And I shall come and see you as often as I can. You never know, Grandmother might decide that she wants to come and see you too.'

Olivia smiled, really smiled, for the first time in weeks. 'I think there's very little chance of that happening,' she chuckled. 'Mother washed her hands of me the day I ran away with your father. And yet I still don't hate her. I think she was, and probably still is, a very unhappy woman. Between you and me I don't think my parents' marriage was a happy one. At least, I don't think it was after I was born. My mother had a difficult birth with me and added to that was the disappointment that I was a girl. After that my father slept in a different room. My mother wanted to groom me into being a perfect wife and marrying well but I was always too independent for that. Believe it or not, I always wanted to be a teacher much as you do. And then I met your father and everything changed. Love can do funny things to you.'

'But how do you know when you've met the person you want to spend the rest of your life with?' Saffie questioned innocently.

Her mother smiled tenderly as she stroked Saffie's silky locks. 'Oh, you'll know all right. But now, hadn't you ought to be getting some rest? You have a very early start in the morning.'

Saffie rose and kissed her mother's cheek and once she had gone to bed Olivia stared into the fire as a solitary tear slid down her cheek. She had resigned herself to the fact that she would never see her husband or her son again, and now she had to wonder if she would ever see Saffie again too. But then she knew that when her time came Ginny and Lucy would be safe at least with Granny Doyle and that was the best she could hope for.

The goodbyes the following morning were tearful and Saffie was feeling low as she gave Stanley a final pat on the head and went to wait for the carrier cart that would take her into Banbury where she would begin her journey. The day passed slowly but at last the train pulled into Trent Valley Station and she began the walk on the final leg of her journey to her grandmother's house in Tuttle Hill.

Minnie met her at the door and from her at least she received a warm welcome. 'Eeh, I've been so lookin' forward to you arrivin'.' She took Saffie's bag from her and Saffie followed her into the hallway where Minnie's smile faded as she leaned forward to whisper, 'But the missus says to tell yer that as of now you're to use the back door when comin' or goin' from the house.'

'Did she now?' Saffie took the pin from her hat and hung it on the hallstand as Minnie squirmed with embarrassment. Fancy having to tell the missus's own granddaughter that she was to use the servants' entrance. It didn't seem right to her at all but then, Mrs Bishop had allus been a law unto herself an' Minnie doubted she'd change now.

'In the drawing room, is she?' Saffie asked.

Minnie nodded as she hurried away to put the kettle on. 'Yes she is, but you'd best come to the kitchen wi' me till she sees fit to send for yer.'

Saffie gave a wry smile as she followed Minnie down the hallway. She'd hardly expected to find the red carpet rolled out for her but it wouldn't have hurt her grandmother to at least make the effort to say hello, surely?

The kitchen was warm and cosy and there was a delicious smell issuing from the oven. 'Mr Berrin'ton dropped us a leg o' pork in earlier on,' Minnie told her. 'So we've got a nice roast dinner to look forward to this evenin'.'

'Lovely.' Saffie sank down onto the chair next to the fire and yawned. It had been a long day and it was then it struck her that this would be her home for the foreseeable future. It wasn't a particularly pleasing prospect and she blinked back tears as she thought of her family back at Granny Doyle's. She was missing them already.

Chapter Ten

'The missus says she'll see yer now in the drawin' room,' Minnie told Saffie when she came back from the dining room with a tray full of dirty dishes following dinner.

'Oh, will she now! How *very* kind of her!' Saffie instantly felt guilty for being so sarcastic. After all, it wasn't as if she hadn't understood that she was only here to do a job of work, so she supposed the sooner she got used to the situation the better.

'Sorry, Minnie,' she said, looking contrite as she made her way to the kitchen door. 'I didn't mean to snap.'

'Eeh, yer don't 'ave to apologise to me,' the good-natured woman assured her. 'I reckon I'd feel just the same if I were in your shoes. But why don't yer go an' get it over, eh? Then we can 'ave a nice evenin' sat at the side o' the fire.'

Saffie tapped at the door of the drawing room and almost instantly her grandmother shouted, 'Come in.'

She entered and went to stand in front of the woman with her hands neatly clasped at her waist.

'Good evening, Grandmoth— I mean, ma'am.'

Clara Bishop stared at Saffie. She really was remarkably like her mother had been at her age, but it didn't soften her attitude towards the girl.

'Oh, for goodness sake, do sit down, Sapphire,' she said crossly. 'You're making my neck ache having to look up at you like this. Sit there opposite me where I can see you properly.'

Saffie obediently sat and after a moment the woman went on, 'I have already written to the matron at Hatter's Hall and told her that you will shortly be going to remove the girl I told you about from her care. My husband was paying a ridiculous amount to keep her there and I can no longer afford to do so. I had thought of putting her into the workhouse,' she continued, showing no sign of sympathy for the child in question whatsoever. 'It certainly couldn't have done her any harm. She's obviously a simpleton to be in there in the first place. But . . . shall we say certain things have come to light that prevent me from doing that so the only alternative is to bring her here and keep her out of sight. And that's where you will come in. I shall expect you to keep her confined up in the attic and make sure that I never have to see her. You and Minnie may prepare the rooms with the basic necessities for her tomorrow.'

'But surely such a young child shouldn't be shut away from the sunshine and daylight?' Saffie was appalled that the woman could be so cruel.

Clara's lip curled with contempt. 'Oh, please don't tell me that you're as romantic as your mother!' she ground out. 'Look where it got her, eh? A life of drudgery with a herd of children clinging to her skirts on a dirty little canal boat.'

'Our boat was *never* dirty and my mother loved each and every one of her children,' Saffie snapped back before she could stop herself. 'The space we lived in might have been a little cramped but it was packed with love and we had a happy childhood!'

She saw a glimmer of a smile touch her grandmother's lips. 'Hm, it seems you have your mother's spirit as well,' she observed. 'And in this instance, it won't be a bad thing. I dare say you're going to need to be strong to care for a simpleton. But now you may go. Minnie has prepared a room for you and as I said, tomorrow you may both work on preparing the attic rooms for the girl. You will have to move anything that is stored up there into the stables.'

'As you wish,' Saffie said stiffly, and rising she left the room without giving the woman so much as a backward glance. The more she saw of her the more she could understand why her mother had run away all those years ago. But a job was a job and she intended to do it to the best of her ability for as long as it lasted.

As she lay staring at the ceiling that night, unable to sleep, she had to bite back tears as she wondered what her father, Archie and Elsie were doing at that moment.

It was perhaps as well that she could have no way of knowing, for as she lay in her warm bed, Archie was lying on stinking straw in the bowels of a ship headed for Australia. Earlier that evening, one of the other prisoners had died of the dysentery that was sweeping through the ship. It had taken three hours of the rest of the men confined there shouting and crying out before the guards finally came and dragged the poor soul away. His body would join the rest of the prisoners who had died in a watery grave over the side of the ship, and Archie thought of all the families left behind who would never know what had become of their loved ones.

The smell below decks was appalling but he was getting used to it now. There were buckets, which the prisoners had to use for their toileting, along one wall, which was bad enough, but the dysentery had made the smell a hundred times worse. Archie's ankles were chained and the skin beneath the shackles was raw and bleeding, which attracted the rats that were the prisoners' constant companions. Once a day they were led up on deck where they were allowed to wash as best they could in barrels of sea water that left their skin sore and stiff with salt. After being confined in total darkness most of them would stumble when they saw daylight until their eyes adjusted to the brightness, and that would earn them a crack of the whip across their bare backs from the prison guards.

The food was abysmal too, and as the journey progressed it got worse. Twice a day the guards would open the door and throw in a few loaves of stale bread and a bucket of clean drinking water. Only the strongest amongst them could get to them before the food was all gone and now men were dying from weakness and malnutrition as well as dysentery. At the start Archie had been determined to survive, but as the journey continued, he began to wonder if death wouldn't be the better alternative. After all, what would he have to look forward to when and if they reached their destination? Years of hard labour? Now as he curled on his side, tears rolled down his pallid cheeks as he thought of the family he had left behind and of what a fool he had been. He wondered how his father was faring in prison. Surely even that must be better than what he was enduring? And then his thoughts turned to his mother and his siblings. Who would care for them now?

Then slowly, from somewhere, his will to survive slowly returned. Ten years seemed like an interminably long time at the moment but it would pass and one day, he promised himself, he would return to the ones he loved and make them proud of him.

The following day was wet and dismal with leaden clouds scudding across a grey sky as Minnie and Saffie went to look at the attic rooms that would soon be home to the child from Hatter's Hall.

'Crikey, it's worse than I thought.' Minnie shuddered as she eyed the cobwebs hanging from the ceiling. 'An' it's so cold up 'ere an' there's so much stuff. It'll take us the best part o' the day just to empty it!'

'Then we'd better make a start.' Saffie rolled up her sleeves. She had never been afraid of hard work so she wasn't fazed in the least.

They spent the best part of the morning carrying the boxes and cases across to the empty stables and then Minnie left Saffie to it while she hurried away to prepare the lunch. Busy as they were, she knew the mistress would still insist on her meal being on time.

By mid-afternoon, the two rooms were clear and Saffie opened the skylight window to let some air in and some of the dust out.

'I'll give the rooms a good sweep before we do anything else,' she told Minnie. 'Then we can start to mop them out. All this dust is making me sneeze.'

Minnie grinned as she stared down at her clothes. They were grubby and caked in dust, as was her hair. 'We're both goin' to need a good bath after this,' she commented. 'But I still can't understand why the missus can't let the girl sleep in the spare room at the back o' the house. She's goin' to feel very isolated stuck up 'ere all on 'er own, the poor little sod. Who did you say she was anyway?'

'My grandfather's cousin's child, I believe my grand-mother said,' Saffie answered as she began to wipe the thick layers of grime from the inside of the window.

Minnie shrugged. 'Strange that. I can't remember either of 'em ever mentionin' a cousin before. Still, it ain't none o' my business who the missus 'as 'ere; I'm just a skivvy.'

Saffie paused to stare at her thoughtfully. She had noticed already that her grandmother never had a kind word for Minnie, even though she had served her loyally for many years. 'I really don't know how you've put up with the way my grandmother treats you. Haven't you ever considered leaving?' she asked. Minnie was such a kind, gentle soul, she deserved to be happy.

'Where would I go? An' anyway, you 'ave to remember she fetched me 'ere outta the work'ouse an' I felt like I'd landed in 'eaven after bein' in that awful place. At least 'ere I got enough to eat an' me own bed to sleep in, an' I didn't get beaten either so I owe it 'er to do me best fer 'er, don't I?'

'I should think you repaid what you felt you owed her many years ago,' Saffie said solemnly. 'And it's time you thought of yourself.'

'Well, we'll see.' Minnie grinned and side by side they went down to fetch the cleaning things they would need.

They finished cleaning the rooms by the light of an oil lamp later that evening and when they were finally done, they stared about in satisfaction.

'I reckon we've done a bloody good job o' that, even if I do say so meself,' Minnie declared as she leaned on the handle of the mop. 'We can start movin' some furniture in tomorrow but I reckon we should go an' carry the tin bath into the kitchen an' 'ave a good bath now. What do you say?'

'I say that sounds like an excellent idea,' Saffie agreed and they set off to fill the bath with water from the copper.

The next morning, straight after breakfast, the two girls were busy once more in the attic. Behind all the boxes and packing cases they had found in there they had discovered an old brass bedframe and once they had assembled it and it had had a good polish it looked almost as good as new.

'But what shall we do for a mattress?' Saffie asked worriedly. 'I doubt Grandmother will pay out for a new one.'

Minnie smiled. 'Don't worry about that. I always save the feathers when I pluck a goose and I've got bags full of 'em in the stable. I'll edge a sheet and stuff it with them and it'll be really comfy. We can carry the washstand from the spare room up here and I'm sure there's an old chair in the stables as well.'

By lunchtime the room looked cosy. They had carried up a carpet for the side of the bed and placed fresh sheets and blankets on the mattress and now it was all ready for the new occupant.

'I reckon you can tell the missus the room is about as ready as we can get it,' Minnie said, and so Saffie went downstairs to find her. She knew her grandmother would be in the drawing room, she rarely ventured out of there, apart from mealtimes.

She tapped tentatively on the door, before opening it. 'Grandm— I mean ma'am, I just came to let you know that

101

we've prepared the room for the child now. When would you like me to fetch her?'

'I'll speak to Marcus later today,' Clara told her coldly. 'Minnie can walk over to the farm and leave a message for him telling him that I wish to see him and hopefully he will drive you there in the carriage at his earliest convenience. Was there anything else?'

Saffie shook her head and once she was back in the kitchen with Minnie her hands bunched into fists. 'I'm sure that woman has a swinging brick in place of a heart,' she said angrily. 'It's hard to believe that she gave birth to my mother, who is one of the kindest people I know! And to think of that poor child locked away in that awful place for so long.'

Minnie shrugged as she kneaded the dough for the bread she was making. 'You get used to the missus after a time. An' as fer the child . . . well, once we get 'er outta that place we can do a bit o' spoilin', can't we?' Minnie was actually quite looking forward to having a child in the house.

'She says she's going to send you over to the house to leave a message for Marcus Berrington to call. She wants him to take me in the coach to fetch the little girl.'

Minnie grinned from ear to ear as she covered the dough with a wet cloth and set it on the hearth to prove. 'I'm 'appy enough to do that. It'll give me an excuse to see Davey.'

And so after dinner that evening Minnie set off with a note Clara had written to Marcus and when she returned over an hour later her eyes were sparkling. She took the reply Marcus had given her straight in to Clara and when she came back, she informed Saffie, 'Mr Berrin'ton will take you to Hatter's Hall at a quarter past four tomorrer afternoon after school 'as finished.'

'That's fine.' Saffie smiled. 'And am I to assume the smile on your face is something to do with a certain gentleman who works at the farm?' Although Minnie was much older than Saffie, she found they'd easily settled into a happy friendship and she was pleased to see Minnie so happy.

Minnie nodded. 'Davey 'as asked me to go the fair in the Pingles Fields wi' 'im on Sunday afternoon. That'll be somethin' to look forward to, won't it?'

'It certainly will.' Saffie was pleased for her; Minnie deserved some enjoyment. She always worked so hard for no praise whatsoever. 'We'll have to sort through your clothes and make sure you're looking your best.'

Minnie blushed. 'Oh, I ain't got that many clothes,' she admitted. 'Mainly cos I don't often go anywhere to wear owt special. I usually just save me wages an' I've got a nice little nest egg tucked away.'

'Then perhaps on Saturday after lunch you should walk into town and treat yourself to something nice,' Saffie suggested. 'Perhaps a new bonnet and a new shawl? I can hold the fort here.'

Minnie looked quite excited at the prospect. 'Ooh, do yer really think I should? I can't remember the last time I 'ad a new bonnet.'

'Then it's way overdue,' Saffie assured her and for the rest of the evening Minnie floated around with a big grin on her face and stars in her eyes.

Chapter Eleven

As arranged, Saffie walked to the farm to meet Marcus the following afternoon. The light was already fading from the day but when she arrived she was a little early, so the maid showed her into the day room where Marcus's wife was sitting with a book. Saffie had never met his wife before and her first sight of Mathilda almost took her breath away. She was a tiny, slender woman who looked as if one good puff of wind might blow her away, and she was also breathtakingly beautiful. Her hair was the colour of ripened corn and her eyes were the colour of grass in the spring. There was an almost ethereal quality about her and Saffie was happy to find that her personality and her nature matched her looks.

'Oh, my dear, you must be Sapphire!' she greeted her, standing up and coming towards Saffie with her hands outstretched. 'How lovely it is to meet you at last. Marcus has told me so much about your mother and her lovely family. I do so envy her having all you beautiful children. Marcus and I are longing for a family but I'm afraid it hasn't happened for us yet. Still, I'm sure it will when the time is right. I'm a great believer that everything happens for a reason, aren't you? But listen to me, rattling away. Come over here and sit by the fire. You must be frozen. Marcus won't be long. He's usually very punctual. Would you like some tea?'

'Oh no, no thank you,' Saffie told her as she drew off her gloves. Even though she was wearing her best outfit she felt quite shabby next to Mathilda who was dressed in a very pretty gown of shot silk in a delicate lemon colour. Her hair was drawn into two bunches of ringlets tied with matching ribbons high on either side of her head and Saffie was sure she had never seen a prettier woman in her whole life.

'So tell me how are you settling in with your grandmother?' Mathilda asked as she gently led Saffie to a chair by the fire. But before Saffie could answer Mathilda began to cough.

'Oh, do excuse me,' she gulped. 'I'm recovering from a horrible winter cough and cold. It might not sound like it, but I promise I'm much better than I was.'

A little shudder of fear traced its way up Saffie's spine as she thought of her mother's cough, but she pushed it firmly away and managed a smile. 'Oh, I'm settling in quite well, thank you,' she said quietly.

'Good. I did ask her if you might come over to take tea with me one afternoon,' Mathilda went on. 'Marcus has insisted I shouldn't go out in this cold weather until I'm better and I've been awfully lonely left to my own devices all day, but your grandmother hasn't replied to me yet. Still, I'm determined to be out and about again very soon.'

Saffie was saved from having to respond when the door suddenly opened and Marcus appeared.

'Hello, darling.' He gave his wife a warm smile and Saffie couldn't help but think how handsome he was before he turned to her apologising, 'I'm so sorry I'm late, Sapphire. Something cropped up at the school with one of the children.'

'It's quite all right. It's very good of you to take me,' Saffie assured him with an answering smile.

'Then perhaps we should be on our way?' he suggested. 'I'm sure the young lady we are going to fetch will be waiting for us with bated breath. Poor thing, imagine a child being incarcerated in such a place.' He quickly crossed to his wife to plant a gentle kiss on her cheek and they then went out into the fast-darkening afternoon and he helped her into the carriage, telling the driver, 'Hatter's Hall if you please, James.'

They rattled up Tuttle Hill at a rare old pace and soon they were passing through Ansley Common and the dark forbidding walls surrounding Hatter's Hall loomed ahead of them. It was a place that was feared by the locals who kept their distance from it as much as they could, insisting that at night they could hear the wails of the poor unfortunates who were incarcerated there.

When the carriage drew up at the enormous metal gates, Marcus climbed down from the carriage to speak to the old gateman who had appeared as if from nowhere. A thick fog had fallen and everywhere looked silent and menacing.

'We are expected,' he told the man. 'And we are here to collect a young girl who has been staying here.'

'Mr Berrington, is it, sir?'

When Marcus nodded the old man fumbled amongst a large bunch of keys before inserting the largest of them into the lock on the gates and then, with some effort and a loud creaking, he pushed them open.

'Just follow the drive an' you'll come to the hall.'

Marcus thanked him and hopped back into the carriage and soon they were driving down a long tree-lined avenue that seemed to stretch forever. Eventually the dark façade of the hall appeared through the fog and Saffie shuddered at the sight of it. Thick ivy clambered up the walls and all the windows that she could see had heavy metal bars across them. It looked like the haunted house out of a ghost story she had read as a child and she clasped her hands together as pity for the poor people trapped inside ripped through her.

'Here we are then,' Marcus said as the carriage drew up outside two enormous oak doors, and they climbed down and mounted the three stone steps leading up to them. Marcus rang the bell and seconds later they heard the sound of footsteps approaching.

The door was opened by a stern-faced woman in a nurse's uniform who was clearly expecting them. She had arms like a wrestler and her thin grey hair was pulled into a tight bun in the nape of her neck. There was no welcoming smile as she asked, 'Mr Berrington and Miss Doyle, is it?'

When Marcus nodded, she stood aside to let them enter. The first thing Saffie noticed was that it was almost as cold inside as it was out. The entrance hall was enormous with a sweeping staircase on either side of it leading up to a galleried landing. The floor was covered in black and white tiles and a child in a drab grey shift dress with her hair shorn was on her hands and knees scrubbing away at them.

'Come with me,' the woman ordered and as they passed the child she hissed, 'Make sure you do a good job of it, girl, or I'll make you start all over again.'

Saffie noticed that the child didn't even dare to raise her head, she just renewed her efforts, and a stab of pity sliced through her as they moved on to a door further along the corridor.

The nurse stopped and rapped on it before opening it to announce, 'Mr Berrington and Miss Doyle to see you, Matron.'

'Thank you, Nurse, please show them in.'

Saffie meekly followed Marcus into a large office where another stern-faced woman was sitting behind a large leather-topped desk. She peered at them over the wire-framed spectacles perched on the end of her nose before telling the nurse, 'Have Catherine Herriot brought down here, please.'

'Yes, Matron.' The nurse quietly closed the door behind her as the matron pushed a form towards Marcus, telling him bluntly, 'Sign that and get Miss Doyle to witness your signature. This is Catherine Herriot's release form and it is *very* irregular. Mr Bishop should have made provision for the continuation of payments for Herriot's keep should anything happen to him. But be warned, once it is signed, we will take no further responsibility for her, is that *quite* clear?' The matron was clearly displeased at the loss of an income.

'Perfectly, ma'am.' Marcus had taken as much of a dislike to the woman as Saffie had, but he picked up the pen and signed his name with a flourish before dipping it back into the ink and handing it to Saffie for her to do the same.

The matron then took up a sheet of blotting paper and blotted their signatures before telling them, 'You may go and wait in the hallway for the nurse.' And just like that they were dismissed.

They quietly left the room and went to stand by the door where they saw the same child still diligently scrubbing away at the tiles. It was as they stood there that wails from the people incarcerated above floated down the stairs to them, and Saffie shuddered. But they had no time to comment on it before footsteps sounded on the stairs and glancing up they saw the same nurse who had admitted them approaching with a small girl walking beside her. The breath caught in Saffie's throat at first sight of the child. Her grandmother had informed her that she was about ten years old and yet she was so small that she looked much younger, and was so painfully thin that the ugly, shapeless grey shift dress that she was wearing hung off her. Her feet were clad in wooden clogs and the child's hair had been roughly chopped and hung lankly to her chin. It was hard to distinguish what colour it was as the light in the hallway was dim.

As the nurse approached them she gave the little girl a hard, spiteful push in the back towards them that almost sent her flying. Saffie's first instinct was to reach out to her to stop her from falling, but when she did the child flinched away from her. She looked questioningly at the nurse with her eyebrow raised. 'And does she have no clothes to take with her?'

The nurse snorted. 'The inmates leave with what they came with. Or at least, those that ever leave here do! She's long since grown out of hers,' she said shortly and without another word she crossed to the front door and flung it open allowing the fog to creep into the hallway.

'Come along, dear.' Marcus tried holding his hand out to the child but again she stepped back, wrapping her stick-like arms about herself and ducking as if she expected to avoid a blow. Hunkering down to her level, Marcus said gently, 'We have a carriage outside waiting for you, Catherine. Do you understand what I'm saying? You don't have to stay here anymore.' Very gently he took her shoulder and led her towards the door and she allowed herself to be led, although she never once looked up and she remained rigid.

Once outside she finally raised her head and stared round as if she could hardly believe what she saw, but then, to her alarm, Marcus lifted her into his arms and gently set her in the carriage where Saffie quickly wrapped a warm blanket across her skinny legs.

'We're taking you to my grandmother's house, you have nothing to fear.' Saffie reached out to touch the child's hand, but again she flinched away from her as far into the corner as she could get where she huddled into a ball beneath the blanket. Saffie shrugged helplessly at Marcus as he joined her.

As the carriage swayed away down the drive, Saffie silently prayed that she would never have to visit this godforsaken place ever again.

The short journey was made in silence and when the carriage drew up outside Clara's cottage, Saffie again held her hand out to the child, saying, 'We're home now, Catherine. Won't you come in and meet Minnie and my grandmother?'

The child made no sign that she had even heard her so once again, slowly so as not to frighten her, Marcus gently lifted her and carried her around the side of the house to the back door. Minnie must have been waiting for them because she threw the door open before they had even reached it and gave a beaming smile as she looked at the little waif huddled stiffly in Marcus's arms.

'Come on in outta the cold,' she urged with a shiver. 'It's enough to cut you in two out there. I've got a pan o' soup simmerin' away on the range an' a nice fresh-baked loaf and butter to go wi' it.'

When the child didn't even look towards her, the smile slid from Minnie's face and she glanced at Saffie with concern.

'I think Catherine is a little overwhelmed with everything that's happening,' Saffie told her in a falsely bright voice. 'But I'm sure she'll feel better with some of that nice soup inside her, Minnie.'

Marcus gently placed the little girl in the chair at the side of the inglenook fireplace and again the child curled into a ball with her arms wrapped about her knees and her head bent.

Minnie nodded and pottered away to fill a bowl with soup, which she placed on the table, and for the first time the child raised her head just enough to watch what she was doing as Marcus and Saffie looked on. Next Minnie cut some thick slices of bread and spread them with soft, creamy butter before telling the little girl, 'There y'are then, pet. Why don't you come an' 'ave it while it's nice an' hot?'

They held their breath as very slowly the child uncoiled her legs, then with her eyes darting from one to the other of them, as if she half expected them to steal the food, she cautiously slunk towards the table and sat down. Seconds later she lifted the spoon and although the soup was hot, she slurped it down as if she hadn't eaten for a month. In no time at all the dish was empty and she began on the bread, stuffing her mouth so full and swallowing it so quickly that she made herself heave. Once it was all gone, she swiped the back of her hand across her mouth and before their astonished eyes she leaned forward and was promptly sick all across Minnie's nice clean floor. She instantly looked terrified and raised her arm as if she expected a blow, but Minnie took it all in her stride as she hurried off to fetch the mop and bucket, telling her, 'Don't get worryin' about that, pet. I can clean it up in a jiffy. You just go an' get warm by the fire again, eh?'

Clearly embarrassed, Marcus moved towards the door. 'Right, if there's nothing more I can help you with I'd best get back. Bye for now.'

Saffie quickly followed him and once outside he shook his head. 'Poor little soul. Did you see the way she attacked that

111

food? I'm afraid you're going to have your work cut out to gain that child's confidence. Oh, and by the way, I should check her hair when she lets you near her. I think I saw head lice in her parting when I was carrying her.'

'I shan't even attempt it today.' Saffie looked sad. 'I think it's best to just let her rest and hopefully she'll see then that we mean her no harm. But do you think she's . . .' She bit on her lip worriedly as she sought for the right words. 'Do you think she can talk? She hasn't said a word so far and when she leaned over to vomit, I noticed that the top of her arms were covered in bruises.'

Marcus sighed as he looked towards the carriage where the horses were growing impatient and pawing at the ground. 'I have heard that the people who are locked away in Hatter's Hall are very cruelly treated. Do you have any idea how long she's been there?'

'No, Grandmother didn't say. But anyway, thank you for taking me and bringing us back. I dare say I'd better go and let my grandmother know she's arrived.'

'Good luck with that.' Marcus gave her a wry smile. He knew that Clara Bishop could be a hard woman and she had made it more than obvious that she had only taken the child because she had no other option. He wondered if the poor little girl was doomed to living the whole of her life with people who didn't want her, but then he looked at Saffie and he somehow knew that she took after her kind-hearted mother and that she would do her best for her.

He swung into the carriage and Saffie stood for a moment and watched it drive away before turning to go and start her new job in earnest. She had an idea that it was going to be a lot more difficult than she had thought.

112

'I just came to inform you that Catherine is here, Ma'am,' Saffie told her when she entered the drawing room a few minutes later.

Her grandmother was reading and she raised her head and frowned. 'Then take her to her room and keep her there. The last thing I want is a brat rampaging about the house. And make sure you keep her quiet too.'

Saffie was shocked. Surely her grandmother would at least want to meet the child, but no, she had already turned her attention back to her book and showed no interest whatsoever. With a sigh, Saffie left the room and made her way back to the kitchen.

Catherine was sitting where she had left her with her head still lowered and Saffie glanced at Minnie who shook her head.

'Poor little soul is scared to move,' Minnie whispered when Saffie joined her at the sink. 'I dread to think what the poor kid 'as suffered up at Hatter's Hall. An' she's so dirty an' all! I'd love to wash 'er 'air for 'er an' sit 'er in the bath in front o' the fire.'

'I know what you mean but I think we'd be better to leave that until another day,' Saffie said sensibly. 'Let's let her settle in a bit and build her trust up first.'

'Ar, yer probably right but it's a cryin' shame, the way I see it. I'd love to sit 'er on me lap an' give 'er a cuddle but if I so much as go near 'er she shies away from me.'

'Things will improve,' Saffie told her, but deep inside she wasn't so sure.

Chapter Twelve

'I shall call you Cathy,' Saffie told the little girl as she led her up to her attic bedroom that evening, with Minnie close behind. 'It's a little less formal than Catherine, don't you think?'

The child said nothing. Minnie was fussing over her like a mother hen, or at least as much as she was allowed to, and had clearly taken a shine to the little girl. She had been up there minutes before to light the oil lamp and now as they entered the room it looked warm and cosy.

Cathy's eyes were like saucers as she lifted her head just enough to glance around her. It was cold up there admittedly but after the cell she had lived in at Hatter's Hall it looked like heaven. Minnie had put lots of nice warm blankets and a colourful patchwork quilt on the bed, and rugs were strewn across the floor. There was a chest of drawers that had been polished to a mirror-like shine and a small table and chair where the child could sit and read or write, if she was able to, that was. A pretty, if slightly chipped, jug and bowl stood on a marble-topped washstand against one wall and Minnie had placed some big fluffy towels on the chair for her to dry herself with. Saffie had laid one of her own nightdresses across the bed. It would be far too big for the child but she reasoned it would be better than nothing until she could get out and buy Cathy some of her own.

'Do you think you'll be comfy in here?' she asked with a smile but again the child hung her head and there was no answer. 'And Minnie has put a hot-water bottle in the bed,' Saffie went on. 'So I'm sure you'll be snug as a bug in a rug once you've snuggled down. I shall be just below you on the next floor so if you need anything during the night just ring that little bell over there and I should be able to hear you.' She and Minnie hovered for a second more, hoping for some sort of a response, but when none was forthcoming, they glanced at each other and backed towards the door.

'Well, goodnight, sleep tight,' Saffie said softly and she left the room closing the door quietly behind her.

'Eeh, I hope the little mite'll be all right!' Minnie said worriedly as they descended the stairs.

Saffie patted her arm. 'I'm sure she'll be fine; it's bound to feel a bit strange after being cooped up in Hatter's Hall, but give her a few days and she'll be as right as ninepence.'

Neither Saffie nor Minnie slept much that night. They both lay listening for sounds from the attic room but all was quiet and the next morning they were both up early to check on the child and met on the landing.

'There ain't been a peep out o' her,' Minnie commented as they climbed the stairs together.

'Well, let's take that as a good sign, eh? Perhaps it means she slept well.'

At the top of the stairs, Saffie gently tapped on the door and when no answer was forthcoming, she inched it open.

Cathy was sitting up in bed with her bedclothes pulled up to her chin, her eyes huge in her small face.

'Good morning, Cathy. Did you sleep well?' Saffie deliberately kept her voice cheerful as she entered the room and approached the bed, but the little girl instantly recoiled from her. Her eyes didn't look quite so dull this morning and it occurred to Saffie that perhaps the staff at Hatter's Hall had given her drugs to keep her quiet. 'Hungry, are you? Minnie does a lovely breakfast; do you like bacon and eggs?' She didn't expect Cathy to answer so wasn't surprised when she didn't. 'Right, so shall we go down to the kitchen then? It will be lovely and warm down there once we've made the fire up.'

The child tentatively crept from the bed, her arms wrapped protectively around herself and her eyes fixed firmly on Saffie's face as she followed her back to the door. Just once Saffie reached out to take her hand but the child shrank away from her so Saffie quickly took a step back as she led them all down the stairs. She was realising that it was probably going to take a lot longer than she had thought to gain the child's trust.

They had almost reached the bottom when the door to the drawing room suddenly opened and Clara appeared, still clad in her nightdress and robe.

'You're up early,' Saffie commented pleasantly but the smile slid from her face when she saw the way her grandmother was watching Cathy. Her eyes were wide and her lips were curled back from her teeth as if there was a vile smell under her nose.

'What is that that . . . *brat* doing down here?' Her voice shook with venom as she waved a quavering finger at Cathy whose neck seemed to have shrunk down into her shoulder blades.

'I was . . . I was just bringing her down for her breakfast,' Saffie answered in a small voice.

After fiddling in the pocket of her night robe, Clara extracted a key, which she flung towards Saffie, telling her, 'Get her back to the attics and *keep* her there, and make sure that the door is locked at all times. I don't want to set eyes on her again, do you *hear* me?'

'Yes, Grandmother, but—'

'It's *ma'am* when you address me,' Clara snarled. 'Now get her out of my sight!'

All three turned as one and fled back up the stairs, almost tripping in their haste. None of them spoke until they were back in the attic room where Minnie let out a long breath. 'Eeh, I don't know what's come over 'er.' She shook her head in bewilderment. 'She were like a woman possessed! Are you all right, pet?' Cathy had fled to the bed and buried herself beneath the blankets but it was clear that she was utterly terrified.

Saffie placed a hand on Minnie's arm and told her gently, 'Why don't you go and bring Cathy some breakfast up on a tray, eh? I'll stay here with her until you come back and we'll talk when I come down.'

'Aye, I'll do that.' Minnie cast one last anxious glance at the quivering little body on the bed and quietly left the room.

Saffie slowly approached the side of the bed. 'It's all right, Cathy, she won't hurt you. She's not usually like that.' She didn't quite know what to say. What *could* she say to excuse her grandmother's abominable behaviour? After a moment she sat down in the chair and waited for Minnie to come back and when she did, carrying a laden tray with all sorts of delicious smells issuing from it, she urged, 'Come on, sweetheart. Look what Minnie has brought you.'

Cathy showed no sign of emerging from the sheets so Saffie pointed to the small table at the side of the bed, saying, 'Minnie and I will leave you in peace to eat your meal, shall we? But don't worry, we'll be back soon.'

She nodded towards the door and minutes later, when they had closed it behind them, Saffie reluctantly locked it and silently followed Minnie down to the kitchen.

'So what did yer make o' that then?' Minnie shook her head. 'I don't know what's gettin' into the missus. *Surely* she don't expect us to keep the little 'un locked away? It ain't natural.'

Saffie shrugged. 'I really don't know why she's taken such an unnatural dislike to the child,' she agreed. 'And you're quite right. Cathy needs fresh air and exercise – every child does. She's spent enough time locked away in Hatter's Hall as it is. But let's just give it a few days to see if Grandmother settles down a bit to the idea of the girl being here and see what happens. Meantime I'm going to ask her for some money so that I can go into town and get Cathy some new clothes.'

'Huh! I can't see 'er bein' none too 'appy about that!'

'I know, but she's got to have something to wear, hasn't she?'

At that moment the front door bell rang and Minnie hurried away to answer it to find Marcus standing on the step.

'Hello, I thought I'd just call in and see how Catherine is settling in on my way to the school,' he said pleasantly.

Before Minnie could answer, the mistress appeared in the doorway of the drawing room and said, 'Ah, Marcus, do come in. Minnie, fetch us some tea.'

'No, no, please don't bother on my account,' he said in a rush. 'I have to be at the school in less than fifteen minutes. As I was just saying to Minnie, I was just wondering how the child is after her first night with you? And Mathilda was thinking of calling later to introduce herself.'

Clara's mouth set in a straight, grim line. 'She is fine, thank you,' she said in a strained voice. 'But I don't believe she is up to visitors just yet. In fact, I would be grateful if as few people as possible know that she is here, please, Marcus.'

He gave a slight frown. 'Oh . . . very well. But what about school? I thought she might like to join my class.'

'Thank you, but that won't be necessary.' Clara's eyes were as cold as marbles. 'Sapphire will be teaching the child here.'

'I see. Then in that case I'm very sorry to have disturbed you.' He doffed his hat and without another word turned and walked away as the mistress disappeared into the drawing room again and Minnie was left chewing her lip. She had no idea what was going on but she didn't like it one little bit.

'You want *what*?' Clara questioned irately when Saffie approached her a short time later.

Saffie kept her head high as she stared coolly back at her. 'I want some money for clothing for Cathy. She has only what she came in and she had to sleep in one of my nightdresses last night. But rest assured I shall only buy what is absolutely essential for her.' For a moment she thought her grandmother was going to refuse but then she sighed and lifting her reticule she began to extract some coins from her purse.

'Here,' she said begrudgingly, handing them to Saffie. 'I believe there is a rag stall in the market place where decent second-hand clothing can be purchased cheaply. But make sure you don't buy anything that she doesn't absolutely need.'

'Of course.' Saffie gazed down at the meagre amount in her hand, thinking that chance would have been a fine thing with that paltry amount, and then she turned and left the room, leaving her grandmother, who was clearly agitated, pacing up and down like a caged animal.

In the kitchen with Minnie once more she slammed the money down on the table. 'I'm not going to buy her much with that, am I?' she groaned.

'Hm.' Minnie grinned. 'The missus 'as allus been a bit tight when it comes to payin' out. But never mind, if the worst comes to the worst an' you can't get what you need we can allus buy some material and make some clothes for her, or failin' that we can always alter things.'

'I hadn't thought of that,' Saffie admitted, handing her the key to Cathy's room. 'Will you be all right with her until I get back?'

'Course I will. Go on, you get off an' I'll go up an' check on 'er.'

And so, Saffie went to fetch her cloak and bonnet and set off for the town centre.

It was a cold, frosty day and by the time Saffie got there her nose was glowing and although she was wearing the warm mittens her mother had knitted for her, her hands were numb. When she reached the market place, she quickly stepped past the cages full of farm animals where the farmers were loudly arguing and bartering with each other and moved on until she came to the stalls that seemed to sell everything from buckets to bowls to food.

Eventually, she came to the rag stall. Women were clustered around it, busily searching through the heaps of clothes piled on it and Saffie reluctantly joined them. She soon discovered why it was called the rag stall as most of the items were indeed little more than rags but at last she pounced on a gown made of a soft fine wool in a pretty pale green colour. It was obviously made for a woman and would be far too large for Cathy but the material was so good that Saffie felt it would be worth cutting down for her, so she held on to it for dear life as the search continued. Half an hour later she felt she had found the best of what was available and she went to haggle with the stallholder, who eventually reluctantly knocked a few pennies off the asking price.

Her next stop was the second-hand shoe stall, but there she bit her lip in consternation. She had no idea what size feet Cathy had, so in the end she settled for a small pair of black buttoned boots. They were very dirty and slightly down at heel but Saffie could see that they would clean up with some elbow grease and a bit of polish and there was still a lot of wear left in them. At any rate, she reasoned that they had to be a lot better than the wooden clogs Cathy had been forced to wear at Hatter's Hall, and if they were too big, she could always stuff the toes with newspaper. Finally, she stopped at the fabric stall and bought a length of clean white linen that she and Minnie could make a couple of nightdresses out of, and satisfied that she had most of what she needed, she set off back the way she had come, keen to get out of the cold.

She had almost reached the edge of the market place when she saw a beautiful woman heading towards her and she recognised Mathilda, Marcus's wife. She had only met her briefly but Mathilda had the sort of looks that once seen would never be forgotten. Today she was dressed in a bright red two-piece costume trimmed with fur, which showed off her fairness to perfection.

'Sapphire!' She rushed forward and gave Saffie a warm hug, evidently happy to see her. Then glancing down at Saffie's loaded basket, she grinned. 'Someone's been busy, by the look of it.'

'These are things for Catherine,' Saffie explained. She knew that her grandmother wanted as few people as possible to know about the child's existence but seeing as Marcus already did, she assumed that his wife would too.

'Ah, of course, and how is the dear little soul?' Even Mathilda's voice was beautiful and Saffie could see why Marcus loved her so much.

Saffie shrugged. 'Still very traumatised, I'm afraid,' she confided. 'And it's hardly any wonder after being locked away in that awful place. She hasn't said so much as a single word yet.'

'I imagine that's to be expected, but I'm sure she'll come round,' Mathilda said kindly. 'Do you have everything you need for her now? I'd be more than happy to help if there's anything I can do.'

Saffie gave her a grateful smile. 'That's really kind of you but I think I've got all she needs for now.' Mathilda's lovely nature clearly matched her looks and Saffie felt that in her she had found a friend and ally.

'Well, just remember where Marcus and I are and don't hesitate to ask if there's anything at all we can help with.'

'I will, thank you, but I'd best be getting back now else my grandmother will be wondering where I've got to.'

122

'Very well, but I insist on giving you a lift in my carriage. It's only just along here in Stratford Street and I've done my shopping now too,' Mathilda told her, gently taking Saffie's elbow and leading her through the stalls.

Saffie's stomach began to rumble as a million smells wafted towards them from the food stalls that sold everything from hot faggots and peas, pies, and fish. She realised that she hadn't had any breakfast, so she didn't protest as Mathilda led her towards her carriage. It would be nice to be out of the cold and to ride in style for a change, especially with such nice company.

Chapter Thirteen

'So 'ow did yer get on then?' Minnie asked the second Saffie stepped through the kitchen door.

Saffie dropped the heavy basket onto the table and after removing her mittens she blew on her hands then rubbed them together to try and get some feeling back into them. 'Not as well as I would have liked.' She sighed. 'Nearly everything will need altering.'

'That's all right.' Minnie filled the kettle from the pump on the sink and placed it on the range to boil, before saying worriedly, 'The missus 'as been behavin' very strangely while you've bin gone. She's walkin' about the place muttterin' to 'erself an' she ain't even bothered to get dressed yet.'

'Really?' Saffie was surprised. From what she'd seen of her, her grandmother seemed to take great pride in her appearance. 'And how is Cathy? Have you checked on her?'

'O' course I have,' Minnie huffed, offended. 'I've been runnin' up an' down them stairs like a blue-arsed fly but I still ain't had a peep out o' her, although she did eat all her breakfast. An' she looks a bit brighter this mornin' an' all. I reckon they were druggin' the kid up at the hall to keep her quiet.'

Saffie shook her head; she had thought the same thing herself. 'Right, well, I'll go up to see her when I've thawed out and had a hot drink,' she said as she started to unpack the things she had bought and spread them out on the table. She had almost finished when the door from the hall opened and her grandmother appeared looking wild-eyed and dishevelled.

'So did you get what you wanted?' she asked abruptly and it was all Saffie could do to remain civil.

'I'm afraid I was unable to with the amount you gave me,' she answered coldly. 'But I have managed to get some garments that can be unpicked and made into clothes that will fit her.'

'And you didn't mention to anyone who they were for?'

'Of course I didn't,' Saffie responded indignantly. 'You specifically told me not to. But I did bump into Marcus's wife and she was fully aware of who they must be for.'

Clara scowled. 'Hm, Marcus must have told her about the girl then. I was hoping he wouldn't. The fewer people who know she is here the better.'

'But isn't it usual for a husband *not* to have secrets from his wife? And why shouldn't people know about Cathy? I'm sure they would think you were a very charitable person for taking her in.'

There was another frown from her grandmother before she snapped at Minnie, 'And are you quite sure the door to her room is securely locked?'

'Yes, missus, I am, though why it 'as to be I can't fathom. The child is 'armless. It ain't right for her to be kept locked away. Surely she 'ad enough o' that up at the hall?'

'Don't you *dare* question my orders, otherwise you'll find yourself looking for another job,' Clara hissed and, turning about, she slammed out of the room leaving Minnie to shake her head.

The next two days were fraught with anxiety as Minnie and Saffie attempted to bring Cathy out of her shell, but although she ate everything they put in front of her, all their efforts were in vain and she didn't say a word, until Minnie finally said, 'Right, we've tried the kid-glove approach an' got nowhere so now I reckon we should be a bit firmer wi' her. We'll start wi' a bath cos every time I go into her room the smell makes me gag.'

'But how are we going to do that?' Saffie looked concerned. 'Grandmother has told us she can't come downstairs.'

'Well, I sure as 'ell ain't goin' to attempt to lug the bath up there,' Minnie answered with a toss of her head. 'I tell yer, if she carries on like this it'll be 'er as ends up in Hatter's Hall next,' she muttered with a shake of her head as she proceeded to warm the teapot. 'Soon as everythin' is quiet this evenin' an' we've got dinner out o' the way I'll fill a warm bath in 'ere in front o' the fire an' we'll bring her down whether she likes it or not. Then when she's nice an' clean we'll let her wear that nightshirt we've stitched for her. That should cheer her up a bit.'

And so that night when Clara was settled reading in the drawing room, Minnie carried the tin bath into the kitchen and filled it with hot water from the kettle.

'Right, shall you go an' fetch her or shall I?' she asked in a determined voice as she laid some towels out ready. She had rolled her sleeves up and clearly meant business.

'I'll go,' Saffie answered doubtfully.

'On yer way then, an' don't stand fer no nonsense. It's fer her own good!'

Saffie mounted the stairs after checking that all was quiet in the drawing room and moments later, she unlocked the door of Cathy's room. As usual the child was huddled under the blankets and she stared up at her fearfully. Remembering what Minnie had said Saffie smiled. 'Up we get, Cathy. You're coming with me to have a nice warm bath and then you can put on the pretty nightgown that Minnie and I have made for you.'

Cathy cringed away from her as she approached the bed but Saffie ignored the look on her face and gently peeled the blankets away before saying firmly, 'Come along, I don't want to have to carry you!'

Realising that she meant what she said, the little girl slowly slung her legs over the side of the bed, her head bowed, and once she was standing Saffie took her hand and drew her towards the door. Inside she was crying for the child who was clearly terrified but she kept up a cheerful chatter as she led her down the stairs.

Once they entered the kitchen Cathy's eyes seemed to pop from her head as she saw the steaming bath of water and she pulled back, but Saffie hung on to her as Minnie smiled.

'That's a good girl. Now let's get that shift off you, shall we?' And before Cathy could protest, Minnie flipped the shapeless garment over the child's head, leaving her shivering with tears in her eyes. It was then that Saffie and Minnie saw the extent of the bruises that covered the child's body and they glanced at each other in dismay. Some of the bruises were faded and yellow whereas the most recent ones were still purple and blue. They had noticed how thin she was but nothing could have prepared them for her poor skeletal little frame. Every rib was visible and her arms and legs were as thin as matchsticks, but even so Minnie's voice was light as she encouraged, 'In you hop, pet. It's lovely an' warm, not too hot, I promise.'

Cathy eyed the water with a deep frown but all the same she stepped into it and slowly sat down. Minnie instantly took up a bar of soap and began to rub it into her hair and as she did so they saw that it was a lovely strawberry blonde colour. It had been so dirty that it had been hard to distinguish what colour it was.

'There now, that ain't so bad, is it? An' think how lovely an' clean you'll feel when we've finished.'

Very gently she washed the child's body and when she was content that she was spotless, she fetched some jugs of fresh water she had standing on the draining board and rinsed her off. She helped her out of the water onto the rug in front of the fire and wrapped her in a voluminous towel before beginning to rub at her hair vigorously with a smaller one. 'That'll do nicely, I reckon,' she said after a few minutes. 'Now you sit down there an' let the fire dry yer 'air and then you can 'ave yer new nightie on an' a lovely cup o' cocoa an' a biscuit. How does that sound?'

The child obediently did as she was told and as the warmth of the fire dried her hair it began to form a little halo of curls about her head. Soon after, Saffie helped her into the night-dress they had made for her, and suddenly the little girl was almost unrecognisable.

Minnie meanwhile made her the promised cup of cocoa but as she took it to her the child started to cry and spoke for the first time when she whimpered, 'I want my mama!'

Minnie was so shocked that she almost dropped the mug. It was the first time they had heard her speak, but why would she ask for her mother if her mother had died giving birth to her? She would never have known her.

'I think sadly yer mama died a long time ago when she had you,' Minnie said gently but the girl shook her head.

'No, she didn't. She was poorly and had to go away and I got put into the bad place until she was well enough to come and fetch me.'

'And how long ago was this?' Saffie asked gently.

The child shrugged. She clearly didn't have a good concept of time but she did tell them, 'I think it was just after Christmas last year?'

Saffie and Minnie were shocked. This flew in the face of everything Clara had told them, but how could they know if the child was telling the truth? And if she was, why had Clara lied to them? Could it be that Cathy's mother was still alive somewhere?

It seemed that now Cathy had started to speak she couldn't stop and she rushed on, 'My mama was pretty and kind and she promised me she would come for me just as soon as she could when they took me away.'

'I see, and do you know where you lived?' Saffie prompted.

The child had no time to answer for at that moment the door burst open and Clara stood there with murder in her eyes as they lit on Cathy.

'*What* is she doing down here?' she ground out, shaking with rage.

Saffie bravely turned to face her. 'We had to bring her down to give her a bath,' she said firmly. 'And she's just told us something quite surprising.'

A look of fear flitted across Clara's face but it was gone in seconds. 'Oh yes, and what would that be?'

'Cathy has informed us that her mother didn't die in childbirth but is possibly still alive somewhere.'

'*Rubbish!* Surely you don't believe a word that comes out of her mouth! She's a simpleton. In fact, I'm amazed that she can even speak.' And before anyone could utter so much as another word, all hell broke loose as Clara flew forward like a woman possessed and thumped Cathy resoundingly across the ear, knocking the poor child sideways.

''*Ere*, there ain't no call fer that, missus!' Minnie shouted as she rushed forward and stood protectively in front of the child. At the same time Saffie put her arms about her grandmother's waist and pulled her away from the little girl who was trembling like a leaf, tears streaming down her waxen cheeks.

'She's *filth*,' Clara spat as Saffie held her back. 'Get her out of my sight this instant else I won't be responsible for my actions. It'll be woe betide her if I have to set eyes on her again!'

Without a word Minnie bent and lifted Cathy into her arms before rushing away with her while Saffie held on to her grandmother for dear life until she felt it was safe to let her go. Clara was shaking violently and when Saffie finally released her she staggered and gripped the back of a chair. The sudden silence was deafening until Clara turned and barged from the room, and Saffie hurried upstairs to see how Cathy was. Suddenly she was wondering if taking this job had been such a good idea after all, but how could she go home now and leave Cathy to the mercy of this woman?

She found Minnie sitting on Cathy's bed with the child on her lap. Cathy was sobbing uncontrollably and Saffie's heart went out to her. To have to suffer this after all she had been through seemed so unfair.

'I want my mama,' Cathy sniffled over and over again. It was like a mantra and Saffie and Minnie could only look on helplessly.

Eventually the sobs turned to sniffles and after Minnie tucked the child into bed, they wearily made their way to the kitchen.

'I don't know what to do or how to handle this,' Saffie admitted.

'Hm, I know what yer mean.' Minnie began to ladle the scummy water from the fast-cooling bath and throw it down the sink. 'I wonder if Marcus could help?' she suggested. 'The missus seems to take notice of him. One thing's for sure, we've got to sort somethin' out! We can't keep that little 'un penned up like an animal.'

'I think you're right,' Saffie agreed. 'I'll try and catch him tomorrow and explain what's going on.'

Chapter Fourteen

A steady drizzle was falling from a leaden sky as Saffie set out on her mission the following morning, clutching her cloak about her. When Canal Farm came into view she quickened her pace, and soon she was tapping at the heavy oak entrance door. It was answered almost immediately by a young maid.

'Good morning, I was wondering if Marc— Mr Berrington was in please?' Saffie smiled at her.

The maid shook her head, setting her mobcap wobbling. 'Sorry, miss. The mister left fer the school some time ago, but the missus is in, if you'd like to see her?'

Saffie chewed on her lip for a moment then making a hasty decision she nodded. 'Yes, that would be fine, thank you.'

'Step inside an' I'll go an' tell her you're 'ere.'

Saffie did as she was told, marvelling at how luxurious the inside of the farmhouse was as the little maid scuttled away. She was back within seconds to tell her, 'The missus says you're to come through to the drawin' room, miss. Would yer foller me?'

Saffie entered the large airy room to find Mathilda waiting for her with her hands outstretched. 'Ah, Sapphire, how lovely it is of you to call.' She gave her a beaming smile. 'Do come in and, Libby, could you organise some coffee for us, or perhaps you would prefer tea, Sapphire?'

'Coffee would be lovely, and please call me Saffie,' Sapphire answered, thinking again how pretty Mathilda was. Today she was dressed in a pale lilac shot silk gown with a voluminous skirt that showed off her tiny waist to perfection, and her lovely hair was piled high on her head.

'Now do come and sit down,' Mathilda insisted as she helped Saffie off with her cloak.

Saffie couldn't help but notice that there was a radiance about Mathilda and she seemed excited. The reason soon became clear when she whispered conspiratorially, 'I'm so glad you've come. I feel as if I might burst if I don't share my good news with someone. But before I do, you must promise not to tell a soul, not just yet anyway.'

'Of course,' Saffie promised.

'Well, the thing is . . .' Mathilda blushed prettily. 'Dr Jones is calling to see me later this morning. Marcus insisted I should see him as I've been feeling rather sick in the mornings for the last few weeks. But . . . I think he might be able to tell me that I am carrying a baby at last. I haven't told Marcus my suspicions, not until it is confirmed. It would be just too cruel to dash his hopes if I am wrong. We've wanted a child for so long but now I have missed two courses so . . .'

Genuinely pleased for her, Saffie clapped her hands together. 'Why, that's wonderful,' she exclaimed. 'You must be feeling over the moon.'

Mathilda nodded, but then frowned. 'I am but I'm afraid I shall be very disappointed if I'm wrong. It has happened so many times before. Still, there's not long to wait now to find out. But hark at me rambling on, I haven't even asked the purpose of your visit, which is very remiss of me. Is this a social call or is there something I can help you with?'

'Well . . . it was just advice I wanted really,' Saffie admitted hesitantly. 'You see, things aren't going well with Cathy, the little girl who Marcus kindly took me to fetch from Hatter's Hall. My grandmother has told me and Minnie that we're not to let her out of her room but last night we had to give her a bath and . . .'

She paused while Libby came in with the coffee and after it had been poured, Saffie went on to tell Mathilda about the way her grandmother had attacked the child.

Mathilda listened carefully, looking appalled. 'But what has the poor little mite done to make Clara hate her so?' she questioned. 'When Marcus told me that she was fetching a relative's child to live with her from Hatter's Hall I thought what a wonderful charitable thing it was to do, but it sounds like Clara doesn't even like her!'

'She acts as if she truly hates her,' Saffie confided. 'But how are we supposed to keep the child locked away? Even an animal deserves to get out in the fresh air and exercise. I suggested that perhaps we could register Cathy at Marcus's school but Grandmother has said that I must teach her at home.'

Mathilda looked mildly surprised. 'Oh, so is that something you feel you could do?'

'Oh yes,' Saffie said confidently. 'I've always dreamed of being a teacher, but circumstances . . . But that isn't the issue. I feel that Cathy would benefit from being with other children her age. And that isn't all – you see Cathy told us that her mother didn't die giving birth to her as Grandmother told us, but that she had become ill some time ago and Cathy was placed in Hatter's Hall by my grandfather until her mother was well enough to have her home again.'

'How very strange.' Mathilda frowned. 'But why would Clara lie? And if Cathy's mother is still alive, where is she?'

Saffie shrugged and after a moment Mathilda said, 'I might be able to find out. I believe Marcus has a former pupil who works at Hatter's Hall. I shall ask him to approach her and see if she can get to the bottom of it.'

'That would be wonderful,' Saffie answered with a smile, but immediately felt guilty. Mathilda had been so happy when she arrived and now she had spoiled it for her. 'I'm so sorry to burden you with this on such a happy day,' she apologised. 'But I didn't know who else I could talk to.'

Mathilda waved her hand airily. 'Oh, don't worry about that. Just leave it with me. I shall speak to Marcus as soon as he comes in.'

As Saffie rose, Mathilda crossed the room in a rustle of silk skirts to kiss her gently on the cheek. 'We shall find a way to resolve this so try not to worry,' she urged. 'And I shall get word to you about the doctor's verdict so keep your fingers crossed it is what I am longing to hear. And do please call again soon.'

'I shall,' Saffie promised as she left. Somehow, she thought as she walked back to her grandmother's house, she sensed that she and Mathilda were going to become close friends and it was a comforting thought.

She was so lost in thought that it came as a shock when she heard someone call her name and glancing behind her she saw a tall young man who looked vaguely familiar making his way towards her. He was smartly dressed in a warm overcoat and a hat but try as she might, she couldn't recall how she knew him, so she waited for him to catch up with her.

'Ah, Miss Doyle, I'm so glad I've caught you,' he said, blushing to the very roots of his hair as he swept off his hat.

It was then that she recognised the young constable who had been kind enough to come and tell the family what had become of her brother and father when they were still living on *The Blue Sapphire*.

'Constable Denning.' He looked so different out of his uniform. 'Whatever brings you to this neck of the woods?' Her stomach churned with fear. Could it be that something had happened? 'Are my father and my brother all right?'

'Oh yes,' he reassured her quickly. 'Or at least as far as I know they are. I haven't heard otherwise. But your granny asked me to come and bring a message,' he went on solemnly. 'I've kept in touch with your mother and your siblings since they settled in the cottage.' He didn't enlighten her that he'd only done so in the hope of seeing her again. 'And I'm afraid that I'm the bearer of bad news. Your mother has taken a turn for the worse and she's asking for you, so your granny wondered if it would be possible for you to come and see her. She sent me because it's quicker than you having to wait for a letter.'

Saffie's heart began to thump like a caged bird in her chest. Things must be very bad indeed if Granny Doyle had seen fit to send for her. But how could she leave Cathy? Her other grandmother wouldn't take kindly to her clearing off and leaving her to do it. And if she did, she dreaded to think how Cathy would be treated.

'You're lucky to have caught me,' she told him. 'I was just paying a quick visit to our neighbour. But come along, we'd better go and see if me coming back with you is going to be possible.' She felt as if she was being rent in two. Half of her wanted to fly to her mother's side but the other half was fearful of what might happen to Cathy if she did.

Constable Denning placed his hat back on and fell into step beside her and for a while they continued in an uncomfortable silence until she said, 'It was, er . . . very kind of you to come and tell me.'

'Oh, it was no trouble at all,' he assured her. He could hardly tell her that she was never far from his thoughts and that he dreamed about her most nights. 'And my name is Bernard, by the way, but it would be nice if you called me Bernie,' he told her shyly.

They had reached the house now and Saffie forced a half-hearted smile as she headed around the back to the kitchen door.

Minnie was kneading dough on the table and as Saffie entered with Bernie Denning close behind her, she raised an eyebrow.

'Minnie, this is . . .' Saffie glanced at Bernie, wondering how she should introduce him. 'Mr Bernie Denning. I met him when my family and I lived on the boat and he's brought a message from my granny. It seems that my mum is very poorly and is asking for me. But how can I go with Cathy to look after?'

Minnie brushed her hands down her apron. 'O' course yer must go,' she said in a firm voice. 'I can look after Cathy till you get back.'

'But you already have so much to do,' Saffie objected.

'Rubbish. She ain't no bother at all so go through an' settle it wi' the missus. An' once you're home take as long as you need to. I shall be just fine an' so will Cathy. An', Bernie, come an' sit down. I dare say a cuppa wouldn't go amiss if you've travelled from Banbury.'

And so Saffie took a deep breath and headed for the drawing room where she found her grandmother sitting in the window overlooking the garden, nervously twisting her fingers together.

'I'm afraid I have some bad news,' Saffie told her without giving her a chance to speak and she hastily went on to tell her what had happened. 'I intend to go,' she ended. 'And of course, you could always come with me. She is your only daughter, after all.'

Just for a moment she saw a flicker of something like concern flit across the woman's face but then her lips set in a grim line and she shook her head. 'No, I shan't be going. Your mother chose the path she wished to take many years ago. And what about . . .' She cocked her head towards the ceiling. '*The girl!* I thought I was paying you to take care of her!'

'Minnie has said that she'll care for her just until I get back,' Saffie told her. 'And I promise I won't stay a day longer than necessary.'

'Huh! Seems to me you're set on going whether I like it or not,' Clara replied huffily, turning her attention back to the window.

Saffie knew that there was no more to be said so she left the room quietly and hurried upstairs to pack a few things in her small carpet bag before hurrying off to join Bernie in the kitchen. 'I'm ready to go, Mr Denning.'

'Oh please, I'd rather you call me Bernie,' he insisted as he blushed again.

Minnie stifled a giggle. It was more than obvious that this young man was smitten with Saffie.

'Go on, get off wi' yer,' Minnie encouraged. 'An' don't get worryin' about anythin' 'ere. We'll be right as ninepence. If you get a shufti on yer should be able to get a train to Banbury from Trent Valley Station. It'll be quicker than the coach.'

And so with a grateful smile, Saffie set off with Bernie hot on her heels.

Thankfully they only had to wait for twenty minutes at the station before a train arrived that would take them to Coventry, and from there they were able to get another train to Banbury. The journey was silent for the most part as Saffie was so worried about her mother she couldn't think of much else. And Bernie was so tongue-tied to be in her presence that while she stared sightlessly from the window his gaze stayed firmly on her.

They entered the station in a hiss of steam and smoke and soon they were heading for the banks of the canal and Granny Doyle's cottage.

'I, er . . . should leave you now,' Bernie told her as they reached the little picket gate.

Saffie shook her head distractedly and waved her hand at him. 'No, no you've been so kind. The least I can do is offer you a cup of tea before you go on your way.'

And so Bernie followed her into the comfortable warmth of the cosy kitchen where the twins instantly whooped with delight at the sight of her and flung themselves at her.

'Ooh, we're ever so glad you've come,' Ginny gushed as she wrapped her arms tightly about Saffie's waist. 'Mum has been ever so poorly. Granny is upstairs with her now.'

'Then be a dear and put the kettle on and make Mr Denn—Bernie a nice cup of tea, would you, while I go up to them?'

She kissed both Ginny and Lucy on their cheeks and after nodding at Bernie she shot away up the stairs without even waiting to take her bonnet and cloak off.

Granny Doyle was leaning over the bed mopping her mother's fevered brow when she entered and, glancing across her shoulder, she shook her head sadly before saying, 'I reckon you've got here just in time, lass. I don't think she's much longer for this world.'

Saffie gasped as she stared down at her mother's waxen face on the pillow. It was so thin that it looked as if the skin had been stretched across her bones, and it was clear that each breath she took was painful for her.

'Oh, *Mammy*.' Dropping down beside her, Saffie lay her head on her mother's chest as tears slid down her face.

'I'll leave yer to 'ave a few minutes alone wi' 'er. Call me if yer need me,' Granny Doyle said quietly and she slowly limped from the room. Saffie removed her outer clothes and immediately began to gently sponge her mother's forehead, as she had seen her granny do, keeping up a gentle chatter all the while.

'Come on now,' she urged. 'What will Dad say when he comes home if you're not here to greet him, eh? You've got to get well for all our sakes. We can't manage without you.'

It was a good half an hour later when Olivia's eyes suddenly blinked open and as they focused on Saffie's face a rare smile lit her features. 'Why, my darling girl. You've come,' she wheezed.

'You should have known I would.' Saffie forced a smile. 'And now that I have, I want to see you improving.'

Olivia's head wagged from side to side. 'No, my love. I think we both know that that isn't going to happen. But before I go, I wanted to tell you to make the best of your life. The girls will be staying with Granny so I know they will be well cared for. But keep an ear open for Elsie. We haven't heard a peep from her, and when your dad and Archie come home, tell them . . . tell them I loved them. And you, well, you must know how special you have always been to me. You were my firstborn and the first time I held you in my arms I felt like the richest woman in the world.'

Saffie's tears started to flow again as she gripped her mother's hand. It felt so frail and delicate. 'Shush now,' she ordered brokenly. 'I won't have you talking like that.' But her words fell on deaf ears. Olivia had already lapsed into a laudanum-induced sleep again.

Chapter Fifteen

By the time her granny forced Saffie down to the kitchen to try to get her to eat some supper, Bernie had long gone and the twins were in bed.

'I dare say you've noticed Bernie is soft on you?' Granny said as she ladled soup into a bowl.

Saffie frowned. 'Whatever makes you say that?'

Granny smiled, showing the gaps in her teeth. 'Why, a blind man on a gallopin' donkey could see it a mile off. An' from what I've seen o' him yer could do a lot worse an' all. But never mind that for now. Sit here an' get some o' this down yer. I'll go up an' sit wi' yer ma fer a while.'

Saffie stirred the food about her dish but when she tried to swallow it, it tasted like sawdust and stuck in her throat, so in the end, she gave it to the dog, who delightedly wolfed it down, and went back upstairs.

Olivia's breathing had become worse and she told Granny Doyle, 'You go and get some sleep now. I'll stay with Mam.'

'If yer sure?' Granny didn't take too much persuading. She was feeling her age now and ready for a good night's rest.

Once she had gone Saffie settled herself in the chair at the side of the bed and took her mother's hand in hers. After a time, she had to keep blinking to try to keep herself awake, but eventually she lapsed into an uneasy doze from sheer exhaustion – it had been a long day.

'Wake you, lass!'

Saffie sprang awake guiltily to find Granny standing over her, clutching an oil lamp. Her long grey hair was tied in a thick plait across her shoulder and she was wearing a warm shawl over her white nightgown.

'Oh, sorry . . . I must have dozed off.' Saffie knuckled the sleep from her eyes with her free hand, still holding tight to her mother's with the other and it was only then that it hit her. Her mother's hand was cold and stiff and when she looked at her she knew in an instant that she was gone. Strangely, in death Olivia looked peaceful and the pain lines had smoothed from her face.

'No . . . *Oh no*,' she gasped as she started to cry.

Granny gently patted her shoulder. 'It's all right, pet. She's out o' pain now. I reckon she only held on as long as she did so as she could see yer. But now you get yerself off to bed. There's nothin' more yer can do 'ere. You'll 'ave to squeeze in wi' Lucy an' Ginny. I'm goin' to lay yer mam out an' first thing in the mornin' yer can fetch the undertaker. No point disturbin' 'im till then.'

Saffie lay awake for the rest of that night and grieved for her mother. Once again, she had lost a beloved member of her family and she was heartbroken. As dawn broke, she crept downstairs and fanned the fire into life, and when Ginny, Lucy and Granny came down shortly after they found a pan of porridge simmering on the stove and a pot of tea waiting for them – not that any of them particularly felt like eating and drinking. The twins were distraught at the loss of their mother and Saffie left them with Granny Doyle while she went to fetch the undertaker.

He followed her home with a pine coffin and took Olivia's body on the back of his cart to lay in the chapel of rest until the funeral, which was to be two days later. She would be laid to rest in the tiny churchyard close to Granny's cottage, where Ginny and Lucy could tend her grave, but it gave none of them any comfort.

Bernie Denning appeared later that day in his uniform to offer his condolences and Saffie thanked him once more for fetching her.

'If there's anything I can do . . . anything at all . . .' he said falteringly as he awkwardly twisted his helmet. This family seemed to have had more than their share of heartache in the time he had known them and it didn't seem fair.

'You could perhaps get word to my dad,' Saffie told him tearfully. 'It's no good me writing to him because he can't read and we have no way of knowing where Archie is, or Elsie.'

He nodded, wishing that things could be different, and left shortly after.

The day of the funeral dawned grey and dismal, just like the family's mood, and as they prepared to leave for the service, Saffie wondered what else life was going to throw at them.

At the church they found a few of the boat people who had been in the vicinity, and who had heard of Olivia's death, waiting to pay their respects and Saffie gave them a grateful smile. The service was short and sweet and when it was over Olivia's coffin was lowered into the cold earth as

Lucy and Ginny clung to their big sister, sobbing uncontrollably. A simple wooden cross marked her resting place. There would be no wake – Granny's cottage was hardly big enough to accommodate them let alone mourners – and so they made their way back to it with empty hearts.

'What will you do now?' Granny asked as she poured them all a cup of hot sweet tea.

'I suppose I should get back to Grandmother Bishop's.' Saffie sighed, not relishing the thought at all. But what alternative did she have? If she didn't go back to her job, she would need to get another one, and at least Cathy and Minnie would be there. 'I'll leave first thing in the morning,' she declared, making a hasty decision.

Bernie Denning appeared again that evening bearing a posy of flowers consisting of snowdrops and violets, which he self-consciously handed to Saffie as Lucy and Ginny giggled behind their hands and Granny looked on with a smirk on her face.

'Er, what will you do now?' he asked awkwardly.

'I've decided to go back to my job in Nuneaton tomorrow, there seems no point in staying any longer.' Saffie took the flowers from him, her cheeks flushed. No one had ever bought her flowers before.

Bernie's face fell. 'Oh . . . I was hoping you'd stay a little longer.' He was acutely aware of everyone listening.

'Well, there's no point in delaying. Granny has kindly agreed to let the girls live here with her and at least if I'm earning, I can help out with their board and keep.'

'I've told you there'll be no need fer that,' Granny huffed, frowning. 'We shall be fine, so you just worry about yerself.'

145

Bernie left soon after but before he went, he drew Saffie to one side. 'Would you mind if I came to see you from time to time?'

Saffie blinked, not sure how to answer before replying, 'Um . . . no, I wouldn't. But please don't put yourself out. We're all very grateful for what you've done for us.'

His face lit up and after nodding to Granny he left them.

'Didn't I tell yer he 'ad a soft spot fer you?' Granny teased and Saffie blushed again.

Bernie Denning was a thoroughly nice young man but she didn't have any feelings other than friendship for him.

Saffie left early the next morning, and when she entered the kitchen of her grandmother's home in Tuttle Hill shortly before lunchtime, Minnie beamed at her. 'Why, this is a nice surprise,' she stated. 'I didn't expect to see yer back so soon, pet. How is yer mam?'

Saffie opened her mouth to speak but somehow the words stuck in her throat and before she could stop them, large tears were rolling down her cheeks. Minnie rushed over to her to place a comforting arm about her shoulders as she led her to a chair.

'Sh-she died,' Saffie gulped, the emotions of the past few days suddenly catching up with her. 'We buried her yesterday so there was no point in me staying there any longer.'

'Eeh, love, I'm right sorry to 'ear that.' Minnie gave her shoulders a little squeeze before rushing away to put the kettle on. As Saffie had discovered, Minnie thought a nice hot cup of sweet tea was the cure for all ills.

146

'And how is Cathy?' Saffie enquired eventually when she had managed to compose herself a little.

'Doin' well, an' a lot better than she were when she first arrived. But the little mite is still sayin' that her mam is alive somewhere. But when I asked what 'er mam's name was, she just said it was "Mama". Bless her. I reckon her memory's been messed up, what with all the terrible things that 'ave 'appened to her. Oh, an' there's been some good news from the farm. Marcus called in yesterday to see the missus an' I 'eard 'im tell her that 'e an' Mathilda are expectin' a baby. I'm that pleased for 'em. They've been tryin' fer years to 'ave a family so let's just 'ope that all goes well for 'em, eh?'

'That's wonderful news.' Saffie was genuinely pleased that Mathilda's pregnancy had been confirmed. 'They must be thrilled to bits.' It was good to hear something nice after all the bad things that had happened and she determined to pop over that evening, once Cathy was in bed, to congratulate them.

The door opened then and Clara appeared and blinked with surprise when she saw Saffie. 'Oh, you're back,' she said rather unnecessarily.

'Yes, I am, and I'm afraid I have some bad news for you.' Saffie paused for a moment, wondering how to tell her. But there was no easy way to break it to her so she just rushed on. 'Mother died shortly after I arrived at Granny Doyle's. We laid her to rest yesterday.'

'Oh . . .' Clara took a deep breath, then turned and left the room.

'Hard-faced old bugger,' Minnie ground out. 'Yer'd think yer were tellin' 'er about the death of a stranger rather than 'er own daughter. I reckon she's got a swingin' brick in place of a 'eart!'

Saffie shrugged before rising to remove her cloak. 'I think I might just pop up and say hello to Cathy while you make the tea. I shan't be long.'

She took the key to the child's room and when she entered the attic space, Cathy was standing on the bed staring wistfully from the high window.

'Hello, Cathy. I'm back. How are you?'

The child shrugged then hopped cautiously down off the bed. 'I'm all right . . . will you be going away again?'

'Hopefully not,' Saffie reassured her. 'And I thought that now that I am back, we might do some reading together. You can read, can't you?'

'*Of course* I can. I used to go to school and my mama used to read to me,' Cathy said scathingly.

This again confirmed to Saffie that the child had told the truth when she had said that she hadn't lived in Hatter's Hall all her life. She didn't comment on it, but silently promised herself that she would talk to Marcus as soon as she could to find out if his friend who worked at the hall had managed to find anything out about the child.

'And how are you feeling now?' Saffie was pleased to see that Cathy was wearing a dress that Minnie had fashioned from one of the larger gowns bought from the rag stall and it fit her like a glove. Now that Cathy's hair was clean it was shining and had formed a halo of little curls about her face, which had gained some colour since she'd last seen her, and Saffie realised with a little shock that the little girl was actually quite pretty.

'When can I see my mama?' Cathy questioned.

Saffie bit her lip. 'Well, first of all we shall have to find out where she is and if she is better, won't we? So if you could tell us where you lived and what her name is, then that might help.' She gave Cathy an encouraging smile.

Cathy frowned, thinking hard. 'We lived in a little cottage somewhere . . . but I don't know where. And I just called her Mama.'

'And what about other people? What did they call her?' Saffie pressed.

Cathy's face screwed up in concentration, until finally she whispered, 'I can't remember. Does that mean you won't be able to find her?'

'Well, it does make it more difficult,' Saffie said, not wanting to give her false hope. 'But we'll do our very best, all right? In the meantime, you will be quite safe here with me and Minnie and I promise you'll be very well looked after.'

Cathy stared at her solemnly. 'And I won't have to see the nasty lady who hit me again?'

'Not if I can help it,' Saffie reassured her. 'So now I'm going to go and see if I can find any books that you might like to read. It'll help pass the time.'

Sadly, down in the room where her grandmother kept all her books, she found nothing suitable for a child to read, but then a thought occurred to her, and she went into the kitchen. 'Do you know which room my mother slept in?' she asked.

'O' course I do an' it ain't much changed since she left,' Minnie told her. 'The missus just locked the door an' as far as I know she ain't been in there since.'

'Good,' Saffie said with satisfaction. 'In that case there might be some of my mother's old toys or books in there that might be suitable for Cathy. The poor child hasn't got anything to play with or read and it must be so boring shut away up there by herself for most of the day. I thought I might ask Marcus to set some lessons for me to do with her. You wouldn't happen to know where the key to my mother's old room is, would you?'

'I reckon it will still be on the hook wi' the rest of 'em.' Minnie obligingly went into the large walk-in larder where the house keys were kept and soon returned with three keys. 'It could be one o' these. Go up an' try 'em. It's the second door on the left on the landin', the one next to yours.'

Upstairs again, Saffie inserted the second key and smiled with satisfaction when it squeaked indignantly before turning in the lock. Pushing open the door, she stared around at the room. It was clear it was as her mother had left it, although now everything was covered in layers of dust, and cobwebs hung from the ceiling. Tears filled her eyes as she looked around at her mother's belongings. The grief she felt at her loss was still very raw, but she was there for Cathy so she took a deep breath and tried to compose herself. The room was a mix of a young adult's and a child's, as some of the favourite childhood things her mother must have been reluctant to part with were still there. Saffie felt sad to think that she hadn't been allowed to take any of these precious things with her when she had left home so hastily.

Her perfume still stood on a smart mahogany dressing table along with a silver-backed hairbrush and comb, and propped up against the pillows on the bed, which were also covered in dust, was her favourite rag doll. Olivia had once told Saffie the doll was called Polly and she had been given her when she was a very small child. There was a selection of books on a shelf to one side of the bed and Saffie quickly picked two that she thought might be suitable for Cathy. The first was *A Christmas Carol* by Charles Dickens and the second was a book of poems that she hoped Cathy would enjoy. She also collected Polly and a wooden jigsaw that she found in a chest of drawers.

She had almost finished rooting around when the door opened abruptly and her grandmother appeared, her lips set in a grim line and her eyes flashing with anger.

'What the *hell* do you think you are doing in here!' Her fists were clenched but Saffie refused to be intimidated and stared steadily back at her.

'Cathy is shut up in the attic with nothing to occupy her so I thought I would come in here and see if I could find anything that might keep her amused,' she replied calmly as she clutched Polly to her.

'You have no right to come in here without my permission.'

'And from where I'm standing you have no right to keep an innocent child locked up like an animal.'

Her grandmother's face was so red now that Saffie feared she might burst a blood vessel.

'Why . . . how *dare* you speak to me like that in my own home!' Her grandmother raged. 'For two pins I'd . . . well, I'd—'

'*Sack me*?' Saffie butted in bravely. 'Go ahead. But who will look after Cathy then? Minnie certainly doesn't have the time to run the house and look after her full-time.'

Clara's mouth opened and shut a number of times, reminding Saffie of some goldfish she had seen when visiting a fair with her parents once, but still she stood her ground until Clara turned and barged from the room with a face like thunder.

That's one to me, Saffie thought as she followed her grandmother from the room, holding the things she had found for Cathy. At least now Clara would know that she wasn't some soppy little girl she could boss about. Her mother had once told her that the best way to deal with a bully was to give them as good as you got and it appeared that she had been right!

Chapter Sixteen

Elsie sprayed herself liberally with the cheap cologne she had bought with the last of her wages.

Sitting on the bed watching her, Josie's eyes watered and she gagged. 'Are yer quite sure about goin' to meet Master Silas?' she asked worriedly. He was home from university for a couple of weeks and Elsie had agreed to meet him in the stable block when the family and their visiting friends were all in bed. 'What I mean is – it speaks fer itself that 'e only wants to meet after dark in the stables, surely? He's only after one thing so be careful!'

'Of course he isn't, he genuinely likes me and I'm not the sort off girl to be free with my favours. You're just jealous cos he's interested in me an' not you,' Elsie retorted as she yanked a brush through her hair and patted it into place. She then pinched her cheeks to bring some colour into them and smoothed down the skirt of the lilac silk dress that belonged to her young mistress Emma. She had never worn anything like it before and felt like a princess.

'Eeh, you'll be fer the chop if Miss Emma discovers you've been wearin' 'er clothes,' Josie warned.

Elsie tossed her head. 'She won't know if you don't tell her, will she? I've only borrowed it after washing and ironing it.

It'll be returned to her room in the morning along with the rest of her clean laundry and she'll never be any the wiser.'

'She will if yer get spotted!'

'But I won't be, and Silas won't tell. I shall go out down the servants' stairs into the yard and who is going to be about at this time of night?'

Realising that she was wasting her breath, Josie sighed and yanked the blankets up to her chin. 'On yer own 'ead be it then, but don't say as yer hadn't been warned.' Disgruntled, she snuggled down between the cold sheets and turned to the wall.

Elsie sniffed before quietly slipping out onto the landing, closing the door softly behind her and pausing to make sure all was quiet. Then, satisfied that no one was about she crept down the bare wooden stairs, avoiding the ones that creaked. In truth, she was weary after spending the whole day in the laundry scrubbing the family's and their visitors' dirty clothes, but this was the first time Silas had ever cornered her and asked her outright to meet him and there was no way she was going to miss this opportunity. She could already picture herself as his wife, living the life of Riley, and her heart pounded with excitement at the thought. There would be no more scrubbing dirty laundry for her. She would be dressed in satin and lace and driven about in a fine carriage with servants of her own to wait on her. She didn't admit to herself that she had flirted with him every chance she got and that she'd almost thrown herself at him.

The door at the bottom of the stairs that led into the yard squeaked alarmingly after she had turned the key and she paused again. After a moment she was satisfied that no one had heard it and lifting the heavy skirts of the dress she stepped into the yard, pulling the door softly to behind her.

It was almost pitch black outside and she went forward with her hands in front of her until she reached the stables. As she stepped inside the smell of the horses and the sound of them snorting wrapped itself around her. Elsie was disoriented as her eyes adjusted to an even greater darkness than that outside.

'Psst, Elsie, I'm up here in the hayloft.'

When Silas's voice came to her, she stumbled forward until her hands found the ladder that led up to the loft. Her heart was beating so loudly now that she feared he would hear it and, encumbered by the gown, she struggled to climb the steep steps. She was breathless with the effort by the time she reached the top but she had no time to compose herself before a strong pair of arms wrapped themselves around her and she was dragged forward. She tripped and landed heavily in a pile of hay and seconds later she felt Silas's hand on her breast and his hot breath on her neck.

Suddenly nervous, she brushed his hand away and tried to sit up but he was breathing heavily now as he pressed her back down.

'Now don't be a prick tease, you know you want it. Why else would you have come?' he jeered and the first flutterings of fear sprang to life in her stomach, making her feel slightly sick.

'I-I thought you liked me,' she whimpered as she desperately tried to control his wandering hands.

'*Of course* I do,' he answered as his hand began to prise beneath the low-cut bodice of her gown. His fingers were teasing her nipples and although she was afraid, all sorts of feelings she had never known she had sprang to life. She knew what he was doing was wrong. Hadn't her mother drummed into her and her sisters that no man should be allowed to touch their most private parts until they were sure it was the man they wanted to spend the rest of their life with? What she hadn't told them, though, was how good it felt. And then suddenly she heard the sound of the fabric on the gown tear as he roughly dragged it up her bare legs and before she knew what was happening, he was lying on top of her as he wrestled her drawers to one side.

'St-stop . . . please,' she implored weakly.

'I knew you'd be a game little filly,' he whispered throatily as he forced a finger inside her. She gasped at the pain of it but then as he gently began to stroke her innermost private parts she was overcome with desire. Seconds later he forced her legs open and before she knew what was happening, he plunged his stiff manhood into her and began to grunt and groan like an animal as he bucked up and down. The pain was brief and soon she felt herself moving with him until he suddenly tensed and groaned.

'There, that wasn't so bad, was it?' he said breathlessly as he rolled off her and collapsed in a heap on the hay.

Elsie felt warm tears on her cheeks and a sticky wetness between her legs. She felt as if she should say something but had no idea what, so for a while, she remained silent until she whispered, 'Does this mean I am your girl now?'

She heard him titter in the darkness. 'Of course it does . . . but you mustn't mention it to anyone yet, mind. It wouldn't do for my parents to find out until I've got them used to the idea. And I'll be going back to university soon so let's just keep it to ourselves for now, eh?'

'Yes, all right.' Elsie felt deflated. She wanted to shout it from the rooftops but then she didn't want to upset him and she would have done anything he told her now.

In the gloom she saw him yank his trousers back up and stand. 'Right, I'll see you soon.' And with that he went to the ladder and disappeared from view, leaving her lying there in the darkness with her drawers askew.

Surely there was more to making love than that? she thought. It had all been over in the blink of an eye and had left her feeling strangely unfulfilled. Still, she told herself, at least he had admitted that she was his girl now so surely it would get better?

At that moment two red eyes appeared just feet away from her and Elsie started. *A rat*. They had always been plagued with them on the narrowboat and she had been terrified of them ever since she was a little girl, so she quickly crawled to the ladder and half climbed half fell down it, suddenly wishing she hadn't worn Miss Emma's gown. Silas hadn't even noticed what she was wearing in the dark. She knew that it was torn and could only imagine how the young mistress would react when she saw it, the spoiled cow! But she would face that when she got back to her room. Hopefully, if the damage wasn't too bad, she could repair it by the light of a candle before she went to sleep and Emma would never be any the wiser.

She crept back up the stairs of the servants' quarters and quietly pushed the door of her bedroom open. Josie stirred as she came in and lit the candle that stood on the stand between their beds.

'Crikey!' She looked at the dishevelled state of her friend and the torn gown, and whistled softly through her teeth.

'No need to ask yer what you've been up to, is there? An' what's Miss Emma gonna say when she sees the state of her gown. That's one of her favourites!'

Elsie plucked a piece of hay from her hair and blinked to hold back the tears that were threatening. 'I'm going to repair it now,' she said in a small voice. 'And it's not what you think. Silas has told me that I'm his girl now. He's going to get his parents used to the idea and then we'll be married.'

'Huh! An' you fell fer that old line, did yer? There's about as much chance o' that happenin' as hell freezin' over, but on yer own head be it. I reckon it'll all end in tears you just mark my words.'

'I don't *care* what you think,' Elsie snapped as she fiddled about in the shared chest of drawers trying to find a needle and cotton. So why then, she wondered, did she feel so miserable?

Chapter Seventeen

Saffie and Minnie were enjoying a well-earned tea break in the kitchen towards the end of February when Minnie commented, 'Don't you find it odd that Cathy never mentions her pa?'

'Hm, I suppose it is odd now you come to mention it.' Saffie frowned thoughtfully. 'Perhaps he died when she was young and she doesn't remember him? She doesn't talk about where she lived either.'

'I thought Marcus was trying to find out from someone he knew up at Hatter's Hall?'

'He is but apparently they've been off sick with this influenza bug that's been sweeping the town, so we'll just have to be patient.'

Minnie shook her head. During the time they had been caring for Cathy the child had put on a little weight, thanks to Minnie's wholesome cooking, but she was still ghostly pale, no doubt because she never got out in the fresh air and sunshine, a fact that continued to trouble them both.

Twice a day they emptied her chamber pot and every morning Minnie took up a jugful of hot water so the child could wash. Once a week, Marcus delivered lessons for Saffie to do with her, and Saffie was impressed by how intelligent

Cathy seemed to be. Marcus, meanwhile, was impressed with how Saffie taught her.

'I could do with you helping at the school,' he had told her on his last visit but Saffie had merely smiled.

'There's nothing I'd like more than to be a teacher,' she admitted. 'But I'm committed to Cathy now. Goodness knows what would happen to her if I left her to my grandmother's tender mercies. I'd hoped when Cathy first arrived that she would get used to her and soften a little but if anything she seems to have become more and more agitated about the poor lamb being here.'

Marcus had frowned. He too had noticed how erratic Clara's behaviour had become and he was growing concerned for her.

'Perhaps we should get the doctor to check her over?' he'd said.

Saffie had shaken her head. 'Minnie already suggested that to her as tactfully as she could and my grandmother almost snapped her head off,' she told him with a wry smile. 'But something will have to change soon. The spring will be here in no time and it will be just too cruel if we have to keep her cooped up upstairs. It isn't healthy for her.'

'Well, hopefully Martha will be fit enough to return to work at Hatter's Hall next week so with a bit of luck she'll be able to root out the answers to a few of my questions and then we can go from there.'

'And how is Mathilda doing?' Saffie had asked, and immediately he was smiling again.

'Apart from the morning sickness she seems to be blossoming,' he told her proudly. 'She's still busy planning the nursery at present and things for the baby seem to be arriving by the day. The doctor expects the birth to be around the end of June or beginning of July.'

Saffie was genuinely pleased for him, for both of them. He was such a lovely man and Mathilda was sweet too. Saffie visited her as often as she could and the two had become good friends. She had no doubt they would make wonderful parents but for now all her concerns were focused on Cathy, and Minnie's were too.

It was later that evening when Saffie and Minnie were sharing a pot of tea in the kitchen that Minnie said cautiously, 'I, er . . . suppose I'm talkin' out o' turn 'ere, but you don't suppose the master, yer grandfather, could 'ave been Cathy's pa, do yer?'

'The thought had occurred to me,' Saffie admitted. 'That would certainly explain why my grandmother hates her so, but let's wait to see what Martha comes up with, eh?'

Four days later Marcus visited again and this time he had news for them. 'Martha went back to work yesterday,' he told them. 'And today she was able to sneak into the matron's office and look at Catherine's file. It appears that she had been in Hatter's Hall for approximately eighteen months, so the child was telling the truth.'

'And did it say who put her in there? Or who the mother might be?' Saffie leaned forward in her chair, staring at him eagerly.

'Nothing about the mother, but er, yes it does say who put her in there.' Marcus looked distinctly uncomfortable. 'She was placed in there by a Mr Charles Bishop.'

Saffie gasped and her hand flew to her throat. 'But that's my grandfather!'

'See!' Minnie said. 'It looks like my suspicions were right. Cathy were your gran'father's child.'

'We have no proof of that,' Marcus pointed out hurriedly, but Minnie was having none of it.

'Why else would 'e pay all that money to keep the child there?' She raised her eyebrows. 'He would 'ave known 'e couldn't bring 'er back 'ere. The missus would never 'ave stood fer it an' how would 'e have explained the child away?'

They sat in silence for a time until Marcus rose, saying, 'Nothing is certain as yet. But at least we know now that Cathy was telling the truth about not living there all her life. I suppose we should consider trying to find out if her mother is still alive somewhere.'

Both Saffie and Minnie nodded in agreement.

'Definitely. But how would we go about it? She doesn't even know her mother's name,' Saffie questioned.

'Perhaps just gently ask a few questions about if she remembers her father and go from there?' Marcus put his hat back on and after wishing them a good evening he left.

'We'll start tomorrer,' Minnie said and they nodded at each other. It seemed that they had opened a can of worms but now, for Cathy's sake, they would try to get to the bottom of things.

The following morning, as Saffie was sitting with Cathy in her room helping her with her spelling lesson, there was a tap on the door and Minnie stuck her head round it to tell her with a cheeky wink, 'That young Bernie Dennin' is 'ere to see yer, Saffie. And he's brought yer some flowers again. You go on down to see 'im. I'll sit wi' Cathy fer a while.'

Saffie blushed as she rose from her seat. 'Oh . . . er, right, thank you, Minnie.'

When she got downstairs, Bernie was standing in the kitchen clutching his hat in one hand and a bunch of early flowering daffodils in the other and when Saffie entered his face lit up.

'Hello, Saffie. It's my day off so I thought I'd drop by and see you. Oh . . . and I have a letter here for you from the twins.' He self-consciously pushed the flowers towards her and when she had taken them, he fumbled in his pocket, all fingers and thumbs, and thrust an envelope at her.

'Thank you, Bernie. And are the girls and Granny Doyle well?'

'Yes, I saw them yesterday and they are all fine,' he assured her. 'I've also found out which jail your father is in. I thought perhaps you might like to write to him.'

'Really?' Saffie's eyes shone, but then she sighed. 'It's a lovely thought but it wouldn't be much use. He can't read,' she confessed.

'Neither can a lot of other prisoners but there's always someone who can who is willing to read their letters to them,' he explained. 'So if you do decide you'd like to, he's in Warwick Gaol.'

Saffie shuddered. She'd heard about how awful the conditions in that place were and she wondered how her father was faring. 'And did you manage to find out if he was all right?'

He shook his head. 'I'm afraid not but I'm sure he'll survive,' he assured her kindly.

They stared at each other awkwardly; Saffie wasn't sure what to say to him now. She had never had a young man try to court her before and certainly not during the hours when she should be working.

Just then the door burst open and her grandmother appeared looking dishevelled and with a grim expression on her face. She'd obviously seen Bernie arrive. 'And who is this?' she demanded rudely as she eyed him up and down. Bernie returned her stare. Once again, she hadn't bothered to change her clothes or brush her hair but he could see that she must have been a beauty in her time.

'This is my, er . . . friend,' Saffie introduced him.

'I see!' Clara sniffed. 'Then perhaps your *friend* should know that I pay you to work and refrain from calling during your working hours!'

Colour flooded into Bernie's cheeks as he mumbled, 'I'm so sorry, Mrs Bishop, I didn't think. I'll go now.'

'Yes, I think you should.'

Saffie was mortified as he backed towards the door. Admittedly she didn't feel romantically inclined towards Bernie but he was so nice that she couldn't help but like him and he certainly hadn't deserved to be spoken to that way.

'May I ask when your day off is?' Bernie asked before making a rapid escape and Clara answered for her.

'Sapphire is allowed every Sunday afternoon off. I suggest you restrict your visits until then, although I feel she is far too young to be walking out with a gentleman friend!'

Bernie made a hasty retreat as Saffie swallowed her indignation. Her mother had told her that her grandmother had been married and had given birth to her by the time she was eighteen and Saffie was already older than that, and more than old enough to have a beau should she choose to.

164

She opened her mouth to object to the way her grandmother had spoken to her visitor but Clara turned before she had the chance and barged back the way she had come leaving Saffie to fume.

When she got back upstairs Minnie raised a questioning eyebrow but Saffie didn't feel it was right to speak in front of Cathy so Minnie left the two of them while she went back to preparing the dinner.

Saffie was aware of the letter from her little sisters in her pocket and was longing to read it but quelled her impatience until lunchtime when Minnie brought Cathy's meal – a tasty cottage pie and vegetables – up to her and she went down to eat hers in the kitchen.

Only then did she slit the envelope and avidly read what her sisters had written. They had clearly each written a part and it was easy to see who had written what as Lucy was much better at spelling than Ginny.

Dear Saffie,

We hopes you are all right as we are. Granny Doyle has had a cold so we made her stay in bed for two days and she didn't half mone but she's much better now. We ain't managed to get out much apart from to take Stanley for a walk or to go to the churchyard and we're still missin our mum something terrible. How are you doin? And how is the little girl you are looking after?

Saffie smiled as tears pricked at the back of her eyes and a wave of longing for their old life when they were all together washed over her. She moved on to Lucy's news.

Bernie Denning comes to see us regular. I reckon he likes you, Saffie, and he talks about you all the time. Are you going to marry him? Me and Ginny would like to wear posh frocks and be your bridesmaids if you do. Bernie is kind and the other day he brought us a big slab of sticky toffee but Ginny was greedy and ate too much of it all at once and it made her sick. Granny didn't half tell her off. We still see some of the boat people when they moor up by Granny's cottage and they always ask after you. We all miss you very much and hope you will come and see us soon,

Lots of love

Lucy and Ginny xxx

'Bless them.' She sighed as she folded the letter and put it back in the envelope. Soon, though, it was time to resume the lessons with Cathy so she made her way back upstairs in a solemn mood.

It was late afternoon and the light was fading fast when Cathy finished the lessons Marcus had set for her and said, 'I wonder why my papa didn't come back for me? He said he would come and take me back to Mama when she was better.'

Saffie's heart beat faster as she asked cautiously, 'Was your papa nice?'

'Oh yes. He was kind and he used to come and see Mama and me.'

'How nice.' Saffie smiled at her encouragingly. 'And what did your papa look like?' she asked innocently.

Cathy frowned for a moment. 'Well, he was big and he used to bring me presents. His hair was light like mine and he had a big moustache.'

Saffie felt the room swim around her. She only knew what her grandfather had looked like from the portrait that hung in the drawing room, but even so it was clear that this was who Cathy was describing. It appeared that Minnie had been right. Her grandfather was Cathy's father! Which explained why her grandmother hated the child so. It also occurred to her that if this was the case the child was actually her aunt!

Chapter Eighteen

'I thought as much!' Minnie remarked later that night when Saffie told her what Cathy had said. 'That would explain why the mistress 'ates the poor little sod so much, wouldn't it? But what do we do now?'

'I don't know,' Saffie admitted. 'I thought I might speak to Marcus again and find out if there's any way we can find out where Cathy lived before she got put into Hatter's Hall.'

'Hm, I might be able to help there.' Minnie patted her lip as she stared thoughtfully into space. 'If the mister really were Cathy's father there might be some clue in his office. It's just as he left it before he died. The missus locked the door and far as I know she's never stepped inside it since, but I know where the key is.'

'But isn't that rather risky?' Saffie looked worried. 'What if she caught you in there?'

Minnie shrugged. 'I'd wait till I were sure she were asleep afore goin' in, an' if she did show up I'd just say as I couldn't sleep so I'd decided to go in an' give it a tidy up.'

Saffie wasn't entirely happy with the idea but she supposed it was worth a try. It wasn't as if they had any other line of enquiry to follow.

And so later that night when Cathy was fast asleep and Clara had gone to her room, Saffie whispered to Minnie,

'When are you planning on going into my grandfather's office?'

'There's no time like the present,' Minnie told her. 'You just go on up an' forget all about it an' soon as I feel happy that the missus is asleep, I'm goin' in there.' She tapped the voluminous pocket of her large apron. 'I've already got the key.'

'Oh dear!' Saffie wasn't at all sure what they were doing was right but then something had to be done so she supposed they had little choice.

After checking on Cathy she retired to her room but she slept fitfully.

When Minnie came down to the kitchen the next morning she found Saffie already there.

'Well, did you manage to find anything that might help us?' Saffie raised an eyebrow.

Minnie shook her head. 'Not a sausage! I didn't even get into the bloody office. The missus were on the prowl all night an' a couple o' times I heard her go up to the attic room.'

'She didn't try to go in, did she?' Saffie asked anxiously.

'No, I crept to the bottom o' the stairs to check but she just stood outside her bloody door listenin'. I tell yer, I reckon she's losin' her marbles. There's somethin' ain't right wi' her, sure as eggs is eggs.'

'Hm, but if she's just found out that her husband had an illegitimate daughter, she's bound to be shocked,' Saffie pointed out. 'Perhaps when she has time to get used to the idea, she might settle down a bit?'

Minnie shrugged before turning to answer a tap on the back door. It was Davey from the farm come to deliver the fresh milk and eggs and Saffie noticed the way he blushed when his eyes lit on Minnie. He was such a nice man and it was more than obvious that he had feelings for her. It was just such a shame that he was so shy.

'Thanks, Davey. Comin' in fer a cuppa, are yer?' Minnie asked as she took the things from him.

'So long as it's no bother.' He dragged his hat off and nodded towards Saffie then made for the table while Minnie put the kettle on the range to boil.

'I wouldn't 'ave asked yer if it were any bloody bother, would I?' Minnie said in her blunt way as she set the cups out.

Saffie had the urge to bang their heads together. It was clear they were perfect for each other if only they could see it.

As Minnie poured the tea, a thought occurred to her and she asked casually, 'So the old master at the farm, Marcus's dad, him an' my master spent a lot o' time together, didn't they?'

'Aye, they did.' Davey nodded in agreement. 'Both in an' out o' work. Mr Bishop used to go to all the shoots an' whatever wi' him.'

'Oh yes, anywhere in particular?' Minnie asked innocently.

'They spent a lot o' time at Lakeside House on the Spencer-Hughes' estate on the way to Bedworth. The master there allus had a shoot or a ball or somethin' goin' on.'

'He's the owner o' the mill in Attleborough, ain't he? The one wi' all the pretty daughters?'

'Aye, that's the one, although I wouldn't say as they were all pretty.' Davey lifted the cup she pushed across to him and took a long drink. 'One o' the girls got wed a couple o' years or so ago. A big posh affair it was. People come from all over the country to attend it. She passed away end o' last year givin' birth to her first child. Knocked Mrs Spencer-Hughes about somethin' terrible

170

it did, but I think Georgina, the youngest is still at 'ome, far as I know. Now there's one to avoid, she's a right plain Jane wi' a tongue on 'er like a viper so I'm told. The oldest left 'ome years ago. She took up wi' a bloke the family didn't approve of an' cleared off wi' him when her parents wouldn't give her permission to wed 'im. It caused a right scandal at the time.'

'Did she really?' Minnie's mind was working overtime but she didn't have time to ask any further questions as Davey drained his cup and rose to leave.

'Right, be seein' yer in the mornin',' he said shyly and he slunk away as Minnie thoughtfully drummed her fingers on the table.

'I just wonder if the runaway daughter couldn't be somethin' to do wi' Cathy,' Minnie mused. 'I mean if the master spent a lot o' time there he'd 'ave had the chance to get to know her very well.'

Saffie grinned. 'Don't you think you might be letting your imagination run away with you?' she teased.

Minnie sniffed. 'Well, we 'ave to explore every possibility if we're to solve the mystery, don't we?' she huffed. 'But anyroad, the missus will be up in a minute an' screamin' fer her breakfast an' a fresh pot o' tea so I'd best get a shufti on.'

'And I'd better go and check on Cathy.' Saffie stifled a yawn as she rose and lifted the hot water jug Minnie had put out for Cathy. She didn't feel as if she'd been to bed and didn't know how she was going to manage to get through the day.

She found Cathy sitting on her bed staring forlornly up at the only window in the room and again it struck her how cruel it was to keep the child locked up in there.

171

'Good morning,' she said cheerily, hoping to lift the little girl's mood, but Cathy merely dropped her chin and didn't even look towards her. 'I thought we'd start with an English lesson after you've had breakfast, you like that, don't you?' Saffie went on as she placed the jug next to the bowl and went to lay out Cathy's clothes for the day. 'Now, why don't you get washed and dressed while I pop down to fetch your breakfast and then we'll begin.' Not waiting for, or even expecting, a response she lifted Cathy's chamber pot from beneath the bed and left again, reluctantly locking the door behind her.

Her grandmother, who was still in her nightclothes, was just leaving her room as Saffie reached the lower landing and she glared at the pot with distaste. 'That . . . that *girl* has thrown the whole house into turmoil. She's got you and Minnie running around after her like mad things,' she complained.

Saffie bristled. 'Perhaps we wouldn't have to so much if you allowed her to leave her room,' she shot back, refusing to be intimidated. 'As it is she can hardly do anything for herself, can she?'

Her grandmother's eyes narrowed and she clenched her hands at her waist. 'Actually, you might not have to pander to her for much longer. I've been thinking about making enquiries at the workhouse. They take orphans, don't they?'

Saffie looked horrified. 'Why, *surely* you wouldn't be so cruel? The poor child has no one and to just abandon her there would be heartless.'

Clara shrugged and continued down the stairs, shaking her head.

Once Saffie had emptied the chamber pot into the outside cess pit she rinsed it beneath the tap in the yard before going in to tell Minnie what her grandmother had threatened and, like her, Minnie was horrified.

'The wicked old bugger,' she hissed. 'She'll do that over my dead body. I tell you now, I'll leave this place an' get a little place o' me own where I can look after the kid afore I'd let her do that. I ain't never 'ad much to spend me wages on an' I've got a fair little nest egg put away. The missus'll soon realise just 'ow much I do about the place then, an' it'll serve her bloody right.'

Saffie chewed on her lip. 'If you don't mind keeping an ear out for Cathy I reckon I might go and see Marcus when she's had her breakfast.'

'But he'll be at the school,' Minnie pointed out.

'That's all right. I'm sure he'll spare me a moment for something as serious as this,' Saffie answered and lifting Cathy's breakfast tray, she carried it upstairs, far more concerned than she cared to show.

Three-quarters of an hour later, Saffie set off for the little school on Abbey Green. When she got there, she searched the classrooms for a sign of Marcus. There were three classes in all, dependent on the children's ages, although there were pitifully few children in any of them. Many parents couldn't afford the luxury of allowing their children to attend school and preferred to put them out to work as soon as they were old enough.

Saffie hovered by the half glass panel in the door and soon, Marcus, who was standing at a blackboard at the front of the class with a piece of chalk in his hand, glanced up and saw her. He immediately said something to the children, who instantly bent to the slates in front of them, before striding down the room to join her, closing the door softly behind him.

'What's wrong? Is Mathilda all right?' he asked worriedly.

'Oh, it's nothing to do with Mathilda,' Saffie assured him hurriedly. 'It's Cathy I've come to see you about. I need your advice because my grandmother is threatening to have her admitted to the workhouse.'

'She's *what*?' Marcus was incensed. 'But she can't do that. It would be too cruel.' He glanced through the glass in the door and seeing that the children were beginning to lark about said, 'Look, I'll call in and see her on the way home from school. And try not to worry. She'll listen to me.'

She gave him a grateful smile and hurried away but she still felt uneasy. Her grandmother's hatred of the child seemed to be growing by the day and her behaviour was becoming more and more erratic. Still, at least she had enlisted Marcus's help now, she consoled herself, and as he had said, Clara did seem to take notice of him, if no one else.

True to his word, Marcus called in at four thirty that afternoon on his way home. It was Saffie who admitted him and she nodded towards the drawing-room door. With a grim smile he went and tapped on it.

Almost instantly Clara called, 'Come in.' She had seen him coming and now stood before the roaring fire in the grate waiting for him, looking as if she had been pulled through a hedge backwards. He saw at a glance that the gown she was wearing was grubby and creased and had not been changed for days, and her hair, usually so neatly arranged, hung in rats' tails about her face.

'Good afternoon, Mrs Bishop.' He removed his hat and gave a slight bow as she gestured towards a seat. 'And how are you today?'

'Perfectly well, why shouldn't I be?' There was a note of irritation in her voice but he kept his smile firmly in place.

'I'm pleased to hear it. I thought I'd call in to see how Catherine is settling in.'

She sniffed. 'She is fine, thank you.'

'Good, and have you given any more thought about allowing her to start at the school?'

'That is totally out of the question,' she answered tersely. 'The child is . . . almost feral!'

'*Really?*' Marcus looked surprised. 'I'm shocked to hear it because after looking at the lessons I set for her to do with Sapphire I would have to say she has above average intelligence for a child her age. That's why I would strongly urge you to allow her to attend school. I think it's very beneficial for children to mix with others their own age and she's clearly very bright.'

Clara looked uncomfortable and gazed towards the window to avoid looking at him. 'Actually, I've been thinking the same thing . . . but not regarding school. She is amongst adults here so I was considering admitting her to the workhouse.'

Now Marcus made no attempt to be pleasant as he stared at her coldly. 'I'm afraid that won't be possible. You see, Charles put a clause in his will that if anything should happen to him the child should remain here until she comes of age. Should you decide to go against his wishes, he requested that the house and everything else he left you should go to his daughter.'

Two high spots of colour flooded into Clara's cheeks. 'But seeing as Olivia has passed away that couldn't happen, could it?' she sneered.

'No, you're quite right, it couldn't. But he had made allowances for that too, so should you decide to abandon the child to the workhouse, the property and everything else would pass to Sapphire as his oldest surviving relative after you.'

Clara's hand flew to her throat and the colour drained from her face as she thudded down onto the nearest chair.

'*Sapphire!* Inherit my house! *Never!* She is nothing more than a common . . . *boatie*!'

'And a very clever one,' he went on, not giving her an inch. 'You should be proud of Olivia for doing such a good job with the girl, she's an absolute credit to her. Her manners are impeccable and she's as bright as a button.'

'I . . . I think it's time you left now, Marcus,' Clara croaked in a shaky voice.

He rose, lifted his hat from the seat at the side of him and rammed it onto his head. 'Very well, Mrs Bishop. If that is what you wish. Good day to you.'

And with that he strode from the room leaving the door open behind him.

Chapter Nineteen

'Oh dear, she ain't gonna be in a very good mood now,' Minnie said from her position at the kitchen door, which she had left slightly ajar. The words had barely left her lips when they saw Clara sail from the drawing room and head for the stairs. 'What do we do now?'

'Nothing. We leave her to calm down,' Saffie answered sensibly as she began to prepare Cathy's tea tray. Minnie had made her a selection of cucumber sandwiches and a large slice of apple pie, which just happened to be Cathy's favourite. Next, she went to fill a glass with milk but she had barely lifted the jug when a noise made her pause and ask Minnie, 'Did you hear that? It seemed to come from upstairs.'

They both stepped into the hallway, listening intently, and when a faint scream reached them they both shot forward as one, almost colliding as they reached the foot of the stairs. Minnie was up the first flight like a greyhound with Saffie close behind and the higher they rose the louder the screams became. It was clear by then that the screams were coming from Cathy's room and they tumbled up the attic stairs to see the door swinging open. There, they skidded to a halt and stared in open-mouthed horror at the sight that met their eyes.

Cathy had been thrown across the bed and lay on her belly with her drawers pulled down to her ankles and her skirts pushed up about her neck, and Clara was laying into her with a thick leather belt that had belonged to her husband. Even from the doorway they could see the welts rising on the child's tender skin as the belt rose and fell across the delicate flesh. Minnie screamed as she ran forward and tried to wrest it from her mistress. But it was as if Clara was possessed and she threw Minnie aside. Her face was red with exertion and she was panting as she ground out, '*You little scum! You're nothing but a bastard, you should never have been born!*'

'*Stop it!* Stop it, you'll kill her!' Saffie cried as she too flung herself at her grandmother, and finally, after a wrestle, she managed to snatch the belt from her hands. Clara sagged to the floor like a rag doll crying uncontrollably, but Minnie and Saffie's thoughts were all for Cathy at that moment. The buckle of the belt had broken the skin on her back and buttocks in places, and blood was seeping down her sides and pooling on the mattress.

'Dear God, run down to the kitchen, pet, an' fetch me up a bowl o' warm water an' a cloth,' Minnie urged.

Saffie did as she was told without even a glance in her grandmother's direction. Once she'd filled the bowl, she rushed back to the attic, half of the water sloshing over the sides in her haste. She was struggling to stop herself from crying; how could her grandmother have done such a wicked thing? She was sure had she and Minnie not intervened the woman would have killed the child and then what would have happened? She would have been hanged for murder!

Cathy's heartrending screams, that only minutes before had been loud enough to waken the dead, had dulled to whimpers now and Minnie was whispering reassurances into her ear as she tried to comfort her.

178

'It'll be all right, pet,' she soothed, her own voice choked with tears, for in that moment she realised just how much the child had come to mean to her. 'We'll have you right in no time, you'll see.'

She looked over her shoulder at Saffie and ground out, 'Get 'er outta 'ere else I won't be responsible fer what I might do. Why she's almost killed the poor little bugger.'

Leaving Minnie to tend to Cathy, Saffie took her grandmother's arm none too gently and almost hauled her from the room. Clara was strangely calm now and thankfully offered no resistance. Her eyes had an eerie, vacant look to them and when Saffie dumped her unceremoniously onto the bed in her own room she just lay there staring up at the ceiling.

'Do you think we should fetch the doctor?' Saffie asked when she joined Minnie again.

'Not yet.' Minnie shook her head as she continued to gently dab at the wounds. 'I've got some ointment downstairs that'll help but if that don't work or if she develops a fever we'll have to.'

Half an hour later, when she had cleaned the wounds as best she could, she lifted Cathy into her arms and headed for the door.

'She'll be sleepin' downstairs tonight in the kitchen on the settle so as I can keep me eye on 'er an' bugger what the missus says!'

'But that's the job I'm paid to do,' Saffie pointed out as she lifted her skirts and hurried after her.

'I reckon you're gonna be more needed lookin' after the missus,' Minnie said caustically. 'If anythin' I reckon it's *'er* as needs a doctor – one from Hatter's Hall! I think she's finally gone off her trolley!'

Saffie wrung her hands as she nodded in agreement.

By the time they reached the kitchen it was clear that Cathy was in shock. Every inch of her body was trembling like the leaves on the trees and as Minnie laid her on the settle and continued to dab gently at the angry red wheals that were popping up all over her small back and buttocks, her tears fell onto Cathy's back.

'The evil old cow!' she muttered. Some of the wheals were still oozing blood and it was clear that even when they healed, the child would be scarred for life. As gently as she could, Minnie patted ointment onto them until there was nothing more she could do and she straightened.

'I think I should fetch Marcus,' Saffie said in a small voice.

Minnie nodded in agreement. 'Aye, that ain't a bad idea. Happen he'll know what to do cos as sure as 'ell I don't!'

Saffie ran all the way and by the time she reached the farm she was sweating and had a stitch in her side. Even so it didn't slow her down and she hammered on the door until the maid answered.

'I . . . I need to see Marcus,' Saffie stuttered, pushing her way into the hall and, to the little maid's consternation, racing towards the drawing room and barging in unannounced. Mathilda was embroidering a tiny nightgown ready for the new arrival and Marcus was reading the newspaper but they both glanced up startled as she almost fell into the room.

'M-Marcus . . . you must come.'

He threw the paper aside and crossed to her hurriedly. 'Why, Sapphire, whatever is the matter?'

Mathilda was on her feet and looking worried too as Saffie blurted, 'It's my grandmother. M-me and Minnie heard a ruckus upstairs and when we went to see what was happening, we found grandmother thrashing Cathy. I . . . I think she would have killed her if we hadn't intervened.'

'Good grief!' Marcus was shocked and turning to his wife he told her, 'I should go and see if there's anything I can do, darling.'

'Of course, I'll come too,' Mathilda offered but he held his hand up.

'No, you stay here. I don't want you upset in your condition. I shall be back very soon.' And with that he ushered Saffie ahead of him out into the corridor where he found the maid staring at them both with her eyes on stalks. She had obviously heard everything, but for now he was needed at Clara's; he would speak to her about keeping what she had heard private when he got back.

Side by side they rushed back to Clara's house and when he entered the kitchen and saw the state Cathy was in, he was shocked.

'Where is Clara?' he enquired when he was able to speak.

Minnie curled her lip and cocked her head towards the ceiling. 'She's upstairs where Saffie left 'er far as I know, but to be honest I don't much care *where* she is!' She was emptying the water in the bowl that she had used to clean Cathy's back and he was horrified to see that it was blood red.

Marcus gritted his teeth and nodded before marching purposefully into the hallway and climbing the stairs.

It was some time before he came down again to tell them, 'It seems that she's had some sort of a breakdown. I think perhaps we should send for Dr Jones.'

'Huh! Who for? Cathy or 'er?' Minnie asked scathingly. She was so angry with her mistress at that moment that she didn't much care what happened to her. All her concerns were for the little soul in front of her.

'For both of them, I should think.' Marcus ran his hand distractedly through his thick thatch of fair hair. He had never come across a situation like this before and he prayed that he never would again.

'But my grandmother doesn't want anyone to know that Cathy's here,' Saffie pointed out.

Marcus shrugged. No matter what he said to his maid when he got home, he had an idea that word of Cathy's arrival would spread like wildfire now and it was obvious that both Cathy and Clara required urgent medical attention. 'Even so I think we have to put the child's needs above your grandmother's wishes. Shall I fetch the doctor or shall you?'

'I will,' Saffie answered meekly, although she dreaded what her grandmother would say when she found out.

Luckily the doctor was in when Saffie got to his house in Swan Lane, and he followed her back to the house, looking somewhat confused. The poor girl was obviously deeply distressed and he had struggled to make head or tail of the garbled story she had told him about Clara Bishop whipping a child. Clara had always been a pillar of the community and what child was the girl on about anyway? As far as he knew there was only Clara and her maid living at the house since her husband had died.

His first sight when they entered the kitchen was of a child lying flat on her stomach on the settle, her back and buttocks raw with deep wheal marks, and he sucked in his breath.

Instantly, he snapped his bag open and withdrew his stethoscope. The child's face was beetroot red and even without examining her he could see she was running a very high temperature.

'Hm,' he muttered when he rose and looked pointedly at Marcus. 'This child is in shock. So perhaps you'd like to tell me exactly what's gone on?'

Marcus stumblingly told him as much as he knew and when he had finished the doctor stroked his chin thoughtfully before asking, 'Who exactly is the child and what is she doing here?'

Marcus glanced at Minnie and Saffie before saying cautiously, 'We believe she may be the illegitimate child of Charles Bishop. Clara didn't know about her until after his death. The little girl has spent some time in Hatter's Hall. Clara seems to think that she had lived there all her life after her mother died in childbirth, but Cathy is adamant that she only went there recently when her mother became ill. Mr Bishop was paying for her keep but after he died obviously he didn't pay any more and Clara, as his next of kin, was informed to fetch her home.'

'Goodness me.' The doctor raised his eyebrows. 'So that would explain why Clara hasn't taken to the child if she's the result of her husband's infidelity. Even so, that is no excuse for beating the child half to death. Where is she now?'

'She's in her room,' Saffie told him falteringly. 'And I fear that she's had some sort of a breakdown.'

The doctor shook his head. It seemed that things were going from bad to worse. 'Very well, I'd best see her next.' And lifting his bag he followed Saffie up the stairs.

It was some time before he came down again. 'You are right,' he said quietly. 'It does appear that she had had some sort of a mental breakdown, although physically I can find nothing wrong with her.' His eyes rested on Cathy again and he nodded his approval at Minnie's ointment. 'You've made a very good job of cleaning the wounds, m'dear, and I suppose I have no need to tell you how important it is that they are kept clean. The last thing we need now is for any of them to become infected. Unfortunately, I have no magic cure for either of their ills but this at least should help them sleep.' Extracting two small glass phials of clear liquid from his bag he handed them to Saffie. 'About three drops in water for your grandmother nearer to bedtime and just two drops for Cathy should the pain become too much for her. And make sure you get as much liquid into her as you can; we don't want her to become dehydrated on top of everything else. I shall call again tomorrow to see how they both are but should you need me before, you know where I am.'

After he'd gone, they stared at each other in consternation for a few moments, until Marcus said, 'I suppose I should be getting back to Mathilda. Will you two be all right?'

'Of course we will,' Saffie assured him with a confidence she was far from feeling. 'And thank you for all your help. But what will we do now?'

'Let me have a night to think about it.' He gave her what he hoped was a reassuring smile. 'I'll be back first thing and hopefully by then we'll all have decided what's best to do. Goodnight.'

'Eeh, 'e's a good man is Marcus,' Minnie said when he'd left.

Saffie nodded in agreement. What had started as a straightforward job looking after a small child had suddenly taken a drastic turn for the worse and she wondered what the future held, not just for her but for all of them. For how could they ever trust her grandmother again?

Chapter Twenty

'Who is the girl with Silas in the garden?' Elsie hissed peevishly to Josie, who had just come to the laundry room to bring her yet more dirty washing.

Josie peered through the steam that was escaping out of the open door into the cold air.

'Oh, that's Selina Dryden. Her family an' Silas's parents are great friends an' they come to stay regular. Pretty, ain't she? I reckon the families hope they'll be a couple afore too much longer.'

Selina was a little too pretty for Elsie's liking and she didn't like the attention Silas was paying her at all, or what Josie had said – particularly as he hadn't turned up for their liaison in the hayloft the night before. She had sat in the freezing cold for well over an hour until she could no longer feel her hands and feet before miserably making her way back to the room she shared with Josie with tears on her cheeks. Sensing her bad mood, Josie hadn't uttered a word, but had merely snuggled further down into the bed and gone back to sleep.

'Now do yer believe me when I said he's usin' you?' She stared at her friend anxiously.

'No, I don't,' Elsie snapped as she tossed another load of washing into the steaming sink and wiped her sweaty brow.

'He's probably only entertaining her to get out of the way of the parents.'

Josie shrugged. She could see that Elsie was still well and truly under his spell and if that was the case, she would have to learn the hard way.

'Suit yerself!' She lifted the empty wash basket and stormed off.

Elsie edged towards the door and peeped out at the two young people. Selina Dryden had hair the colour of spun gold and the bluest eyes she had ever seen. She had an hourglass figure too, accentuated by the tiny jacket with a peplum waist that she wore, and Elsie stared enviously at her beautiful velvet costume. It was in a lovely shade of pale green, trimmed with a darker green braid, and on her head was a matching jaunty little hat. The outfit looked as if it had cost more than she could earn in a whole year.

At that moment Silas glanced towards the wash house and seeing Elsie watching him he scowled as she quickly shot back to the sink. Furious, she promised herself that she would make him pay – when she could get him alone that was.

That night she made her way to the hayloft but again there was no sign of Silas and she went to bed disappointed once more. The only thing that gave her any joy was knowing that the Drydens were leaving the next day, and when she heard their coach pull away after breakfast the following morning, she almost cheered. Soon after, from her place at the sink in the laundry room, she saw Silas striding across the yard looking handsome in his riding gear, and without stopping to think she hurried to the door and hissed, '*Silas!*'

He looked towards her then glanced quickly about to make sure she hadn't been heard before striding towards her and pushing her none too gently back into the room.

'Haven't I *told* you *not* to speak to me when we could be overheard?' he snapped as he tapped his riding whip against the side of his high leather boots.

Elsie's face fell. 'B-but I just wanted to speak to you.' Her lips trembled. 'I've waited for you for two nights on the trot but you didn't come and Josie said that you and that Selina had an understanding. Is it true? Because if it is I—'

His attitude changed immediately and kicking the door shut behind him he placed his arm about her waist. He hadn't had his fill of her yet, so it would be worth keeping her sweet for a little while longer, just until the novelty had worn off, and then he would drop her, just as he had a number of the maids before her. 'Of course it isn't true, you silly little goose,' he chided gently as she stood rigid in his arms. 'You should know you're the only girl for me, but as I explained, we have to take it slowly. To be honest, I think Mother and Father have always hoped that Selina and I would become betrothed one day but neither of us wants that.' He traced her chin with his finger and instantly she became like putty in his hands.

'Oh . . . I'm sorry,' she muttered, but she had no time to say any more before his lips found hers and she melted against him.

It was he who broke the embrace. 'Look, I really have to go now.'

'But will you meet me tonight?'

He stared down into her hopeful face, then shook his head. 'Sadly, I have to go out this evening, but we will get together again very soon, I promise.'

After he'd gone, Elsie wasn't sure whether to laugh or cry, and slowly she turned back to the mountain of laundry the visitors had made.

'Surely you ain't goin' out to meet him *again*?' Josie looked exasperated as she shrugged herself into her nightgown. It was late the next evening; they had only just finished their work and Josie, at least, was exhausted and ready to tumble into bed.

'Why shouldn't I?' Elsie retorted as she stepped out of her work clothes and began to wash in the cold water she had poured into the large ceramic bowl.

Noting the sparkle in Elsie's eyes, Josie chewed her lips worriedly. 'Didn't you 'ear a word I said? Silas and Selina Dryden will be announcin' their betrothal soon, you just mark me words, an' then he'll drop yer like a ton o' 'ot bricks. Let's just 'ope as yer ain't got a bun in the oven by then, eh? You'll wish you'd listened to me!'

Elsie ignored her as she pulled on her best blouse, then with a toss of her head she sailed out of the room. Josie sighed and, knowing there was no more she could do, she hopped into bed and blew out the candle.

For once, Elsie was rewarded when she found Silas waiting for her in the hayloft and the next hour passed in a blur of ecstasy as she gave herself up to the sheer pleasure of being in his arms.

Later, as they dressed, she asked hopefully, 'Shall I see you at the same time tomorrow evening?'

His face was in shadow and he hesitated before answering, 'No, I, er . . . forgot to mention that I shall be away for a few days, but I'll see you when I get back.'

'But how long is a few days? Two? Three? A week?' Elsie couldn't keep the disappointment sounding in her voice.

'About a week,' he answered irritably.

'A *week*!' Elsie was horrified. A week away from the man she loved sounded like a lifetime. 'But where are you going?'

'Good Lord, do I have to tell you my whereabouts now?' he snapped as he moved towards the ladder that led down to the stables.

Elsie sensed that she had upset him and was instantly contrite. 'I-I'm sorry, I didn't mean to upset you. It's just that . . . I shall miss you so much.'

Her lips were trembling and her eyes were bright with unshed tears, and he softened a little. 'I shall miss you too but a week isn't so very long. Goodbye for now.'

Once he was gone, Elsie allowed the tears that had been threatening to fall as she finished getting dressed and slowly tiptoed back to her room.

It was the mistress's lady's maid who informed the staff at breakfast the following morning, 'The family will all be going away this afternoon for a week, so you can take advantage of a bit of a rest. I only wish I didn't have to go too. Anyway, I hadn't better stand about here gossiping; I have all the mistress's clothes to pack and no doubt she'll want to take enough to last her for a month.'

'And where are you all going? Somewhere nice?' the cook enquired as she poured herself another cup of tea. Now that the family and staff were fed, she could relax for a while until it was time to start preparing the lunch.

'We're going to the Drydens'.' Miss Tattersall glanced across her shoulder and lowered her voice before going on conspiratorially, 'Between you and me I think we might be going to celebrate young Master Silas and Miss Dryden's engagement, although I haven't officially been told that, of course.' She grinned. 'But I picked up a beautiful ball gown for the mistress from the dressmaker yesterday, and she seems very excited about something.'

Elsie was sitting next to Josie at the table and had just bitten into a slice of toast, which she almost choked on as the colour drained from her face. 'B-but surely the family would have told us?' she managed to squeak.

Miss Tattersall shook her head. 'Why would they? We are merely here to serve. But are you all right, my dear? You've gone dreadfully pale.'

Aware that all eyes were upon her, Elsie rose so suddenly that her chair almost overturned, and dashed from the room without a word. Everyone watched her go but then shrugged and returned their attention to what else Miss Tattersall had to say.

'Ooh, fancy that.' The cook grinned as she crossed her arms and heaved her ample bosom higher. 'They managed to keep that quiet, didn't they? That would explain why we've seen so much of the Drydens recently.'

Elsie fled into the laundry room and leaned heavily against the wall as she tried to catch her breath. She felt as if all the stuffing had been knocked out of her and was cursing herself for a fool. If what Miss Tattersall had said was true then Josie had been right all along: Silas had merely been toying with her affections and had never had any intention of marrying her. As all her dreams of becoming a lady turned

190

to ashes, the bitter tears began to flow. And yet even then she couldn't quite make herself believe that it was true. She loved him with all her heart. *Surely* he couldn't be so cruel!

Slowly the heartache turned to anger and her small hands clenched into fists. He would marry Miss Dryden over her dead body! She wiped the tears from her cheeks and straightening her back marched back out into the yard and into the kitchen, ignoring everyone's shocked stares as she strode towards the green baize door that led into the hallway.

'Girl ... you can't go in there.' Miss Tattersall leapt towards her but her words were lost as the door banged resoundingly shut behind her.

Once in the hallway, Elsie's eyes widened, and she paused to gawp around. This part of the house was like another world to that in which the servants lived. There were fringed Turkish carpets on the floor and expensive silk-patterned paper on the walls. She hesitated as her courage started to desert her, but then she took a deep breath and straightening her back she marched on.

She knew the mistress would be taking coffee and reading the newspaper in the day room now that breakfast was over, the only problem was, never having been in this part of the house, she wasn't at all sure where that was. She paused outside each door until she heard what sounded like a cup being placed back on a saucer and before she could stop herself, she tapped on the wood, and pushed it open, without even waiting for an answer.

As she had hoped, the mistress was sitting in a chair at the window with a newspaper spread out on a small table in front of her and a pair of spectacles perched on the end of her nose. At the disturbance she glanced up and examined the girl who had burst in on her, taking note of the coarse apron and rough serge dress.

'Who are you, girl? And just *what* do you think you are doing barging in here uninvited?' she demanded coldly.

'Please, ma'am . . . I'm Elsie, your laundry maid, and I'm sorry to disturb you but there is something I must speak to you about.'

The mistress scowled and turning her attention back to the newspaper she waved her hand dismissively in Elsie's direction. 'I suggest you speak to Miss Tattersall, the housekeeper, about any issues you may have,' she said icily. 'And in future *do not* disturb me or you will wish you hadn't!'

When Elsie stood her ground, the woman looked back up at her in disbelief. This girl was a lowly laundry maid and yet here she was having the audacity to ignore her. She waved her hand at her again, 'Didn't you hear what I said? Go along.'

'Oh yes, ma'am, I heard.' Elsie's chin was set. 'But this isn't something I can speak to Miss Tattersall about. It's something that only you can deal with.'

The mistress was so flabbergasted at the girl's nerve that her mouth fell open – although she couldn't help but admire her spirit. Most of her staff would have scurried away like frightened mice at one cross word from her but Elsie here clearly wasn't going to leave until she had told her what was on her mind.

'Very well. Just this once tell me what is wrong and make it quick!'

Elsie's courage wavered and she licked her dry lips before beginning, 'The thing is . . . there is talk in the kitchen that Silas and yourselves are going to stay with the Drydens today and that you are going to announce his engagement to their daughter. Is this true?'

The woman positively bristled at the sheer nerve of the girl. 'That is absolutely *none* of your business. How could what my son does *possibly* have anything to do with you?'

Elsie's pretty face flushed as she glared right back at her. 'It has *everything* to do with me,' she retorted. 'Because, you see . . . he is already betrothed to me and he loves me . . . he told me so!'

The woman's shoulders sagged and as she removed her spectacles, she rubbed her forehead. 'Oh, not again,' she said wearily. 'And I suppose you believed him?'

'Yes, ma'am.' Elsie nodded vigorously.

'Then more fool you. Perhaps you should be aware that you are not the first maid that my son has . . . shall we say, dallied with? And I have no doubt you won't be the last. Unfortunately, he has an eye for the ladies, just like his father.'

As Elsie stared at her in disbelief, the woman sighed. Standing up, she walked over to a small ornate escritoire set against one wall. Taking a small key from her pocket she unlocked one of the drawers and reached for something inside it. Turning, she handed Elsie a crisp white five-pound note. 'Here, take this in lieu of any wages we owe you and make sure you have left within the hour.'

'What? You mean you are *sacking* me?' Horrified, Elsie shook her head in distress. 'But you can't! Silas loves me, I tell you. Ask him, he'll tell you himself—'

She had no time to say any more, for at that moment the door barged opened and Silas himself appeared as if speaking of him had conjured him up by magic. He visibly paled when he saw Elsie and the look on his mother's face, and he quickly turned to beat a hasty retreat but his mother's words stayed him.

'Silas, come *here* this instant.'

Silas quietly turned, avoiding eye contact with Elsie. 'Yes, Mother.'

'This girl is saying that you and she have been having a relationship, is this true?'

He shook his head vehemently.

Tears started to roll down Elsie's cheeks and she stared at him in disbelief.

'She's been throwing herself at me,' he lied. 'Every time I so much as set foot in the stable yard, she's there. I've tried to avoid her but what's a chap to do?'

'That's not true and you *know* it,' Elsie sobbed. 'You told me we were going to be married and that you loved me.'

'I really don't think so.' His eyes were as cold as his mother's as he glared at her contemptuously. 'Why would I want to marry a common little laundry maid like you?'

Elsie felt as if she had been doused in cold water.

'That's quite enough!' Mrs Worthington knew her son only too well and had no doubt whatsoever that the laundry maid was telling the truth, but his union with the Drydens' daughter would be advantageous for both families so she had no choice but to get rid of the girl. 'I suggest you go and pack your things and leave immediately,' she instructed Elsie, who was still looking at Silas, unable to believe what she was hearing. 'I would like you gone within the hour, otherwise I shall have no choice but to have you removed forcibly!'

Elsie wavered for a second but then gathering what dignity she had left she turned and stomped from the room.

Within minutes she was in the little attic room ramming her few possessions into her carpet bag.

The door opened and Josie came in. 'What's goin' on?' she asked nervously.

'I've been sacked!' Elsie took off her apron and flung it to the floor, then snatched her shawl from the nail on the back of the door and draped it around her shoulders. 'I told the mistress about me and Silas and he denied everything!' There was a wobble in her voice but the tears had stopped now and she was angry. 'And don't bother to say "I told you so"! I don't need to hear that.'

'I wasn't goin' to,' Josie said shakily. 'I was just goin' to say I shall miss yer.'

'I shall miss you too,' Elsie answered in a softer voice and after giving her friend a quick hug she set off to she knew not where, with all her dreams in tatters and her heart broken.

Chapter Twenty-One

It was now three days since Cathy had been thrashed, and Minnie and Saffie had taken it in turns to care for her day and night, as well as having to keep a close eye on Clara. They were both exhausted but at least Cathy's temperature had come down a little and she seemed to be slightly better, although her back was still sore and weeping.

Dr Jones and Marcus had been constant visitors and Saffie didn't know what she would have done without them, although there had been very little either of them could do for the child. For the first twenty-four hours, on the doctor's advice, Saffie had kept Cathy in a laudanum-induced state but now she was only administering the drug when the pain became unbearable. Every hour she or Minnie bathed the wounds in warm salt water, which made the little girl wince and cry out, but that was better than risking an infection. Now, Saffie was sitting at the side of the bed trying to persuade the child to eat a little of the porridge she had brought upstairs for her. 'Just try one spoonful,' she coaxed. 'You'll feel so much better with something in your tummy, and look, Minnie has put honey in it for you and lots of sugar.'

Cathy was still lying on her stomach to allow the air to get to her open wounds and she shook her head and turned it to

196

the wall, so eventually Saffie gave up and with a sigh rose to take the bowl back downstairs.

'Any luck?' Minnie asked the second she set foot in the kitchen.

Saffie smiled briefly at Davey, who had become a regular visitor over the last few days and was seated at the table drinking a cup of tea, then shook her head. 'Not even a taste of it.'

'Why don't you let me see if she'll take somethin' from me?' Davey suggested, looking embarrassed. 'I'm told I 'ave a way wi' kids.'

Saffie was about to object when Minnie stepped in to say, 'Why not let 'im try? We ain't had any luck, have we? So what have we got to lose?'

Seeing the sense in what she said, Saffie nodded and handed the dish to Davey who loped away up the stairs while Saffie went to check on her grandmother who was still lying in bed just gazing at the ceiling with a blank expression on her face. Crossing to the window, Saffie drew the curtains aside allowing the light to flood into the room. 'We're almost into spring now,' she commented cheerfully as she turned to lift her grandmother's dressing robe from the back of a chair. 'Let's get you downstairs, eh? Then when you've had breakfast, we'll get you dressed before the doctor calls.'

Clara meekly allowed Saffie to help her on with the robe and soon she was seated at the dining-room table, although she made no move to eat the breakfast that Minnie carried in to her. It seemed to the girls that both their patients had lost their appetites.

'Eat up,' Saffie told her as she and Minnie left the room.

'I doubt she'll touch her food again,' Saffie said worriedly.

Minnie shrugged. 'Well, there ain't a lot we can do about it is there? We can 'ardly force-feed 'er.'

They were sitting together enjoying a cup of tea when Davey joined them ten minutes later and they were both shocked and pleased to see that at least half the porridge in the bowl had been eaten.

'Well done,' Saffie praised him, making him blush again. 'How did you manage to get her to do that?'

He shrugged. 'Just a bit of encouragement an' praise, I suppose. But I'd best get back, I've work waitin' to be done. I'll be back later to see if there's owt yer need doin'.'

Saffie noticed how his eyes lingered on Minnie as he left. 'You do realise that man still loves you, don't you?' she said teasingly to Minnie, and now it was her turn to blush.

'Then why didn't he say so when we were walkin' out together? He 'ad enough bloody chances.'

'Happen he did, but Davey is so shy,' Saffie pointed out.

Minnie sniffed, and Saffie realised that she still had feelings for him too. It was such a shame, she thought, because they would have been so good together. But then, who was she to interfere?

Later that morning Dr Jones arrived and went in to check on Clara first. Saffie had dressed her and styled her hair into a neat chignon on the back of her head, but she was still sitting as still as a waxwork in the chair where Saffie had placed her and seemed to have no idea of where she was.

'So, still no change?'

Saffie shook her head and he sighed.

'Right, well you get off while I examine her,' he said as he took his stethoscope from around his neck.

Out in the hallway, Saffie found Marcus waiting for her.

'How is she? And how is Cathy?' he asked.

'Cathy seems fractionally better, Davey managed to get her to eat a few spoonfuls of porridge this morning, but my grandmother . . .' Her voice trailed away.

He patted her arm and led her towards the kitchen where Minnie was just making another pot of tea.

Saffie smiled ruefully; lately all they seemed to do was drink one cup of tea after another as they rushed between Cathy and Clara. When she had agreed to the job of caring for Cathy, she had had no idea that she would end up caring for Clara too. More and more she found herself thinking back to her life on the canal. It had been hard, admittedly, but it had seemed so uncomplicated and she wished she could turn the clock back to happier times.

They sat in silence sipping at their drinks until Dr Jones reappeared with a worried frown on his face.

'I'm beginning to think your grandmother might benefit from a stay in Hatter's Hall,' he said tentatively and seeing the look of horror that crossed Saffie's face he quickly held his hand up. 'In her current state I really can't say what she might be capable of. Ideally, we could get Cathy away from here for a while until Clara is slightly better, but that's out of the question at present. Cathy isn't well enough to be moved as yet and the thing is, I really can't say that Clara isn't a risk to herself or the child in her current state. Who knows what she might be capable of? At least in Hatter's Hall she would get the treatment she needs, whereas all I can give her is laudanum to try to keep her calm. What do you think of the idea?'

'I reckon it's a good 'un,' Minnie said without hesitation. 'Wi' the missus the way she is, I don't mind admittin' I'm almost afraid to close me eyes come night time. An' what wi' runnin' up an' down them stairs after her an' Cathy, me an' Saffie are fair worn out.'

Saffie sighed. She knew Minnie was right and yet she felt as if she was betraying her grandmother somehow having her put away in such a place. But then, the sensible side of her questioned, what other option did they have? Neither she nor Minnie were trained to care for someone suffering with a mental illness. But how much would all this cost? she wondered.

It was as if Marcus had been able to read her mind for he said, 'I think it might be for the best, Saffie, and don't get worrying about the cost. Your grandfather and my father were the very best of friends and my father would want me to do this for her.'

Saffie stared down at her hands, which were clasped tightly in her lap, before slowly nodding. 'Very well, Dr Jones, would you mind making the arrangements? And thank you, Marcus.'

He inclined his head and shortly after he and the doctor left, promising to let them know when the arrangements had been made.

Seeing Saffie's glum expression, Minnie wagged the spoon she was using to stir sugar into yet more tea at her. 'Now don't you get thrashin' yerself over this,' she warned. 'None o' this is your fault, nor mine if it comes to that. Truth be told the missus ain't been right since yer grandfather passed away, God rest his soul, and havin' Cathy 'ere just seems to 'ave tipped her over the edge. I've no doubt it's 'er guilty conscience – she were never much of a wife to 'im.'

She quickly drained her tea and rose to make a start on the lunch while Saffie divided her time between checking on the two invalids.

There was a welcome diversion later that afternoon when Mathilda arrived, looking breathtakingly pretty in a sky-blue costume and matching bonnet. Thankfully, both Clara and Cathy were taking a nap so she and Saffie went to sit in the drawing room.

'I came to see if there was anything I could do,' she said as she settled in the chair with her silken skirts billowing about her. Saffie hadn't been able to visit so often since having two invalids to care for and she had missed her. 'Marcus told me what had been decided for your grandmother and I have to say I think you've done the right thing agreeing to it. Marcus and the doctor are at Hatter's Hall making the arrangements for her to be admitted even as we speak.'

Saffie's eyes strayed to the window and she shrugged her slim shoulders. 'I just wish I could care for her here,' she answered in a small voice, although deep down she knew that wasn't strictly true. Her grandmother had never done anything to endear herself to her, although initially Saffie had hoped they would become close. She wondered what her mother would have thought about Clara being incarcerated in such a place, but the decision had been taken now, so there was no point worrying about things she couldn't change.

Early the next morning a carriage driven by two coal-black horses arrived from Hatter's Hall, and with tears in her eyes, Saffie helped her grandmother into her coat. Two burly male nurses entered the house to take Clara away but she offered no resistance. In fact, she went with them meekly, like a lamb to slaughter, and in no time at all she was gone.

'It's fer the best, pet,' Minnie said wisely as she noted Saffie's distress. 'An' no doubt they'll 'ave her right in no time. Meanwhile we can concentrate on gettin' young Cathy better an' try an' find 'er mother for her, eh?'

Saffie nodded, although she had no idea how she was going to go about it.

Marcus called later that day after speaking to the matron at Hatter's Hall who had told him that she felt Clara would benefit from cold water treatments and leeches to suck the badness out of her. Saffie shuddered at the thought, although she supposed they knew what they were doing.

During the next week Cathy slowly made progress until finally the doctor said he felt she was well enough to come downstairs each day for a few hours.

Saffie and Minnie gently carried her down the stairs between them that very afternoon and propped her up with pillows in a chair by the back door where she could look out over the garden. It was now the middle of March and the outside was coming back to life after the long hard winter. Primroses peeped from beneath the hedgerows and daffodils pushed through the earth as the green buds on the trees slowly began to unfurl in the watery sunshine.

'You'll be out there playin' in the sun in no time,' Minnie told the child cheerily as she tucked a warm blanket around her knees, but Cathy didn't answer. Since the thrashing she had retreated into her own little word of silence and this time Saffie worried that she might never leave it. It seemed unfair that the poor little girl had been through so very much heartache in her short life but all Saffie and Minnie could do was try to make things better for her. At least she was in no imminent danger now that Clara was gone.

That same day they had a surprise visitor when Bernie Denning appeared, looking very smart in a new pinstriped suit. It had been a few weeks since he had visited following Clara's tantrum about him coming during Saffie's working hours, and she found she was pleased to see him. He was the only link she had to Granny Doyle and her sisters, and she was eager to hear how they all were.

'They're all in the best of health and doing very well,' he assured her. 'And they asked me to bring this to you.'

He produced a rather dog-eared envelope from his coat pocket and passed it to her.

Saffie frowned. 'But who is it from?'

'I believe it's from your father. He wrote to your mother; he obviously didn't know of her passing. Granny Doyle thinks that he perhaps got another prisoner to write it for him, and they thought you might like to see it.'

'Oh, I would,' Saffie said with a lump in her throat. It would be the first time they had heard from him since he had been arrested and she was eager to hear what he had to say.

'Thank you, I shall read it later,' she told him as she tucked it into the deep pocket of her apron and she went on to tell him of all that had happened since they had last met.

It was not until much later that evening when Cathy had been settled in bed and Minnie had retired for the night that

Saffie finally sat down on the settle at the side of the fire to read the letter.

My deerest Olivia,

I dare say yu'll be surprised to ear from me an I don't quite know where to begin. Peraps I shud start by tellin yu ow sorry I am for bein such an idiot. We was appy till I got in wi the wrong crowd an went off the rales, I can see that now an I promis I'll make it up to yer when I cum 'ome. As yu can see im usin me time wisely when I aint workin and lurnin to read an write. Jacko Barnes, the chap I share a cell wi is teechin me. Yu allus wanted me to but I didn't feel the need fer it bak then. Now I do an I'm gonna make yu proud o me I promise. I ope the kids are all wel? I miss em an yu an the blu saffire sommat terrible. The guvnor ere is a fare bloke an he told me that if I keep beavin meself I mite get out a bit early. Sory fer the bad spellin' iv still got a lot to learn but im tryin me best me darlin. I know Archie got transported an it breaks me eart but opefully one day we'll both be back wi yu all where we belong. Until then me love know that I think of yu every minute o the day and long fer the day when we'll be together again.

I luv yu all wi all me 'eart,
Yur lovin usband Reuben xxxxxxx

Tears began to course down Saffie's cheeks as she slowly folded the letter and placed it back in the envelope. Her father would be shocked when he came home and discovered just how much had changed, and she was heartbroken that her mother had died without the love of her life at her side. But none of that could be helped now and all she could do was make the best of things.

Even after what had happened, the majority of the memories she held of her father were happy ones. She remembered idyllic days leading old Nellie along the towpath as she pulled the barge behind her with the sun blazing down on them from a cloudless blue sky. Happy times sitting with her mother on the deck of *The Blue Sapphire* when they were moored, polishing the horse brasses until they gleamed, and chatting of where they might go next. Playing in buttercup meadows and making daisy chains with her siblings in the fields along the canal. Snuggling down into bed at night knowing that her family were all safe and sound around her. Happy times that could never come again, but she had her memories and they would last a lifetime.

Chapter Twenty-Two

During the first week in April Granny Doyle had an unexpected visitor when Elsie turned up on the doorstep looking thin and bedraggled.

'Oh, so you ain't forgot us altogether then,' Granny quipped in her usual forthright way, ushering her into the kitchen. The girls had gone to market so she was alone in the house.

'Where's me mam?' Elsie asked as she glanced around the room. 'And Saffie and the girls?'

Granny Doyle took a deep breath and told her all that had gone on in the last few months, and by the time she had finished Elsie was sitting at the table, tears of disbelief and shock rolling down her cheeks.

'B-but I had no idea!'

'Well, you wouldn't 'ave, would yer? You never even bothered to let us know where yer were so 'ow were we supposed to get in touch?'

If Elsie had expected sympathy, she certainly wasn't going to get it from Granny Doyle.

'So why 'ave yer come back now wi' yer tail atween yer legs,' Granny asked as she filled the kettle from the bucket and placed it on the fire to boil. 'Got the sack, did yer?'

Elsie flushed. 'Y-yes I did . . . but it wasn't my fault,' she whimpered. 'It was the son of the house where I worked.

He told me he loved me and that he wanted to marry me but then . . .'

'Oh, let me guess,' Granny Doyle snorted. 'He 'ad 'is wicked way wi' yer an' then dropped yer like a ton o' hot bricks!'

Shamefaced, Elsie stared down at her joined hands. 'Something like that,' she muttered.

'An' now you've got a bun in the oven, eh? So you've come back 'ere expectin' yer ma to sort it.'

When Elsie didn't answer, she sighed. 'Well, me girl, yer ma ain't 'ere anymore, is she? An' there certainly ain't room fer anyone else 'ere.'

'I shall have to go to Saffie then and see if she can help me,' Elsie answered in a small voice.

'Huh, you know our Saffie, she's got a 'eart as big as a bucket but it won't be up to 'er. She's livin' in her other grandmother's 'ouse doin' a job o' work, may I add, an' it'll be up to 'er if you can stay there or not. Although she's ill an' in Hatter's Hall at present so Saffie told us in 'er last letter.'

There was a tap on the door just then and Bernie Denning appeared. He often visited Granny and the girls on his day off and he stared at Elsie curiously. He could vaguely remember seeing her on *The Blue Sapphire*. He'd been told that she had taken a job in a big house in Coventry so wondered why she was there now, unless she was just visiting.

'Hello, it's Elsie, isn't it?' He smiled at her and she nodded back. 'Come for a visit, have you?'

'She needs to get to Tuttle Hill to our Saffie,' Granny told him unfeelingly and Elsie's head bowed even lower.

For weeks she had been staying in a dirty room in a cheap bed and breakfast place in the seedy part of Coventry as she tried to search for another job, but what little of her wages she hadn't squandered on fancy clothes was gone now and she didn't know where to turn. One thing was already for certain, she wasn't going to find any help at Granny's so Saffie and her other grandmother – who she hadn't even known existed until today – were her last hope.

'I'm going to see Saffie later this afternoon, as it happens,' Bernie told her. 'You could travel on the coach with me if you like.'

Elsie blushed. 'I, er . . . haven't got the fare.'

Realising that something was amiss, Bernie smiled. 'Oh, don't worry about that. I can pay for you; the fare isn't that much and I'm sure Saffie will be happy to see you.'

'Th-thank you.' Elsie had never felt more miserable in her life, although she supposed she had deserved the welcome she had been given. She really should have kept in touch more and she couldn't believe that she would never see her mother again. She hadn't even got to say goodbye. As she sat there feeling thoroughly miserable, Granny made another pot of tea and after fetching a freshly baked loaf from the pantry she carved two large slices and pushed them towards her with a heel of cheese.

'Get that down yer,' she ordered. 'Yer as thin as a rake.'

Elsie wanted to tell her to keep her food, but her stomach was rumbling and so forgetting her pride she wolfed it down in seconds.

Bernie sat down by the fire keeping his eyes averted until she had finished and during that time the twins returned and whooped with delight when they saw their sister.

'Are you staying?' Ginny's eyes were sparkling as she raced to give her a hug.

'No . . .' Elsie glanced at Granny Doyle but saw that there was no chance of her changing her mind. 'I just called in to see you then I'm off to see Saffie. Mr Denning here is going to take me.'

'Aw.' Lucy pouted. 'I wish we could come too.'

'Well, you can't.' Granny frowned at her. 'Saffie 'as enough on 'er plate at present.' But seeing the girl's face fall her voice softened. 'But soon per'aps, eh?'

For the next hour the twins chattered away to Elsie like little magpies as they asked her all about what she had been up to since she left them. Elsie chose her words carefully but was almost relieved when Bernie finally said, 'We should be leaving now. The coach leaves in less than an hour.'

Elsie said her goodbyes and promised she would come and see the twins again very soon and then they were on their way, Elsie clutching her old carpet bag, which contained all her worldly possessions.

She was unnaturally quiet during the journey but Bernie supposed that was to be expected. She had only just found out about her mother's passing and all that had gone on, after all, so it was understandable that she would have little to say.

Once they had alighted close to the market place in Nuneaton, Bernie gallantly took Elsie's bag and they set off for Clara's house nestling close to the canal in Tuttle Hill. The family had moored there many times when they lived on *The Blue Sapphire*, but Elsie had never paid the place much attention. Now she knew her mother used to live there, though, she was curious to see what it was like.

'So, are you and Saffie, er . . . walking out together?' she asked as she almost ran to keep up with Bernie's long strides.

He flushed. 'Oh no, nothing like that,' he assured her, although he wished with all his heart that it was otherwise. 'Saffie and I are just friends.'

'Oh, I see.' Elsie wondered why he would go to so much trouble and keep making the journey to see her if that was the case, but she didn't say it aloud. She had enough troubles of her own to worry about without giving too much thought to what Saffie was up to, so she fell silent.

When they reached the house, which was much grander than Elsie had imagined it would be, Bernie led her around to the back door where he found Minnie beating a carpet that was flung across a line that extended across the yard. Seeing the visitors she turned and looked at Elsie suspiciously.

''Ello, Bernie, an' who is this then?'

'This is Elsie, Saffie's younger sister. She's come to see her.'

'Oh 'as she now?' Elsie eyed the girl up and down. She had thought that Saffie was pretty but this girl was positively beautiful, even if she did look slightly bedraggled. But she supposed she shouldn't have been surprised. Their mother had been beautiful too until the hard life she had chosen on the canal had prematurely aged her.

'So how are Cathy and Mrs Bishop?' Bernie asked.

Minnie shrugged as she dropped the carpet beater and walked towards the kitchen door. 'The missus is doin' as well as can be expected, accordin' to Mr Marcus, an' Cathy, well, yer can see fer yerself. She's in the kitchen an' on the mend now 'opefully, at least, physically she is.'

Bernie and Elsie followed her into the kitchen where Saffie was washing up pots in the deep stone sink, and much as her younger sisters had done earlier in the day, she whooped with delight when she saw her.

'Why, Elsie, what a wonderful surprise.' She quickly wiped her hands on her calico apron and hurried across the room to give her sister a hug. 'But what are you doing here? I thought you were working in Coventry? Have they given you a holiday?'

'Not exactly. I'll, er . . . explain everything later. But I've come to see if I might stay for a little while?'

'I see.' Saffie didn't quite know what to say. It wasn't up to her who stayed in her grandmother's house after all. She glanced at Minnie, who shrugged.

'It ain't as if the missus is 'ere at the minute to object so I can't see why she shouldn't,' she stated.

Elsie let out a sigh of relief. At least she would have a roof over her head again, for the time being at least. She glanced towards the little girl who was sitting in a chair propped up with pillows and guessed that this must be Cathy, the child Bernie had told her about. She seemed to be locked away in a world of her own, staring sightlessly at the flames that were flickering up the chimney, and Elsie felt sorry for her. From what Bernie had told her the poor kid had had a rough time of it.

'So how long were you thinking of staying?' Saffie asked.

Acutely aware of Minnie and Bernie listening, Elsie shrugged. 'I, er . . . I'm not sure yet. As I said, we'll talk about it later, eh?'

It was much later that evening before Saffie and Elsie got the chance to speak alone and when Elsie told her sister about the predicament she was in, Saffie was horrified.

'What a louse,' Saffie breathed. 'And you must have fallen for his patter hook, line and sinker. How far gone are you? And what are you going to do now? I have to tell you, our grandmother is a hard woman and I can't see her taking pity on you and letting you stay when she comes home. She'll have you out of that door faster than you can say Jack Robinson.'

Elsie sniffed back a tear. 'I reckon I'm a couple of months, I've just missed my second course, and as to what I'm going to do . . .' The tears came in earnest then as Saffie sat worrying her bottom lip with her teeth.

'Let's just take each day as it comes for now, eh?' she said eventually. 'I don't even know what's going to happen to me yet. It's obvious that Cathy isn't going to be able to stay here now and if Grandmother sends her away there'll be no job for me and I'll be in the same boat as you.'

'Apart from the fact that you're not carrying a baby,' Elsie pointed out dejectedly. And lowering her voice, she went on, 'Actually, I was wondering if you knew of anyone around here who might be able to help girls like me?' she whispered hopefully.

Horrified, Saffie slammed her small fist on the table, making the pressed glass sugar bowl dance.

'We'll have *none* of that talk,' she spat. 'I'll not have you going to some backstreet butcher, do you hear me? Let's just see what happens. Meantime you can come and help me make up a bed for you.'

She flounced away leaving Elsie with no choice but to follow her.

Chapter Twenty-Three

Davey was in the kitchen drinking tea with Minnie when Saffie got up the next morning. The fire was glowing in the hearth and a pan of porridge was already bubbling on the stove.

She smiled at him. 'You're an early bird.'

'Aye, I came wi' a message from Master Marcus. He's visiting Mrs Bishop at Hatter's Hall this afternoon an' he wondered if you wanted to go along o' him.'

Saffie frowned. 'Well, I . . .'

'Don't worry,' Minnie assured her, adding another spoonful of sugar to her mug. 'I'm quite capable o' keepin' me eye on everythin' 'ere fer a while.'

'In that case could you tell Marcus that yes I'd like to go.' She glanced around the room. 'No sign of Elsie stirring yet?'

Minnie shook her head. 'No, an' little Cathy is still fast asleep an' all so I thought I'd leave 'er be. She must be comfortable so that's a good sign that 'er back is healin' if she can rest now.'

Saffie nodded as she fetched another cup from the cupboard and joined them. Soon after Davey left to begin his day's work and Saffie said slyly, 'He really is a lovely chap, isn't he? Cathy seems to be quite taken with him.'

'I suppose he is.' Minnie scowled at her. 'But don't you get readin' anythin' into it now. He's comin' purely to bring us things that we need an' to see Cathy.'

'If you say so.' Saffie tried to hide her smile behind her cup as Minnie bounced away from the table to go and give the porridge a stir.

It was almost ten o'clock that morning before Elsie appeared looking grey and drawn.

'Ah, the spirit stirs!' Minnie joked. 'Do yer want a nice dish o' porridge, luvvie?'

At the mention of food, Elsie clapped her hand across her mouth and dashed off to the outside toilet.

'I take it she's havin' a bairn then?' Minnie said drily.

Seeing no point in lying, Saffie nodded. 'Yes, I'm afraid she is. It's the son of the people she was working for. He told her he loved her and was going to marry her and she fell for it.'

'Aye well, she ain't the first an' I doubt she'll be the last but what's she gonna do now?'

'I have no idea. In fact, I don't know what's going to happen to either of us,' Saffie admitted. 'You and I both realise that Cathy can't stay here once my grandmother comes home. We would have to be with her every second of every day to make sure that she was safe and that isn't always possible. So I imagine that Grandmother will send her away somewhere and I'll be without a job too.'

'Let's not think too far ahead just yet.' Minnie had grown fond of Saffie and hated the thought of her leaving. 'Yer know the old sayin', "When one door shuts another door opens." Let's just 'ope as it's true, eh?' She lifted the large

214

basket of washing she had just put through the mangle and carried it out to the yard.

Marcus picked Saffie up in his carriage at two o'clock that afternoon. She had changed into her Sunday best skirt and blouse and her best bonnet, which Minnie had trimmed with yellow ribbon for her, and she had left her hair loose and brushed it until it shone like a raven's wing.

'You look very nice, my dear,' Marcus commented as she settled back against the leather squabs.

She blushed prettily. 'Thank you.'

His face became solemn as the horse drew away from the cottage. 'I'm sorry I haven't managed to get to see any of you for a few days. I've been very busy with school, and added to that, after what you told me about Spencer-Hughes, I've been doing a little detective work regarding the eldest daughter.'

'Really?' Saffie couldn't keep the edge of excitement from her voice. 'And have you had any luck in finding out what happened to her?'

'I think I have, as it happens. The first time I visited last week, Mr Spencer-Hughes was present so it seemed pointless to bring the subject up. He made it more than clear when he disowned her that he would never have her name mentioned in the house again. But yesterday when I visited, I had more luck when I found Mrs Spencer-Hughes alone. Mathilda visits her sometimes for morning coffee and she confided to her some time ago that she still misses her daughter, so I tentatively mentioned her name. The poor woman was instantly in tears and eventually admitted that she knows where Margaret is now.

'It seems she married the young man she ran away with but sadly he was killed in an accident shortly after they were wed. For some time, her mother had no contact with her and had no idea where she was. Then when Margaret did get in touch some years later, she had a small child who fits Cathy's description. It's too much of a coincidence, wouldn't you say? I feel we must be on the right track, particularly as Mrs Spencer-Hughes told me that Margaret had been very ill some time ago and she had no idea who was caring for the child now.

'She is too afraid of her husband to make further enquiries but everything fits with what Cathy told us. I would imagine that it was when Margaret became ill that your grandfather placed Cathy in Hatter's Hall, but whether or not he was Cathy's father I have no idea. But she couldn't have been her husband's child because her mother confided to me that he was killed some two years before Cathy was born, so everything certainly points to her being your grandfather's, especially considering the way your grandmother has reacted to having her in the house.'

'And is Margaret still alive?' Saffie asked eagerly.

Marcus nodded. 'Yes, and I have a feeling that it's her mother who has paid for her to be cared for during her illness, but she hasn't told me where she is – not yet at any rate.'

'But surely if Cathy is her granddaughter, she would want to care for her?'

Marcus sucked his teeth and sighed. 'You would think so, wouldn't you? But it's well known that Mr Spencer-Hughes is the boss in that house and Mrs Spencer-Hughes is a very meek woman who wouldn't dare say boo to a goose.'

Saffie sagged back against the squabs and stared from the window at the fields. It was all just so sad and she wondered how they were ever going to resolve everything.

Soon after they reached the imposing gates of Hatter's Hall and Saffie broke out in goosebumps as the old gateman came to open them. Just the sight of the place was enough to give her nightmares and she was sure that most people who had to stay there would be mad in no time, even if they hadn't been when they arrived there.

They were admitted by a mousy-haired nurse who led them up a sweeping staircase. As they climbed, the sounds of the patients grew louder and without thinking, Saffie reached out to take Marcus's hand. They could hear crying and some were wailing and she had to stifle the urge to cry. The poor souls sounded so helpless and hopeless. Marcus gave her fingers a reassuring squeeze and they moved on until they reached a long landing.

'Mrs Bishop is in a room along this way,' the nurse informed them as they stopped at a door. She fumbled with a chatelaine about her waist and selected a key, and after unlocking the door she ushered them ahead of her before stopping to lock it securely behind her again. On either side of the corridor were doors with small grills in the top, and as they went along Saffie glimpsed people sitting on narrow wooden beds inside. Many of them were groaning and rocking backwards and forwards and she felt as if her heart would break as she thought how dreadful it would be to be locked up in such a confined space all day. It was no wonder they were ill.

At the very end of the corridor the nurse took another key from the bunch and opened yet another door. 'This is

Mrs Bishop's room,' she told them. 'And Dr Saville will be along to talk to you presently. Meanwhile, do please try to keep her calm. She had a bad night and we had to sedate her this morning.'

Saffie's first impression of the room gave her some relief. It was much larger than the cells they had passed and more comfortably furnished, although the bars that were fitted to the window made her suppress a shudder. A neatly made brass bed stood against one wall and a hard-backed chair and a wooden table stood in the window. There was a chest of drawers and a washstand with a china jug and bowl on it against another wall and two small rugs, one on either side of the bed. Other than that, the room was bare. Clara was sitting in the chair by the window but she didn't even glance up when they entered.

Saffie took a tentative step towards her, shocked to see how old and frail she looked. 'Grandmother . . . it's me, Sapphire.' She knew that Clara had told her never to address her as such but under these circumstances Saffie felt she might be forgiven. But when Clara didn't even acknowledge her presence but continued to stare blankly from the window, a flutter of unease started in Saffie's stomach. She had hoped to find her slightly improved but if anything, she seemed even worse. She glanced helplessly at Marcus who removed his hat and stepped forward.

'Hello, Mrs Bishop. How are you feeling today?'

Again there was no response. They stood for a while, unsure what to do and were relieved when they heard the key turn in the door and a small, bald-headed doctor with a bulbous red nose appeared.

'So how is she, Doctor?' Marcus enquired.

The doctor sighed and stroked his chin. 'She seems to be in some sort of shock,' he replied. 'And as yet she hasn't responded to treatment, although of course it's still very early days.'

'And may I ask what sort of treatment that is?'

'We've tried cold water treatment and blood-letting up to now.'

Saffie shuddered. They both sounded dreadful, although she supposed the doctor must know what he was doing.

'I see, and do you have any idea how long she could remain in this state?'

The doctor shook his head. 'I'm afraid not, sir. Each patient is different. She could come out of it very suddenly or she could remain like this for some time. We are going to try leeches next. We have had a measure of success with them.' He crossed to feel Clara's wrist and smiled with satisfaction. 'Her pulse and her temperature are excellent so it is clearly purely a mental condition and I assure you we will do all we can. Now, unless you have any more questions, I have other patients waiting to be seen, so if you will excuse me?'

When he had gone, Saffie gently placed her hand on Clara's arm and just for a moment she got a reaction as the woman flinched away from her. It appeared that even in her current mental state she couldn't bear to have her granddaughter close.

It was then that a thought occurred to Saffie and turning to Marcus she asked, 'Is this a private room?'

He nodded.

'But how much is all this costing?' she asked with concern. 'And does Grandmother have sufficient funds to pay you back?'

'Don't get worrying about that,' Marcus said. 'I told you I am seeing to that. It was what my parents would have wanted me to do. They were very close to Mr and Mrs Bishop and I assure you I can afford it.'

Saffie didn't quite know what to say and looked back at her grandmother. They might as well not have been there and so a few moments later they left and started the short journey back to the house. As they turned into the long drive that led to the farm and the house, they saw Mathilda, wearing a smart burgundy velvet riding habit, trotting across the fields on her snow-white horse.

Marcus frowned. 'I do wish she would stop riding, at least until after the baby is born. I admit she's an excellent horsewoman and the doctor has told her that it will do no harm for a few more weeks, but I wish she would listen to me all the same.'

'I'm sure she'll be fine,' Saffie assured him as she watched Mathilda's horse jump a gate with ease. 'She looks very competent.'

The next month passed uneventfully and May arrived in a blaze of colour as the flowers in the garden burst into life. Cathy was improving by the day. Her back had healed well and she was able to wear clothes once more. She had even started to say a few words again, no doubt because in Clara's absence she was no longer afraid of what she might do to her. Clara, however, still showed no signs of improvement and Elsie was quiet and withdrawn.

Bernie visited at least twice a week and had become the odd job man about the house, along with Davey who was always ready to lend a hand, and as much as Saffie hated to admit it, all in all the house was a happier place without Clara, even with Elsie moping about the place.

Thankfully Clara had always allowed Minnie access to money for food and bills so they had no concerns on that score, although Saffie felt slightly guilty that she was now there under false pretences. Minnie still insisted on caring for Cathy as well as doing the majority of the cooking and cleaning, and sometimes Saffie felt a little like a spare part. But then, she tried to convince herself, things would be different when her grandmother came home. Minnie would have much more to do again and she could take on the role of caring for Cathy full-time.

But things took a drastic change when Marcus suddenly turned up one day looking pale and worried.

'What's wrong, lad?' Minnie asked when he barged into the kitchen.

Marcus took a deep, steadying breath. 'It's Mathilda,' he told her miserably. 'She's been thrown from her horse and broken her leg and it looks as if she might lose the baby!'

Chapter Twenty-Four

'Oh Lordy!' Minnie sucked in her breath. 'What can I do to help?'

'Actually, it's Saffie I've come to see.' He shuffled from foot to foot as he glanced towards her. 'I shan't be able to attend the school for a few days at least. I need to be at home with Mathilda and I wondered . . . well, I know it's a lot to ask, but I wondered if you might possibly be able to take my place and keep the school open until I can go back?'

Saffie was shocked. 'But I don't have any qualifications,' she pointed out, although the prospect of doing what he was asking filled her with excitement.

He waved her concerns aside. 'I'm fully aware of that. I'm also fully aware that you'd be more than capable of keeping the place going.'

'But . . . I'm needed here,' she faltered.

At which point Minnie interrupted. 'No, you ain't . . . at least not until the missus comes 'ome. I'm more than able to manage things 'ere an' I'm sure Elsie is capable of lendin' a 'and if necessary. Ain't that right, Elsie?'

Elsie nodded somewhat reluctantly. She had quite enjoyed being looked after.

'There you are then,' Minnie said with satisfaction. 'Problem solved. When would yer like 'er to start?'

'Tomorrow, if possible. I can set out the lessons for you each evening to make things a little easier if you think you could manage it.'

Saffie felt as if she could burst with pride. Like her mother, she had always dreamed of being a teacher but because of her upbringing she had thought it would never be possible, and now here Marcus was offering her a post, albeit temporary, at his little school.

'In that case, I'd be honoured to help out,' she told him. 'Although I do hope Mathilda is soon well again. Please send her my love. I'll be keeping you all in my prayers.'

'Thank you.' He withdrew a key from his pocket and handed it to her. 'That is the key to the school and I'll drop tomorrow's lessons in to you first thing in the morning. But now I really must get back to my wife.' And with that he jammed his hat back on and strode away, looking like he was carrying the weight of the world on his shoulders.

'Eeh, fancy that, you a teacher, eh?' Minnie said delightedly. But her expression changed quickly. 'But poor Mathilda. They've longed for this baby an' if owt should go wrong now they'll both be heartbroken, poor loves. Still, let's not look on the black side, eh? Happen Mathilda'll be as right as rain after a good night's sleep.'

Sometime later Minnie found Saffie spreading her few clothes out across the bed.

'What's up?' she asked. 'Not sure what to wear?'

Saffie sighed. 'I don't really have a lot of choice. I only have my Sunday best skirt and blouse and even they are well past their best and the costume I altered to come and meet grandmother in is far too grand.'

'Hm.' Minnie fingered the brown calico skirt. As Saffie had stated it was well darned and certainly not what anyone would expect to see a teacher wearing. Then suddenly she smiled. 'I've just 'ad a thought. You an' yer gran are round about the same size. Why don't yer borrow somethin' o' hers to wear?'

Saffie looked horrified. 'Oh, I couldn't! What would she say?'

'She ain't 'ere to find out, is she?' Minnie pointed out. 'An' no doubt by the time she is, Marcus will be back at school an' she'll never know. Come on, let's go an' see if we can find somethin' suitable.' She set off purposefully, leaving Saffie no choice but to follow her.

Once they were in Clara's room, Saffie looked about uncomfortably. It didn't feel right being in here but, she reasoned, Minnie was probably right. What she didn't know surely couldn't hurt her, could it?

Crossing over to the ornately carved walnut wardrobe that stood against one wall, Minnie threw the door open and Saffie's eyes stretched as she stared at the array of gowns, skirts and blouses in all the colours of the rainbow. There were day gowns in soft velvet and ball gowns in satin and silks. Skirts and more blouses than Saffie had ever seen in one place before.

'What about this one?' Minnie took out a long black skirt in a soft cord material and held it up to Saffie's waist. 'That's smart, try it on while I look fer a blouse that ain't too fancy to go wi' it.'

Saffie reluctantly slid out of her own skirt and slipped into it. It was slightly large about the waist but it was nothing that a few stitches wouldn't remedy.

'An' what about this blouse?' Minnie held up a soft lawn blouse, white with ruffled cuffs and neckline and Saffie instantly fell in love with it. 'Come on, try it on.'

She did as she was told and when she was dressed, Minnie hurried over to a large chest of drawers and returned with a wide petticoat that she jiggled up beneath the skirt and over Saffie's hips. Then she turned her around to survey herself in the cheval mirror and Saffie gasped.

'We'll put yer 'air up an' all. It'll make yer look a bit older an' wiser,' Minnie suggested as she turned to the dressing table to grab a handful of hair clips. She plonked Saffie down on the stool and took up the mistress's hair brush and ten minutes later she told her, 'There, yer can look now. Yer certainly look the part.'

Saffie stared at her reflection in awe. Minnie had twisted her coal-black hair into a neat chignon, and together with the expensive clothes she was sure she could have passed herself off as gentry.

'Goodness,' was all she could say and Minnie chuckled.

'Right, I suggest yer get a good night's sleep. You'll 'ave to be up early in the mornin an' I'll take that waistband in fer you this evenin'.'

'But are you quite sure you'll manage here on your own?' Saffie fretted.

'Like I said afore, I ain't on me own, am I? Young Elsie can pull her finger out an' earn 'er keep fer a change. Now go on, be off wi' yer. I've got a skirt to alter!'

Sleep didn't come easy to Saffie that night as she tossed and turned feeling nervous about the next day and worried for her friend, so by the time the dawn broke she was exhausted and her stomach was full of butterflies. She was being thrown in at the deep end and she wouldn't even have Marcus there to advise her if she was doing right or wrong. But it couldn't be helped, so she dressed quickly and went down to the kitchen. Minnie was already pottering about and she smiled at her approvingly. Saffie had managed to put her hair up by herself, not quite as neatly as Minnie had done it admittedly, but she looked very nice all the same.

'You'll do,' Minnie told her with a satisfied smile. 'Now get some o' this porridge down yer.'

That proved to be easier said than done. It seemed to lodge in Saffie's throat and now she was seriously wondering if she had bitten off more than she could chew! What if she made a hash of things and let Marcus down?

All her concerns flew out of the window when he arrived shortly after with a sheaf of papers under his arm. He was unshaven and looked worn out, with dark circles beneath his eyes and wearing crumpled clothes.

'These are the lessons for today,' he told her without preamble as he thrust them into her hands. 'It's all very basic stuff: spelling and the times table.' He blinked as he properly looked at her for the first time, wondering what was different about her. He had always looked upon her as a very pleasant girl but suddenly she was standing in front of him looking like a very presentable young woman.

'I shall be just fine,' Saffie told him with a confidence she was far from feeling. 'But how is Mathilda today?'

He hung his head and she thought she detected tears on his eyelashes. 'I'm sorry to say she lost our child in the early hours of this morning. The doctor is still with her and I'm afraid she's . . .'

Saffie gasped and blinked back her own tears as she remembered how excited Mathilda had been when she told her about her pregnancy. 'Oh, Marcus, I'm so sorry,' she said softly, laying her hand gently on his arm.

He turned abruptly. 'Thank you, but now I must get back. If you'll excuse me . . . and, Saffie, thank you.'

'Eeh, the poor buggers,' Minnie sniffled when he'd gone, wiping her tear-stained cheeks on the edge of her pinny. 'They must both be 'eartbroken – Mathilda especially. She'll no doubt blame 'erself, poor lass. But come along now, you 'ave a school to open, so goodbye fer now, Miss Doyle, an' good luck.'

Saffie took a deep breath and wrapping the pretty shawl that Minnie had selected for her around her shoulders, she set off for the little school in Abbey Green.

There were children already assembled outside in the small yard when she got there and they stared at her curiously as she took the key from her pocket and unlocked the door.

They followed her into one of the classrooms where small desks and rows of chairs were set out in front of a large blackboard and silently took their seats. Soon others began to trickle in until the desks were all full, and Saffie asked, 'Is everyone here now?' She had counted fifteen children and the largest of them nodded.

'Yes, miss.'

'Good. Then before I begin, I shall introduce myself. My name is Miss Doyle and I shall be your teacher for the next few days until Mr Berrington returns.'

'Please, miss, is Mr Berrin'ton poorly?' A small, snotty-nosed boy with his hair freshly slicked down asked her.

'No and I'm sure it won't be long until he is back,' she told him with a smile. 'But now shall we take the register? That will help me to learn all your names, although I probably won't remember them straightaway so you'll have to forgive me.'

'I's Tom Ballard,' the same boy told her and she added a tick by the side of his name.

'An' I'm Cissy, 'is sister.'

The children continued to shout out their names until all but three of the names in the book had been ticked.

'Right then, children, we shall begin with some sums,' Saffie told them as she handed out their slates and pieces of chalk.

The morning seemed to pass in a flash and before she knew it, it was time to ring the bell for lunchtime. All but one of the children scattered, leaving Saffie to eat the sandwiches Minnie had packed for her in peace.

'Aren't you going to go home for your lunch, Sylvie?' Saffie enquired of the little girl. She was stick thin and Saffie was sure she could see head lice running across the uneven parting in her mousy-coloured hair.

'Ner, miss,' the child answered. 'There'd be no point. Me mam will probably be entertainin' a gen'leman at 'ome be now an' she won't thank me fer interruptin' 'em.'

Saffie was so shocked she almost choked on a mouthful of sandwich. Sylvie's mouth was almost watering as she stared at it hungrily and lifting the other half of it, Saffie offered, 'Would you like to share this with me?'

Sylvie hesitated but then leaning forward she snatched it and bit into it hungrily, sending crumbs scattering in all directions. The poor little mite was clearly starving so laying the rest of her own sandwich on the desk in front of her, Saffie told her, 'You can finish that too if you like. I'm not very hungry today.'

Sylvie needed no second telling and very quickly that had gone the same way as the other.

'Cor, that were luvly, miss, thank you,' she said, swiping her grubby hand across her mouth.

Saffie smiled at her before turning her attention to preparing the blackboard for the afternoon's lessons, but inside she was sad. Many of the children who attended the school were dressed in little more than rags and were severely undernourished. Now she understood why Marcus was so keen to help them improve themselves. Most of their fathers worked in the local mines or brickworks and he hoped that by getting some sort of education, the little ones might grow up to have more opportunity than their parents.

There was a spring in Saffie's step when she set off for home later that afternoon.

'No need to ask how that went if your face is anythin' to go by, eh?' Minnie smiled. 'Why, yer beamin' like a Cheshire cat!'

'Oh, I loved it, Minnie!' Saffie removed her shawl and smiled at Cathy who was sitting in her usual chair by the window. 'Perhaps you might like to come along and join the classes when you feel better?' she suggested but Cathy shook her head and for now Saffie didn't press the point.

Marcus visited later that evening with the lessons he had set out for the next day and he was pleased to hear that all had gone well.

'How's Mathilda?' Saffie asked as soon as he arrived.

Marcus smiled sadly. 'Her leg is badly broken, and she's been given something to make her sleep, which is the best thing for her . . .' His voice trailed away as he stared off into the distance, his expression bleak.

'You know, I'd be more than happy to pick up the lessons from you, so you don't have to leave her,' Saffie said, her heart breaking for both of them.

Marcus shook his head. 'Thank you for offering, but to be honest, the walk does me good. Now, tell me, how did you get on?' Marcus asked, anxious to change the subject.

Saffie smiled. 'I enjoyed it immensely. But I hadn't realised how poor some of the children were.'

Marcus nodded. The few parents who could afford it sent the odd penny in to him but the majority of them got their learning for free. He was aware that if he tried to charge them, they would get no education at all, but the sparse amount he collected barely covered the cost of the hire of the building they used as a school.

'I had thought of trying to supply some food for those that wanted it each lunchtime,' he admitted. 'But the problem with that would be they would just be turning up to eat and then clearing off.'

'Perhaps we could think of doing some sort of fundraising to cover the cost of the food?' Saffie suggested, but it was clear that Marcus was still far too upset about the loss of the baby and Mathilda's health to worry about much else so she didn't pursue it.

'Poor chap,' Minnie said when he had left. 'This 'as proper knocked the stuffin' out o' him, ain't it? Oh, an' by the way, young Elsie ain't been too grand today neither. She won't say what's up wi' her though.'

'Oh, where is she?'

Minnie nodded towards the door that led to the hallway. 'Up in 'er room. She's barely ventured down 'ere all day only fer a drink o' water. She ain't eaten a thing.'

Saffie made her way towards the stairs just as a tap at the door sounded and Bernie arrived.

'I shan't be long, Bernie,' Saffie told him over her shoulder. 'Elsie isn't too well so I'm just popping up to see how she is.'

She found Elsie lying on the bed looking very pale and sorry for herself. There were dark bags beneath her eyes from lack of sleep and Saffie could see that she'd been crying.

'What's wrong?' Saffie asked gently and Elsie's eyes instantly filled with tears again.

'I'm frightened,' she admitted. 'What's going to happen to me, Saffie? When the baby comes, I mean. I shall have to get a job and who will look after it? And where will we live? I won't be able to stay here once our grandmother comes home, will I? She'll send me packing straightaway when she knows I'm with child and then we'll end up in the workhouse.'

'Let's just take one day at a time, shall we?' Saffie said as she hugged her younger sister to her. But inside she was afraid too. It appeared that all their lives would change when Clara was discharged from Hatter's Hall and it was possible they could find themselves homeless.

Chapter Twenty-Five

'June already,' Minnie sighed on the first day of the month. It was early in the morning and Saffie was busy packing sandwiches to take to school for some of the children for their lunch. She knew that she shouldn't without Marcus's consent but she couldn't bear the sight of their hungry little faces.

The last month had passed in a blur and Saffie had loved every minute of it, but now she knew that her time as a teacher was fast coming to a close as Marcus had told her the evening before that he felt Mathilda was almost well enough to be left in the care of the servants now, although she still wasn't up to receiving visitors. Saffie was disappointed not to be able to visit, but she understood. Over the last weeks she had taken to sending notes and small gifts to her, so she would have to content herself with that until Mathilda felt well enough to see her.

She had an inkling that Marcus was planning to return to school the following week and so she intended to make the most of every second. Not only would she miss the job, she would also miss the children, but she was grateful that she had been given the chance and hoped that one day in the future she might be able to find a post as a teacher full-time.

Meanwhile they were also planning for her grandmother's return with trepidation. Marcus had visited Hatter's Hall the week before and had been told that she was almost well enough to be discharged. Saffie was looking forward to it and dreading it in equal measure as she had no idea what state Clara would be in when she returned, and what was going to happen to Elsie? she wondered. She couldn't see her grandmother being pleased to find her there, especially when she discovered that she was carrying a child.

And then there was little Cathy, who was finally beginning to relax a little after her horrendous thrashing. Thanks to Minnie's tender loving care the wheals on her back had completely healed, although it was clear that the poor child would be scarred for life. Would Clara be any more kindly disposed towards her after her own stay in Hatter's Hall? Saffie doubted it, in which case they would be back to square one.

Despite these grim thoughts, as she set off for school in the warm, balmy morning, she was determined not to spoil the day. Bees were buzzing from flower to flower and the leaves on the trees were now a lush green. The children were waiting for her in the yard and Saffie frowned when she saw that Johnny Grimes had a black eye. It was a well-known fact that his father was a bully and frequently knocked his wife and children from pillar to post. They regularly went hungry too as his father's wages usually ended up over the bar of the local inn, and Saffie wished that things could be different.

Now as she looked back on her own childhood, she realised how lucky she had been. They may have struggled for money from time to time but her father had never lifted his hand to any of the children as these poor little waifs' fathers had. Admittedly she could remember her father hitting her mother occasionally, although he had always bitterly regretted it afterwards. She sighed, wondering how different their lives might have been if their father had never got involved with Seth Black. Still, she couldn't change the past and at least the twins were happy and settled with Granny Doyle, so she just had herself and Elsie to worry about, which she did almost every waking minute.

The day passed quickly and as she neared her grand-mother's home late that afternoon, she saw Marcus's horse tethered outside.

'Hello, Saffie,' he greeted her when she entered the kitchen. 'I have news for you. Your grandmother will be coming home on Monday, so I thought we should have a little chat.'

Minnie was busy mashing a pot of tea, and Elsie and Cathy were nowhere in sight so she took a seat at the table as he went on, 'Minnie and I have been talking and we both agree that it wouldn't be wise for any of you, especially Cathy, to stay here once she's back. We can't risk what happened to Cathy happening again, so Davey and I have had our heads together and I think we may have come up with a solution. There's an empty cottage at the back of the farm. It needs some doing up, admittedly, but Davey has offered to help with that and I think you, Minnie and Cathy could be quite comfortable there. I would, of course, only charge you a very small peppercorn rent.'

Saffie gulped. She hadn't expected this. 'But who will look after Grandmother?' she asked. 'And how will we live?'

'I thought Elsie could stay here and care for Mrs Bishop,' Marcus informed her.

'Aye, an' I've got enough saved to see us through fer some time to come,' Minnie piped up. 'Once we've settled in, I could look after Cathy an' you could per'aps take a little job, then we'll be in clover!'

234

It sounded idyllic but Saffie knew she would have to inform Marcus that Elsie was expecting a baby. She had promised her sister she wouldn't and had avoided doing so up until now, but Elsie wouldn't be able to care for a new baby and her grandmother.

'Unfortunately, I don't think that will work, you see, while Elsie was working in Coventry the son of the house took advantage of her and she is with child . . .' Her voice tailed away and Marcus frowned.

'Then we shall have to rethink things,' he said quietly. 'Perhaps she could manage her grandmother just for a while and then Elsie could go to the cottage with you and Minnie, and I could ask one of my maids if they'd be willing to care for Mrs Bishop.'

It sounded a perfect solution but Saffie's pride kicked in. 'But that would mean yet more expense for you,' she pointed out, colour flooding into her cheeks.

Marcus smiled. 'Oh, don't worry about that. My mother and father would have wanted me to take care of Mrs Bishop.'

'I see.' It didn't sound like an ideal solution but Saffie couldn't think of another option for the moment so she nodded reluctantly.

Marcus smiled, although it didn't quite reach his eyes. He had so much going on in his life at present that Saffie felt sorry for him. 'In that case I shall set Davey and some of the men to work on the cottage first thing in the morning,' he decided. 'And in the meantime, you and Minnie might like to go and take a look at it. I have a spare key here for you. My father's gamekeeper and his wife lived there and when they retired, Father let them both stay on until they passed away so it should be fairly comfortably furnished. If there's anything you need that isn't there, I'm sure you could take a few things from here.'

He placed a key on the table and Saffie stared at it, still not feeling comfortable with the idea. But what other option did she have? she asked herself. Had she just had herself to worry about she could have left for pastures new and found another position but as it was, she felt responsible for Elsie.

'Thank you,' she said awkwardly as Marcus rose from the table. 'And may I ask, how is Mathilda now? Do you think I might visit her?'

He shook his head. 'Physically, she is much recovered, but I fear mentally this is going to take a long time for her to get over,' he answered in a small voice. 'But anyway, I'll leave you now. I shall be fetching your grandmother home after school on Monday and hopefully when things have settled down a bit I can start to try and trace Cathy's mother again. Thank you for doing such a grand job of keeping the school open. From what I hear the children have quite taken to you.'

'It was a pleasure,' Saffie assured him, blushing at the compliment. And she meant it as she realised how sad she would be not to be teaching anymore. Tomorrow would be her last day. But then, she consoled herself, she had known it would only be a temporary post.

Davey and Bernie turned up after dinner that evening and Davey suggested shyly, 'I thought yer all might like to come an' 'ave a look at the cottage. Me an' the men are goin' to make a start on it tomorrer but I've just 'ad a good look an' it's in a lot better shape than I thought it would be. There's a couple o' leaks in the roof, the garden's badly overgrown an' it needs a good clean but other than that it seems to be fine.'

Minnie seemed excited at the prospect. This would be the nearest she had ever been to having her very own home and she certainly wasn't going to miss working for the mistress, who had never shown her a scrap of kindness.

'I shan't bother coming, I'm not feeling too well,' Elsie told them and Saffie noted that she did look flushed and hoped that she wasn't sickening for something.

'In that case I'll stop here with Elsie and keep an eye on Cathy,' Bernie offered, and once again Saffie thought what a lovely young man he was. It was a shame that she didn't feel romantically inclined towards him, because not only was he kind, but he was quite good-looking too. Saffie had no doubt that he would make someone a good husband one day.

Soon after, when Cathy had been settled in bed, Minnie and Saffie set off to look at what was soon to become their new home. It was dusk by then so there was no time to be wasted and they hurried along. The cottage was located a stone's throw away from the canal and Saffie had a lump in her throat as she glanced at the slow-moving water and thought of *The Blue Sapphire*. How her life had changed since then. She had passed the cottage many times but had never taken much notice of it before but now she was pleasantly surprised at the size of it.

A picket fence, badly in need of a lick of paint, surrounded the garden and Minnie beamed as they stepped through the gate. As Davey had told them, the garden was badly overgrown with weeds and brambles, but sprouting amongst them, she could see clumps of cranesbill and ragged robin along with lupins and hollyhocks.

'Eeh, this'll be a blaze o' flowers when we've got it sorted,' Minnie declared, unable to contain her glee, and

Saffie couldn't help but smile – anyone would have thought that Minnie was viewing a palace.

They picked their way through the tangle of undergrowth and when Saffie unlocked the door, which squeaked alarmingly, they found themselves in a large kitchen-cum-living room. A big inglenook fireplace with tarnished copper pans suspended on the beam above it took up one wall, while beneath the window against the opposite wall, a range cooker stood next to a deep stone sink and wooden draining board.

'It looks like that were a vegetable garden,' Minnie said, peering through the grimy glass. 'And look, there's a pump on the sink connected to the well. We'll have as much water as we like wi'out havin' to go outside to fetch it.'

The room was well furnished with somewhat dated but solid furniture and again Minnie couldn't conceal her delight. 'This'll come up a treat wi' a bit o' lavender polish an' a lot o' elbow grease,' she chortled. 'An' all the curtains are good an' all, they just need a wash to freshen 'em up.'

There were flagstones on the floor, which were covered in a thick layer of dust that whirled into the air as they walked across it, but other than that they looked to be in good condition, which delighted Minnie even further. They explored two doors set into another wall and found that one led into what would be a pretty little parlour once it had been cleaned. The other door opened on to a narrow, steep staircase and at the top of it they discovered three good-sized bedrooms, again all furnished with beds and drawers. One of them even had a large wardrobe.

'Eeh, I can 'ardly wait to get crackin' on it,' Minnie declared as she began to hook the slightly faded floral curtains down. 'An' I'm goin' to start by takin' all the curtains back wi' us to give 'em a good wash. I reckon we'll be really 'appy 'ere! Cathy can 'ave 'er own little room, bless 'er.'

Saffie bit her lip. 'Just as long as you realise that she might not always be with us,' she pointed out gently. It was obvious how much Minnie doted on the child and Saffie feared that if or when Marcus managed to locate her mother, Minnie's heart would be broken.

The smile instantly slid from Minnie's face and she sniffed as she folded her arms and hitched her breasts up. 'Yes, well . . . we'll face that if an' when it 'appens,' she retorted sulkily and she stamped off to the next room to retrieve the curtains from the window in there.

They arrived back at the house laden down with curtains and linen they had found in the cupboards in the cottage, and that very evening Minnie set about soaking them in the tin bath ready for washing the next morning.

'I might take Cathy on a little walk to the cottage an' make a start on cleanin' the windows in the mornin' when I've got this lot on the line,' she told Saffie. 'An' while we're there she can choose which bedroom she'd like to sleep in. I've no doubt she'll want the one that overlooks the canal so she can watch the boats go by.'

Saffie gave her an indulgent smile before retiring to bed. She still had one day of teaching ahead of her and she intended to enjoy every minute of it, because who knew what lay ahead for her? Once again, her future looked very uncertain.

Chapter Twenty-Six

By the following Monday morning the cottage was gleaming like a new pin and even Cathy seemed mildly excited at the prospect of moving there.

'I need to give this place a good clean now ready for the mistress comin' 'ome,' Minnie declared after breakfast as she rolled her sleeves up ready to start work.

Both she and Saffie had worked from early morning till late at night over at the cottage while Elsie had watched over Cathy. Elsie had surprised them when she had offered to stay on and care for her grandmother, for a while at least. She realised that once the baby began to show properly she would have to make alternate arrangements, but for now she seemed happy to take on the carer's role. And so now, between them, Saffie and Minnie scrubbed the house from top to bottom, and as they went through each room Minnie loaded a barrow with any last-minute things they wished to take with them.

Thankfully they needed very little apart from a few sheets and blankets, and odds and ends for the kitchen. Minnie had been to the market at the weekend and had stocked the pantry up for Clara and Elsie, as well as doing the same for the larder at the cottage. Davey had chopped enough logs to keep both places warm for weeks to come and by early afternoon there was little more to do. Minnie had a large pan of stew simmering on the stove to try and tempt Clara to eat, as Marcus had told them that she appeared to have lost a lot of weight, and all that remained was for Minnie to go upstairs and collect the few toys they had bought for Cathy and load them into the barrow.

'That's that then,' she said when the job was done. She glanced around the kitchen. It had been her home for so long that she knew every nook and cranny of it. She had expected to feel sad to be leaving, despite the fact that Clara had never been the kindest of mistresses, but to her surprise she didn't. All she felt was excitement at the thought of the new home she was going to where she would be her own boss. There would be no more of anyone telling her what to do and she could hardly wait. A new chapter of her life was opening up and she wanted to embrace it. Now she brushed Cathy's hair until it shone and tied a yellow ribbon in it before holding the little girl at arm's length and exclaiming, 'My, you're as pretty as a picture an' just look 'ow much yer 'air 'as grown, eh?'

Cathy stared solemnly back at her. She was still saying very little, apart from to Davey who was endlessly patient with her.

'Right, we'll go on ahead,' Minnie told Saffie as she took Cathy's small hand in her own red, calloused one. 'Yer can say yer goodbyes to yer sister in private then. An' don't fret about the barrer, Davey's comin' over at some stage this afternoon to drag it over to the cottage fer us.' As if speaking of him had conjured him up from thin air, Davey appeared at the door and dragged off his cap. Minnie smiled at him. 'Well, that were good timin'. We're all ready fer the off, ain't we, sweet'eart?' She squeezed Cathy's hand and after saying her goodbyes to Elsie, she and Davey set off with little Cathy and the barrow between them.

'Are you quite sure you're going to be all right?' Saffie asked her sister.

Elsie fiddled with the fringe on the green chenille table-cloth and nodded. 'I'll be fine. Although goodness knows what will happen when our grandmother discovers I'm going to have a baby.'

'We'll cross that bridge when we come to it,' Saffie answered. 'And don't forget what I said – you mustn't be insulted if Grandmother is rude to you. She never did take to me. Just remember I'm only half a mile or so away, so don't hesitate to come and get me if there's anything you're worried about.'

'I will,' Elsie promised with the hint of a tear in her eye and after kissing her cheek, Saffie set off to catch the others up.

It was a beautiful day with not a cloud in the sky, but despite that Saffie felt unsettled. Of course, she was more than grateful to Marcus, and Minnie for that matter, that she would have a roof over her head but she didn't want to be a burden to them and intended to look for work at the earliest opportunity.

She saw Minnie and Davey up ahead, pointing out the wildflowers and things of interest to Cathy, and it struck her again how right they looked together, almost like a little family.

By the time she had caught up with them the cottage was in sight and Minnie was beaming from ear to ear. The small leaded windows that she had so diligently scrubbed were glistening in the sunshine and, although there was still a lot to do outside, Davey, under Minnie's instruction, had made a good start on clearing the front garden, careful not to dig up any of the plants. Even so, Saffie felt no pleasure. Both Marcus and Minnie had such big hearts and she knew they would give her free lodgings for as long as she needed, but she was too proud to impose on them for longer than she had to.

The cottage was almost unrecognisable from when they had first seen it. The furniture had been polished to a mirror-like shine and the freshly washed curtains flapped gently in the soft breeze blowing in through the slightly ajar windows. Cathy gripped Minnie's hand as she looked around.

'We'll be 'appy 'ere, pet,' Minnie promised, squeezing Cathy's hand in return.

Cathy nodded solemnly. 'But just till Mama comes home, eh? And then she'll fetch me and we'll live together again, won't we?' she whispered hopefully.

Saffie could see that Minnie was struggling to keep her smile in place. 'Of course, sweet'eart,' she answered, but deep down she was selfishly hoping that day would be a long way away. She had come to look on Cathy as the little girl she had never had and she loved her as her own. 'But now how about we unpack that fruit cake we baked yesterday? An' I think we've got a jug o' lemonade somewhere too.'

They spent the rest of the day putting the things they unloaded from the cart away and by bedtime everything was just as Minnie wanted it. Cathy had gone to bed as meekly as a lamb in the little bedroom that overlooked the canal and now with the back door open to the balmy evening air and the oil lamp casting a pool of light across the scrubbed oak table, the cottage looked warm and cosy. Minnie was sitting sewing some new cushion covers to go on the stuffed horse-hair sofa and Saffie thought that she looked more content than she had ever seen her.

'Davey's comin' over in the mornin' to clear some more of the back garden,' she informed Saffie. 'An' when he's done, he's goin' to build me some coops so we can 'ave a few chickens of us own. Imagine that, eh? Our own eggs whenever we want 'em. We've got plenty o' time to get some vegetables planted an' all.'

Saffie smiled. It was nice to see Minnie so happy.

'I thought I might try to see Mathilda tomorrow,' she said as she sipped at the cocoa she had just made for them both. 'Marcus tells me she might be ready for visitors and I'm anxious to see how she is. That is, if you don't need me for anything?' she added.

'I think that's a grand idea,' Minnie agreed. 'Poor love, she's still grievin', I expect, but she'll 'ave to try an' get back to normal at some stage so a visit from you might just set her off in the right direction.'

They went to bed soon after and Saffie fell asleep almost as soon as her head hit the pillow.

The next morning, Saffie set off bright and early to visit Mathilda, collecting a bouquet of wildflowers on the way. Mathilda's maid let her into the house and left her standing in the hallway while she shot off to see if her mistress was accepting visitors. Saffie half expected to be turned away so she was relieved when the maid came back to tell her, 'The mistress is in the drawin' room, miss, an' she's says you're to go in.'

Saffie was shocked at her first sight of Mathilda. She was sitting in a chair by the open window overlooking the copse at the back of the enormous farmhouse, with a warm rug tucked around her legs, and she seemed to have shrunk to half her size. She had always been dainty but now she looked frighteningly thin and her clothes hung off her. Her eyes had sunk into her head and had deep dark circles beneath them and her beautiful hair looked limp and lacklustre.

Even so, she raised a weak smile when she saw Saffie and held her arms out to her. 'How lovely it is to see you, I've missed you,' she greeted her in her own sweet way as Saffie held the flowers out to her and gave her a gentle hug. She looked so fragile that Saffie was almost afraid of hurting her. 'And how did your first night in your new home go?'

'Well . . .' Saffie sat on a chair close to her. 'To be honest I don't really feel that I belong there. I only came here to look after Cathy and now Minnie has rather taken over that role, so I'm thinking that as soon as possible I shall find a new position and me and Elsie will probably move on.'

'Ah, Marcus told me about Elsie. She's your sister, isn't she? How lovely that she came to join you. I always wanted a brother or sister, but unfortunately I was the only child.'

Saffie felt a stab of guilt. It seemed so unfair and rather ironic that Mathilda who had longed for a child had just lost hers while Elsie was carrying one that was unplanned and unwanted. Not that Mathilda was aware of that, she hoped. It would seem just too cruel for her so perhaps that was another reason for leaving sooner rather than later. She would have hated to hurt this kind, gentle woman who she had grown so fond of.

'Marcus told me that Elsie will be caring for Clara now she's come home, is that right?'

Saffie sighed. 'It all depends, really, on whether or not my grandmother will allow her to,' she admitted. 'I would have willingly taken the job on but she made it clear from day one that she couldn't stand to have me close to her, although she never hated me as much as she does poor little Cathy! Let's just hope she feels differently about Elsie.'

'How sad!' Mathilda stared out of the window almost as if she had forgotten that Saffie was there for a moment, but then remembering her manners, she rang a small bell at the side of her and minutes later the maid appeared. 'Could we have a pot of tea, please, and perhaps some of Cook's excellent seed cake, if Marcus hasn't eaten it all?'

'Of course, ma'am.' The maid bobbed her knee and disappeared and an awkward silence settled between them for a time as Saffie tried to think of something to say. Mathilda had lost her sparkle and all Saffie could do was pray that it would return. She had been so vivacious and beautiful but now there was a haunted look in her eye.

Once the maid returned with the tea trolley, Saffie poured tea into two bone china cups with saucers and after adding two lumps of sugar, as she knew Mathilda liked it, she handed one to her.

'So, how is Minnie finding the cottage?' Mathilda asked.

Saffie smiled. 'Oh, she really loves it. I think she feels at home already. It's remarkably kind of Marcus to let her rent it.'

'Why not? It was only standing empty,' Mathilda pointed out. 'And Marcus is very kind.'

Saffie steered the conversation to happier things then as she told Mathilda about the short time she had spent teaching at the school. Eventually, though, Saffie could see that Mathilda was tiring so after thanking her for the tea and hospitality she took her leave, promising to call again soon.

She was halfway back to the cottage when she suddenly veered off in another direction. She was painfully aware that her grandmother probably wouldn't wish to see her but she desperately needed to know how Elsie's first night with her had gone, so she decided to risk her wrath.

Once at the house she skirted round it and went through the yard before peering through the kitchen window. She was shocked to see Bernie sitting at the kitchen table. Elsie was washing up at the sink and when Saffie quietly entered through the back door, she looked at her in surprise, while Bernie blushed as red as a beetroot.

'Hello, Bernie, I didn't expect to see you here. I thought you would be working,' Saffie said, and he blushed even redder if that were possible.

'I, er . . . had a few days leave owing to me so I thought I'd pop along and see how things were going,' he muttered with a quick glance at Elsie.

'Oh, I see.' Saffie turned her attention to her sister. 'And how is Grandmother?'

'It's hard to judge seeing as she hasn't uttered so much as a word since she got here.' Elsie dried her hands on her apron and for the first time Saffie noticed that she'd had to let her waistbands out. It wouldn't be long before everyone guessed that she was going to have a baby so perhaps it would be as well if they left sooner rather than later. At least if they moved to another area, Elsie could pretend that she was a young widow and no one need ever be any the wiser.

'And has she eaten?'

'A bit,' Elsie told her. 'She had a boiled egg this morning and a few nibbles of toast. But she's just sitting in the drawing room staring from the window. I don't think she has any idea who I am and I haven't enlightened her or she might object to me like she did you.'

'That's perhaps a good idea,' Saffie agreed, wondering why she suddenly felt as if she was interrupting something. 'Anyway, I'd better get back and see what Minnie wants me to do, but do shout if you need a hand with anything.'

'Oh, it's all right, I'll do anything she needs doing,' Bernie said quickly and then clamped his mouth shut and flushed again. It all felt very strange and Saffie was almost pleased to leave them to it.

'I was really surprised to see him there,' she told Minnie over a cup of tea when she got back to the cottage. 'I almost felt like a spare part.'

Minnie chuckled. 'I ain't a bit surprised,' she confessed. 'You've been so busy what wi' teachin' at the school an' movin' us in 'ere that you ain't noticed how much attention he's been payin' 'er. But I 'ave, an' atween you an' me I wouldn't be surprised if he didn't propose any time now. He's clearly smitten wi' the lass an' not worried about the fact that she's carryin' another chap's bairn. An' let's face it, she could do a lot worse. Bernie is a nice bloke; he's got a good job an' all an' I reckon he'd do right by 'er.'

Saffie was shocked. It didn't seem so long ago that Bernie had been sweet on her, but somewhere along the way he had obviously transferred his affections to her sister and she wasn't sure how she felt about it. 'Oh!' she said and Minnie giggled.

'Had yer nose put out o' joint, 'ave yer?' she teased. 'But then you've only yerself to blame. Yer did make it fairly obvious that yer weren't interested in the poor lad an' then along comes Elsie and, *wham*, he falls fer 'er 'ook, line an' sinker.'

'I suppose I wasn't very encouraging to him, was I?' Saffie admitted as she tried to take it in. But if Bernie was willing to marry Elsie as Minnie thought, would it really be such a bad thing? It would mean that she herself wouldn't have to worry about her anymore and she would be free to go on her way with only herself to worry about.

'Let's just wait and see what happens, eh?' she said and for then at least the subject was closed.

Chapter Twenty-Seven

Over the next few days Saffie spent her time in the garden. Minnie had everything running like clockwork in the cottage and she began to feel more and more unsettled. And then on Sunday morning Bernie unexpectedly turned up at the door bright and early and stood in the kitchen wringing his hat in his hands and looking thoroughly uncomfortable.

'I, er . . . was wondering if I might have a word?' he told Saffie.

'Why, of course you can, go ahead,' she answered.

He shook his head, glancing at Cathy and Minnie who were watching him avidly. 'Er, could we go somewhere a little more private?'

Saffie rose and ushered him into the tiny parlour. 'So what is it that you couldn't say to me in front of Minnie?' she asked, but she had a good idea what was coming.

'Well . . . I can't speak to your father at present,' he said, looking thoroughly awkward. 'So I thought it would be right to speak to you first. You see, I want to ask Elsie to marry me. Would you give us your blessing if I did?'

Saffie stared at him for a moment before asking, 'Have you quite thought this through, Bernie? It's a lot to take on someone else's child. And where would you live?'

'I've thought of nothing else since I met her,' he told her shyly. 'And I know I can love the child as if it was my own when it comes. As far as I'm concerned it *will* be my own. As for where we'd live, I've spoken to my sergeant back in Banbury and there's a police house coming vacant next month, which he has told me I can have if I wish. I'm sure Elsie would like it. It's in a very respectable neighbourhood.'

'I see.' Saffie tapped her lip. 'I must admit, it does sound as if you've thought this through,' she told him. 'But do you think Elsie will want to marry you? What I mean is, do you think she returns your feelings?'

He shrugged. 'I won't know until I ask her, will I? But I didn't want to do that until I'd spoken to you.'

'In that case go ahead.' She smiled at him, feeling quite emotional. It would be the best outcome she could have hoped for her sister and the unborn baby – if Elsie wanted to marry him, that was.

His face lit up like a ray of sunshine and again she thought what an attractive young man he was. And kind too. Yes, Elsie could certainly have done a lot worse for herself.

'Thank you,' he said sincerely. 'I'll go over to the house right now and pop the question. There's no time like the present, eh? And perhaps if I get the answer I'm hoping for, you could maybe help us arrange the wedding? I have no idea how to go about something like that.'

'Let's see what Elsie has to say first, shall we?' Saffie gave him a warm smile. 'Now go on, get off with you, I can see you're longing to.'

He rammed his hat on and was off like a whippet before the words had left her mouth and as she watched him striding away, she sighed. If Elsie accepted, they would have to find someone else to care for her grandmother but that would be a small price to pay for Elsie's happiness, so she crossed her fingers that her sister would accept his offer. It would certainly stop her worrying about what they would do when the baby came.

'What did I tell yer?' Minnie whooped when Saffie relayed what he had said to her. 'I could see he were keen as mustard!'

'Well, we shouldn't have to wait too long to find out what her answer is.' Saffie smiled. 'I'll go over there after lunch to find out what's going on.'

As it happened, she didn't have to wait to find out because Bernie called in again an hour later on his way to catch the coach back to Banbury. He was on duty later that afternoon and didn't want to upset his sergeant by being late.

His face told Minnie and Saffie all they needed to know the minute he set foot through the door and while Minnie congratulated him and gave him a hug, Saffie pecked him on the cheek and wished him and Elsie all the best. She just hoped that Elsie was marrying him for the right reasons and not for a way out of her predicament. She loved her sister dearly but was also fully aware that Elsie had a selfish streak.

'So when is the weddin' to be?' Minnie asked. She loved a good wedding, although she hadn't had the chance to go to many.

'I suppose as soon as we can arrange it.' Bernie couldn't stop smiling. 'There doesn't seem much point in delaying, although we will of course wait until you have time to find someone else to care for Mrs Bishop.'

'Don't you get worryin' about that,' Minnie told him. 'There's allus someone in the town who's glad of a job. Just go ahead an' see the vicar the next time yer over 'ere an' let

252

us worry about that side o' things. You do 'ave somewhere to live I take it?'

'Oh yes,' Bernie assured her. 'As I explained, I've been promised a house so there's no problem there.' He glanced at the clock and reluctantly moved towards the door. 'I'm really sorry but I have to go. I'll be back on Sunday and Elsie and I thought we might go and see the vicar then if one of you wouldn't mind keeping an eye on Mrs Bishop for a while?'

'I can do that,' Minnie assured him as she shooed him towards the door. 'But now go on an' be off wi' yer. We don't want yer to lose yer job just afore the weddin', do we?'

As Bernie set off with a spring in his step, Saffie sighed. She was delighted for Elsie, but now more than ever she felt that she had no purpose there and it was time to really think about her future.

Later that afternoon, when Saffie was sure that her grandmother would be having her nap, she went to see Elsie.

'I'm so pleased for you; Bernie is a lovely young man and I'm sure he'll be good to you and the baby,' she told her. 'Are you happy?'

Elsie gave a weak smile. 'Of course I am, although . . .' She shrugged. 'I'm very fond of Bernie. As you say he's so kind and lovely, but I don't feel for him what I felt for Silas, the baby's father.'

'I've no doubt the love will come in time,' Saffie assured her. 'But you mustn't feel that you *have* to marry him. If you really don't want to, we'll manage somehow.'

'I do want to marry him. Things are so different now. Most of the boat people didn't bother much about being properly married – our own parents included. But it's different here. I don't want my child to be known as a flyblow and I *am* fond of him so I'm sure I'll have a good life with him. We're even going to have our own house in Banbury so I'll be able to see more of the twins and Granny Doyle. But what will you do?'

'Oh, don't you get worrying about me,' Saffie said with a cheerfulness she was far from feeling. 'I'm realising for the first time what a sheltered life we've had in some ways. What I mean is, although life on the canal was hard, we always had Mam and Dad there to care for us and now suddenly . . . But never mind about that. We'd better start to think about your wedding dress. I'm not having my sister look anything less than beautiful on her wedding day. Would you like me to go into town and get the material for it? I have a little money saved and I'm sure you and I could make it between us, and Minnie will help too, no doubt. She's a dab hand with a needle and thread.'

'That would be nice.' Elsie smiled. 'I was thinking something lacy . . .'

'Then lacy it shall be,' Saffie assured her. 'Leave it with me.'

And so, the following morning bright and early, Saffie set off for the market and once in the haberdashery shop, she began to rifle through the bolts of material, sighing with dismay when she saw how expensive they were.

'Can I help you, m'dear?' the kindly owner asked as she approached her and saw the anxious look on her face.

'I, er . . . I'm looking for some material to make a wedding gown for my sister,' she said, flushing. 'But I, er . . . wasn't aware of how expensive it all is.' It was no wonder, she thought, seeing as she and her siblings had always had second-hand clothes when they lived on the canal. But that just made her all the more determined that Elsie should wear something brand new on her wedding day.

'I see . . .' Mrs Downes, a plump middle-aged lady, stroked her chin thoughtfully. She liked the look of this young lady. 'I might be able to help you. I have some end of roll satin and lace that could be just what you're looking for and seeing as it's the last of its kind I could let you have it cheap.' She pottered away to return with a length of pale pink satin and another of white lace. Saffie sighed with delight at the sight of it. 'I thought you could make the underskirt with the satin and do an overlay of lace,' Mrs Downes suggested. 'And there should be enough to do lace sleeves too if you don't do the skirt too full. What do you think?'

'I think it's beautiful and Elsie would love it,' Saffie admitted as she fingered the delicate material. 'But how much is it?'

When Mrs Downes named a very reasonable price, Saffie nodded immediately. At that price she might even be able to afford a bonnet for her sister.

Mrs Downes carefully wrapped it in brown paper and tied it with string, and after thanking her profusely, Saffie set off for the milliner's where she found a pretty bonnet that she could decorate with a pink ribbon to match the satin underskirt.

Excited to see what Elsie thought, Saffie made her way back to her grandmother's house.

Elsie was often exhausted after running around for Clara all day while pregnant. But luckily Clara's stay in Hatter's Hall did seem to have mellowed her slightly. More often than not she would sit quietly by the window for most of the day and Saffie realised that there definitely wasn't the shouting and carrying on that she had had to put up with when she had been staying there.

Elsie was thrilled when Saffie showed her her purchases, and after deciding on the pattern they set to on making the dress immediately, working on it each evening when their grandmother was in bed. Minnie helped too, which was just as well as Bernie turned up the following Sunday to tell them that he had been to see the vicar of Coton Parish Church who had agreed to marry them in three weeks' time, as soon as the banns had been read.

'We'll 'ave a little do for 'em afterwards back at the cottage,' Minnie told them. 'An' I'll see to that as my weddin' gift to 'em.'

Elsie was touched that they were going to so much trouble for her but was beginning to worry about what would happen if they couldn't find someone to care for her grandmother in time. There was no way Clara would allow Saffie to again and Minnie wouldn't even consider Cathy being in the same house, but thankfully they discovered that Marcus had it all in hand.

'Don't worry, I already have someone in mind,' he promised them. 'Our housekeeper, Mrs Jenkins, is finding it all a bit too much running the house now and she's been considering retiring. But she gets on fairly well with your grandmother, and I think they'd rub along rather well together if she decides to take the post.'

For a few days after this, Mrs Jenkins came regularly to Clara's house to see how they might get along and finally, much to everyone's relief, she agreed to take on the post of Clara's carer for as long as she was needed.

It seemed no time at all before the day of the wedding dawned and there was furious activity in the cottage. Elsie had stayed at the cottage the night before, and Minnie woke her with a tray of tea and breakfast in bed. The wedding was set for twelve o'clock that day. It was going to be a very simple service with few attending, although Bernie's parents were coming from Banbury. Granny Doyle had been invited too but had decided the journey would be too much for her. Seeing as she rarely ventured far from the cottage, Elsie didn't mind that, although Ginny and Lucy were heartbroken to not be able to be bridesmaids.

Directly after the small reception at the cottage, Elsie and Bernie were to take the coach to Banbury to take up residence in their new home. The Sunday before the wedding, Bernie had taken her to see it and she was looking forward to making it her own.

'So let's be havin' you then, miss,' Minnie said cheerfully after she had drawn the curtains and placed the tray across Elsie's lap. 'We want you lookin' yer best today.'

In actual fact Elsie looked unnaturally pale and Minnie correctly guessed that she was having a severe attack of pre-wedding nerves.

'What if Bernie doesn't turn up?' Elsie fretted, rubbing her eyes. 'After all, he might have second thoughts and decide that I'm not good enough for him. I mean . . . he's a policeman, isn't he? With a good career ahead of him. I've no doubt he could have had any girl he wanted

257

let alone a boat girl who's already carrying someone else's child!'

'Now that's quite enough o' that sort o' silly talk,' Minnie scolded, wagging her finger at her. 'Have yer looked in the mirror lately? Why, yer beautiful an' I'm sure he thinks he's lucky to 'ave yer so get that breakfast down yer an' then we'll start to get yer ready.' And with that she sailed from the room to put the finishing touches to the wedding feast.

Both Saffie and Minnie were thrilled when they helped Elsie into her wedding dress sometime later. They had chosen a simple style with a rounded neck and long sleeves. It fitted tightly into the waist and then flared into a hooped skirt. Saffie had piled Elsie's beautiful hair into curls high on her head and teased out some ringlets, and with her new bonnet sat atop them, which had been lavishly trimmed with white satin roses and pink lace made from oddments of material, she looked radiant.

Minnie, who was looking rather grand herself in her best two-piece blue costume, swiped a tear from her cheek as she stood back to survey her as Saffie handed her a small posy of sweet-smelling freesias and white rosebuds. 'Eeh, luvvie, I don't reckon I've ever seen a lovelier bride,' she said, her voice full of emotion, and Saffie could only agree.

She'd been pleased to see a gradual change in Elsie since she had come to her grandmother's house and it was a change for the better. She seemed to have grown up and wasn't nearly so self-centred anymore, and she prayed she would have a happy life. But it would also be a sad day for Saffie, for after the wedding she was painfully aware that she would be truly alone. Her other siblings were all being taken care of and now it was up to her to pave her own way in life.

258

She pushed that thought away for now. This was Elsie's day and nothing must be allowed to spoil it.

Marcus had called in his own splendid carriage to take them all to the church, although Mathilda had stayed at home, as she still didn't feel well enough to leave the house. Once they arrived Marcus, Minnie and Cathy scuttled inside to take their seats, leaving Saffie and Elsie to have a few moments on their own.

'Now, are you quite sure you want to do this?' Saffie asked as she arranged the small train on her sister's wedding dress. She truly did look beautiful. 'It isn't too late to change your mind, you know?'

'I'm sure.' Elsie squeezed her hand as they went through the lychgate and up the path. 'And thank you, Saffie . . . for everything. A lot of sisters would have turned their back on me when I showed up out of the blue in the pickle I was in.'

'Don't be silly.' There was a catch in Saffie's voice. 'Now come on, let's do this.' And they walked on beneath a cloudless blue sky with nothing but the sounds of the birds and the church organ to be heard.

At the sight of his bride walking down the aisle on Saffie's arm, Bernie's face lit up like a ray of sunshine and in that moment, Saffie knew that he would always be good to her sister and she felt happy.

When the short service was over, the happy couple left the church in a hail of rice and rose petals. And then it was time for Elsie to throw her bouquet and turning she tossed it across her shoulder and it landed squarely in Minnie's arms. The poor woman blushed until her face was the colour of a beetroot.

Back at the cottage, the wine flowed like water and the food Minnie had prepared went down a treat. Even Cathy came out of her shell a little and seemed to be enjoying herself. Bernie's parents were lovely warm people too, but Saffie couldn't help but think of those who were not present. It should have been her father who gave Elsie away, not her, and how her mother would have loved to see her in her wedding dress. But she pushed the sad thoughts aside and all too soon it was time for Elsie and Bernie to leave. Bernie had taken what few possessions and clothes Elsie had to their new home the day before and now all that was left to do was for them to say goodbye.

'Thank you, Marcus, for everything,' Elsie told him as he slipped her an envelope containing money as his wedding present to them. 'And thank you too, Minnie, for working so hard on my dress and the wedding feast, it's all been perfect.'

'Oh, get off wi' yer, it were nothin'.' Minnie sniffed as she gave her a sloppy kiss on the cheek before ushering Davey, who was looking very uncomfortable in his best and only suit, into the kitchen ahead of Cathy. And then there was only Saffie and Elsie to say goodbye and Bernie tactfully walked a little way away to give them a little privacy.

'Be sure to write to us and let us know how you're getting on,' Saffie urged as she gave her sister a hug.

Elsie giggled. 'You talk as if we're never going to see one another again. I'm only going to Banbury. I shall expect you to visit.'

'Of course,' she answered, but seeing Bernie glance at his pocket watch she ushered her towards Marcus's carriage, which was going to take them into town to catch the coach. 'Now be off with you, Mrs Denning, you mustn't keep your husband waiting.'

Elsie chuckled and minutes later she hung out of the carriage window and waved until it turned a bend in the road and was lost to sight.

A wave of loneliness engulfed Saffie as she stood there, until suddenly she became aware of someone standing at the side of her and turning she saw Marcus.

'It's been a good day,' he said quietly and, blinking back the tears that were threatening, she nodded. 'And hopefully it's about to get better.'

She frowned at him in confusion.

'The thing is, Minnie told me that you've been feeling a little like a spare part.' He smiled. 'So I've been making a few enquiries and I think I might just have found the ideal position for you if you're interested. Let's go inside and I'll tell you all about it.'

Chapter Twenty-Eight

'So,' Marcus said when they had taken a seat in the kitchen while Minnie and Davey were busy washing up a pile of dirty pots. 'I visited the Spencer-Hugheses the other day and during the course of a conversation with Eugenie she happened to mention that her lady's maid would be leaving shortly to have a baby. I instantly thought of you and if you're interested, she's happy for you to go along for an interview to see if she thinks you would be suitable.'

'*Me* a lady's maid!' Saffie was shocked. 'B-but I wouldn't know what to do!'

Marcus chuckled. 'If you can control a class of cheeky urchins, I'm sure you could pander to one middle-aged lady. You're very presentable and very bright, I think you'd be perfect for the job. And of course, with you working at Lakeside House we might just get a little closer to finding out where Cathy's mother is, if indeed it is Margaret. What do you think?'

'Well . . . I-I suppose I could go along and see if she thinks I'd be suitable,' Saffie answered uncertainly.

'Too bloody right yer will,' Minnie announced – her ears had been flapping. 'She'd make a lovely lady's maid, wouldn't she, Davey?'

'Aye, I reckon she would,' Davey said quietly as he finished drying a plate.

'In that case I'll get in touch tomorrow and arrange for you to go, but now I really must be off. I need to see how Mathilda is.'

'Hm, that were a turn up fer the books,' Minnie said when he'd gone. 'Though I'll miss yer if yer do decide to go. It'll be lonely 'ere of a night once young Cathy's tucked up in bed, but I know yer've been growin' restless since we moved 'ere.'

Saffie smiled but said nothing until much later that evening when Cathy was in bed and Davey had retired to his rooms above the stables at Marcus's house.

'What you were saying earlier about being lonely if I should get the job at the Spencer-Hugheses' house . . .' she began cautiously.

Minnie looked up from the cardigan she was knitting for Cathy and raised her eyebrow. 'Aye, what about it?'

Saffie glanced towards the bouquet that Elsie had thrown, which was now sitting in a glass vase in the centre of the table. 'Well, I don't think you need be lonely,' she went on. 'Not if the way Davey looks at you is anything to go by. He's practically lived here since we moved in, and it's obvious he still worships the ground you walk on.'

'Oh, don't start *that* again,' Minnie snapped irritably, colour flooding into her plump cheeks. 'If I wait for 'im to make a move hell'll freeze over, the big oaf!'

'So why don't *you* make the move then?'

Minnie's mouth fell open. '*Me?* Propose to 'im! B-but it's 'ardly the done thing, is it? Fer the woman to ask the bloke, I mean?'

'And why not?' Saffie laughed. 'You clearly still have feelings for him if you didn't reject the idea out of hand.'

263

'Er . . . I-I . . .' For once Minnie was at a loss for words, a rare occasion indeed.

'Anyway, just think on it.' Saffie yawned as she rose from her seat. 'I'm going to bed now. It's been a long day, hasn't it? And I have a funny feeling that if you did give Davey the nod, we could have another wedding sometime very soon. But don't leave it too late, life is short. Goodnight.'

Minnie watched Saffie leave the room, then her eyes strayed to the bouquet and she chewed on her lip thoughtfully. She had a lot to think about.

The following afternoon Marcus arrived at the cottage looking worried.

'An' what's wrong wi' your face, then?' Minnie asked in her own inimitable way. She was never one for beating about the bush.

'It's Sylvie Preston, a little girl that attends my school.'

Saffie's head snapped up from the book she was reading. 'Sylvie? Why, what's wrong with her?'

'It's not her exactly,' he said, shaking his head sadly. 'It's her mother. She sent Sylvie off out of the way as usual so she could entertain one of her gentlemen friends in their room and when the child got home she found her mother with a knife sticking out of her ribs.'

'Oh no!' Both Saffie and Minnie exclaimed in unison.

He nodded. 'It looks like the poor child will end up in the workhouse unless one of the neighbours takes pity on her and takes her in, but I doubt that will happen. Everyone around there is as poor as a church mouse. They can barely afford to feed themselves let alone another mouth. I was tempted to bring her home with me but with Mathilda as she is . . .' His voice trailed away and Saffie stared at him in horror.

'But who would do that to her mother?'

Minnie snorted. 'Huh! It could 'ave been any Tom, Dick or Harry. It were a well-known fact that Lil Preston earned 'er money lyin' flat on 'er back fer anyone who'd pay 'er. But that poor little mite.'

She chewed on her fingernail before suddenly suggesting, 'She could come 'ere to stay wi' us? That's if you wouldn't mind? I reckon 'aving another little 'un about would be good fer Cathy.'

Marcus stared at her in surprise. 'What, you mean you would be willing to care for her? I have to warn you before you decide that she's rather, er . . . shall we say "a rough diamond", and her language when anyone upsets her could turn the air blue.'

Minnie chuckled. 'I can cuss meself when anyone upsets me so that wouldn't be a problem. Where is she now?'

'From what I could gather from the other children she's still in the room in a shared house where she lived with her mother for now. The undertaker has taken her mother's body away but if I know their landlady, she'll be turning Sylvie out in no time and have another family in there.'

'Then we'd best go an' find 'er, 'adn't we?' Minnie removed her apron and reached for her shawl. 'Come on, there's not a minute to spare if what yer say is true. Let's go an' look fer 'er. You'll watch Cathy fer me, won't yer, Saffie?'

'Of course.' As Saffie watched them go, she offered up a little prayer that they would find the child. Goodness only knew what would happen to her if they didn't. She checked on Cathy, who was happily playing in the garden, before setting about preparing the vegetables they would have with the steak and kidney pie Minnie had cooked that afternoon.

Davey arrived just after six o'clock after he had finished his chores on the farm and when Saffie told him what had happened, he sucked on his teeth and shook his head.

'Crikey, Minnie'll 'ave her 'ands full wi' two little 'un's to look after, won't she?' he commented. 'But then, it don't surprise me. Heart as big as a bucket that lass 'as got.'

'She'll cope,' Saffie agreed and they settled down to wait for Minnie's return.

It was gone seven o'clock before they spotted her coming along the lane with Sylvie's hand in hers, and Saffie breathed a sigh of relief. Minnie and Marcus had found the child cowering in a corner of the filthy room she had lived in with her mother and she had been appalled at the state of it. A filthy mattress, which was now spattered with blood, was thrown on the floor in one corner of the room and the smell of stale urine had been so overpowering that Minnie had retched.

Now, Minnie gently ushered the child ahead of her into the kitchen and Cathy stared at her curiously. The poor child's face was as pale as putty, although her eyes were puffy and red from crying, but after the shock she must have had after finding her mother murdered, Saffie wasn't surprised.

'This lady's brought me to stay wi' yer, Miss Doyle,' Sylvie informed Saffie sadly. 'Cos somebody's killed me mam, see? Stuck a knife right bloody through 'er they did!' She blinked rapidly to stop the tears that were shimmering on her lashes, and Saffie hurried over to her and put her arms about her.

'I know, Sylvie,' she said gently. 'And I'm so sorry.' The child's stick-thin arms were covered in bruises again, Saffie

266

noted, and she had a black eye, but it was no surprise: Saffie had never seen her without injuries of some sort or another.

'Come on, sit down at the table and I'll get you a meal. Oh, and this is Cathy, by the way.'

Sylvie glanced towards Cathy and the two girls nodded solemnly at each other as Sylvie took a seat at the table. Then she stared around at her surroundings in amazement. Everything in the little cottage gleamed and she felt as if she had died and gone to heaven.

'It's posh 'ere, ain't it?' she muttered and Minnie preened.

'I do me best, pet. But now let's get some food inside yer. I bet yer 'aven't eaten yet today, 'ave yer?'

Sylvie swiped her bare arm beneath her runny nose, leaving a trail of snot. 'I ain't got no money to pay for it,' she answered suspiciously and Minnie chuckled.

'Bless yer, child. I don't want payin'.' She went to the stove and ladled a generous portion of thick chicken soup into a bowl and as Sylvie watched her, she almost drooled.

When Minnie placed the bowl and a plateful of freshly baked bread in front of her, she hesitated for a moment but then her belly growled ominously and she snatched up the spoon and began to ram the food into her mouth, swallowing it so quickly that she retched now and again.

'Slow down, lass, there's plenty more where that came from. Yer can ave some steak an' kidney pie an' all when it's cooked, if you've still got room,' Minnie assured her. The poor little mite was clearly starving, but Sylvie paid her no heed and just continued to gobble the food until every drop of soup and every crumb of bread was gone.

'There now,' Saffie said gently. 'That must feel better. And as Minnie said, you can have some more to eat when the main meal is ready and after that we'll get you bathed. I'm sure Cathy won't mind lending you one of her nightdresses.'

'*Bathed!*' Sylvie looked horrified. 'I don't do baths; I 'as a wash at the pump sometimes.'

'Well, if you're going to live here for the time being I'm afraid you'll have to have one,' Saffie told her firmly. 'And we'll wash your hair too. Think how much better you'll feel.'

Sylvie crossed her arms about her skinny chest and glared at Saffie mutinously.

'Let's see about that later on, eh?' Minnie suggested quickly, sensing that a row was brewing. 'Cathy, why don't you take Sylvie out to look at the chickens? You can check if they've laid any eggs while you're out there.'

Somewhat reluctantly Cathy crossed to the door and after a final glare at Saffie, Sylvie followed her.

'Phew, I thought she was going to make a run for it for a moment there.' Saffie went to the window and watched the two girls cross the yard. They looked as if they were from two different worlds, but she supposed they were. Cathy looked angelic in the pretty dress Minnie had made for her, and her shiny hair was tied up with a blue ribbon that matched the dress, whereas poor Sylvie's clothes were little more than rags. Even the colour of her dress was indistinguishable and it hung off her thin frame. 'I think we're going to have trouble trying to get her clean,' Saffie remarked.

Minnie nodded in agreement as she headed outside to fetch the tin bath that hung on a nail on the wall. 'Happen she'll feel a bit more obligin' later on when she's filled 'er belly again, but one thing's fer sure – I ain't keen on 'er sleepin' in one o' my clean beds in the state she's in. Did yer see the nitties runnin' amok in 'er hair? She must 'ave 'ad 'em that long the poor little mite don't even scratch, an' I don't want Cathy catchin' 'em, so one way or another she's goin' in the tub tonight whether she likes it or lumps it!'

Saffie stifled a smile. Minnie was strong-minded but she had an awful feeling she might have met her match in Sylvie. Time would tell.

Later on, they had their evening meal and once again Sylvie attacked it as if she was afraid someone was going to snatch it from under her nose.

'Her table manners leave a lot to be desired, don't they?' Minnie hissed as she and Saffie stood at the sink washing the pots up.

Saffie nodded. 'I know, but in fairness it isn't Sylvie's fault. From what I could make of it while I was teaching at the school, her mother kicked her out on the streets in all weathers to fend for herself most of the time while she entertained her men friends. She hasn't really had anyone to teach her manners.'

At that moment, Davey appeared with a jug of fresh milk and, drawing him aside, Minnie quickly told him, 'I'm goin' to try an' get 'er in the bath now. Will yer stay in case she tries to do a runner?'

Davey nodded obligingly as Minnie began to fill the bath with buckets of hot water from the copper in the corner and Sylvie watched her suspiciously. She looked like a little bird ready to take flight at any moment so Davey stood quietly by the door smoking his pipe to discourage her from trying to escape.

At last the bath was ready and Minnie fetched some big fluffy towels and a bar of carbolic soap as well as one of Cathy's clean nightdresses and laid them ready to warm in

269

front of the fire, before telling Sylvie brightly, 'There we are, pet. Do yer want to come an' pop in? I've tested the water wi' me elbow an' it's just right, not too 'ot an' not too cold so yer should enjoy it. Then when yer clean you'll feel brand new. Davey 'ere will turn 'is back, won't yer, Davey?'

Sylvie's face darkened as she glared round at them and Davey hastily turned to face the door to save her modesty.

'If you think I'm gerrin' in there, missus, yer've gor another bleedin' think comin',' she ground out through clenched teeth.

As Minnie advanced on her, rolling up her sleeves with a determined look on her face, Sylvie growled deep in her throat like a little animal. Saffie gasped with dismay as Cathy looked on in amazement.

'I've told yer – I *ain't* goin' in there so *piss off* afore I kick yer,' Sylvie shouted threateningly.

At this point Davey turned to intervene. 'Look, why don't you all go and sit in the parlour fer a bit?' he suggested. 'So me an' Sylvie 'ere can 'ave a little chat, eh?'

Minnie stared at him as if he had lost his mind. 'An' what good do yer think that will do?'

He winked at her. 'Go on now, there's a good lass. Just five minutes is all I'm askin', an' then I'll fetch yer, all right?'

Minnie stared at him dubiously before turning and ushering Saffie and Cathy ahead of her towards the parlour.

'Five minutes,' she warned.

Once they were gone, Davey calmly crossed to the table and patted the seat of the chair at the side of him. 'Why don't yer come an' join me, pet?'

Sylvie hovered uncertainly for a moment as she gauged the distance between him and the back door but then with a sigh she approached and perched on the very edge of the chair.

'Now, what I was thinkin' were this . . .' he began.

Five minutes later he summoned Saffie and Minnie back into the kitchen and told them, 'I'm goin' outside to smoke me pipe fer a while so's you can get Sylvie bathed.'

'*What?*' Minnie's mouth dropped open. 'Yer mean she's agreein' to it?'

'O' course she is, an' when yer done yer goin' to make 'er a nice cup o' cocoa an' she's goin' to 'ave it wi' some biscuits while I read 'er an' Cathy a bedtime story. Ain't that right, Sylvie?'

Somewhat reluctantly Sylvie nodded as she eyed the water. Despite this, though, the second Davey had left the room, she stripped off her clothes and cautiously stepped into the bath.

Minnie immediately began to rub the soap into her hair and to wash every inch of her, and although Sylvie clearly wasn't enjoying it, she sat as still as a stone and allowed it.

Once she was clean, Minnie produced a nit comb and painstakingly went through Sylvie's tangled hair, which was no mean feat and she was red in the face with exertion by the time she eventually sat back on her heels and told the child, 'There, I reckon that'll do fer tonight.'

As the little girl stepped out of the bath, Saffie wrapped her in a towel and dried her thoroughly before slipping one of Cathy's pretty little broderie-anglaise-trimmed nightshirts over her head. With her face glowing and her hair hanging in damp ringlets about her face, the child was almost unrecognisable to the little waif who had arrived merely hours before.

'You'll do,' Davey said approvingly when Minnie summoned him back in. 'Now why don't I empty that bath fer you while you an' Saffie make the cocoa an' then we'll 'ave that story I promised yer wi' Cathy, eh?'

Sylvie nodded and smiled for the first time, transforming her little face, and Saffie and Minnie gawped at each other, scarcely able to believe their eyes. Davey really did have a knack with children there was no denying it, and Saffie couldn't help but think what a wonderful father he would make.

Chapter Twenty-Nine

'All right then, tell me 'ow yer did it?' Minnie questioned later that evening when the children and Saffie had retired to bed. 'Got 'er into the bath, I mean.'

Davey chuckled. 'Just common sense, really,' he said as they sat looking out over the garden. It was a lovely evening with stars twinkling above them in a velvet black sky. 'A bit o' bribery goes a long way wi' young 'uns. Remember that, cos I reckon that poor kid would do just about anythin' fer food. I thought Cathy were in a bad enough state when she first got 'ere but that little scrap is even worse. She obviously never knew where 'er next meal were comin' from, which is why she crams every morsel she can get into 'er mouth as fast as she can.'

As Minnie stared at him the strangest feeling came over her. He was a good man was Davey and she was *very* fond of him. And, unbidden, she suddenly thought of what Saffie had said to her, *So why don't you make the move then?*

She gulped as she summoned every ounce of courage she had, knowing that what she was about to say might well change the course of her life forever. And then she blurted out, 'Me an' you were good together, weren't we, Davey?'

He looked momentarily surprised before blushing and nodding, 'Aye . . . we were, lass.'

'So why did yer never ask me to marry yer? Yer must 'ave known I'd 'ave said yes.'

'I, er . . . allus meant to,' he said in a thick voice. 'But I never seemed able to find the right words or the right time some'ow! But it weren't cos I didn't want to. I suppose I were a bit scared yer'd turn me down.'

'I see.' Minnie looked up at the moon. 'Then why don't I do it? What I mean is, why don't I ask you? Davey Webb, will you make an honest woman o' me an' marry me? I know I ain't no spring chicken anymore an' I'll never win no beauty competition but I would be loyal an' good to yer, if that'd do.'

Davey almost choked as he swivelled in his chair to look at her. And then his face broke into a smile and he nodded. 'That'd do me just fine. You're beautiful in my eyes an' I'd be delighted to, lass. You just name the day.'

And it was done as simply as that.

'Why, that's absolutely *wonderful*,' Saffie whooped the next morning when Minnie told her the news. 'I can't believe we have another wedding to plan so soon after Elsie and Bernie's.'

'Now slow down,' Minnie warned. 'We ain't no kids an' we just want a very simple do. We talked about it last night. We'll just slip off an' do it quietly wi' just a couple o' witnesses present.'

'You most certainly *will not*!' Saffie said indignantly. 'A wedding is a wedding, no matter what age you are. We'll have to organise a new gown for you, and Davey will have to have a new suit. I dare say Marcus will help him with getting that.

Then we could have a little wedding breakfast back here for you.'

At that moment Marcus appeared and when Saffie told him the news, he beamed. 'And about time too! You two should have been wed years ago. Congratulations. But now, how did the first night with young Sylvie go?'

'In actual fact, thanks to Davey, it went very well,' Saffie told him. 'She's outside with Cathy collecting the eggs.'

'Aye, an' she loved the little shaky down bed I made up fer 'er,' Minnie went on. 'I reckon she's allus slept on the floor before.'

'Excellent.' Marcus looked towards Saffie. 'And I have some rather good news for you. At least I hope it is. Mrs Spencer-Hughes is prepared to give you an interview tomorrow afternoon for the post as her lady's maid.'

'As soon as that?' Minnie looked slightly dismayed. 'But that means you could be gone in no time if she takes yer on.'

'And quite right too.' Saffie smiled. 'I don't want to be here playing gooseberry to two newly-weds, it'll be bad enough you having two young children under your feet.'

The rest of the day was spent helping Sylvie to come to terms with her mother's death and settling her in, and they were heartened to see that by bedtime Cathy seemed to be coming out of her shell a little, and was even speaking to Sylvie, albeit briefly.

Davey called in as soon as his jobs at the farm were done and he was in high spirits. 'The gaffer said you told him we was gettin' wed an' he were tickled pink. An' guess what?' He could hardly contain his excitement as he beamed at his bride-to-be. 'He's giftin' this cottage to us as his wedding gift. Do you realise what that means, lass? We'll be settin' out in our very own little 'ome. What do yer think o' that, eh?'

Minnie's mouth opened and shut like a goldfish as she tried to take the wonderful news in.

'B-but why would 'e do that?'

'He says it's cos I've worked fer the family since I was knee 'igh to a grass'opper an' 'e feels I deserve it. You an' all, if it comes to that. An' that ain't all, pet. I've been to see the vicar an' we can get wed in three weeks' time just as soon as he's read out the banns in church.'

'As soon as that?' Minnie gasped. There was so much going on her head was in a whirl.

Saffie discreetly made her way upstairs, leaving the two lovebirds to discuss their bright future and she was pleased as she passed the girls' bedroom door to hear them chatting to each other. It seemed that Minnie had been right when she said that Sylvie might bring Cathy out of her shell.

Once in the privacy of her own room, though, the doubts crept in. Everything was working out for all those she cared about and she couldn't have been happier for them, but what was to become of her? Especially if she didn't get the role of lady's maid to Mrs Spencer-Hughes. She would have nowhere to go and it was a daunting thought.

Pushing the thoughts aside, she laid her Sunday best blouse and skirt over the chair in readiness for her interview the next day. Marcus had agreed to take her in his carriage and she was grateful for that as she wasn't quite sure where it was.

Eventually she undressed and got into bed, listening to the old owl hooting in the tree outside. What would tomorrow bring? she wondered, before finally she slept.

The next morning Saffie helped Minnie get the girls dressed, and as they trotted off outside, she marvelled at the change in Sylvie already. Once her hair had been washed, they had discovered it had a tendency to be curly, and it shone in the late June sunshine. For now, she was wearing some of Cathy's clothes until Minnie could stitch her some of her own. Thankfully they were of a similar height, although Cathy was now more sturdily built than Sylvie so they were slightly big on her, but she looked a treat.

'I thought she were a plain little thing when she arrived, but now she's clean an' dressed nice she's quite pretty, ain't she?' Minnie said as she watched them with satisfaction. 'Oh, an' I thought on yer way back from yer interview yer could per'aps drop into town an' pick me up some material to make her a little gown of 'er own, if yer don't mind. I've got some money to pay fer it.'

'I'd be happy to,' Saffie told her. 'And while I'm there I'm going to get you some material for a gown for your wedding dress too. It'll be my wedding present to you. But we'll have to get cracking on it straightaway. We haven't got long to the wedding.'

Minnie flushed. 'There's no need to do that,' she objected. 'I can wear the outfit I wore to your Elsie's weddin'. I've only worn it the once an' there's no way we'll 'ave time to make another one.'

Saffie was disappointed but she supposed Minnie was right. It would be pushing it to try and get another gown done in time but that wouldn't stop her buying her friend a new bonnet at least.

By the time Marcus arrived to pick her up, her nerves were frayed and Minnie chuckled as she walked out to the carriage with her.

'Stop worryin' an' just be yerself,' she advised her and she waved as the carriage rattled away over the grass.

'Feeling all right?' Marcus asked.

Saffie nodded. 'I think so. Just nervous, I suppose.'

'Please don't be. I'm sure Mrs Spencer-Hughes will love you. You're a very presentable, polite and intelligent young woman, so just do as Minnie said and be yourself.'

When the carriage finally turned into the long drive of the Spencer-Hugheses' home and Lakeside House came into view, Saffie's eyes almost popped out of her head. She had thought that Marcus's farmhouse was big but this was positively huge.

'I-I didn't expect it to be quite so grand,' she said in a strangled voice and Marcus chuckled.

'Victor Spencer-Hughes is one of the richest men in the town,' he informed her. 'He owns the mill in Attleborough as well as a number of other businesses and houses.'

'Oh!' Saffie watched two gardeners scything the lawns as they rattled past and soon after the carriage drew to halt in front of three curved marble steps, polished to a mirror-like shine, that led up to two enormous oak doors.

'Just remember, be yourself,' Marcus told her as he helped her down from the carriage, but Saffie already felt at a disadvantage. She had no doubt that the clothes she was wearing wouldn't even be as grand as the ones the servants wore in this place and it knocked her confidence even more.

The door was opened by a maid in a broderic anglaise mobcap and a starched white pinafore and Marcus led her into a hallway that to Saffie's mind was bigger than the entire cottage put together.

'It's very big, isn't it?' she whispered to Marcus as the maid took his hat, and he patted her arm encouragingly.

'Miss Doyle is here to see your mistress and is expected,' he informed the maid. 'And I shall see Mr Spencer-Hughes. Is he in his study?' Marcus had clearly been there many times before and Saffie suddenly wished that he could have stayed with her.

'I'll tell them both you're here if you'd care to take a seat, sir,' the maid said and bobbing her knee she disappeared as Saffie and Marcus sat down on a gilt-legged chaise longue.

'The mistress will see you now, miss.' The maid was back in no time and as she led Saffie away, Marcus gave her a gentle pat on the back and went off in search of Mr Spencer-Hughes.

When they finally stopped at one of the many doors that led off the hallway, the maid tapped on it and entered. After announcing Saffie, she discreetly left, leaving Saffie in the most enormous drawing room she had ever seen. Two huge windows draped in thick green velvet curtains overlooked the sweeping lawn and a rose garden to one side of the house, and the rest of the room was lavishly decorated in lighter shades of green, giving it an airy feel.

She was so intent on looking around that she wasn't at first aware of a small lady sitting to one side of the fireplace regarding her solemnly from a velvet chaise longue, wringing a lace handkerchief between her fingers.

'Good morning.' The woman's voice made Saffie start and she looked towards her, colour burning into her cheeks. 'You must be Miss Doyle. Do come and take a seat.'

Saffie hesitantly did as she was asked. The woman had a gentle voice and when she smiled at her, Saffie relaxed a little. She certainly seemed nice enough.

'I believe you have come to apply for the position of my maid. And I must say you have come very highly recommended by Marc— Mr Berrington.'

'Yes, ma'am.' Saffie's voice came out as a squeak.

'And have you ever held a position like this before?'

Saffie shook her head. 'No, ma'am . . . but I'm a very fast learner.'

The woman was so tiny and delicate that she might have been taken for a child from a distance. And despite her kindly voice, she appeared to be almost as nervous as Saffie. Her fair hair, which had streaks of grey running through it, was piled onto the top of her head and fell in soft ringlets about her face, which was showing signs of age, but Saffie guessed that she must have been very beautiful in her younger days. She was still a very attractive woman and the heavy satin gown she was wearing and the beautifully matched pearls that hung about her neck and dropped from her ears looked as if they had cost more money than Saffie had ever known in her life before.

'Then I suppose I should tell you what the job entails and what would be expected of you,' Mrs Spencer-Hughes went on and Saffie listened avidly. 'You would live in but have every Sunday afternoon off,' she finished after she had explained what would be expected of her and told her the wage. It was far more than Saffie had expected and the job didn't sound that hard. After all, she reasoned, it couldn't be too different from pandering to her siblings and her mother when she was ill.

'I'm sure I could do that,' Saffie told her, feeling more confident. 'If you think I might be suitable that is?'

Mrs Spencer-Hughes surveyed her thoughtfully for a moment. Marcus had been truthful and had told her that Saffie had been raised on the canal, which had given her a few misgivings, but after meeting the girl she was pleasantly surprised. Her clothes were poor but spotlessly clean and she was nicely spoken. She seemed intelligent too, and honest, so after a moment she nodded. 'Why don't we give it a month's trial to see if we are right for one another?'

Saffie felt a little flutter of excitement in her stomach as she nodded enthusiastically. 'I'd like that very much, Mrs Spencer-Hughes.'

'Very well, I would like you to report here at seven o'clock sharp three weeks on Monday morning and then the housekeeper, Mrs Beasley, will show you where you are to sleep and issue you with a uniform. Your room will adjoin mine in case I should need you during the night.'

Saffie nodded again as she rose and started to back towards the door where she bobbed her knee. It seemed that the interview was over and now she could hardly wait to tell Marcus and Minnie the good news. 'Thank you very much, Mrs Spencer-Hughes.' She quietly slipped out of the door closing it behind her and was relieved to see Marcus further down the hallway with a stern-faced gentleman. The man said something to Marcus after giving her a cursory glance and then Marcus came towards her.

'Well, how did it go?'

Her face lit up as she told him breathlessly, 'I'm to have a month's trial starting three weeks on Monday. I can't thank you enough for putting a good word in for me, Marcus.'

His smile almost matched hers as he patted her on the shoulder. 'Why, that's excellent news,' he said, leading her towards the front door where the maid stood waiting to let them out. 'I think you'll like working for Eugenie. She's a very gentle woman.'

Soon they were back in the carriage and his face grew serious as he told her, 'I should warn you about Georgina. She's the youngest daughter and as spoiled as they come, unfortunately. Sadly Elizabeth, the middle daughter, died some months ago and Eugenie took it very badly. The child she was carrying died with her, which was a double blow to the family. Eugenie was a nervy woman before that happened but since then she's become almost reclusive. But Victor . . . well, let's just say Georgina was always the favoured one and now with her older sister disinherited and Elizabeth deceased she has become the heir to the Spencer-Hughes estate and makes sure everyone knows it.'

Seeing the look of dismay on Saffie's face, he hurried on, 'But I doubt very much you'll see a lot of her. She spends some of her time at the Spencer-Hugheses' London house and until recently was rarely here. Even when she is she has a very busy social life so don't get worrying about it please.'

Saffie nodded and stared from the carriage window. So very much had happened to her and her family in such a short space of time that she could barely get her head around it all, and now here she was about to start yet another chapter in her short life. She could only pray that it would be a happy one. In the meantime, she was grateful that she would not be starting until after Minnie's wedding, at least she would be there to share her big day with her.

Suddenly the thought of leaving Minnie, who had been almost like a second mother to her, hit her like a blow to the stomach and it occurred to her that this job would be the very first she'd had without someone like Minnie behind her. It was then that the pride her mother had instilled in her kicked in and blinking back the tears she straightened her back. *You can be anything you want to be*, her mother had always told her, and now it was up to her to prove it.

Chapter Thirty

'Oh Minnie, you look . . . just *beautiful*!' Saffie breathed on the day of the wedding as she helped Minnie to get ready. Minnie was wearing the pretty bonnet trimmed with silk roses that had been Saffie's present to her, and with her eyes shining and her face glowing she truly did look beautiful.

'Aye, well let's just 'ope as the bridegroom thinks so too,' she said with a grin. She could hardly believe the day had dawned. She had long since thought she would be a spinster forever and now here she was finally about to become a wife.

Downstairs they could hear Sylvie and Cathy, who were now the best of friends, chatting together as they each admired the new dresses Saffie and Minnie had sewed for them. They'd had to sit up until the early hours of the morning each night to get everything done on time, but seeing both the girls looking so pretty made it worth it. Marcus had insisted on paying for a small wedding breakfast for the bride and groom and their guests at a hotel in town following the service and they would also spend their wedding night there while Saffie returned to the cottage with the girls. Unfortunately, Mathilda was still not well enough to attend, so much like Elsie and Bernie's wedding it would only be a small affair, but that suited Minnie down to the ground.

'I never wanted a big fuss an' palaver,' she'd confided to Saffie. And now here she was, all done up in her wedding finery, and at the joy on her face Saffie felt a lump form in her throat as she wondered if she would ever find such happiness. She handed Minnie her bouquet of pale pink rosebuds just as they heard Marcus's carriage, which he had sent to take them to the church, pull up outside.

'Are you all ready?' Saffie asked.

Minnie smiled and nodded, and when they reached the bottom of the stairs Marcus beamed at Minnie.

'You look absolutely stunning,' he said sincerely and Minnie blushed prettily.

'Why thank you, kind sir. But now, come on – let's be gettin' this show on the road. I've waited long enough fer this day an' I don't want to keep me groom waitin', do I?'

They all piled into the coach and as Saffie glanced at Marcus, she couldn't help but feel sorry for him. His life had changed since Mathilda had lost the baby and he'd confided to her that sometimes he felt lonely because Mathilda seemed to have locked herself away in her own little world where the pain of her loss couldn't touch her. In addition to that, Mathilda had not completely recovered physically from the miscarriage, so not only was he coping with his own grief, he was also having to support and look after Mathilda. All they could do was pray that with time she would return to her usual sparkling self.

Even so, it was a merry group that arrived at the church and while Saffie ushered the two little girls inside, Marcus stayed behind to walk the bride down the aisle. The service was short but sweet and as Minnie and Davey took their vows with the light from the stained-glass windows shining down on them, Saffie gulped back tears. It was clear to everyone that they were meant for each other and she hoped they would grow old together.

The wedding breakfast that followed was a happy affair too and the wine flowed like water. Even Saffie, who rarely drunk alcohol, was tipsy by mid-afternoon and Marcus teased her as his carriage took her and the two girls back to the cottage, leaving the two lovebirds to enjoy their first night as Mr and Mrs at the hotel.

'You've done them proud. It's been a wonderful day,' Saffie praised him as the girls giggled and pointed out things from the window.

'It was my pleasure. I've known Minnie and Davey for most of my life and they deserve to be happy.'

Saffie couldn't have agreed more and once he had dropped them off and returned to his own home, she hurriedly got the two girls changed out of their new finery and let them go out to play in the garden for a while. Davey had made them a swing, which hung from a branch of a large oak tree, and Saffie smiled as she watched them taking it in turns to push each other on it. All in all, it had been a grand day, there was no doubt about it, and she was in a mellow mood.

It wasn't until much later that evening when the girls were fast asleep that her thoughts turned to her new job again and she nibbled her nails nervously. Davey and Minnie would be back the following morning to begin their married life, but Saffie would be leaving the cottage forever for her new life at Lakeside House. *Still, there's no use fretting about it*, she scolded herself. It was high time she learned to be independent, and on that thought she carried the candle upstairs and went to bed.

Minnie and Davey were in fine spirits when they arrived home the next morning.

'Eeh, can yer believe Marcus had ordered room service an' we got served breakfast in bed,' Minnie chuckled. 'It made a rare change from me waitin' on everybody, I don't mind tellin' yer.'

'From now on yer shall 'ave a cup o' tea in bed every mornin' afore I leave fer work,' Davey promised. He smiled at her, and Saffie could almost feel the love between them.

The day passed mainly in happy reminiscing about the wedding and before she knew it, it was bedtime and time to say goodbye to Davey, as he would already have left for work by the time she departed the next morning.

'Take care o' yersen, lass,' Davy told her as he shyly pecked her on the cheek. 'An' don't get mitherin' about this brood. I'll see as they're all well taken care of.'

'I know you will,' she answered and she meant it. Davey was marvellous with both the little girls and they adored him.

'Well, I shall get up bright an' early to see you off,' Minnie insisted. 'So I won't say me goodbyes just yet.' And with that she followed her new husband up the stairs.

'Now don't get frettin' if you've forgotten owt,' Minnie told her the next morning. 'I can soon get Marcus to drop it in to yer.' True to her word she had risen early and by the time Saffie came downstairs there was a pan of porridge simmering on the stove. The only problem was, Saffie was so nervous after a night spent tossing and turning that she couldn't eat a bite of it. 'An' just make sure as yer come to see us sometimes on yer afternoon off,' Minnie went on tremulously. 'We'll allus be 'ere fer yer, just remember that. Yer don't 'ave to stay anywhere if you ain't 'appy.'

'Thank you, I appreciate that,' Saffie said in a wobbly voice. 'But I'm a big girl now and it's time I learned to stand on my own two feet.'

Saffie turned her attention to the two girls who were standing by with solemn faces. Suddenly realising how much she was going to miss them, she kissed their cheeks and ruffled their hair, then, not wanting to prolong the goodbyes, she lifted her bag and felt her way blindly to the door. The girls and Minnie stood on the step and waved until she turned a bend in the road and only then did Saffie allow her tears to flow.

Marcus had offered to take her to her new home but she had chosen to walk and now she was glad she had because it would give her time to compose herself. It was a long walk and on the way she passed many of the pit workers who were hurrying to their jobs, their hob-nailed boots sparking on the cobbles. By the time she had passed through the town and reached Griff Hollows her arm felt as if it was going to drop off with the weight of her bag, but at least she knew she was nearing her destination so she ploughed on until, at last, she reached the long driveway that led to Lakeside House.

It was when she finally reached it that she made her first mistake when she climbed the steps and pulled the bell on the huge door. The same maid who had admitted her previously opened the door and glanced nervously across her shoulder before hissing, 'Sorry, miss, if you're the mistress's new lady's maid you'll have to enter round the back by the servants' entrance.'

She hastily closed the door, leaving Saffie to chew on her lip before turning and making her way around the side of the house as she silently scolded herself for making such an error. She came to an enormous yard bordered by outbuildings and stables with horses hanging their heads over the top of their stalls. They whinnied at her as she passed and Saffie felt a pang of regret as she thought of old Nellie. How easy her life had been back then, she mused, but she set her chin and quickly moved on. It wasn't the time to get nostalgic; this was the start of a new life.

Another maid was hanging washing on the long line that was strung across the yard and she stared curiously at Saffie when she asked, 'Could you tell me where I have to go to see the housekeeper, please? I'm expected.'

The girl gestured to a door on the other side of the yard. 'Ah, you must be the boatie that's come to be the missus's new lady's maid. Just go in there an' someone'll sort you out.'

Thanking her, Saffie walked over and tapped on the door. She could hear activity from within and when yet another maid in a pretty starched mobcap and apron opened the door, Saffie introduced herself with a smile. 'Hello, I'm Sapphire Doyle. I believe Mrs Beasley is expecting me.'

'You'd better come in,' the maid said shortly, holding the door wider, and Saffie walked into what appeared to be a hive of activity in the most enormous kitchen she had ever seen.

'We're preparin' breakfast for the family so sit over there till Mrs Beasley has time to see you. I'll get someone to let her know you're 'ere.'

Saffie self-consciously went and perched on the edge of the chair the girl had pointed to, very aware that all eyes were on her and that her welcome hadn't been particularly warm. On the table in front of her were silver dishes full of devilled kidneys, fat juicy sausages, crispy rashers of bacon and another of eggs fried to perfection.

Within seconds the girl who had opened the door began to whisk them away to the dining room, while another followed with silver pots full of steaming tea and coffee. Saffie's stomach rumbled at the tempting smells and she wished she'd eaten some of the porridge Minnie had made for her. The cook, a large round woman with a red face, stared at her suspiciously as she wiped her hands on her calico apron, but when Saffie smiled at her she turned her head away and Saffie flushed. They had clearly all been discussing her before she arrived, if the covert glances she was receiving were anything to go by, and she began to feel distinctly uncomfortable. It certainly wasn't the welcome she had hoped for.

At that moment the green baize door to one side of the room opened and a stern-faced woman in a black, full-skirted bombazine gown with a chatelaine of keys about her waist appeared. She was tall and thin, and her grey hair was tied into a severe bun in the nape of her neck. Her nose was slightly hooked and her cold grey eyes scanned the room, until they settled on Saffie.

'Miss Doyle, I presume?' Her voice was as cold as her eyes.

Saffie nodded nervously.

'Come this way,' she said shortly, turning away.

Lifting her bag Saffie hastily followed her, feeling more uncomfortable by the minute. Soon she found herself in the hallway she had waited in with Marcus, but she had no time to admire it before the woman reached a door and threw it open. Inside were long floor-to-ceiling shelves stacked with clothing. The woman examined her briefly before selecting a gown off one of them.

'I believe this will fit you. Any slight alterations you will be responsible for doing yourself. Please try it on, I shall be back shortly.' She turned and left, closing the door with a loud click behind her.

Saffie could feel the disapproval coming off the woman in waves and wondered what she might have done to upset her already, but all the same she quickly dropped her bag and struggled out of her best blouse and skirt before trying the gown on. She was pleased to find that it was actually very nice: plain and serviceable and in a soft dove-grey colour. The material was superior to any she had ever worn before and as Saffie did up the row of tiny buttons that stretched from the waist to the neckline, she wished she had a mirror to admire herself in. The gown fitted snugly into the waist and had long sleeves and a high neckline that was trimmed in a darker grey braid. The skirt was full and Saffie was stroking it when Mrs Beasley reappeared.

'Hm, that will do, Doyle,' she observed, reaching for another identical one. 'A little long, but you can see to that in the evenings when the mistress no longer requires you.'

'Of course, Mrs Beasley,' Saffie said pleasantly, hoping to soften the woman's attitude towards her a little. 'And my name is Sapphire.'

The woman snorted with derision, her lip curling scorn-fully. '*Sapphire!* What sort of a name is *that*? But then I sup-pose I should expect no more from a . . . a *boat* person. Kindly

291

remember that while you are here you will be addressed as *Miss* Doyle, and think yourself lucky. The maids are only referred to by their surnames. And this . . .' She lifted a lock of Saffie's shimmering hair, which was hanging loose down her back. 'Make sure it is securely tied up before you present yourself to the mistress. You are not running wild on the canal banks now, my girl. You must behave with decorum!'

'I am quite aware what is expected of me!' Saffie retaliated, smarting. 'And I assure you I never ran wild.'

Mrs Beasley handed her the other gown. 'You will have one to wash and one to wear. You may present your soiled gown to the laundry maid once a week. Now I shall show you to your room and a maid will bring you up some petticoats and other essentials shortly while you settle in. The mistress is having breakfast in bed this morning so you will go to her when she rings a bell that will sound in your room. You must be polite and respectable at all times. Is that *quite* clear?'

'Quite!' Saffie's voice was as sharp as the housekeeper's now. Already it was clear they were never going to be friends and Saffie was too proud to allow the woman to talk down to her. From now on she would give as good as she got and see how the pompous woman liked that! It wasn't the best of starts and Saffie wished it might have been different.

The woman sailed from the room and snatching up her bag and discarded clothes, Saffie hurried after her.

The magnificent staircase swept up from the hallway to a galleried landing and under other circumstances Saffie would have enjoyed looking about her and getting acquainted with her surroundings but at that moment she felt resentful. She guessed that all the staff must know that she had been raised on the canal and had already passed judgement on her, hence the icy reception she had received from them in the kitchen, but she'd show them!

At the top of the stairs the woman led her to a door and throwing it open told her, 'This will be your room. The mistress's is just there.' She pointed to the adjoining door. 'You will take your meals with the staff in the kitchen or alternatively you may have a tray brought to your room.'

She turned and left without another word as Saffie entered the room that was to be hers. Instantly her bad mood lifted slightly as she looked about her. To her eyes it was enormous. There was a large brass bed, easily big enough to fit herself and the twins in, she was sure, and she had her own wardrobe, chest of drawers, dressing table and wash stand as well as a small desk and chair that stood in the window. Pretty floral curtains hung at the long window and there was a matching bedspread on the bed. She noted there were some hair pins on the dressing table so she quickly braided her hair into one thick plait and coiled it on the back of her head securing it with the pins. She hardly recognised herself in the smart gown when she looked in the mirror. She looked almost like a lady and very grown up and she wondered what her mother would have thought if she could have seen her now.

But there was no time to stand admiring herself, the mistress might ring for her at any minute so she quickly began to unpack her bag until a tap came on the door. She crossed to answer it to find a young maid standing there.

'Mrs Beasley said as I was to fetch these to yer, Miss Doyle,' she said as she handed Saffie another armful of assorted garments, giving Saffie the first smile she had received since entering the house.

'Oh, that's very kind of you. Could you put them on the bed please? I'm just putting my things away.' Saffie returned the smile. 'And my name is Sapphire by the way, but everyone calls me Saffie.'

'Ooh, I couldn't call yer that,' the girl said fearfully. 'It'd be more'n me job were worth. She's a tartar fer everyone obeyin' the rules is Mrs Beasley, an' she'd 'ave me guts fer garters if I didn't follow 'em. Oh, an' I'm Boss – daft name, ain't it? But that's what it is. Grace Boss an' I'm the under 'ousemaid, or general dogsbody in other words. I get to do all the shitty jobs like lightin' the fires first thing while everyone else is abed.'

'It's very nice to meet you, Grace . . . I mean Boss.' The girl was quite small with mousy-coloured hair and a heart-shaped face, but Saffie guessed that they must be round about the same age.

'Right, I'd best be off,' Boss said before pausing to ask, ''Ave yer 'ad any breakfast? Cos if you ain't, I could fetch you some up on a tray while yer finish puttin' yer things away. I doubt the missus will stir fer at least another hour or so, so yer should 'ave time to eat it. An' they call me Bossy in the kitchen, by the way.'

'I haven't actually, and that would be lovely, Bossy,' Saffie admitted, and with a nod the girl scuttled away leaving Saffie feeling slightly better to think that there might be at least one person who hadn't prejudged her in the house.

Chapter Thirty-One

After Mrs Spencer-Hughes had retired to her room that evening, Saffie made her way downstairs for some supper, which she was told she could eat, if she so wished, in the kitchen with the rest of the staff.

She entered the room quietly and was surprised to see so many people seated around the table. But the second her presence was registered, silence descended and Saffie felt herself flush.

'Come over 'ere an' sit by me,' Bossy invited and Saffie was only too pleased to do as she was asked.

'Hello, everyone,' she introduced herself, determined to try and make a good impression. 'I'm Saffie Doyle. I started today as Mrs Spencer-Hughes's lady's maid.'

The cook sniffed. 'We know who you are,' she said with no warmth in her voice and Saffie felt herself shrink inside.

'Right, well 'elp yerself to some o' this lovely steak an' kidney pie,' Bossy said quickly. 'An' you ain't tried nuthin' as good as Cook's roasties. They're all crispy on the outside an' soft in the middle.'

'Thank you.' Saffie helped herself to a small portion. She had eaten in her room at lunchtime while her mistress ate in the dining room with her husband and daughter, but tonight she had wanted to join the rest of the staff to hopefully get a little better acquainted with them.

'Has anyone told yer that the lady's maid, the butler an' the 'ousekeeper usually eat in their own rooms?' the cook questioned.

Saffie shook her head. 'Er . . . no, they haven't. May I ask why?'

'It's cos they hold the most important jobs,' Cook said. 'Though o' course, *most* people who climb to those positions 'ave usually earned 'em.'

Her voice was loaded with sarcasm but Saffie chose to ignore it. The last thing she wanted was to get embroiled in an argument on her first day here. Instead, she quietly began to pick at her food and eventually the conversation around her resumed, although everyone apart from Bossy excluded her from it.

She was relieved when it was finally over and she bade them all a quiet goodnight and scuttled away, but she had only just reached her room when Bossy tapped on the door.

'Don't mind them lot,' she said in a quiet voice. 'This is all Miss Georgina's doin'. She's turned 'em all again yer afore they've even got a chance to know yer. She's a spiteful little cow, she is, as you'll find out.'

'But why would she do that? I haven't even met her and she knows nothing about me!'

'Yer came 'ere wi' Mr Berrington an' that'd be enough to make 'er jealous. She's 'ad 'er sights on 'im fer years even though 'e's married an' years older than 'er.'

Saffie's eyes widened. 'But surely Georgina Spencer-Hughes could have any man she wants? Her father is one of the richest men in the county, isn't he?'

'Aye, he is, but she's got a face on 'er like a slapped arse an' a nature to match. It'd 'ave to be a very brave man who'd take her on! But anyway, that's enough about 'er. How did yer first day go?'

'Very well, actually,' Saffie told her. 'Though it will be much easier when I know where everything is. Every time the mistress asked me for anything I had to search for it. I have a few of her clothes to repair this evening. But she does seem very nice.'

Bossy nodded, setting the mobcap above her mousy hair dancing. 'She is, it's just Mr Spencer-Hughes an' Georgina you've to look out for,' she warned. Then glancing at the door, she whispered, 'I'd best gerroff to the servants' quarters now. I ain't supposed to be on this floor less I'm lightin' fires or cleanin'. Ta-ra fer now, see yer in the mornin'.' And with a cheery wave she was off, leaving Saffie to spend her first night in her new room.

Once again Saffie braved the kitchen the next morning and once more, she was amazed at the number of staff present.

'How many people actually work here?' she whispered to Bossy, who was tucking into her food as if she hadn't eaten for a week. Before working at Lakeside House, she had been one of nine children living in a two-up, two-down terraced house in the town. They had never had enough to eat and now Bossy took full advantage of the plentiful food that was always available to them.

'Hm, I ain't really sure, I ain't never counted 'em. Not that I can count,' Bossy admitted. 'But there's the butler, Mr Spencer-Hughes's valet an' you, o' course. Then there's the 'ousekeeper, the gardeners, the stable lads an' the groom.

There's me an' the parlourmaid an' the laundry maid an' Cook an' the kitchen maids.'

Saffie was shocked. How could just one family of three people need so many servants? she wondered. The atmosphere in the kitchen was still frosty towards her and she decided that from now on she would take all her meals in her room, at least for the time being until some, or all of them hopefully, got used to having her there.

On a happier note, she was at least getting along well with Mrs Spencer-Hughes. She was a very quiet, inoffensive little woman who Saffie doubted would dare to say boo to a goose. When Saffie thought back to how her own parents and all her siblings had slept in the cramped quarters aboard *The Blue Sapphire*, she found it strange to find that both the master and the mistress had their own bedrooms and dressing rooms. But as she was fast discovering the gentry seemed to live an entirely different way of life, although whether it made them any happier, she had no idea. It certainly seemed to suit Eugenie Spencer-Hughes, who trembled every time her husband entered a room.

Immediately after breakfast Mrs Spencer-Hughes rang her bell and Saffie hurried to her room to draw the curtains.

'Good morning, ma'am,' she said as she threw a few nuggets of coal onto the dying embers. It really should have been Bossy's job but Saffie didn't mind getting her hands dirty.

'Would you like me to bring your breakfast up to you on a tray?' she asked and Mrs Spencer-Hughes nodded.

'If you wouldn't mind, Doyle. Just a pot of tea and some lightly buttered toast, I think. I have a terrible headache and I'm afraid I didn't sleep well again.'

Saffie crossed to the bed and helped the woman up onto her pillows before bustling away to fetch her food.

She was ignored in the kitchen as she prepared the tray but she was getting used to it by now and quietly went about her duties.

It was as she was leaving with the tray that she heard the parlour maid hiss to Cook, 'Stuck up little madam! Who does she think she is anyway? Why, she's the lowest of the low. I still can't believe the mistress gave that position to *her* when *I*, who've worked here for years, wanted it!'

At least now Saffie understood why that woman didn't like her and she sighed as she carefully made her way to the stairs. It seemed they had all made up their minds not to like her before they had even met her, but at least she had made a friend in Bossy.

She had just started to climb the stairs when she had another unpleasant encounter as the daughter of the house started to descend, or at least she assumed this must be Miss Georgina.

'Oh, so *you* must be the one everyone is on about – Mama's new maid,' she said nastily as they drew level.

'Yes, miss.' Saffie concentrated on the tray she was carrying. Despite her fancy clothes, the young woman was as plain as a pikestaff. She was tall and plump and her hair was a dull brown colour.

'Hm, well just remember, Mama only took you on because Marcus put in a good word for you.' The look she gave Saffie was scathing. 'Though why he'd do that I have no idea. Everyone knows your sort is untrustworthy.'

Saffie bristled. 'I assure you, miss, I am *totally* trustworthy,' she defended herself indignantly.

'Time will tell, but I shall be watching you,' the older girl sneered. 'Now be off with you, you're not paid to stand about.'

Mustering what dignity she could, Saffie went on her way and once she reached Mrs Spencer-Hughes's bedroom she took a deep breath before entering. It wouldn't do to repeat what Georgina had said, it could only cause trouble.

While the woman was picking at her breakfast like a bird, Saffie busied herself laying out the clothes that Mrs Spencer-Hughes had told her she wished to wear that day and then she hurried off to fetch a jug of hot water for her to wash in. Her next job was to help Mrs Spencer-Hughes dress and to style her hair. Saffie found it strange that a grown woman should need anyone to help her do such things, but she was being paid for it and so she was happy to do it.

'I think I shall wear my pearl necklace and the matching earrings today, Doyle,' Mrs Spencer-Hughes told her when Saffie had managed to dress her hair to her satisfaction. She still found that rather difficult but hoped she would get better as time went on.

Saffie crossed to the large jewellery box standing on Mrs Spencer-Hughes's dressing table and withdrew the pearls and earrings before handing them to her. The first time she had been asked to get something from the box she had been shocked to see the array of jewels it contained. There were precious stones in all the colours of the rainbow set into fine gold, but she had soon discovered that Mrs Spencer-Hughes seemed to favour her pearls above any other.

'I have a visitor calling to take morning coffee with me later on,' Mrs Spencer-Hughes told her as she fastened the earrings into her ears. 'I shall receive her in the drawing room.

You may be present when she arrives and fetch us some coffee and biscuits, then you may go about your chores for the rest of the visit.'

'Very well, ma'am.'

'Oh . . . and Doyle.' The woman stared at her for a moment as if she was trying to make a decision before saying in a low voice, 'Mrs Parker-Bates, my visitor, is my oldest and dearest friend. When she arrives, she may have a letter for me. I would like you to take it to my room and put it in my jewellery box, but no one must see it. I shall read it when I am alone. Do you think you could do that for me?'

Saffie thought it was a rather strange request but it wasn't up to her to question the mistress so she nodded. 'Of course, ma'am.'

She waited until the woman had made her way downstairs before beginning to tidy the room. It seemed that the gentry were waited on hand and foot and when she thought of the hard life her mother had led on *The Blue Sapphire* she shook her head. As always it appeared that there was one lifestyle for the rich and one for the poor, and they were worlds apart.

Later that morning, Saffie sat with Mrs Spencer-Hughes awaiting the arrival of her friend in the drawing room and when she arrived promptly at eleven a.m. she was shown in by the maid.

'Maude, my dear, how lovely it is to see you,' Mrs Spencer-Hughes greeted her effusively when the maid had left the room. Mrs Parker-Bates was a short, plump woman and because of the many frills and furbelows on her outfit she looked even bigger, and the hat she was wearing was so enormous that Saffie could scarcely take her eyes off it.

301

'This is Doyle, my new maid,' Mrs Spencer-Hughes told her friend, and the woman gave Saffie a smile.

'How do you do, my dear. And how are you finding my friend to work for? Is she a slave driver?' There was a mischievous twinkle in her eye and Saffie warmed to her immediately. Despite the grand carriage pulled by two matching coal-black stallions she had arrived in, and the clothes she was wearing, she was clearly very down to earth.

'She's very kind, thank you, ma'am.' Saffie returned her smile before asking Mrs Spencer-Hughes, 'Shall I order your coffee now, ma'am?'

'Yes please do, but first . . .' Mrs Spencer-Hughes glanced anxiously towards Mrs Parker-Bates to ask, 'Do you have anything for me today, Maude?'

'I do, as it happens.' Mrs Parker-Bates rummaged in her small reticule before handing an envelope to Mrs Spencer-Hughes who instantly passed it to Saffie.

'Could you put it in the pocket of your gown?' she suggested. 'Remember, no one else must see it, and you know where to put it, don't you? Order the coffee first and take it straight upstairs.'

Saffie nodded and once out in the hallway she almost bumped into the housekeeper who was evidently heading for the kitchen. 'Mrs Beasley, would you mind asking in the kitchen for coffee to be sent to the drawing room for the mistress and her visitor, please?'

The woman looked at her with disdain but nodded and went on her way and as Saffie made her way back upstairs, she sighed. Mrs Spencer-Hughes and Bossy were still the only ones who spoke to her but she supposed it was still very early days. She could only hope that as the rest of the staff got to know her, they might give her a chance, but only time would tell.

On the landing she encountered Georgina once more. The girl was dressed in an elegant dark green velvet riding habit, with a matching hat trimmed with feathers perched on the side of her head and she was carrying a small riding whip. Saffie pitied the poor horse she'd be riding if she was as brutal with him as she was with her, but thankfully Georgina merely glared at her as she passed, so Saffie hurried on to her mistress's room.

Once inside she hastily went to put the letter where the mistress had requested, but not before she had noticed that the envelope was addressed to Mrs Spencer-Hughes, c/o Mrs Parker-Bates at an address in nearby Fenny Drayton. She briefly wondered why it couldn't have been sent straight to Lakeside House, but just as she opened the lid of the jewellery box the door banged open and Georgina stood there.

'I thought you looked shifty,' she snarled. 'Just *what* do you think you are doing going into my mother's jewellery box? Got your eye on something in there, have you? I know what you boat people are like! Thieving *scum*, the lot of you.'

Colour flared in Saffie's cheeks. She wanted to tell this awful young woman to go to hell but realised that it would be more than her job was worth, so instead she quickly pushed the envelope back into her pocket and turned to face her.

'I was just putting something away, if you must know,' she said quietly. 'Here . . . come and check that everything is still there if you like!'

303

Georgina's lip curled back from her teeth, which were surprisingly straight and white and about the only thing that was attractive about her as far as Saffie could see. She crossed the room smartly and elbowing Saffie aside, she quickly checked the contents of the box. 'Hm, it seems that I caught you just in time. But just remember, I'm on to you and I shall be watching you like a hawk.' And with that she turned in a flurry of velvet skirts and slammed out of the room, leaving Saffie to break out in a cold sweat.

That had been a little too close for comfort. What if Georgina had found the letter Mrs Spencer-Hughes had entrusted to her? Perhaps she should suggest to Mrs Spencer-Hughes that she think of another hiding place to put her private mail? Trying to put the unpleasant incident from her mind she settled in the window to sew some buttons on to one of her mistress's gowns. It was part of her job to keep Mrs Spencer-Hughes's clothes in good repair and now she was grateful that her mother had taught all the girls to sew from an early age. Admittedly she would never make a seamstress but at least she could do what needed to be done reasonably well.

Over an hour later she heard Mrs Parker-Bates's carriage being brought round to the front door from the stables and shortly after the woman left.

'Did you do as I asked?' Mrs Spencer-Hughes asked as soon as she returned to her room.

Laying aside her mending, Saffie nodded. 'Yes, I did, Mrs Spencer-Hughes, but your daughter almost caught me in the act and seemed to think I was about to steal from you. Perhaps in future you might think of somewhere else to hide your private mail?'

Mrs Spencer-Hughes sighed. 'You could be right,' she admitted. 'But now perhaps you could take my laundry down to the laundry room while I read it in peace?'

Saffie hastily lifted the pile of clothes she had placed ready, and as she hurried from the room she saw Mrs Spencer-Hughes ripping the envelope open as if she could hardly wait to read whatever was inside it.

The second Saffie reached the landing she heard the key turn in the door behind her and she was even more intrigued. Whoever was writing to the mistress was clearly very important to her, but she found it strange that she didn't want any of the rest of her family to know about it. Still, it was nothing to do with her, she decided as she hurried to the laundry room. Her first afternoon off couldn't come quickly enough now and suddenly seemed a very long way away.

Chapter Thirty-Two

'Aw, lass, it's lovely to see you, we've missed yer,' Minnie greeted her when Saffie arrived at the cottage on her first Sunday afternoon off. The sun was shining in a cloudless blue sky and the little front garden was now ablaze with colourful flowers. Cathy and Sylvie had run to meet her up the lane when they had spotted her and after the hostility she had met from most of the staff at Lakeside House, it warmed Saffie's soul to know that she was still loved. 'So how's it goin'?'

Saffie sighed as she sat down at the table. 'Mrs Spencer-Hughes is actually very nice but all the staff, apart from one, haven't taken to me and seem to resent me being there.' Saffie studied Minnie, who was filling the kettle at the sink, and it did her heart good to see her friend looking so happy. She was positively blooming – married life clearly suited her.

'Davey's outside plantin' some more veg,' Minnie informed her with a smile. 'But come on, tell me what life in the big 'ouse is like, apart from the stuck-up servants, I mean.'

Saffie quickly told her about her duties and Minnie nodded.

'Hm, that don't sound so bad. An' what about the daughter o' the house? Miss Georgina, ain't it? Marcus reckons she's a right tartar.'

'She is.' Saffie sighed again. 'Like the staff she obviously resents the fact that someone who was brought up on the canals should be given such a position, but that only makes me all the more determined to do the job well.'

'Good fer you.' Minnie spooned tea leaves into the large brown teapot. 'Never forget yer just as good as them, me gel. But 'as Margaret been mentioned?'

'Not as yet.' Saffie fiddled with the fringing on the green chenille tablecloth. 'But hopefully when Mrs Spencer-Hughes gets to know me a little better, she might open up to me a bit more. Oh, and have I had any mail? I hope you don't mind but I wrote to Granny Doyle and the twins and told them to write to me here. I don't think Mrs Beasley approves of the staff having letters delivered to the house.'

'There's one come yesterday, as it 'appens. There on the mantelpiece, look.'

Saffie hurried over to get it, and recognising Ginny's handwriting, she slit the envelope and started to read while Minnie prepared the cups for the tea. The girls were outside playing on the swing, and the sound of their laughter drifted into the room.

'Everything is fine at Granny Doyle's, thank goodness,' Saffie told Minnie once she had partially read it, and her face lit up as she exclaimed, 'Oh, and they've heard from Archie! How wonderful!'

'Really, tell me what he says then.'

Saffie was only too happy to oblige. '"Because of me age when we arrived in Australia, a farmer took me on to work on his ranch with him till I've served me time. And I love the life. Farmer Boyd and his missus treat me like family and I'm loving working on the land. They have a son, Thomas, who's just a bit younger than me and two daughters, Miriam and

Ruth. Miriam is a year younger than me and we get on like a house on fire. She's a really grand lass.'"

'*Ooh*, do I detect the start of a romance there?' Minnie giggled gleefully and Saffie laughed, before continuing.

'"You wouldn't believe how different some things are here. We have kangaroos with little joeys in their pouches (that's baby kangaroos) and wallabies and parrots in the trees. The only downside is they have a lot of snakes and spiders too, some of them venomous! Working the land is hard but I'm learning all the time. I think of you all often and hope that you are well. I'm so sorry for letting you all down. Have you heard from our dad, Saffie? I know he was sentenced the same day as me but I have no idea what happened to him, and how is our mam?"'

Saffie's smile faded at this point. Of course, Archie could have had no way of knowing that their mother had passed away, so she decided she would write him a long letter and fill him in on all that had transpired since his arrest.

Minnie, who was standing close beside her, gently squeezed her shoulder and Saffie blinked her tears away. At least Archie sounded happy, and even if his life was hard, he seemed to be enjoying it. 'I shall write to him tonight before I go to bed,' she told Minnie. 'Though goodness knows how long it will take the letter to get there.'

Davey came in at that moment and his eyes instantly found Minnie's, who blushed with pleasure at the sight of him.

'I swear this husband o' mine can smell a cup o' tea from a mile off,' she said jokingly. 'And I dare say he wouldn't say no to a slice o' my fruit cake neither!'

'Not 'alf.' Davey smiled and nodded at Saffie before crossing to his wife to plant a sloppy kiss on her cheek.

'I've missed yer, lass.'

She gently punched his broad chest. 'Oh, get off wi' yer, yer daft ha'p'porth. You've only been out in the garden.'

They were so in love and so wrapped up in each other that Saffie suddenly felt in the way, even though they were both clearly pleased to see her. So she dutifully ate the delicious slice of cake Minnie cut for her and drank the tea before telling the newly-weds, 'Right I shall be off.'

'What already? Why – that were a flyin' visit, weren't it? You've barely been 'ere 'alf an hour. What's the rush?'

'I thought I'd call and see Marcus and Mathilda before I set off back,' Saffie explained. 'I haven't see Mathilda for some time and it's a fair walk back to Lakeside House.'

'I could take yer in the pony an' trap,' Davey kindly volunteered but she shook her head.

'Thanks, Davey. I appreciate the offer but I'm looking forward to the walk in the fresh air. But don't worry, I shall be back next Sunday, if I'm welcome, that is?'

'Huh! Don't talk such nonsense, yer know yer allus welcome,' Minnie scolded, giving her a hug.

As she set off, Cathy and Sylvie waved to her from the garden.

Marcus's maid admitted her when she arrived at the farmhouse and she was shown into the parlour where Mathilda and Marcus were taking afternoon tea.

'Do have a cup,' Marcus urged after greeting her but she shook her head as she smiled at Mathilda, who, she was shocked to see, seemed to have lost even more weight.

'Thank you but I just had tea with Minnie and Davey.'

'Ah, and how are they?'

'Very happy indeed from what I could see of it.'

'Good.' Marcus sat back in his chair. 'And how are you settling in to your new post?'

'Very well, although what you warned me about Georgina was quite right,' she said soberly with a little shake of her head.

Marcus grinned. 'Not the nicest of young women, is she? It's no wonder she's still on the shelf, although I believe that now she's set to inherit everything, she's had a few suitors. Her father told me at the gentleman's club last week that there's a chap in London wants to marry her. Trouble is he's a widower who's almost sixty, with three children older than her.' He chuckled wickedly. 'Personally, I think she should snap him up. With her looks and personality, he's possibly the best she could get.'

Normally Mathilda would have scolded him for saying such a cruel thing about anyone, even if it was in jest, but she sat quietly all throughout the conversation without saying a word.

Marcus's face became serious then when he asked her, 'And has Mrs Spencer-Hughes mentioned Margaret at all?'

Saffie shook her head. 'Not once and I don't like to mention her. I'm just hoping she will when she gets to know me a little more.'

'Quite.'

'And how are you?' Saffie gently questioned, turning her attention to Mathilda.

'Oh . . . not too bad,' Mathilda replied. But it was obvious this wasn't true. Her face was gaunt, there were dark circles beneath her eyes and her once lustrous hair was now dull and limp.

They talked of the school for a time until eventually Saffie took her leave. Marcus followed her to the door and much as Davey had done shortly before, he offered to drive her home, but again, she politely refused the offer.

'In that case I shall walk you to the end of the drive.'

They walked in silence for a time until Saffie asked, 'How is Mathilda . . . *really*?'

He shook his head. 'Not good. It's almost like being married to a completely different woman. The doctor has warned us that attempting to have another child could kill her and she's taken it very badly. She always used to joke that she wouldn't stop having babies until the house was full to the rafters, and now here we are, not even able to manage one.'

'It's very sad, but have you thought of adoption?' Saffie suggested. 'I'm told the workhouse nursery is full of babies who need a good home.'

Marcus nodded. 'Yes, I have, but Mathilda won't even consider it. She says if she can't have a baby of her own, she doesn't want somebody else's.'

They were nearing the bend in the lane now and Marcus slowed his steps, ready to take his leave of her. 'Do come and see us again soon,' he urged, noticing how smart she looked in her new dress with her hair neatly pinned up on top of her head. Not for the first time, he also noticed how she had blossomed into a very attractive young lady. No doubt it wouldn't be long before some young man came along and swept her off her feet, he thought.

He watched her until she was out of sight then slowly turned and made his way back to his wife.

Chapter Thirty-Three

On a cold morning in early September, Saffie began her day as usual by going to the kitchen to make up a breakfast tray for Mrs Spencer-Hughes. She no longer ate with the rest of the staff, choosing to have all her meals in her own room, and Bossy was happy to carry them up to her on a tray. Saffie had hoped that the staff would warm to her in time but this hadn't been the case. Even so, she was content enough and she and Mrs Spencer-Hughes were easy in each other's company, to the point that her employer now confided certain things to her – one of them being that her marriage wasn't what she had hoped it would be.

As she was carrying the tray along the landing, she saw Mr Spencer-Hughes leaving his wife's room in his bathrobe, and Saffie's heart flipped inside her chest. When she entered the room, just as she expected, she found the woman sitting up in bed with tears streaming down her cheeks. Mrs Spencer-Hughes hastily snatched up her robe and threw it across her shoulders but not before Saffie had noticed that the pretty nightgown she was wearing was torn and an ugly bruise was forming on her shoulder.

'Morning, ma'am.' Saffie discreetly placed the tray down on the small table to the side of the bed and went to draw the curtains, giving Mrs Spencer-Hughes time to dry her cheeks and compose herself – she was clearly embarrassed to be found in such a state. It wasn't the first time Saffie had noticed bruises on her following a visit from her husband and it was blatantly clear that the woman was afraid of him. He was a bully and Saffie strongly disliked him, not that she could ever voice it.

'Are you all right, ma'am?' she asked softly when she returned to the bed to place the tray across the small woman's lap.

'Yes, Saffie, I'm fine.' Mrs Spencer-Hughes had dispensed with calling her by her surname when they were alone some time ago, a sign that she now felt comfortable with her. 'I am really . . . it's just that Victor can be, er . . . a little rough.'

Saffie didn't reply as she went to fetch the clothes Mrs Spencer-Hughes would wear that day from the wardrobe. She was aware that it wasn't her place to comment and she never took advantage of the woman's kind nature.

Her friend, Mrs Parker-Bates, had visited twice more during the time Saffie had worked there and each time she had brought a letter for Mrs Spencer-Hughes, which she had immediately passed to Saffie to go and hide. Following the incident with Georgina the first time, she now hid the letters discreetly amongst her mistress's silken underwear in one of the drawers.

Saffie watched the woman push the food aimlessly about the plate before she thrust it away from her, saying in a shaky voice, 'Do you think you could organise a bath for me, please, Saffie? I think it might relax me a little. I'm not feeling too well.'

'Of course, ma'am,' Saffie answered obligingly. 'I'll go and ask the maids to carry the water up immediately.'

Minutes later the hip bath was placed in front of the fire in the bedroom and the maids began to carry up buckets of steaming water while Saffie organised some soft fluffy towels. She had found it quite embarrassing to help Mrs Spencer-Hughes bathe the first couple of times, but now she thought nothing of it and as she watched her mistress lower herself into the warm water she bit down on her lip as she noticed yet more bruises on her stomach and back.

'I can tell what you're thinking.'

Saffie blushed as she realised that Mrs Spencer-Hughes was watching her.

'As you've gathered, Victor can be . . . shall we say a little brutal?' Mrs Spencer-Hughes sighed. 'It wasn't always this way. In fact, when we first got married, we were very much in love and Victor was as gentle as a lamb. The trouble started after my first child, Margaret, was born. Victor had so longed for a son that he couldn't hide his disappointment and he paid her scant attention. The same thing happened when I had my sweet Elizabeth, and then when I had Georgina and the doctor told Victor that having any more children would be a risk to my health, he went into a depression. All his hopes for a son and heir died then and I don't think he's ever forgiven me.' She gave a wry smile as she sank down into the scented water. 'Oh, I know he has mistresses and to be honest, I don't mind. At least while he has a woman on the go, he leaves me alone.'

'Oh *ma'am*.' Saffie felt so sorry for her that there was a catch in her voice.

Eugenie heard it and regarded her thoughtfully for a moment before saying gently, 'You're a sweet young woman, Saffie. I understand now why Marcus thinks so highly of you.' And she further shocked Saffie when she went on, 'You must wonder who it is who writes to me at my dear friend's address?'

Saffie flushed uncomfortably. 'Not at all, that's none of my business, ma'am.'

Mrs Spencer-Hughes's gaze didn't leave her face as she said quietly, 'Would I be right in thinking that I can trust you, my dear?'

Without hesitation, Saffie nodded. During the time she had worked at Lakeside House the rest of the household and Georgina had treated her abominably but Mrs Spencer-Hughes had never treated her with anything other than respect and kindness, and Saffie was fond of her.

'I thought as much; I'm usually a pretty good judge of character.' Mrs Spencer-Hughes smiled at her before lowering her voice and going on, 'Were you aware that my firstborn was disinherited and ran away when she fell in love with a man her father didn't approve of?'

Saffie felt there was no reason to lie and nodded. 'Yes, I did hear something to that effect.'

'Hm . . .' Eugenie stared off into space as her mind went back in time. 'Margaret has always kept in touch with me,' she confided. 'Although it would be more than my life was worth should Victor ever find out. That's why she sends her letters to my friend's address.'

'I see.' Saffie's mind was racing. Marcus had been right about Margaret still being alive.

'Unfortunately, not long after Margaret and her husband were wed, he was killed in an accident,' Mrs Spencer-Hughes went on. 'She was living in Cornwall until she became ill.' She blinked back tears. 'In her last letter she informed me that she is now living in a small village close to Skegness.

The doctor who is tending her recommended she go there because the air is said to be bracing.'

'I . . . I'm sorry to hear that.' Saffie's voice came out as a croak. 'Do you have any idea what is wrong with her?'

'She went down with lung fever, God help her, and it has left her with a very weak chest.' The tears were raining down the woman's cheeks now and Saffie felt even more sorry for her. But she also found it strange that Mrs Spencer-Hughes hadn't mentioned Cathy. Surely if she was her only grand-child, she would have been concerned about her?

'Luckily I have a small inheritance left to me by my grandmother and I have been able to pay for her treat-ment without my husband's knowledge, and I've managed to visit her each year. But as time goes by I miss her more and more, and long for her to be able to come back to me.'

There was silence for a time until Mrs Spencer-Hughes suggested, 'Would you be willing to come with me, if I could organise it? I thought I could tell my husband that I feel in need of a little holiday. I can't see that he would object to that, and of course he would expect me to take you along to cater to my needs. My last maid, Daisy, accompanied me each year and my husband never objected, because thank-fully he never realised where I was going.'

'In that case . . . I . . . well, yes I suppose so.' Saffie was so shocked that she could barely get her words out.

'Of course, we would have to be very careful. Should Georgina get wind of what I was planning to do she would break her neck to tell her father.' The woman sighed as she sat up in the water. 'I've long thought that Georgina sus-pects I have kept in touch with her oldest sister and she wouldn't be at all happy at the idea of her returning to the fold. You see, with Margaret gone and my poor Elizabeth deceased she is now the heir to the house and everything my husband owns, and she's well aware of it. For some reason she's always been closer to her father than either of the other two girls, possibly because they are so alike in nature. I love her dearly, of course I do, but I am also aware of her faults, and spite and greed are but two of them.'

Saffie didn't quite know how to respond so she said nothing, and as her mistress rose from the water, she wrapped a huge warm towel about her.

'So, Saffie, will you at least think about it?'

Saffie nodded. 'Of course, ma'am. In actual fact, it would be quite an adventure for me. You see, although I was brought up on the canals, I have never seen the sea and it's always been an ambition of mine to do so.'

'There we are then.' Mrs Spencer-Hughes smiled at her warmly and for now the subject was dropped, although it left Saffie with a lot to think about.

On the way to visit Minnie, Davey and the girls the following Sunday, Saffie called in to see Marcus. He greeted her warmly but she couldn't help but notice the dark circles beneath his eyes, and his usual sparkle was gone.

'Come into the drawing room,' he invited. 'Mathilda is having a lie-down. I'm afraid she tires rather easily since . . . Anyway, come along in.'

Once inside, Saffie stared at him nervously.

'Well? I was rather hoping Eugenie would confide in you once she got to know you.' He smiled at her encouragingly. 'Has she?'

'She has . . . but I told her that she could trust me.'

He nodded. 'I quite understand, but surely if you told me what was said you would be breaking your promise for the greater good. And this could bring us a step closer to finding out if Cathy really is your grandfather's daughter.'

Saffie realised he was right and so she hesitantly told him all that had been said.

'Well, it sounds like we may be able to solve the mystery of Cathy's parentage sooner rather than later,' Marcus remarked when she'd finished.

'But if it's as we think, what should we do about it?' she asked.

'Let's cross that bridge when and if we come to it. I do realise that it could be opening a hornet's nest.'

Saffie raised her eyebrows. 'What do you mean?'

'For a start, your grandmother has forfeited her right to your grandfather's estate now that Cathy is no longer able to live there. Something your grandmother was unaware of until I enlightened her after she threatened to send Cathy to the workhouse. She is, of course, allowed to live there until her death, but it is no longer her house to gift. In fact, according to the will, the estate should have passed to your mother. Which means, now that she is no longer here, by rights it should belong to you as her eldest child. But I imagine that if we can prove Cathy is your grandfather's child, she would inherit over you.'

Saffie shrugged. She hadn't given the financial side of affairs any thought. And as for owning the house . . . well, with her grandmother still living there, whether she owned it or not made no difference since she could never live there while Clara was in residence. The woman clearly couldn't stand her. In any case, it had never entered her head that she might inherit anything at all.

'If Cathy is the one entitled to inherit then that is fine,' she assured him.

Marcus was about to lift the bell to summon the maid to bring them some tea but Saffie stayed him. 'Please, you don't have to order anything for me. I'm on my way to see Minnie, Davey and the girls and I only popped in to give you an update on the way.'

He nodded. 'I think we've taken a major step forward to learning the truth, well done,' he said. 'But when is Eugenie thinking of leaving for this, er . . . holiday?'

'From the way she spoke, I believe it will be sooner rather than later – after all, we're into September already and if she wants to pass the visit off as a holiday it would be more believable if she wished to take it in the good weather.'

'Quite right,' he agreed. 'But do be careful. What I mean is, Georgina would do anything to stop Margaret reclaiming her rightful place in the family and if she should guess that you're going to see her sister . . . Well, there's no saying what she might do. I wouldn't trust her as far as I could throw her, so do take care.' He took hold of her hand, gazing into her face earnestly.

Saffie looked back at him, and for a moment, found she was frozen to the spot as the strangest tingly feeling ran up her arm. She felt a flush rising up her cheeks and hastily pulled away, flustered.

'I, er . . . I'd better be off now.' Suddenly wanting to put some distance between them, she quickly made for the door. 'Do give my love to Mathilda, and should we leave before

I have a chance to see you again, I'll try and write to you to keep you informed of what's going on.'

'Splendid. But remember, take care of yourself, my dear.' He saw her right to the door and once he had closed it behind her, she let out a deep breath. Feeling warm, she removed her bonnet and took the pins from her hair, letting her jet-black locks tumble down her back as she tried to analyse what had just happened.

Marcus must be at least fifteen years older than me, she thought as she wandered along swinging her bonnet by its ribbons. *And he's married to a woman I like very much!* But as her arm tingled again with the memory of how her hand had felt wrapped in his large one, there was no denying to herself that she did feel strongly attracted to him. She closed her eyes, mortified that she should be thinking of Marcus in this way and terrified that she might somehow give herself away one day.

She fretted about her feelings all the way to Minnie's but once she reached the cottage there was no time to think of anything but the two little girls who almost dragged her inside as they gave her a rapturous welcome.

'Eeh, yer lookin' well.' Minnie beamed at her as she wrapped her in a bear hug. 'I reckon workin' up at the big 'ouse must suit yer, lass.'

Saffie just smiled. She didn't dare tell Minnie that the majority of the staff still treated her like she was dirt on their shoes, because Minnie would no doubt be up there like a shot from a gun to give them a piece of her mind, which could only make matters worse.

They all had tea and scones, which Minnie had baked especially, and then Davey took the girls into the orchard to pick some apples for pies and at last Saffie was able to tell Minnie about the planned visit to Margaret. She hated breaking the promise she had made to Eugenie but now that she had told Marcus she felt that Minnie had a right to know too.

'Let's just pray as yer can get to the bottom o' things while yer there an' that little Cathy an' her mam can be reunited,' Minnie said worriedly. She loved Cathy as if she was her own child and the same went for Sylvie. She couldn't imagine living without either of them, although she would if it was for the best for them.

'And have any of Sylvie's relatives come forward to claim her yet?' Saffie asked as she sipped at her second cup of tea.

Minnie shook her head. 'No, Marcus 'as put the word around but nobody's laid claim to 'er as yet. She started back to school last week an' young Cathy went wi' her an' loved it. Marcus reckons she's as sharp as a knife now she's come out o' her shell a bit, bless 'er. I reckon we 'ave young Sylvie to thank for that. It'd be 'ard not to respond to Sylvie. I 'ave to say, Marcus 'as been kindness itself: he takes the girls to school wi' him every mornin' an' drops 'em off to me in the afternoon to make sure they get 'ome safe. He even paid fer a funeral fer Sylvie's mam. Nothin' flash, mind, just plain an' simple. He's a good man, ain't he?'

Saffie nodded and lowered her head, but not before Minnie had seen the flush that rose in her cheeks. It concerned her. Surely Saffie couldn't have developed a soft spot for him? For Saffie's sake she sincerely hoped not because nothing good could come from it. But all she could do was bide her time and hope that she was mistaken.

Chapter Thirty-Four

As Saffie loaded the last of Mrs Spencer-Hughes's clothes into the trunk, she could hear the carriage horses restlessly pawing the ground below the bedroom window, as they waited to take them to the station.

'I think that's it, ma'am.' She snapped the lid of the trunk down and secured it while Mrs Spencer-Hughes jammed an evil-looking hat pin into the enormous hat she was wearing. It was an elaborate affair trimmed with silk roses and feathers in a fetching shade of sea green that exactly matched the travelling costume she was wearing.

'Good, I'll get the footman to carry that down then we must be off, otherwise we're going to miss the train,' Mrs Spencer-Hughes fretted. She had been a bag of nerves ever since waking that morning and now the nerves were beginning to rub off on Saffie.

They left the bedroom together and almost collided with Georgina who was walking along the landing in a silky peignoir trimmed with feathers.

'Off now, are you, Mother dear?' she drawled sarcastically.

'Yes, I am . . . and do please put something decent on,' her mother implored. 'It isn't right to float about in that . . . that . . . outfit in front of the male staff.' She waggled a finger at Georgina's night attire disapprovingly.

'Oh, don't be such a prude, Mama,' Georgina sneered. And narrowing her eyes, she asked slyly, 'Papa and I were wondering why, after going to Cornwall for the last couple of years, you've suddenly decided to go to Skegness?'

'I suppose I just fancied a change. They do say a change is as good as a rest, don't they?'

Georgina eyed her suspiciously for a moment but then with a toss of her head she went on her way while Eugenie gripped the banister rail to compose herself.

'Are you all right, ma'am?' Saffie asked anxiously and after a moment her employer nodded and gave her a weak smile.

'Perfectly. Now let's be on our way or we really will miss that train.'

The journey included a change of trains at Lincoln, which proved to be quite stressful as Saffie had to run about the platform trying to find a porter to move the mountain of Mrs Spencer-Hughes's luggage. She was sure she had brought enough clothes to last her for years let alone a few weeks, but it wasn't her place to question it. Eventually she found one and when the burly man had piled the trunks and cases onto a low trolley he followed the women to the platform where they would catch the next train to Skegness. By that time Saffie was beginning to get excited at the prospect of seeing the sea. Of course, she had seen pictures of it in numerous books but now she was looking forward to seeing it in real life.

She would have liked to leave the station to visit Lincoln Cathedral, another place she had always longed to visit, but there was no time, so instead she and Mrs Spencer-Hughes were directed to tea rooms at the end of the platform while the porter stood guard over their luggage.

Once the train chugged into the station in a smog of steam and smoke, the man loaded the luggage into the guard van, and after tipping him generously, Mrs Spencer-Hughes and Saffie boarded the train for the last leg of their journey.

Saffie peered from the window excitedly.

'You'll notice the land is becoming much flatter,' Mrs Spencer-Hughes informed her indulgently. 'It isn't as hilly here as it is back at home in Warwickshire.'

Saffie would have liked to ask questions about where they were going and when they might get to see Margaret, but Mrs Spencer-Hughes was staring pensively from the window now, and not wishing to disturb her, Saffie stayed silent.

At last, they pulled into a station and Mrs Spencer-Hughes informed her, 'This is it, dear, lift my travelling bag down from the luggage rack, would you?'

As the train slowed, they could hear the sound of the doors being opened for people to alight and once they were sure they had everything, they too stepped down onto the platform. The first thing Saffie noticed was the smell. The air smelled salty and fresh and as Mrs Spencer-Hughes noticed her sniffing, she smiled. 'It's the sea air,' she said. 'Victor and I brought all our girls for a holiday here when they were small and we had a wonderful time.' She was silent for a moment as her mind slipped back to happier times but then with a determined effort, she brought her thoughts back to the present and asked Saffie, 'Would you try to find us a porter again, dear?'

As it happened, Saffie didn't have to because at that moment one approached them. The porters here did very well from the tips they earned from the holidaymakers and were always keen to help.

'Our luggage is in the guard van,' Mrs Spencer-Hughes told him. 'And once we have it all could you direct us to a carriage to take us to our hotel?'

'Aye, wi' pleasure, ma'am.' By the cut of her clothes and from the way she spoke he could tell that this was a lady of quality so he was hoping for a decent tip from this one and couldn't be obliging enough.

At last, the luggage was loaded onto yet another trolley and he led them towards the exit. Saffie looked about excitedly, but there was no sign of the sea from there so she knew she was going to have to be patient for a while longer. Outside the station was a row of horses and hackney carriages and as Mrs Spencer-Hughes approached the driver of one of them to tell him where they wanted to go, the porter loaded the luggage onto the back of the carriage, asking Saffie in a friendly fashion, 'Here on holiday wi' yer mother, are yer, miss?'

'Oh, she isn't my mother,' Saffie told him hastily. 'I'm Mrs Spencer-Hughes's maid and no, we're not exactly on holiday. We're here to visit someone.' Suddenly she realised that she might be saying too much so she quickly closed her mouth and stood quietly until the last of the luggage had been safely transferred.

'There you are, my good man. Many thanks for your help.' Mrs Spencer-Hughes pressed a sum of money into his hand that had him smiling from ear to ear as he tipped his cap at them, then she ushered Saffie ahead of her into the carriage.

'Am I allowed to know exactly where we're going?' Saffie asked as the horses set off at a trot.

'Of course. We're going to a small town called Mable-thorpe, which is the other side of Ingoldmells. And' – Mrs Spencer-Hughes smiled at her indulgently – 'I've asked the driver to take us along the coastal road so you should get your first glimpse of the sea in the next few minutes.'

Saffie's eyes grew wide as the coach rattled along and minutes later it turned on to the sea front and at last, she got her first glimpse of the sea. She gasped with delight. Never in her wildest dreams had she ever imagined it would be so vast. It stretched away into the distance seemingly forever, and on the broad sandy beach late holidaymakers were making the most of the last of the good weather. Children paddled and splashed in the sea, while others were busily making sand-castles, and parents were relaxing on deckchairs and bright towels stretched out across the sand.

'Oh . . . it's so . . . so *big*!'

Mrs Spencer-Hughes smiled to see Saffie so happy. She had always seemed such a sensible, grown-up young woman but now for the first time she saw the child that was still left in her and it did her heart good. Marcus had confided what a terrible time Saffie had had of it during the months before she had come to work for her, and Mrs Spencer-Hughes hoped that this short break would do her good and help to heal the pain that she must have suffered after losing her family the way she had.

Further along, Saffie saw some donkeys with children riding on them along the edge of the water and a little further on still she saw a Punch and Judy kiosk set up with a row of happy children perched in front of it.

'Oh, my younger twin sisters would *so* love this,' she chirped happily, but suddenly remembering who she was talking to she gave Mrs Spencer-Hughes an apologetic glance. 'Sorry, ma'am. I forgot myself for a moment.'

'Don't be.' Mrs Spencer-Hughes smiled. 'It's nice to see you enjoying yourself.'

For the rest of the journey, Saffie was so entranced by the view from the window that she almost forgot Mrs Spencer-Hughes was there. They passed through a town called Ingoldmells and another called Chapel St Leonards, but eventually the carriage turned off the coast road and after a short time it stopped in front of a modest hotel.

'This is where we'll be staying,' Mrs Spencer-Hughes informed her as the driver jumped down from his seat and hurried to open the door for them. 'But I shouldn't expect too much. The larger, more luxurious hotels are in Skegness, but I'm sure this will suffice.'

The driver was now unpacking the mountain of luggage for them and carrying it into a small but spotlessly clean foyer. When it was done, Mrs Spencer-Hughes paid him handsomely, then rang the small bell on the desk. Almost instantly a lady appeared. Although she looked to be quite old with grey hair tied neatly into a bun on the back of her head, she was sprightly and her eyes twinkled in her plump face as she smiled at them.

'Good afternoon. You must be Mrs Spencer-Hughes and Miss Doyle,' she greeted them affably. 'I have your rooms all ready for you. If you'd like to follow me, I shall show them to you. Oh, and I'm Mrs Hawkins, by the way.'

Mrs Spencer-Hughes hesitated as she glanced at their luggage but the landlady assured her, 'Don't worry about that, my dear. Arthur, my husband, will carry it upstairs for you.'

She led them up a narrow staircase that opened on to a surprisingly spacious landing and pointed to two doors. 'I've put you in adjoining rooms. I do hope that's all right.' She flung the first room open and Mrs Spencer-Hughes walked in and quickly looked about. It was nowhere near as grand as her room back at home but the bed linen was snowy white and everywhere was spotless.

'This will do admirably.'

The landlady flushed at the praise. 'Excellent. And now perhaps you'd like to see your room, my dear?'

'Yes, please.' Saffie followed her to the room next door and once Mrs Hawkins had unlocked the door, she found herself in a room almost identical to Mrs Spencer-Hughes's, the only difference being that this room was decorated in shades of pale grey whereas her mistress's room was done in shades of lilac and lavender.

'It's lovely,' Saffie told her and then left to return to Mrs Spencer-Hughes. By then Arthur was labouring up the stairs with the first lot of luggage.

'Now for the house rules,' Mrs Hawkins told her as Mrs Spencer-Hughes removed her hat. 'Breakfast is served between seven and eight in the morning. The dining room is the second door on the left in the hallway. Dinner is served each evening between six and seven.' She fumbled in her pocket and produced two keys, which she handed over to her guests. 'Here are your room keys and I do prefer to have my guests back in the house by ten thirty at night. Finally, may I ask how long you think you might be staying?'

'Hm, I should think for at least three to four weeks, if that is all right?'

'Perfectly. The rush of holidaymakers has long since slowed down and there isn't such a demand for rooms at this time of year. But anyway, I'm sure you must be thirsty after your journey so I'll pop down and make you both a nice tray of tea to keep you going until dinnertime.'

When the kindly woman had bustled away, Eugenie crossed to the window to watch the seagulls that were circling in the sky outside. Very soon she would see her firstborn again and she could hardly wait.

Saffie unpacked her mistress's clothes until it was time for dinner and they went down to the dining room together.

There were only two other tables taken in the dining room, the first by a family with two young children who were chattering excitedly about the things they had done that day, and the second by a young couple who could hardly take their eyes off each other.

'I think they might be on honeymoon,' Mrs Spencer-Hughes whispered with a smile and Saffie blushed. If the way they were staring at each other was anything to go by she had a feeling that Mrs Spencer-Hughes could be right.

The meal – a large meat and potato pie, roast potatoes and fresh vegetables – was home-made, simple and tasty, and it was followed by a jam roly-poly, thick creamy custard and a large pot of tea. It was nothing like the à-la-carte meals that Mrs Spencer-Hughes was served at home but it was extremely tasty and she enjoyed it all the same.

'Will you be going to see your daughter this evening?' Saffie enquired as they tucked in.

'I think so.' Mrs Spencer-Hughes paused to dab at her lips with a napkin. 'I wasn't planning to go until the morning but I find now that I'm here I'd like to.'

'Would you like me to come with you or stay here and unpack the rest of your clothes, ma'am?'

Mrs Spencer-Hughes smiled. 'Actually, I'd like to go alone for the first time. And I was thinking you might like the evening off to do a little exploring? It is your first time at the seaside after all, and the rest of the clothes can be unpacked in the morning after breakfast.'

'Really?' Saffie was as excited as a child and it showed in the sparkle in her eye. 'Then thank you very much, ma'am. I shan't be late back, I promise. I'll be here to help you get ready for bed.'

'I'm sure I shall manage perfectly well for one night,' Mrs Spencer-Hughes said. 'So just go and enjoy yourself, but take care, mind.'

'Oh, I shall,' Saffie assured her, and suddenly she could hardly wait to leave the table. Her only regret was that Lucy and Ginny weren't there to share the experience with her. She was sure they would have loved the seaside as much as she did. Still, at least she knew that they were safe back in Banbury with Granny Doyle and she didn't intend to let anything spoil this special time.

Chapter Thirty-Five

Once Mrs Spencer-Hughes had set off for the nursing home, Saffie quickly put on her bonnet and shawl and went to explore. The high street was much like in any other town: there was a butcher's shop, a bakery, two inns, a hardware store, a dress shop, and set amongst them were the shops selling buckets and spades, and knick-knacks for the holidaymakers to take home as gifts.

Most of them were closed by that time but Saffie enjoyed peering into the shop windows. At the end of the high street was a sharp rise leading up to the seafront and once she had climbed it, she gasped at the panorama spread out before her. A path led all along the front for as far as she could see and concrete steps led down to a beach of soft, white sand. Mrs Spencer-Hughes had told her that from here you could walk for miles, even as far as Hull if you wished, and now Saffie believed her.

The tide was in and the frothy white waves breaking on the shore were so irresistible that she sat down and removed her shoes and stockings. She knew it was a very unladylike thing to do but she couldn't resist it and thankfully, as there was hardly anyone left on the beach apart from the odd person walking their dog, she doubted if anyone would notice.

The sand was still warm as it slid between her toes and she laughed with delight as she lifted her skirts and tripped to the water's edge. She spent some time giggling as the waves ebbed and flowed across her feet and then she began to walk along the waterline, admiring the sand dunes. They were covered in plants, including marram grass that danced in the wind, sea holly and creeping buttercups, as well as many others that she couldn't identify. The further she walked the quieter it became until there was no one else in sight and she sighed with pleasure. But the sky was darkening, so reluctantly she turned and began the long walk back.

Once she reached the steps in Mablethorpe again, she hastily brushed the sand from her feet, put her shoes back on, leaving the stockings in her pocket, and shook her skirts before setting off back to the hotel. She could quite happily have stayed on the beach all night but she didn't want to break her promise to Mrs Spencer-Hughes.

The woman was already back when Saffie entered the lounge of the hotel and she smiled when she saw Saffie's bright eyes and rosy cheeks. 'Come and join me, dear,' she invited. 'And have some of this tea. I fear if I drink all this, I shall be up half the night on the chamber pot.' She quickly poured out a cup for Saffie and asked, 'And how did you like the beach?'

'Oh, ma'am . . .' Saffie hardly knew how to describe how wonderful it had been. 'It . . . it was just incredible.'

'And did you see any seals?'

Saffie frowned. 'Seals?'

'Yes, Seal Island is not too far out to sea from here. On a clear day you can just about see it and sometimes in the early evening, if you're lucky, you might see the babies playing on the beach.'

'Really?' To Saffie the place was becoming more magical by the minute. 'Look . . .' She took a handful of shells from one of her pockets. 'I collected these on the beach. And I saw a crab too in one of the little rock pools that the sea left behind. I've only ever seen them on a marble slab in the fishmonger's before.' But then she became solemn as she suddenly remembered why she was there and asked, 'And did you manage to see your daughter, ma'am?'

Mrs Spencer-Hughes nodded as she sipped at her second cup of tea, despite the advice she had given herself only moments before. 'Yes, I did, Saffie, thank you. And I have to say she doesn't look as bad as I expected. In fact, I thought she was looking much better than the last time I saw her. I think the sea air here must be doing her good. I've arranged to go back in the morning and spend most of the day with her. I may as well while I have the opportunity. Perhaps you would like to come along and meet her?'

'Yes, of course, I would like to very much,' Saffie answered, suddenly feeling guilty. She had promised Minnie and Marcus that she would find out whether there was a connection between Cathy and Margaret, but she had been so busy enjoying herself that she hadn't even thought about it till now. And yet if there was a connection, she found it increasingly strange that Mrs Spencer-Hughes had never once mentioned her. After all, if Cathy was Margaret's child it would make her Mrs Spencer-Hughes's granddaughter, and surely she would want to care for her?

They finished their tea in silence and retired. It had been a long day and they were both tired. In fact, Saffie could

333

hardly stop yawning, but despite her employer's reassurance that she could manage perfectly well, Saffie insisted on helping her undress for bed and hanging her clothes away before she went to her own room. Once there she opened the window as wide as it would go and hung over the sill, drawing in deep breaths of the salty air until exhaustion finally claimed her and she fell into bed and was fast asleep before her head had time to hit the pillow.

Saffie slept like a log and it was only the sound of a bell ringing the next morning that woke her. With a guilty start she realised that it must be the kindly landlady announcing that breakfast was served. Hopping out of bed, she pulled her clothes on and tugged a brush through her hair before racing next door to help Mrs Spencer-Hughes. But she needn't have worried as the woman was already dressed and just putting the last pins into her hair.

'Oh, I'm so sorry, ma'am.' Saffie was embarrassed. She had never overslept like that before. 'I think it must have been the sea air and the travelling.'

Mrs Spencer-Hughes laughed. She was in a good mood at the prospect of seeing her daughter again. 'Don't worry about it. I could have knocked for you had I needed to. I'm quite capable of seeing to myself. But now let's go and see what Mrs Hawkins has in store for us for breakfast. Oh, and by the way, you might like to change out of your uniform dress when we've eaten. I see no reason why you should have to wear it while we're here.'

'Thank you, ma'am.' Saffie instantly thought of the pretty gown Minnie had helped her to make. It was white cotton with little sprigs of rosebuds all over it and as yet she hadn't had the chance to wear it.

The breakfast was just as delicious as the meal the night before and soon they were tucking into bacon, eggs, mushrooms, sausages and thick slices of crispy fried bread, all washed down with as much sweet tea as they could drink.

'Goodness, I shall be as fat as a pig by the time we go home,' Saffie commented as she patted her full stomach.

They went to Mrs Spencer-Hughes's room when they had finished where Saffie continued to unpack her mistress's clothes before shooting off to her own room to change. Once dressed in the pretty gown and with her silken hair hanging down her back like a black velvet cloak, Saffie really felt as if she was truly on holiday.

Soon it was time to visit Margaret and they set off side by side. 'It isn't far,' Mrs Spencer-Hughes said as they made their way down the high street. 'She's in a small nursing home in Quebec Road. I'm sure you'll like it as her room overlooks the sea.'

Eventually they came to a drive that led steeply upwards towards a large house surrounded by trees. After ringing the bell, they were admitted by a young nurse in a starched white cap and apron who led them upstairs to Margaret's room.

'Matron said to expect you,' she said pleasantly as they moved along a lengthy landing. 'So, are you both family?'

'Oh no,' Saffie said quickly, feeling slightly embarrassed. 'I'm actually Mrs Spencer-Hughes's maid.'

'I see.' The nurse looked surprised as she looked at Saffie's pretty gown and her hair hanging loose but she made no comment.

'Here we are.' She stopped at a door and after tapping on it she opened it for them. 'Do enjoy your visit. I'll bring you up some tea and biscuits at eleven.'

After the enormous breakfast, Saffie doubted she would ever eat again but she smiled as they were ushered into the room. Just as Mrs Spencer-Hughes had said there was a glorious view of the sea from the long window but Saffie barely glanced at it. She was too curious to meet Miss Margaret who was sitting up, propped by pillows, in a bed to one side of the room. At sight of her mother Margaret opened her arms and Mrs Spencer-Hughes went straight into her embrace. She was remarkably like her mother: the same smile, the same eyes and hair, and Saffie could almost believe she was looking at a younger version of Mrs Spencer-Hughes, although Margaret was pale and looked frail after such a long illness.

'And you must be Sapphire. Mama has told me all about you,' she said eventually with a warm smile. 'She says you take very good care of her, so thank you for that.'

Saffie shook her head, warming to the woman immediately. 'Actually, I think it's your mother who takes care of me,' she said with a twinkle in her eye.

Saffie went to stand by the window, content to let the two women catch up on all that had happened since they had been forced to live apart, and after a time she felt uncomfortably in the way. They clearly loved each other so much that they had almost forgotten she was even there.

'I don't suppose . . .' Margaret hesitated before rushing on. 'I don't suppose Father's feelings towards me have softened?'

Mrs Spencer-Hughes's face became solemn as she shook her head. 'I'm afraid not, darling. You know what he's like. Once he's made his mind up about something nothing will change it.'

'I see, so I am still dead to him then. Georgina must be happy about that.'

'Georgina is so like him in nature.' Mrs Spencer-Hughes shrugged. 'And now she's an heiress, she's had more interest from men than she's ever had before, and I think she fears that if you came back, that would change. And although it may sound cruel, I believe that could well be the case, because with her looks and nature they certainly weren't queuing for her before.'

'Poor thing,' Margaret said quietly. 'I'm sure she could improve her looks if she made a little more effort.'

They went on to speak of other things while Saffie admired the view. Margaret's room overlooked the sand dunes with the sea beyond and she felt that she could have stood there all day.

At lunchtime she and Mrs Spencer-Hughes left Margaret to have her meal in peace and strolled along the seafront.

'I'm actually delighted with the improvement in Margaret,' she said. 'And I believe if it wasn't for her father and Georgina I could care for her at home now, but I doubt very much if either of them will ever allow that to happen.'

There had not been a mention of Cathy and so Saffie suggested tentatively, 'Perhaps when she does come out of the nursing home, she might meet someone and have a family. She's still young enough, isn't she? And she's very pretty.'

'It's possible.'

But there was still no mention of Cathy and so for now Saffie had to swallow her impatience. They ate a light lunch in a small eating house in the high street and before returning to her daughter, Mrs Spencer-Hughes again gave Saffie the afternoon off to do as she pleased.

'But, ma'am, I've hardly done anything since we arrived,' Saffie pointed out. 'I really don't feel as if I'm earning my wages.'

'You are my companion for now and that is enough. Now off you go and enjoy yourself.'

And so that was exactly what Saffie did. She bought Minnie, Davey and the girls a little gift each, for when she went home, as well as something to send to the twins and Granny Doyle, and then strolled along the beach, enjoying the late afternoon sunshine. There was a nip in the air now and it was breezy but it didn't bother Saffie in the least, she would have happily walked the beach in a gale-force wind.

It was as she was returning to the boarding house for the evening meal that she got the most curious feeling that someone was following her and turning swiftly she glanced over her shoulder just in time to see someone enter a shop doorway a short way up the street. She shook her head and went on her way, wishing that she hadn't been blessed with such a fertile imagination.

Mrs Spencer-Hughes arrived back just as Saffie was making her way down to the dining room.

'I wish I could get my husband to forgive Margaret,' she confided in a low voice as they sat down at the table together. The family they had dined with the night before had gone home and only the honeymoon couple and themselves remained.

Saffie wasn't sure how to reply, so she remained quiet and was glad when the meal was over. Mrs Spencer-Hughes was clearly not in a happy mood.

'I think I shall have an early night, I have a bit of headache,' Mrs Spencer-Hughes declared over coffee, so after helping her mistress to get ready for bed, Saffie bade her goodnight and went to her own room to read a book she had luckily brought with her. She would have liked to go to the seafront again but didn't want to take advantage. Soon her eyelids were drooping, no doubt because of the fresh sea air, and she fell asleep.

In no time at all it seemed, the first week had passed. By then Saffie had explored every nook and cranny of the little town and she could happily have stayed there forever. Mrs Spencer-Hughes was spending every minute she could with her daughter at the nursing home but one evening she and Saffie returned to the hotel to find their landlady waiting for them with an anxious expression on her face.

'Is something wrong, Mrs Hawkins?' Mrs Spencer-Hughes asked with a frown.

'I fear there might be, dearie.' The kindly landlady fumbled in the pocket of her voluminous apron. 'This came for you about an hour or so since. I couldn't get it to you because I didn't know where you were.' She handed Mrs Spencer-Hughes a telegram.

Her face paled as she read it.

'Has something happened?' Saffie asked anxiously, and after taking a deep breath, Mrs Spencer-Hughes nodded.

'Yes, I'm afraid it has. M-my husband has had an accident and Georgina tells me I must go home immediately.'

Chapter Thirty-Six

'You'll not get a train back to the Midlands this evening, dearie,' Mrs Hawkins told Eugenie as she wrung her hands sympathetically.

'Oh!' Mrs Spencer-Hughes stood there speechless with shock for a moment, then pulling herself together with a great effort she told Saffie, 'Then we must be ready to leave at first light to get to the train station in Skegness. Could you start to pack while I go and organise a carriage?'

'Of course, but wouldn't you like me to come with you? It's dark now,' Saffie answered.

'There'll be no need for either of you to go. I'll get my Arthur to go and organise one for you,' Mrs Hawkins offered obligingly. And on a gentler note she told her guest, 'I'm so sorry, me dear. I hope when you get home your husband's accident isn't too serious.'

'That's very kind of you, Mrs Hawkins.' Mrs Spencer-Hughes ran her palms down the side of her skirt. 'In that case we may as well go into dinner as planned.'

She and Saffie went into the dining room and sat down at the table they had adopted as their own, but they both seemed to have lost their appetites.

'I shall have to go back to see Margaret after dinner and tell her what's happened,' Mrs Spencer-Hughes informed

Saffie solemnly. 'I can't just leave without saying goodbye. She would know there was something amiss and worry.'

'Of course, and I'll come with you.' Without thinking, Saffie reached out and took Mrs Spencer-Hughes's hand and the woman hung on to it as if it was a lifeline.

It had been a long time since she and her husband had been close. In fact, Victor was an arrogant bully, and yet she still didn't want anything bad to happen to him.

'Oh Mama, I hope he's all right,' Margaret said later that night when they called back to the nursing home. 'I wonder what's happened?'

'I have no idea but we'll find out soon enough.' Her mother was trying desperately hard to stay strong. 'I'm just so sorry that we have to cut our trip short. I so wanted to spend some more time with you.'

'I know but there will be other times.' Margaret kissed her cheek. 'But now you go and get ready to leave, and don't get worrying about me. I'm feeling better than I have for ages.'

They said a tearful goodbye and once back at the hotel, Mrs Hawkins told them that a carriage would arrive to take them to Skegness train station at seven the next morning and that there would be a train leaving for Lincoln at eleven.

'I shall be up bright and early to make sure you have a good breakfast before you leave,' she assured them kindly. 'I can't have you travelling all that way on empty stomachs.'

She was true to her word and the next morning both Saffie and Mrs Spencer-Hughes tried to do justice to the enormous breakfast she placed in front of each of them, although they failed dismally.

Mrs Spencer-Hughes paid their bill then and left a hefty tip, and soon after they were in the carriage on the first leg of their journey. They had arrived in sunshine but today was dark and dismal to match their mood. As the carriage rattled along the coast road, Saffie gazed sadly out at the crashing waves on the beach, wondering how long it would be before she might get the chance to see them again. The holiday had been magical to her and she knew she would never forget it.

It was early evening when the train chugged into Trent Valley Railway Station in Nuneaton and while Saffie organised a porter to get their luggage from the guard van, Mrs Spencer-Hughes went off to find a carriage.

'Soon be home now,' the woman said gently as Saffie stifled a yawn – all the travelling had tired her out. 'But I just wonder what I am going home to?'

As the carriage pulled into the long driveway leading to Lakeside House the branches of the trees bent towards them in the wind and Saffie shuddered. They were almost into October now; the first leaves were fluttering down and the weather had definitely taken a turn for the worse.

Within seconds of the carriage pulling up outside, the housekeeper, who must have been watching out for them, rushed out onto the steps to greet them.

'Oh ma'am, thank goodness you are home,' she gushed, wringing her hands together. 'We didn't know when to expect you or we would have sent the coach to meet you.'

'It's quite all right, Mrs Beasley.' Then looking towards Thomas, her husband's valet, who had also come out to join them, she told him, 'Could you organise getting the luggage inside please, Thomas.'

As she followed Mrs Beasley into the hallway, with Saffie close behind her, she drew off her gloves and took the pin from her hat. 'So, exactly what has happened, Mrs Beasley?'

Mrs Beasley opened her mouth to reply, but before she had the chance to, Georgina came hurtling down the stairs in a most unladylike manner.

'Ah, so you're back,' she said rather unnecessarily with a glare at Saffie. 'What took you so long? I sent the telegram yesterday afternoon.'

For once her mother was cool with her as she answered calmly, 'You might well have done but unfortunately, we were out when it arrived at the hotel, and by the time we received it last night it was too late to catch a train home. But never mind that – tell me what has happened and how is your father?'

'He fell down the stairs,' Georgina said quickly. 'I think he must have been drinking. I was in bed and it was very late when I heard a commotion and ran out of my room but he was already lying in the hallway. The doctor is with him now.'

Without a word Mrs Spencer-Hughes lifted her skirts and headed for her husband's room and after glaring at Saffie again, Georgina followed her.

Eugenie was shocked at the first sight of her husband. He was lying in bed with the doctor leaning over him and he looked ghastly. He had always been such a handsome, upright man but now he looked like a broken shadow of his former self. The left side of his face seemed to be pulled down, even his eye seemed to have drooped, and there was drool running down his chin, although he did seem to recognise her and

343

attempted to lift his hand. There was a cage over his legs and crossing the room she asked, 'How is he, Doctor?'

Before the doctor could answer the door barged open and Georgina appeared and instantly Victor became more agitated. The doctor turned and told her sternly, 'Please leave the room, miss. You are upsetting my patient!'

With a toss of her head, Georgina turned and left the room, slamming the door behind her so loudly that the sound echoed through the house.

'Perhaps I might speak to you in private, Mrs Spencer-Hughes.' The doctor took Eugenie's elbow and quickly marched her from the room and onto the landing where he shook his head. 'I don't know what that was all about. He becomes that way every time your daughter makes an appearance.'

'*Really?*' Eugenie was puzzled. Georgina had always been Victor's favourite so what could have happened to make him have such a change of heart? she wondered. But then she swallowed and asked, 'How is my husband, Dr Bell?'

He sighed. 'I'm afraid during the fall his leg was broken and he was knocked unconscious. That at least was a blessing because I was able to set his leg in splints while he was comatose. But unfortunately, I believe the shock of the fall has caused him to have an apoplectic attack and that is far more serious. At present he has lost all feeling down his left side.'

'But it *will* come back, won't it?' she asked anxiously.

'I'm afraid I have no way of knowing that, my dear.' He patted her arm, his eyes sympathetic. 'His condition is extremely serious at the moment. If you want me to be brutally honest, I must warn you that it could go either way. I would prefer to have him in hospital but I fear that trying to move him at present would bring on another seizure and that would doubtless prove to be fatal. He is going to need round-the-clock nursing and the next twenty-four hours will be crucial. If he can get through that there might be hope, but I fear he will never again be the man he was. I'm so sorry, Mrs Spencer-Hughes.'

Eugenie stood there in shock, trying to take it in. But then pulling herself together with an obvious effort, she nodded. 'Thank you for your honesty, Doctor. And don't worry, he will be well taken care of.'

'Good, good.' The doctor briefly returned to the bedroom to collect his bag and after wishing her a good day and promising to be back the next morning he went on his way.

When he had gone, she stood there for a time before entering Victor's bedroom again. With tears in her eyes, she took his good hand and squeezed it. They had not been close for some long time now, but nevertheless she hated seeing him reduced to what he was now. He had always been such an energetic, vibrant man.

'Don't worry, my dear. We'll get you well again,' she whispered.

Once more he became agitated as his head thrashed from side to side and he tried to speak. 'G . . . Ge . . .' His voice was strangled and she shushed him.

'Now don't try to speak just yet; you must save your strength and concentrate on getting better,' she scolded gently but still he tried to say something, his voice nothing more than a gurgle.

After a few minutes she lay his hand on the bed and made for the door, promising, 'I shall be back very shortly. Try to get some sleep.' And with that she hurried to her room where she found Saffie unpacking her clothes.

'How is he, ma'am?'

Mrs Spencer-Hughes sighed as she swiped a hand across her weary eyes. She could see dark days ahead for them – if Victor survived that was. He was clearly not going to be a good patient. She briefly told Saffie what the doctor had said and the girl instantly offered, 'I could help with the nursing, ma'am. I looked after my mother when she was poorly and you can't do it all alone, otherwise you'd be ill too, unless you're thinking of getting a nurse in?'

'I had entertained the idea briefly,' Mrs Spencer-Hughes admitted as the tears she had bravely held back finally snaked down her pale cheeks. 'The problem is, knowing my husband as I do, I fear a stranger would make him worse. He has always been a very vain, proud man and he won't want people to see him like this.'

Saffie nodded understandingly. 'Then we shall do it together,' she promised and once more her employer blessed the day that Marcus had recommended Saffie to her.

For the rest of the evening, Saffie and Mrs Spencer-Hughes took it in turns to sit by the master's bed, trying to tempt him with the chicken broth Cook had made especially for him, or giving him sips of water. All was well for the most part, until Georgina attempted to enter the room, when once more he would start to thrash about and become agitated again.

'I really can't understand it,' Mrs Spencer-Hughes confided to Saffie. 'Victor has always openly favoured Georgina above all the other children so why should he suddenly take against her now?'

'It could be that he isn't quite in his right mind. I dare say things will change as he starts to improve,' Saffie comforted her, although she had grave doubts about whether Mr Spencer-Hughes would even survive.

They continued to sit beside him all through the long night that followed but as it progressed, he seemed to develop a high temperature and Mrs Spencer-Hughes grew even more concerned. It was as she was gently mopping his brow that a thought suddenly occurred to her and she frowned. Georgina had said that she'd found her father after hearing a commotion on the stairs but how could she have done? Her room was at the other end of the long landing and it was highly unlikely that she would have heard anything from there. Still, she decided, now was not the time to dwell on it. There would be time to speak to Georgina when the crisis was over.

Saffie came to relieve her mistress at three in the morning when the wind was howling around the house and shaking the window frames as if it was trying to gain entry.

'I'll take over now, ma'am,' she told her. 'You go and try to get a little sleep.' Mrs Spencer-Hughes looked totally worn out.

'Oh . . . I don't know if I should leave him,' the woman said uncertainly.

'I promise if he gets any worse, I shall fetch you straight-away,' Saffie assured her and so Mrs Spencer-Hughes reluctantly did as she was told, although she doubted she would sleep, as exhausted as she was. There was just something about this whole accident that didn't sit quite right with her, but as yet she couldn't decide what it was. Even so within minutes of lying on the bed, she slipped into an uneasy doze and when Bossy wakened her with a tray of tea the next morning she started.

'Oh dear, what time is it?' she asked worriedly as she swung her legs over the side of the bed. She had slept in her clothes and now her gown was crumpled and the pins had escaped from her hair. 'I fear I've overslept and left poor Saffie to care for my husband all alone.'

'It's all right, ma'am.' Bossy poured out a cup of tea and handed it to her. 'I just took her some tea in too an' I'm pleased to say the master seems a bit calmer this mornin'. Saffie says his temperature seems to 'ave gone down a bit.'

'Thank goodness.' Mrs Spencer-Hughes sipped at the tea. 'But now I really must go in to him. Saffie will be exhausted.' And after draining the cup she hurried along the landing. What was it the doctor had said? 'The next twenty-four hours will be crucial.' Well, it looked like he was going to manage that so perhaps there was hope for him after all.

She realised now that the night before she hadn't expected him to survive and a shiver of guilt passed through her as she was forced to admit to herself that she wasn't at all sure that she had wanted him to.

Chapter Thirty-Seven

The rest of the week passed painfully slowly as Mrs Spencer-Hughes and Saffie took turns at nursing the master. Thankfully he appeared to be no worse, although if asked they would both have been forced to admit that there was little sign of improvement either. He still got agitated every time Georgina attempted to enter the room and so for now Mrs Spencer-Hughes had forbidden her to try.

'What time did the accident happen?' Mrs Spencer-Hughes asked Mrs Beasley one morning as she was going to relieve Saffie.

'All I can tell you is it was about midnight.' Mrs Beasley shook her head. 'The first I knew of it was when Miss Georgina came to wake me to tell me she thought her father had fallen down the stairs and that she thought he was dead. Of course, I hurried to check and when I found that he was breathing I sent the groom for the doctor straightaway.'

'But you didn't actually hear anything?'

'Nothing.'

'Hm, thank you, Mrs Beasley.'

That afternoon she found Georgina reading in the drawing room and she asked her, 'Georgina, the night of the accident, what did you actually hear?'

...rgina glared at her suspiciously. 'Well, I . . . er . . . ...d a bit of a commotion as Father came upstairs – he'd been drinking all night in his study. Marcus was with him at one point. Anyway, he was clattering about and I came out to see what the noise was and that was . . . when he fell.'

Her mother narrowed her eyes as her daughter stared calmly back at her. 'How strange. The carpet runner we have all up the stairs is so thick that I'm surprised you could hear anything, particularly from your room – it's so far away from the staircase.'

'Ah . . . actually, I was getting up anyway as it happens. I wanted to go down to the kitchen for a drink.'

'But the maid always leaves you a jug of water on the bedside table, doesn't she?'

Georgina swallowed nervously as she averted her eyes. 'Er . . . yes, she does, but I fancied a cup of tea.'

'In the early hours of the morning?'

On the defensive now, Georgina scowled. 'What's wrong with that? Don't you believe me?'

'I'm just trying to find out what might have caused the accident,' her mother told her. 'But anyway, I'll leave you to your reading now.'

Georgina stared at the door for a long time after her mother had left, but eventually she returned to her book.

Marcus came to see them that afternoon. Georgina had gone riding and Mrs Spencer-Hughes was sitting with her husband so it was Saffie who went to him in the drawing room.

'You look tired,' he greeted her and she smiled.

'I could say the same about you.'

He nodded. 'I am rather tired as it happens. Mathilda isn't sleeping well at all. The doctor has given her some sleeping draughts but she doesn't seem keen on taking them.' He sat down, his hands joined between his knees, and lowering his head he confided, 'As you are aware, she's taken the loss of the baby very badly but now that the doctor has advised her not to try for another one she's even worse. Added to that she's having lots of . . .' He looked embarrassed. 'Shall we say "women's problems". I'm sure she'll explain better than I can when you manage to see her. She would come here but she isn't up to it, I'm afraid. But anyway, that's enough about our problems. How is Victor?'

Saffie shook her head. 'Not good at all, I'm afraid, although he does seem to be holding his own now. When we first got back it was touch and go and of course there's always the chance that he could have another seizure and if he did . . .' When her voice trailed away, he pursed his lips.

'It seems very strange to me,' he said thoughtfully. 'Him falling down the stairs like that, I mean. I've known Victor drink most men under the table and still be able to ride his horse home, and he was perfectly fine when I left him.'

Saffie shrugged. 'Perhaps he slipped or something. We'll never know unless he improves enough to tell us. I suppose it was just lucky that Georgina was here to find him when she did.'

'Hm, lucky indeed seeing as she had only got home that day.'

'Got home?'

'Yes, she went off somewhere the day after you and Eugenie left without saying where she was going. Enough about her, though, did you meet Margaret?'

Saffie smiled. 'Yes, I did, and she's so nice. Her mother was so sad that we had to cut our visit to her short but it couldn't be helped.'

'And did she mention Cathy?'

'I'm afraid not, not once, although I mentioned that a child called Cathy was living with Minnie and Davey for the time being.'

Disappointment clouded his face. 'Aw well, you did your best.'

It was then that they saw Georgina galloping her horse down the drive. The poor beast was frothing at the mouth, and Marcus shook his head. 'She's a cruel madam, she is,' he said in disgust. 'She shouldn't be allowed to own an animal.'

Saffie didn't reply but pulled the bell rope and ordered tea for them and minutes later Georgina strode into the room, her face flushed from the cold air. The green velvet riding habit she was wearing was beautiful but it did nothing to enhance her appearance, and when her eyes settled on Saffie, her lips curled back from her teeth.

'And what are *you* doing here entertaining our visitor?' she demanded. 'Haven't you got work to do? It's about time you knew your place.'

'Actually, your mother asked me to come and see Marcus as she is sitting with your father.' Saffie flushed with humiliation.

'Really! Then you can go now that I'm back, can't you?'

Saffie nodded towards Marcus and made a hasty exit, but as she closed the door, she heard him remark coldly, 'I hardly think there was any call for you to speak to Saffie like that, Georgina.'

She shook her head as she climbed the stairs. It seemed no matter what she did, the daughter of the house was never going to like her. But she had to confess that the feelings were mutual and not likely to change now.

At last, Sunday rolled around and although Saffie hadn't expected to have any time off due to the circumstances, Mrs Spencer-Hughes insisted that she should. 'You've spent far too long cooped up in the sick room. A little fresh air and a break away from here will do you good,' she told her kindly, so after lunch she set off.

It was a cold October day and as she made her way down Cat Gallows Lane the leaves fluttered from the trees like confetti. Very soon she was glad she had thought to wear her warm cloak and she hugged it tight about herself as she hurried along with her head bent and her teeth chattering.

'Why, bless yer, pet. Yer shiverin' through, come on in quickly out o' the cold,' Minnie said as she ushered her into the warm and cosy kitchen when she arrived at the cottage. 'We 'eard what 'appened up at Lakeside House. How is the master now?'

'No better but no worse really,' Saffie told her as she crossed to the fire and held her hands out to it. 'But he's making things no better for himself. He's very agitated about something all the time and frustrated because he can't tell us what it is. He won't even let Miss Georgina into the room without going red in the face. The mistress has banned her from trying to see him for now because she fears the sight of her might bring on another seizure. It's very strange because from what I can make of it she's always been the favourite.'

'Hm, sounds a bit fishy to me,' Minnie stated as she pushed the kettle onto the hob to boil. 'It just makes yer wonder if there ain't more to this so-called accident than meets the eye.'

'To be honest, I've thought the same,' Saffie confessed. 'Although I haven't said as much to Mrs Spencer-Hughes.' She turned her attention to the two girls who were playing with their dolls on the rag rug and asked in a whisper, 'And how are the girls? Have any relatives of Sylvie's come forward yet?'

Minnie shook her head as she warmed the teapot and fetched a fruit cake from the larder. 'Not as yet.'

Saffie noticed a note of relief in her voice. 'An' Marcus tells us Margaret never mentioned young Cathy to you either.'

'Not once,' Saffie answered. Davey came in with a basketful of logs he'd been chopping for the fire and smiled a welcome.

'Marcus 'as problems of his own wi' poor Mathilda an' all,' Minnie said sadly. 'The poor lass seems to get thinner an' frailer by the day. Ever since she lost the baby they've not been able to control her courses. She's bleedin' fer much o' the time now an' she's as pale as lint, but there don't seem to be anythin' the doctors can do, poor love.'

'How sad.' Whenever Saffie thought of Mathilda, she pictured her as she had been when she had first met her but she knew too well that she no longer looked like that.

There was a welcome letter from Elsie who sounded as happy as Larry with her new husband and her new house, and also one from the twins who also sounded content, and Saffie was pleased that at least she didn't have to worry about any of them.

Already the afternoon was darkening and Saffie wanted to call and see Marcus and Mathilda on her way home. There was a hint of rain in the wind so she didn't want to be too late getting back and was hoping to get an uninterrupted night's sleep.

As always, Marcus was delighted to see her and drew her into the parlour where Mathilda was sitting in a large wing chair by a roaring fire with a warm blanket across her legs.

'Saffie, how lovely it is to see you. Marcus told me you were back and about Mr Spencer-Hughes's fall. How awful. How is he?'

'Never mind about him, how are you?' Saffie crossed to take Mathilda's hand in hers and was worried to find it was damp and clammy. She looked as if she'd had the life sucked out of her and bore no resemblance to the Mathilda she had first known.

'Oh, you know . . . I've been better. Marcus, darling, do go and get some tea ordered, would you?'

'Of course.'

When he was gone Mathilda took Saffie's hand and a note of urgency crept into her voice as she whispered, 'I don't think I'm long for this world, Saffie, and there's something I must ask you.'

'Don't talk so silly!' Horrified, Saffie snatched her hand away and frowned but Mathilda would not be silenced.

'Please listen, dear friend. I must say this before Marcus comes back.' She blinked to stop the tears that were glistening on her lashes from falling before rushing on. 'I want you to promise me that should anything happen to me you will keep a close eye on Marcus. He likes and respects you and he's going to need someone he can trust to help him through his grief.'

Again, Saffie opened her mouth to object but Mathilda gently placed a finger on her lips. 'Please. Let me finish. I know he will be sad. The love we share is very special but we mustn't forget that he is still a relatively young man. I want him to meet someone else. Someone who will love and respect him. Do you understand what I'm saying?'

Saffie was about to answer but at that moment Marcus strode back into the room informing them that the tea was on its way and so, to Saffie's relief, the conversation couldn't go any further. She had grown to be very fond of Mathilda during the time she had known her and could hardly bear to think of her life without her in it, and yet some dark sense of foreboding told her that Mathilda could be speaking the truth. All that Saffie could do now was pray that she might make a miraculous recovery. She had lost so many people she cared about in such a short time that she didn't think she could bear to lose another.

She stayed for only a short time longer as she could see that Mathilda was tiring.

'Marcus, you must have the carriage brought around to the front and see Saffie home,' Mathilda told him. 'I don't like the thought of her wandering about in the dark on her own, and it's raining now too.'

'Oh, Mathilda . . . that's very kind of you, but there's no need really,' Saffie objected.

But Marcus added his concerns to those of his wife. 'You wait right here, young lady, and do as you're told,' he ordered bossily. 'My wife is quite right. You never know who's loitering about nowadays.' And he went off to order the carriage to be brought round.

'She's not good, is she?' Marcus said worriedly as they sat opposite each other in the carriage heading for Lakeside House a short time later.

'No . . . I'm afraid she isn't,' Saffie said and to her horror Marcus raised his hands to cover his face and began to cry.

'I . . . I'm so sorry,' he gulped as she rose and sat beside him with her arm across his shoulders. He was trying so hard to get a grip on himself but failing miserably. 'Every day I feel as if she is slipping a tiny bit further away from me and the worst thing is I can't do anything to stop it.'

'I know,' she soothed, wishing there was more she could say to comfort him but knowing there wasn't. So they sat side by side in silence, dreading what might lie ahead, for they both loved Mathilda in their own way.

Chapter Thirty-Eight

On a cold wintry night at the beginning of November, Saffie woke and lay staring into the darkness. Outside a storm was blowing and she wondered what had woken her. Normally she was so tired by the time she got to bed that she slept like a log but now for some reason all her senses were on alert. And then she heard it. A noise coming from the master's bedroom.

That night for the first time since he had had his seizure, she and Mrs Spencer-Hughes had decided they would both try to get some rest instead of taking it in turns to sit beside him, but they had left his bedroom door open so they would hear the bell they had left close to his good hand if he needed them. Saffie instantly clambered out of the warm sheets and pulled her dressing robe on, then slipping her feet into her house slippers she quickly lifted the candle that was flickering on the table beside the bed and hurried out onto the landing.

It seemed that she was not the only one who had heard something because she had gone no more than a few steps when she almost collided with her mistress who was coming out of her bedroom.

'Did you hear something, Saffie?' Mrs Spencer-Hughes asked anxiously and when Saffie nodded, they turned as one and hurried towards the master's room. It was quiet in there but as they reached the door, they found Georgina standing at the side of her father's bed with one of his pillows in her hand.

She started when they barged in but quickly composing herself, she told her mother, 'Send for the doctor quickly, Mama . . . I think Father has had another seizure . . .'

Mr Spencer-Hughes lay very still, his eyes staring sightlessly up at the ceiling with his one good hand raised above his head as if he was trying to ward someone off. Froth coated his lips and his face was frozen in a terrible rictus.

'What happened?' Mrs Spencer-Hughes was beside him in a moment.

'I, er . . . I heard something and came to see what was wrong,' Georgina faltered.

'But why didn't he ring his bell? I always made sure that it was next to his hand. And why are you holding his pillow?'

'I, er . . . moved the bell out of the way as I tried to help him,' Georgina said in a shaky voice. 'And I moved the pillow too, thinking he might be better if he was lying flatter.'

Saffie moved to the side of the bed and gently felt for a pulse before looking at her mistress and sadly shaking her head. Even before doing that it was obvious to all of them that he was dead.

'Oh my dear God!' Mrs Spencer-Hughes's hand flew to her mouth and she swayed with shock as Saffie quickly led her to a chair.

'Miss Georgina, I think you had better go down and wake Mrs Beasley. Ask her to get someone to run for the doctor,' Saffie ordered, taking control of the situation, and with a glare in her direction Georgina muttered something and went off to do as she was asked, although she made it more than clear that she didn't like taking instructions from a servant.

Once she was gone, Saffie stared down at the master and frowned. Something wasn't right. Why would Georgina have moved the bell? Why would she have moved the pillow? And how on earth had she heard any noise coming from her father's room when her room was so far away? She didn't have long to ponder on it before Mrs Beasley rushed in, puffing and panting after running up the stairs.

'I've sent Boss to fetch the doctor,' she told them breathlessly as she crossed to the bed and gently closed the master's eyes. 'But I've told her to tell him there's no need to rush. Miss Georgina said he was already gone. God bless his soul. Now why don't you go down and have a nice stiff drink, ma'am, while I wash him and tidy him up.'

Mrs Spencer-Hughes shakily rose from the chair and allowed Saffie to lead her downstairs to the drawing room where she poured her mistress a generous measure of brandy from the cut-glass decanter. She coughed as she took a great gulp of it but after a moment it seemed to calm her a little. Most of the servants were up by that time, having heard the commotion, and they tiptoed past the door like ghosts. There was no sign of Georgina, and Saffie was disgusted with her. Surely she should have been the one comforting her mother? But Georgina had proved time and time again that she was selfish to the core so she supposed she shouldn't have been surprised. Knowing her, she had probably taken herself back off to bed!

It was almost an hour later when the doctor arrived and he went straight upstairs to Mr Spencer-Hughes's room. Mrs Beasley had washed him and made him tidy but there was nothing she could do about the horrified look on his face.

'I can only imagine that he had another seizure and it proved fatal,' he told Mrs Spencer-Hughes after examining him. 'I'm so sorry, my dear, but it wasn't entirely unexpected, was it?' He shook his head as he accepted the brandy that Saffie handed to him. 'I did say that I didn't think he would survive another attack and sadly I have been proved right. Would you like me to call into the undertaker on my way back into town and ask him to call on you?'

'Y-yes please.'

The doctor quickly swallowed his drink and after lifting his bag and putting his hat back on he nodded towards Saffie and quietly left.

Saffie stood silently with her hands clasped at her waist, not knowing what to say. Mrs Spencer-Hughes hadn't cried as yet, although she was deathly pale.

'Something is not right, Saffie,' she said suddenly and again Saffie didn't know how to answer. She felt exactly the same, although she didn't feel it was her place to agree with her. 'If her father was so ill when she found him, why didn't Georgina fetch me immediately? And how would she have heard him from her room?'

'I-I don't know, ma'am.' Saffie stood, uncertain what to do, before suggesting, 'Shall I go and make you a hot drink? There's nothing more we can do until the undertaker arrives, unless you would like to go back to bed, of course. I can wait up for him.'

Mrs Spencer-Hughes shook her head. 'No . . . thank you, but I should go and get dressed. I'm hardly in a fit state to meet the undertaker.'

'Then I shall come and help you,' Saffie insisted and they went upstairs together.

Half an hour later, Mrs Spencer-Hughes was dressed in the only black gown she possessed. It was the one she had had made for her daughter's funeral.

'Seeing as I shall be in mourning for the next twelve months, I shall have to have some more black gowns made,' she commented as Saffie put the finishing touches to her hair.

'Should I wear black too, ma'am?' Saffie asked hesitantly, but her mistress shook her head.

'No, Saffie, thank you but there will be no need for that. It is usually only close family members who observe the mourning period.'

She went downstairs to wait for the undertaker and with nothing else to do, Saffie made her way to her room. She was shocked when she entered to find Georgina standing by the window. The second the door closed behind her Georgina wheeled about, her face a picture of fury.

'I heard what my mother said just now in the drawing room,' she spat. 'About something not being right! Was it *you* who put the idea in her head?'

Saffie's hand, which was holding the candlestick, trembled violently but she remained outwardly calm as she stared back at the other woman. 'I haven't commented on your father's death, so I suggest if your mother has said something you are not happy with you should take it up with her!'

'*You . . . you . . .*' Georgina was so angry she was red in the face. 'It's about time you cleared off back to where you came from,' she said through gritted teeth. 'Don't think I don't know what you and my mother are up to! I know that she is still in touch with Margaret and I know where she is too! I followed you to the coast when you went off on your "little holiday". But don't you get trying to convince Mother that she can bring her back here. Lakeside House is *mine* now by rights, or at least it will be if anything happens to Mother, and then you'll be out of here like a flash, I assure you!'

Saffie was appalled at what she was hearing, but Georgina hadn't quite finished yet.

'I guessed you were up to something the day I caught you going into Mother's jewellery box and so I waited until you were out of the way and found Margaret's letter. You've been encouraging Mother to keep in touch with the trollop, haven't you!'

'I haven't encouraged your mother to do anything. And now if you wouldn't mind, I'd like you to leave my room.'

Georgina was so red in the face now that she looked in danger of bursting a blood vessel, and as she took a threatening step towards her with her fist raised, Saffie was afraid that she was going to hit her. But thankfully she seemed to think better of it and with a growl she pushed past her and slammed out of the room.

For a while Saffie just stood there shaking as she tried to compose herself, wondering what she should do. Georgina had never pretended to like her but now her hatred was out in the open. Should she tell Mrs Spencer-Hughes about their altercation? After giving it some thought, she decided against it. If she did it would be her word against Georgina's and Georgina was Mrs Spencer-Hughes's flesh and blood, after all, so the likelihood was that she would believe her daughter. Saffie sighed. She knew there would be no point in going back to bed now, she would never sleep, so she quickly washed, brushed her hair and went back downstairs to wait with her mistress for the undertaker to arrive.

The following morning the servants crept about the house like mice. The curtains had all been tightly drawn and the clocks stopped until after the master's funeral as a mark of respect, and the atmosphere was tense.

That afternoon, Marcus was the first to arrive to pay his respects and the second she saw him, Mrs Spencer-Hughes finally broke down.

'I feel so awful,' she sobbed. 'Victor and I hadn't been close for some long time and I feel guilty now.'

'But you shouldn't.' Marcus handed her his clean white handkerchief and patted her back. He knew of Victor's many dalliances with other women and felt sorry for Eugenie. 'Victor lived his life the way he wanted, you must never forget that.' A thought occurred to him, and he asked tentatively, 'Have you let Margaret know what has happened yet?'

She sniffed and dabbed at her cheeks. 'Yes, I wrote to her this morning.' And then she gasped. 'Goodness, now that Victor has gone, she could come home, couldn't she? Although I doubt Georgina would be very happy about it if she did.'

Marcus shrugged. 'But this is your house now and it's entirely your decision,' he pointed out. 'And no doubt Georgina would accept it eventually if you decide that's what you want.'

'Huh! I doubt it.' Eugenie shook her head. 'Georgina was always jealous of her older sisters, even though she was Victor's favourite. I think it suited her when Victor

364

disowned Margaret, and then when my poor Elizabeth died . . .' She gulped. 'Well, I think she began to make her plans about this house straightaway, believing that she would be the one to inherit it if anything happened to Victor and me.'

'But nothing is going to happen to you for a very long time, hopefully,' he said. 'And so for the foreseeable future, who does or doesn't live in this house is your decision and no one else's.'

'It is, isn't it?' Eugenie took a deep breath and offered him a wavering smile. 'But that is not for thinking about now. I must give Georgina time to come to terms with the loss of her father and I have a funeral to arrange. I wondered if you would be the chief mourner at the service seeing as having women at funerals is frowned on? Victor didn't have any surviving male relatives. I will host a wake here after the funeral.'

'Of course,' Marcus agreed graciously. It was nice to see Eugenie smile again, even if it was a shaky one and he had a feeling that before too long Margaret would be back where she belonged. He hoped so because then they would discover the true identity of Cathy's parents.

Chapter Thirty-Nine

The day before the funeral, Victor Spencer-Hughes was brought home to lie in his coffin in the drawing room, and all day the house was full of people coming and going to pay their last respects to him. Saffie was kept busy supplying the women with tea or coffee and the men with something stronger should they prefer it, and by evening she was worn out.

Meantime in the kitchen, the cook was barking out orders like a sergeant major as she and the kitchen staff prepared the meal for after the funeral the following day. There had been no more tears from Mrs Spencer-Hughes. She had been forced to admit that as sad as Victor's untimely end was, any love she had had for him had died a long time ago and now she just wished to bury him with the dignity she felt everybody deserved.

'You must be worn out, my dear,' she commented to Saffie as she and Georgina made their way into the dining room for their evening meal.

'Huh! It makes a change to see her earning her wages,' Georgina responded cuttingly but Saffie ignored her. She was used to her spiteful ways by now, although she had noticed that since the master's death, she had been paying a lot more attention to her mother, even to the point of insisting that it was she who took her tray up to her each morning.

'Now, darling, we don't need any harsh words this evening,' Mrs Spencer-Hughes said wearily. She hadn't been too well for the last few days. She had complained of feeling nauseous and had developed diarrhoea, which Saffie supposed was due to the stressful time she was going through. She hoped that once the funeral was over her mistress would recover but for now, she pointedly ignored Georgina's cutting remarks as Mrs Spencer-Hughes told her, 'Why don't you have your meal now, Saffie? You've done quite enough for one day. I shall get myself ready for bed this evening.'

'Thank you, ma'am. I think I will, if you're quite sure you can manage.' She turned about and made her way upstairs and shortly after, Bossy appeared with her meal on a tray.

'Cor blimey, I shall be right glad when tomorrer is over,' she said as she put the tray down and went to throw some more coal onto the fire. 'It's like a bleedin' mad'ouse down in the kitchen wi' Cook snappin' at everyone. God knows 'ow many people she's expectin' to turn up fer the wake. I swear she's cooked enough grub to feed an entire bloody army.'

Saffie grinned. Bossy would never change and she didn't really want her to. She had been the only real friend she'd had in the house since starting work there. Bossy glanced towards the door, as if she was checking that no one was there, and lowering her voice she whispered, 'There's them that are sayin' there's somethin' fishy about the way the master went.'

'Really?' Saffie responded innocently. Secretly she still thought the same but she wouldn't admit it. She'd never been one to gossip, unlike Bossy, who loved a bit of slander.

'Ar, I mean you think about it, you an' the missus 'ad stayed wi' 'im every night since he'd 'ad 'is funny turn an' the first time yer didn't . . . Well!' She spread her hands and let out a deep breath. 'There 'e is, dead as a dodo wi' Miss Georgina standin' at the side of 'im wi' a piller in 'er 'ands. Makes yer wonder if she didn't bring the last seizure on, don't it?'

'Oh Bossy, you have a very fertile imagination,' Saffie answered, trying to make light of it. 'The doctor did warn us that the master could have another seizure at any time.'

'Hm, you can think what yer like but I know what I think. Anyroad, enjoy yer dinner. I'd best get back else Cook will 'ave me guts fer garters.'

Saffie shook her head and smiled as the girl left. She really was incorrigible.

The next day dawned blustery and wet and once again the house was a hive of activity as the maids ran from the kitchen to the dining room laying out the food for the wake. The funeral was scheduled for eleven o' clock and the undertaker arrived at ten to nail down the coffin lid. Mr Spencer-Hughes was then carried out to the waiting glass hearse, which was pulled by four matching black stallions wearing feathered plumes on their heads.

Mrs Spencer-Hughes watched from the drawing-room window as it pulled away until it was out of sight. She was almost relieved that she wasn't expected to attend the funeral, and she waited sadly for the mourners to arrive following the service as she tried to think back to happier times. She had loved Victor passionately when they were first married and believed that her love had been returned, but his love for her had slowly died when she had given him three daughters, instead of the son he had so desperately craved. Still, she decided, what was done was done and now she must make the best of things.

By the time the mourners returned everything was ready for them and as Cook was heard to say later that day, they descended on the food like a pack of vultures. The maids were kept busy refilling glasses and making hot drinks for those that wanted them as Mrs Spencer-Hughes and Georgina mingled with their guests, accepting their shallow condolences. But at last people began to leave and by teatime they had all departed.

'Eeh, it looks like the place 'as been ransacked,' Bossy declared as she arrived with a tray to start collecting the dirty pots.

'I'll help,' Saffie offered. Mrs Spencer-Hughes had gone to lie down suffering with a headache and there was no sign of Georgina. And so, for the next hour Saffie pitched in and eventually the room was cleared of pots, the floors had been swept and everything was back as it should be.

Next she went upstairs to check on her mistress and as she entered her bedroom, she was just in time to see Georgina spoon something into the cup before hastily handing it to her mother.

When Saffie frowned, Georgina told her quickly, 'It's, er . . . a sleeping draught. The doctor told me it might help her to rest.'

Saffie didn't comment, although she certainly couldn't remember the doctor prescribing anything.

Georgina quickly thrust a small bag of powder into her pocket, and with a smile at her mother, she encouraged, 'Drink it while it's hot.' Mrs Spencer-Hughes did as she was asked.

'I just came to see if you'd like me to bring your evening meal up on a tray,' Saffie said, thinking how drab Georgina looked. Her black mourning gown did nothing to flatter her pale complexion, and her mousy-coloured hair was pulled back into a severe bun on the back of her head.

'Thank you, dear, but I find I don't have much appetite at the moment.'

And to her horror her employer suddenly leaned forward and just managed to vomit into the chamber pot rather than onto the carpet.

'Go away, I'll see to her,' Georgina ordered, yanking on the bell pull to summon Bossy to come and clear up the mess.

Feeling that she didn't have much choice but to do as she was told, Saffie went to her own room to put her feet up for a while. It seemed that Georgina couldn't bring herself to be civil to her even on this sad day, but that was the least of Saffie's worries. She thought back to the powder she had seen Georgina dropping into her mother's tea. Surely if it had been nothing more than an innocent sleeping draught, she would have left it in her mother's room rather than hide it in the pocket of her gown? Slowly she sank onto the side of her bed trying to dispel the awful thought that had just occurred to her, but the more she thought of it the more it seemed that the pieces of a jigsaw were coming together.

Now that Georgina's father was dead, there was only her mother standing between her and her inheritance. Unless Mrs Spencer-Hughes brought Margaret home. Because then, as the oldest surviving child, she would become the legal heiress once more. Could it be that Georgina was trying to poison her mother before she had a chance to do that? Saffie still felt strongly that Georgina could have had a hand in her father's death, although it couldn't be proven. And if that was the case, she would be more than capable of disposing of her mother too.

She thought of the symptoms Mrs Spencer-Hughes had been suffering since Georgina had insisted on serving her meals, and realised with a little shock that they matched the symptoms of arsenic poisoning. They had had to use small amounts of arsenic on *The Blue Sapphire*, which had always been prone to rat infestations, and she knew how potent it was. A large dose could kill an adult within hours, but if administered a little at a time it could cause the symptoms Mrs Spencer-Hughes was suffering from.

As the light faded, she lit the oil lamp at the side of the bed and crossing to the window to draw the curtains she was just in time to see Georgina ride out of the stable block and gallop off down the drive. It made no difference to her if it was light or dark, wet or dry, she went riding every day, but now Saffie realised that this was the ideal opportunity to go and see if she had any suspicious powder hidden in her room.

Before she could lose her nerve, she left her room and crept along the landing. She felt like a thief in the night, but Mrs Spencer-Hughes's life might depend on what she was doing, so with her heart in her mouth she tiptoed on, praying that she wouldn't bump into a member of staff. She would certainly have some explaining to do if she did and it could well cost her her job – she knew that Georgina would jump at any chance to get rid of her. Thankfully, though, the upstairs seemed to be deserted and she made it to Georgina's room in record time, sighing with relief when she found that the door was unlocked.

Inside a fire was burning in the grate and the oil lamp was lit at the side of the bed, so first she cautiously began to open the drawers and glance through them, being careful not to disturb anything. Her search revealed nothing, so she crossed to the ornate rosewood dressing table and in the second drawer she found what she was searching for: a small bag containing white powder. Quickly she dropped it into her pocket and left the room, after checking first that the coast was clear, and once she reached the safety of her room, she let out a sigh of relief.

It was what she should do next that troubled her now. If her suspicions were correct, Georgina would realise the powder was missing in no time and Saffie had no doubt she herself would be the first to be blamed. She wished that Marcus was here so she could ask his advice, but it was doubtful he would be back so soon after the funeral and she knew that if she asked to go out at this time of the evening it would look suspicious. Quickly lifting her mattress, she tucked the bag as far underneath as it would go before taking a deep breath and going to check on how Mrs Spencer-Hughes was. As she hurried to her mistress's room the large grandfather clock in the hallway chimed the hour – they had all been set again now that the funeral was over and Saffie prayed that things might start to return to some sort of normality.

Mrs Spencer-Hughes was still fast asleep when she entered her room, so Saffie quietly began to put away the clean washing that had been brought up from the laundry. Less than an hour later she heard Georgina's horse galloping towards the stables and she waited nervously for her to put in an appearance.

Sure enough, minutes later, Georgina strode into the room still dressed in her velvet riding habit, her face flushed from the cold outside. It was then that Mrs Spencer-Hughes stirred and ignoring Saffie, Georgina crossed to her to ask sweetly, 'Do you feel like you might be able to eat something now, Mama? I'll just go and get changed and then I'll bring you something up on a tray if you don't feel like going down to the dining room; it's been an awfully long day for you.'

Mrs Spencer-Hughes sat up and knuckled the sleep from her eyes. 'Thank you, darling. Perhaps just a little something light. I'm not really that hungry.'

'Very well, just so long as you eat something. You have to keep your strength up.'

Georgina scowled at Saffie and turning in a swish of velvet skirts she strode from the room.

Saffie held her breath. If her suspicions were correct, Georgina would soon discover the powder was missing, but all she could do now was wait as she helped her mistress to get changed into her nightclothes.

Twenty minutes later, Georgina returned with a tray on which were a number of dainty sandwiches, a cake and a pot of tea. She slammed it down so hard onto the small table at the side of the bed that some of the tea sloshed out of the spout of the teapot and without even glancing at Saffie, she stormed from the room with a face like thunder.

'Oh dear, I thought her mood was too good to last,' Mrs Spencer-Hughes commented wryly as Saffie poured her tea into a bone china cup.

'Perhaps she's just tired.' Saffie handed her the cup and saucer but she had a feeling that she knew what had caused

Georgina's sudden change of mood: she had discovered that the powder was missing. Now all she could do was wait to see what she would do about it.

Shortly after, she carried her mistress's chamber pot away to clean it and once outside beside the midden, she cautiously sniffed at the urine. It smelled strongly of garlic, as she had feared, yet another sign that her mistress might be the victim of arsenic poisoning.

The rest of the evening passed uneventfully and at just after nine o'clock, Saffie said goodnight to Mrs Spencer-Hughes and slipped away to her own room where she quickly washed and changed into her nightclothes. After a time she recovered the small bag of powder from beneath her mattress and cautiously sniffed at it. As she had thought there was no smell, another sign that it could well be arsenic, and she chewed on her lip as she worried what she should do. It was all well and good to keep this hidden but Georgina could easily get some more from almost any apothecary.

She returned the bag to its hiding place and listened to the house quietening around her as the servants retired for the night. Soon there was only the sound of the wind howling and the rain pattering against the windows to be heard and Saffie decided she would check on her mistress just once more before trying to get some sleep. She shuddered as she left the warm sheets and slipped into her robe, then lifting the oil lamp, she set off along the landing and almost jumped out of her skin when Georgina suddenly stepped from the shadows like a ghost.

'I thought you'd be along sooner or later to play the dutiful little servant and check on Mama!' Her eyes glittered with hatred as Saffie began to back away from her.

'I . . . I always check that she has all she needs before I settle down.'

'And don't I *know* it,' Georgina scoffed. 'Little Miss Goody Two Shoes, butter-wouldn't-melt, boat *scum* girl! You're trying to ruin my life.'

'No . . . no, I'm not!' Saffie continued to back away until they were at the top of the stairs and she could go no further without pushing past Georgina. It was then that she saw the gleam of madness in Georgina's eyes and for the first time she was truly terrified. 'Look, let me just go and check on your mother,' she pleaded. 'There's no need for any of this. I wish you no harm.'

'Huh!' Georgina's lips curled back from her teeth in a feral snarl. 'So why have you been snooping in my bedroom?'

Saffie opened her mouth to say that she hadn't but thought better of it and snapped it shut again. Georgina wasn't going to believe her whatever she said so it seemed safer to say nothing.

By now her back was tight against the banister rail at the top of the stairs and Saffie was painfully aware that if she should take so much as another step, she would go toppling down them, much as Mr Spencer-Hughes must have done.

Georgina moved closer and now Saffie could feel her breath on her cheek as the girl started to stab her spitefully in the chest with a sharp pointed finger.

'Give me the powder you took or so help me . . .'

At that moment Mrs Spencer-Hughes's door crashed open and she stepped onto the landing. Taking in the scene, she demanded, 'And what exactly is going on out here? Georgina, whatever has got into you? Leave Saffie alone.'

'Oh, I might have *known* that you'd take *her* part,' Georgina shrieked as she whirled about to face her.

Her mother tutted as she advanced. 'Stop being so silly. I'm not taking *anyone's* part.'

With a cry of rage, Georgina turned back to Saffie and lunged towards her, but Saffie managed to throw herself to one side a second before she reached her, landing painfully on the floor. And then everything seemed to happen in slow motion as Georgina's foot caught in the hem of her nightgown. She seemed to hover at the top of the stairs, her arms thrown wide as she tried to regain her balance. A stabbing pain sliced up Saffie's leg and she winced as she desperately tried to lean far enough forward to grab at the hem of Georgina's nightgown, but before she could manage it Georgina toppled forward with an ear-piercing scream, and all Saffie could do was watch as she plunged down the steep staircase.

After what seemed a lifetime, but was in fact no more than a few seconds, she landed at the bottom with a sickening thud. And suddenly the servants appeared, bleary-eyed and clad in their nightclothes.

Saffie began to cry while Mrs Spencer-Hughes stood there in shock, as if she had been turned to stone.

It was Mrs Beasley who went to Georgina's aid and they held their breath, waiting to see if she was still alive. But after bending over Georgina's still form, she stared up at them and one look at her pallid face told them all they needed to know. Mrs Spencer-Hughes dropped to the floor in a dead faint.

Chapter Forty

'She would have died instantly,' the solemn-faced doctor told Mrs Beasley after examining Georgina's body a short time later. The butler had carried her back to her room. 'I'm afraid she broke her neck. But how did it happen?'

'I . . . I don't know.' Mrs Beasley wrung her hands, hardly able to believe that the daughter of the house had died on the same day as her father's funeral. It was no wonder her poor mistress had had to be put to bed in shock. As for Saffie, she was suffering from a severely sprained ankle and she too had been carried to bed.

The doctor shook his head. 'I shall record it as accidental death if she tripped, but do you suppose she might have been pushed? If that's the case the police will have to be involved.' He gently closed Georgina's staring eyes.

'Saffie was present at the time, I believe, but she isn't a violent girl.' Mrs Beasley sighed. Like many of the staff, she had never felt that Saffie was right for the post of lady's maid but she was a fair woman and had seen first-hand how Miss Georgina had victimised her. It was beginning to feel as if the house was cursed.

'Goodness knows how your poor mistress will take this latest tragedy. Perhaps she can throw some light on how it happened? I shall go up and see her now.'

'I doubt you'll get much sense out of her tonight,' Mrs Beasley commented. 'She hasn't said a word.'

'Hm, you're probably right.' The doctor rose and snapped his bag shut. 'But I would like to check on her all the same. And didn't you mention that Miss Doyle was injured too? Perhaps she and Miss Georgina had had some sort of an altercation?'

'As I said, Saffie isn't a violent girl. She tends to keep herself very much to herself, but I am aware that Miss Georgina didn't like her. Saffie was brought up on the canal and Miss Georgina didn't consider that she was good enough to attend her mother.'

'I see. Well, I shall go and see your mistress now.' The doctor strode from the room and once upstairs he tapped on Mrs Spencer-Hughes's bedroom door. When there was no answer, he inched the door slowly open and stepped inside.

Mrs Spencer-Hughes was lying on the bed staring at the ceiling and he approached her cautiously. He had known her ever since she had come to Lakeside House as a young bride, and so he felt that he could speak openly to her, more as a friend than as her doctor.

'So, this is a fine kettle of fish, Eugenie, I am so sorry for your loss. I'm hoping you can cast some light on what might have caused Georgina's fall. Did it have anything to do with your young lady's maid?'

'No, it did *not*!' Suddenly Mrs Spencer-Hughes seemed to come out of her trance-like state and sat up abruptly.

'Ah, so you saw what happened then? Perhaps you could tell me about it.'

She sighed as she swiped her hands wearily across her eyes. 'It . . . it was all Georgina's own fault,' she said in a

378

croaky voice. 'I heard some noise on the landing and when I came out to see what was going on, I found Georgina bullying Saffie. She lunged at her but Saffie managed to throw herself out of the way and . . .' She gulped. 'And then Georgina fell . . . Saffie reached out to try and grab her to save her but she couldn't.'

'Hm.' The doctor stroked his chin. 'In that case I shall record the death as accidental. I shall go and see Miss Doyle now.' And turning on his heel he left the mother to grieve for her child. It said something about the woman's character that although it was her own daughter who had died, she was still prepared to make sure that no one was falsely accused of causing the accident.

Saffie was also lying on her bed when he reached her room and she was sobbing pitifully. She looked towards the door and when she saw the doctor, her expression turned fearful.

'I-I *tried* to save her, *really* I did, but I couldn't.' Her sobs became louder as she relived the awful moment when Georgina fell down the stairs.

'Shush now,' the doctor soothed. 'I'm sure you did, but why was she shouting at you?'

Saffie clamped her mouth shut and a frightened look came into her eyes but the doctor was determined to get to the bottom of things. 'I-I can't tell you,' she whimpered, shaking her head. 'It would be just too much for Mrs Spencer-Hughes if she were to find out and she's been through so much already.'

'Perhaps she doesn't need to find out,' he said gently as he sat on the bed at the side of her. 'But it would help me greatly if you were to tell me. I have to know what to put on the death certificate. Your mistress has already told me that this wasn't your fault. Won't you trust me, Saffie? I only want what is best for your mistress, I promise you.'

Saffie stared at him doubtfully for a moment then with a sigh she rolled towards the edge of the bed. The doctor rose and balancing unsteadily on one leg she reached down and felt beneath the mattress until her fingers closed around the small bag of powder she had stolen from Georgina. She hastily told him the story of how she had seen Georgina sprinkling some of it into her mother's tea and her suspicions of what it might be. 'All the symptoms Mrs Spencer-Hughes was displaying led me to believe that Georgina might be poisoning her, and so I took the powder from her room and hid it in here and she accused me of stealing it. That's what she was shouting about at the top of the stairs. She was demanding that I give it back to her.'

'But what makes you think that Georgina might have wanted to kill her own mother?' he asked appalled.

'She had discovered that Margaret was still alive and I think she was afraid that Mrs Spencer-Hughes might bring her home. I think she might have had a hand in her father's death too.' Saffie went on to tell him about how Georgina had been found in his room at the time of his death.

The doctor frowned. 'Would you mind if I took this powder to find out what it is?'

Saffie nodded. 'Of course, but please don't tell my mistress. She has enough to deal with already, losing her daughter so soon after her husband, and I would like to think she can at least retain some fond memories of her. Think how awful it would be if she were to discover that Georgina had been trying to kill her.'

'Let's hope you are wrong,' he said quietly as he pocketed the small bag of powder. 'Now, let me look at your ankle.'

Saffie winced as he twisted it gently this way and that. Thankfully he could confirm that it wasn't broken but badly sprained and he bandaged it up tightly and ordered complete bed rest for at least the next couple of days. 'I shall have found out what the powder is by that time,' he promised her. 'And I shall tell you when I come back to check on you and Mrs Spencer-Hughes.'

After he left, Saffie lay there wishing she had never set foot in the place. It certainly hadn't been a happy house to live in, although she was very fond of her mistress and Bossy. Now all she could do was wait to see what the doctor's verdict of the powder was, and she silently prayed for Mrs Spencer Hughes's sake that she had misjudged Georgina and that it was as she had insisted, nothing more than a harmless draught.

During the next two days both Bossy and even Mrs Beasley waited on her hand and foot. Her ankle was paining her dreadfully but she knew that soon it would start to heal and so she spent her time reading. On the third day, late in the morning, there was a tap at her door and Bossy told her, 'Mr Berrington is 'ere to see yer, miss. Mrs Beasley says I'm to stay in 'ere wi yer throughout the visit cos it ain't proper fer a young lady to 'ave a gentleman in 'er room unescorted.'

Saffie stifled a smile, the first since the night Georgina had met her death so tragically. Seconds later Marcus followed Bossy into the room.

'How are you, Saffie?' He looked uncomfortable as he stood with his hat in his hands.

'I'm fine, it's just a sprain, more painful than serious.' She pointed to the chair at the side of the bed and he took a seat, one eye on Bossy, who was cleaning the hearth, even though she'd done it that morning. There was so much he wanted to ask her but felt it wouldn't be right in front of the maid.

'What has happened . . .' He shook his head. 'Well, it's just dreadful, so soon after Eugenie losing Victor too. I just hope she'll have the strength to get through this.'

Saffie nodded. She so wanted to confide in him and tell him what had happened, what her suspicions about Georgina had been and what had led to Georgina's fall, but she was feeling as uncomfortable as he was. It felt strange to have a gentleman in her room, even though she was covered from head to foot in her voluminous nightgown with a shawl about her shoulders. Her long hair hung across her shoulders and down her back like a black silken cloak and Marcus couldn't help but think what a beautiful young woman she was.

Bossy, meanwhile, was feeling just as uncomfortable as they were and turning to them suddenly, she told them, 'Look, I's goin' to go an' stand just outside the door so as yer can talk proper wi'out me in the room. If I see anybody comin' I shall 'ave to come back in, though, else I'll be in trouble fer not doin' as I was told.'

'Right, now perhaps you can tell me what happened,' Marcus said the second the door had closed behind her.

And so, haltingly, Saffie told him everything and when she was done, he frowned. 'I always felt that Georgina was spiteful and jealous of Margaret and Elizabeth but I never thought she would go to those lengths. And yet everything you've told me about the way she reacted to you taking that powder points to you being right. If it had been a harmless sleeping draught, why would she have become so upset? She could simply have asked the doctor for some more.' A thought occurred to him and he chewed on his lip. 'Did you think to ask the doctor if he had prescribed the sleeping draught?'

Saffie blinked. 'N-no, I didn't.'

'Hm, in that case I shall ask him when I leave here. I have to get back to the school now anyway so I can call in to see Dr Bell on the way. He might even have found out what the powder you gave him is by now. For Eugenie's sake I pray that you were wrong, because how would she cope with knowing that her own daughter was trying to do away with her?'

'All right, but before you go . . . How is Mathilda?'

Marcus stared towards the window and the sadness in his eyes sent a cold shiver of fear up Saffie's spine.

'No better,' he answered quietly. 'To be honest, she hasn't got out of bed for days now. She's too weak. I called in another doctor for a second opinion but as Dr Jones had already told me, there was nothing he could do.'

'I'm so sorry.' Saffie felt his pain. She knew how much Marcus adored his wife and could only imagine how hard it must be for him to have to stand by and watch her withering away before his very eyes, knowing that there was nothing he could do to prevent it. 'I'll come and see her as soon as I'm up and about again,' she promised, and with a nod and a little smile Marcus quietly departed.

Saffie sighed deeply. She was beginning to wish she had never agreed to care for Cathy at her grandmother's house now. So much had happened since then and there had been so much heartbreak. However, that afternoon her spirits lifted slightly for a time when she received a letter from her sisters, which Davey had kindly delivered to the kitchen, telling her that Elsie had delivered a baby boy. Both mother and baby were doing well, they told her, and now Saffie could hardly wait until she was able to go and meet her nephew. The news was like a little ray of light at the end of a long dark tunnel and she prayed this might be the start of happier days to come, for surely things couldn't get much worse?

Late in the afternoon, however, when the doctor visited her again, she discovered they could.

'I'm afraid your suspicions about Georgina were correct,' he told her grimly. 'The bag of powder you gave me was indeed arsenic.'

Saffie's hand flew to her mouth. 'S-so she was trying to poison her mother?'

He shrugged. 'It would certainly appear so.'

'Will you tell the mistress?'

'Ah, now that's what I wanted to talk to you about, my dear.' Dr Bell flicked his coat-tails aside and sank down into the chair at the side of the bed. 'I should, as a doctor, report my findings to the police and let them make a decision on what to do about this. In fact, it goes against all my medical ethics if I don't . . . but . . .' He shrugged. 'Georgina is gone and Mrs Spencer-Hughes is having to come to terms with the fact. That in itself is bad enough, but if she were to discover that her own child was trying to kill her, I fear . . .'

'It would destroy her,' Saffie ended for him in a shaky voice.

'Quite.' He joined his hands and peered at her over the top of his steel-rimmed spectacles. 'I thought under the circumstances it might be kinder if we didn't inform her. What do you think? It's not as if Georgina is here to take her punishment, so I wonder what we could achieve by laying yet more heartbreak at that poor woman's door. But of course, I think the final decision should lie with you. After all, you are the one she attacked.'

Saffie stared at him thoughtfully before slowly nodding. 'I agree with you. There's nothing at all to be gained. Georgina paid for her wickedness with her life so I would be willing to say nothing if you feel that it's for the best.' And as something occurred to her, she paled. 'B-but I told Marcus Berrington what happened this afternoon when he visited.'

'I shouldn't worry too much about that.' The doctor rose from his seat. 'Marcus and his family have been close friends of the Spencer-Hugheses for many years. I shall have a word with him and I have no doubt he would agree that it would be better for your mistress to put this whole sorry incident down to an unfortunate accident. That way at least Mrs Spencer-Hughes need never know that her own flesh and blood was trying to poison her. But you would have to promise me that no one else would ever know, and are you quite sure that you can live with that secret, Saffie?'

'Yes, I am.' When Saffie nodded vigorously, he sighed.

'In that case I shall write accidental death on Georgina's death certificate and Mrs Spencer-Hughes need never be any the wiser.' He started towards the door where he paused to look back at her and say, 'And for what it's worth, I think you are a very brave young woman. Good day, my dear.'

Chapter Forty-One

Georgina was laid to rest in a grave next to her father's the following week, and once more the house was full of mourners who had come to pay their respects. By that time, Saffie was able to hobble about on a crude crutch that one of the gardeners had fashioned for her. Her ankle was healing nicely but Mrs Spencer-Hughes would not hear of her resuming her duties until it was properly better. Minnie had been to see her twice during the time she had been confined to the house and the last time she had come, the day before the funeral, she had been the bearer of yet more bad news.

'Young Mathilda Berrington is fadin' fast from what I've heard of it,' she had told Saffie sadly. Saffie had wondered why she hadn't seen Marcus for a while and now she understood. 'They reckon she's barely stopped bleedin' since she lost the babe an' now she's as weak as a kitten.'

Tears sprang to Saffie's eyes as she again thought back to how Mathilda had been when she had first met her.

'I don't know how Marcus will cope if anything should happen to her,' she said sadly.

Although she was devastated to hear about Mathilda, Saffie noticed that Minnie appeared to be positively glowing and the reason was soon apparent when she blushed like a schoolgirl and told her, 'An' I've got some more news fer you an' all.'

She licked her lips and looked down shyly as she blustered on, 'Yer see, me an' Davey 'ave just discovered that we're goin' to 'ave another little nipper to look after in a few months' time.'

'What? You mean you're . . .' Saffie's eyes were almost popping out of her head and Minnie chuckled.

'Yes, I mean it's shook us to us roots; we both thought we were past all that at our age. Here's me in me early forties an' havin' me first. Who'd have thought it, eh?'

'Oh Minnie, that's *marvellous* news!' Saffie was genuinely thrilled for her. Having seen how she doted on Cathy and Sylvie she knew that Minnie was going to make a wonderful mother. 'Are you both happy about it? And what do the girls think?'

'We're chuffed to bits.' Minnie beamed 'But we ain't told the girls yet. Thought it best to wait till I'm a bit further on an' we're sure that everythin' is goin' to go well. After all, yer never know, do yer?'

'Oh, I'm sure everything will be just fine,' Saffie reassured her.

'I reckon Davey is secretly hopin' fer a boy, although he says he don't care what it is just so long as it's healthy.'

'I'm absolutely thrilled for you both.' Saffie meant every word. 'But you're going to have your hands full.'

Minnie shrugged. 'The more the merrier, that's what I say. I allus dreamed of havin' a big family an' now it looks like me dream is finally goin' to come true. But what about you, pet? What are you goin' to do when yer better? Are yer goin' to stay on 'ere?'

'I think so . . . for a time, at least,' Saffie answered. 'Just till I'm sure Mrs Spencer-Hughes is all right. Then I might decide to move away and try another job.'

Minnie didn't like the sound of that, although she could understand why Saffie might want to. She certainly hadn't had a very happy time of it in this household, one way and another. 'Well, that is your decision to make but never forget you'll allus 'ave a home wi' us if yer want it.'

'I appreciate that, Minnie, but don't you think you're going to be rather full at the cottage when the new baby arrives?' She giggled and the sound was so infectious that Minnie laughed too.

'There'll allus be room fer one more,' she assured her. 'But now I'd best get back. I've left the girls wi' Davey an' they can run rings round 'im, the little sods. He's as soft as clouts wi' 'em.' She became serious and asked tentatively, 'I know it's early days yet, but do yer reckon the missus will want Margaret to come 'ome when she's got over all this? I'm thinkin' that if she does, Margaret might want Cathy back now 'er father ain't 'ere to condemn 'er.'

'I can't answer that,' Saffie said truthfully. 'And we don't even know if our suspicions are correct. I haven't been able to find out anything about Margaret having a child, let alone it being Cathy. But I would think there's a very good chance that the mistress will want Margaret to come home. After all, she is all she has left now, isn't she? But don't get worrying about it. Let's cross each bridge as we come to it, eh? For now, you just enjoy planning for the new arrival and take good care of yourself.'

Two weeks later, on a cold and frosty Sunday afternoon, Saffie went to visit Mathilda. There was a chill wind blowing and the grass was stiff with hoar frost, standing to attention like rows of tiny soldiers. It crunched underfoot and although Saffie's ankle was much better it began to ache after a while and she was glad when the house came into sight.

Mathilda's maid admitted her and ushered her into the drawing room where Marcus was sitting reading the newspaper. 'Saffie, this is a lovely surprise,' he greeted her warmly. 'How are things up at the house?'

'Settling down now,' she told him as she handed her cloak, bonnet and gloves to the maid. 'In fact, yesterday Mrs Spencer-Hughes confided that she was thinking of bringing Margaret home for Christmas. I think it would be the best thing she could do for both of them.'

'Oh dear, that will set the tongues wagging.' There was a twinkle in his eye and Saffie smiled as she crossed to hold her cold hands out to the welcoming flames roaring up the chimney.

'Do you know, I think the poor woman has gone through so much now that she doesn't care and she'll do as she pleases and shame the devil.'

'Good for her. It's time she had a bit of happiness in her life again, and of course, if Margaret does come home, it might take us a step closer to discovering if she is Cathy's mother.'

'Yes, there is that. But tell me – how is Mathilda?'

'Not good, but I'm sure she'll be all the better for seeing you. But first you must have a cup of tea to warm you up – you look perished. And don't even think of walking home, I shall take you in the carriage. There's something I want to talk to you about as it happens but it can wait until later.' He pulled the bell and ordered them tea then half an hour later he showed Saffie upstairs to Mathilda's bedroom.

'I shan't come in with you, I know how you women like to have a gossip,' he told her and becoming serious he sighed. 'Saffie, I should warn you to prepare yourself,' he whispered as they stood on the landing. 'Mathilda is very, very poorly and . . .'

'I understand.' She squeezed his hand and after tapping lightly on the door she took a deep breath and breezed in with a smile on her face.

'Saffie . . .'

It was all she could do to keep the smile in place as she stared down at the dear soul lying on the silken lace-trimmed pillows. Constant pain had ravaged her once beautiful face and now she looked like an old, old woman.

Mathilda lifted her hand and Saffie took it. It felt hot and sweaty, but Saffie kept her expression cheerful as she lied, 'I think you're looking a little better, Mathilda.' The nurse Marcus had employed to look after his wife was pottering about the room and she smiled at the visitor.

'If you're going to be here for a while, I shall pop down to the kitchen and see if I can persuade the cook to make me a nice cup of tea,' she said and tactfully left the two young women to it.

'I'm so glad you've come,' Mathilda said weakly when she was gone and Saffie had gently sat down on the edge of the bed next to her. 'I-I'm dying, Saffie.'

'Don't talk like that,' Saffie scolded, tears stinging the back of her eyes.

But Mathilda gently shook her hand. 'You know I'm telling the truth. Please don't get upset. I've come to terms with it now. And I might not have had a long life but I've been so lucky. I would rather have had the short time I've had with

Marcus than a whole lifetime with anyone else, which is why I needed to tell you again that I trust you to look out for him when I'm gone. He's far too good to spend the rest of his life on his own. Oh, I know that he'll grieve for me at first, but I want him to meet someone else and perhaps have a family someday.'

Tears were rolling down Saffie's face now and she bent to gently kiss Mathilda's sweating forehead. Even now she was thinking of Marcus above herself, which only went to prove how much she loved him. Once again life was being unfair.

'Will you promise me, Saffie? At least then I can go to meet my maker with a clear mind.'

'I promise I'll do all I can,' Saffie answered with a hitch in her voice. Mathilda's eyes were closing, she was clearly worn out, so for a time Saffie sat gently holding her hand and trying to print every detail of the sweet lady's face into her memory.

An hour later, Marcus summoned the carriage and insisted on driving Saffie home. It was late afternoon and darkness was fast approaching. 'I wanted to have a word,' he admitted. 'And I'm not sure that you'll be able to help me but if you are willing, I shall speak to Mrs Spencer-Hughes.'

'What is it?'

He scratched his head, looking embarrassed. 'The thing is, I've had to close the school for a while because I want to spend as much time as I can with Mathilda. I know that Eugenie employs you as her maid but I wondered if she might allow you to have a few hours off each day just to keep the school running. It would only be for a time until—' He gulped and Saffie's kind heart went out to him.

'I would be more than willing,' she told him. She had loved her time teaching the children when she had worked at the school before. 'And I suppose it might be possible. Once I've helped Mrs Spencer-Hughes in the morning she doesn't really need me until later in the day and I'm sure she'd want to oblige you. Unlike some of the gentry she believes in the working class having an education. Why don't you ask her?'

With a smile of relief, he took her hand and gently squeezed it and Saffie flushed as, once again, tingles shot up her arm. She knew that nothing could ever come of the feelings she harboured for him – Marcus adored his wife and Saffie supposed he always would – but try as she might, she couldn't seem to control her feelings towards him.

'I'll speak to her this very evening,' he promised and Saffie nodded and stared out of the window, glad the darkness hid her blushes.

As soon as they arrived back at Lakeside House, Marcus went off to find Mrs Spencer-Hughes while Saffie went to her room to take off her cloak and bonnet. Ten minutes later, Bossy tapped on her door to tell her, 'The missus wants to see yer in the drawin' room, Saffie.'

Saffie smiled and followed Bossy downstairs to find Mrs Spencer-Hughes and Marcus waiting for her.

'Marcus has told me what he'd like you to do and I'm more than happy for you to help out,' her employer told her with a kindly smile. 'Marcus will send the carriage to take you to the school at half past eight each morning, by which time I shall be up and dressed so you have no need to fret about me. He suggests you start the school day at nine and finish at twelve, which gives the children at least half a day's schooling for now. I think it's a marvellous idea.'

Saffie was thrilled and couldn't wait to be back in the classroom.

'And while you're both here . . . I, er . . . have some news of my own that I'd like to share with you.' She took a deep breath. The last weeks had been difficult for her but now she felt ready to move on. 'I have decided that I would like to bring Margaret home for Christmas. I know it will start the tongues wagging after her long absence, but let them wag! She is all I have left and I want her to take her rightful place back in this house. It has seen enough sadness this year to last a lifetime and I want it to be a happy place again. All Victor's businesses are being run admirably by managers who report to me once a week so I am in a position to devote myself to my daughter and that's what I intend to do.'

'Why, that's marvellous news,' Marcus told her, genuinely pleased. 'And I agree with your decision entirely. When are you planning on bringing her back?'

'There's no time like the present.' Mrs Spencer-Hughes smiled. 'I thought I would start the journey tomorrow and bring her back the next day. The one thing I would ask of you, Saffie, is that you accompany me to help before starting at the school. Would you mind doing that?'

'I'd be delighted to,' Saffie assured her and so it was all decided and later that day Saffie packed an overnight bag for herself and the mistress, trying to imagine how Margaret would react when they both arrived to take her home.

For the first time in some while, things were finally looking up and Saffie hoped that this would be the start of better times to come.

Chapter Forty-Two

Although the house was still in mourning, Margaret's homecoming was a joyous occasion. The journey to the coast to fetch her home had been uneventful and although Margaret was worn out when they arrived back, she wept with joy to be home. Mrs Spencer-Hughes seemed to have developed a new lease of life and spent every moment she could with her daughter, fussing over her like a mother hen.

Saffie couldn't have been happier for them and once Margaret was settled, she went back to the school five mornings a week. She suspected that her employer was so delighted to have Margaret home that she didn't even miss her and the arrangement worked well.

Early in December, Mrs Spencer-Hughes sent one of the gardeners off to fetch two Christmas trees – an enormous one for the hallway and another, slightly smaller one, for the drawing room, and Saffie arrived home one afternoon to find them decorating the one in the hallway with dainty glass baubles that had been in Mrs Spencer-Hughes's family for years. Bossy was there too, sorting out the tiny candles that would go on last, although Saffie suspected that she was more of a hindrance than a help because she was so butter-fingered and kept dropping them. Even so, the atmosphere was light and everyone was smiling, even though they were observing the mourning rituals for Mr Spencer-Hughes and Georgina.

'I'm determined to make this Christmas as happy as it can be for Margaret,' Mrs Spencer Hughes commented with a smile that evening as Saffie brushed her hair for her at the dressing table.

'I'm sure it will be, ma'am.' Saffie was thrilled to see her mistress looking so much brighter.

She was also acting as lady's maid to Margaret, so with that and her teaching at the school her days were completely taken up and sometimes when she went to bed at night, she was so exhausted that she fell asleep the instant her head hit the pillow. Even so she was content, her only regret being that because of her busy schedule she didn't have time to go and see Granny Doyle and the twins to give them the little gifts she had bought for them. Still, she consoled herself, she would no doubt manage to see them after Christmas and at least she knew they were all well from the letters she regularly received.

In no time at all the house was looking very festive. Huge bowls of holly with shiny green leaves bearing bright red berries were placed in all the downstairs rooms and the Christmas trees were a triumph and remarked upon by everyone who saw them. In the kitchen the cook was busily preparing puddings that had been soaked in brandy and the most enormous Christmas cake that Saffie had ever seen.

'I insist that you come into the dining room to eat with Margaret and me on Christmas Day,' Mrs Spencer-Hughes said. 'You're like one of the family now and I really don't know what I would have done without you over the last few months.'

Saffie blushed with pleasure. Some of the staff were being much kinder to her now as well, a sign that she was finally being accepted, so Saffie felt that things were definitely looking up. If it hadn't been for the constant worrying about her father and Archie, she would have been content, but they were always on her mind and she often wondered if she would ever see them again. Still, the twins and Elsie were happy and healthy, so she had to be content with that.

And so on Christmas Eve, she went to her room to wrap the small gifts she had bought for Margaret and Mrs Spencer-Hughes and when she went back downstairs she found Margaret sitting alone in the drawing room staring pensively into the fire. Saffie turned to leave, reluctant to disturb her, but Margaret called her back and when Saffie was seated, she suddenly asked, 'Is Cathy, the little girl you mentioned was staying with Minnie, still with her?'

It was the first time Margaret had ever mentioned the child and Saffie's heart began to race, could Margaret be about to admit that the little girl was hers?

'Er . . . yes, yes, she is.'

'Hm, and is Minnie good to her?'

'She loves her, and Sylvie – who Minnie took in soon after – as if they were her own.'

Saffie watched different emotions flicker across Margaret's face before she said, 'I would like to see her, do you think you could arrange it?'

'I, er . . . I dare say I could?' Saffie had waited for this for so long and yet now that it was happening, she wasn't sure how she felt about it. Minnie would be heartbroken if it turned out that Margaret was Cathy's mother and she lost her, and yet Cathy deserved to be reunited with her if she *was* Margaret's flesh and blood. 'But . . . could we perhaps leave it until after Christmas?' she suggested. 'I know the girls are so looking forward to it. Minnie and Davey are so good to them.'

'Very well. Perhaps we could arrange for her to come and visit the day after Boxing Day?'

'I'll see what I can do,' Saffie promised.

But as things turned out she didn't have to do anything because the next morning when she had gone to fetch Margaret and Mrs Spencer-Hughes a mid-morning cup of tea, there was a tap on the kitchen door and the maid opened it to admit Minnie, with Cathy and Sylvie clutching small presents they had made for her.

'Merry Christmas everyone!' Minnie shook the snow that had just started to fall from her shoulders as the children stood there beaming, their faces rosy from the fresh air. 'I'm sorry to disturb yer all on Christmas mornin' but the girls insisted on comin' fer a walk to see Saffie so I thought I'd bring 'em while the goose was cookin'.'

Saffie's heart felt as if it was beating a tattoo in her chest. She was always happy to see Minnie but now she would have to tell her what Margaret had requested instead of leaving it until after Christmas. The children advanced on her, offering her their gifts and Saffie opened them. Sylvie had made her a handkerchief and had attempted to stitch her initials in the corner of it with embroidery silk. The letters were somewhat wonky but Saffie made a huge fuss of it all the same and promised that she would keep it for her very best. Cathy had attempted to knit her some mittens, under Minnie's guidance, and they too were less than perfect but because of all the time they must have spent on making the gifts Saffie was delighted with them and told them so. She had left their gifts with Minnie the week before.

'I dare say you little ones wouldn't be averse to tryin' a slice o' my fruit cake with a glass o' milk to wash it down, would yer?' the cook asked with a twinkle in her eye, and as the girls eagerly clambered onto the chairs that were placed around the table, Saffie drew Minnie to one side and taking a deep breath she began.

'Minnie, I was going to come and see you the day after tomorrow, but seeing as you're here . . .' She gulped but forced herself to go on. 'Margaret has asked to see Cathy.'

The colour drained from Minnie's face like water down a pipe and she pursed her lips together as she tried to compose herself. 'I see . . . an' when does she want to do that?' She had dreaded this day since she first met Cathy, and yet deep down she supposed she had always known that it might happen.

'I suggested I speak to you about it the day after tomorrow but seeing as you're here . . .'

Minnie nodded as she stared towards Cathy, who was eating the cake as if she hadn't been fed for a month. And then making a decision she took a deep breath. 'Well, seein' as we are 'ere, I suppose yer should go an' ask 'er if she wants to see 'er now.'

Saffie knew how much it must have cost Minnie to say that and she felt for her. 'Are you quite sure?'

Minnie nodded, so lifting the tea tray she had ready, Saffie carried it through to Mrs Spencer-Hughes and Margaret in the drawing room. She poured the tea out and handed the cups to them before saying quietly, 'I should perhaps tell you, Miss Margaret, that Cathy is in the kitchen. Minnie brought her and Sylvie so that they could give me the little presents they had made for me.'

The delicate china cup and saucer Margaret was holding wobbled dangerously and tea slopped all over her gown leaving a dark stain, but she seemed not to notice as she asked shakily, 'Cathy . . . is here? Now?'

When Saffie nodded, she banged the cup back onto the tray and looked towards her mother, who nodded as if she was giving permission for something.

'In that case . . . do you suppose Minnie would allow me to see her now for a few minutes?'

'I'm sure she would. Would you like me to bring her through?'

Margaret nodded and rose, her hands clasped tightly together at her waist as she waited while Saffie quietly left the room. Minutes later she was back, holding Cathy's hand, with Minnie and Sylvie close behind her.

'There's someone in here who you might like to see,' Saffie told the confused child, and with an encouraging nod she drew her into the room.

For a moment Cathy stood looking about her but as her eyes settled on Margaret a look of shock crossed her face and with a squeal of delight she was across the room like a hare. 'Mama, Mama, I *knew* you'd come back one day,' she cried as she flung her arms about Margaret's waist.

'Oh, my dear girl, how I've missed you.' Both Margaret and Cathy were crying happy tears as Minnie looked on dully. She knew in that moment that as much as Cathy loved her, she loved her mother more and it was like a knife in her heart.

'Are you all better now? You won't go away again, will you?' the child babbled as she clung to Margaret for dear life. It was as if she was afraid she would disappear again if she loosened her hold on her.

'Yes, I am much better, darling, and no, I won't go away again,' Margaret soothed as she gently stroked the hair back from Cathy's forehead. Then looking towards Minnie she said quietly, 'Thank you for taking such good care of her. Saffie has told me what a wonderful job you've done.'

Minnie shrugged. 'Anyone would've done the same,' she muttered as she bit back tears. She had been so looking forward to her first Christmas with her girls, as she thought of them, but now it looked like she might only have one of them.

'So shall we go back to our little house now, Mama?' Cathy chattered on excitedly.

Swallowing, Margaret shook her head. 'No, darling, I shall be living here now, but don't worry, we'll sort something out and I shall see you often. But for now, you must go back with Minnie and Sylvie; I believe she's got some lovely things planned for you over Christmas and we don't want to spoil that do we?'

Cathy accepted what she said surprisingly easily and staring towards the window where the snow was falling thickly now, she giggled. 'Davey says he'll help us build a snowman if the snow settles.'

'I shall arrange for the coach to take you all home, my dear,' Mrs Spencer-Hughes said kindly. 'You have a long walk ahead of you and it won't be easy if this continues. It's turning into a blizzard. Saffie, would you mind going to ask Mrs Beasley to have it brought round to the front for our visitors?'

'Of course, ma'am.' Saffie gave Minnie a timid smile and shot off to do as she was asked. She had expected the day to be quiet and uneventful when she had risen that morning but it was fast turning out to be anything but.

Fifteen minutes later the horses and coach were waiting outside the front door and Margaret and Cathy said a tearful goodbye. 'Promise you'll come and see me very soon, Mama,' Cathy pleaded.

After glancing at Minnie, who gave an almost imperceptible nod, Margaret smiled. 'Weather permitting, I shall come the day after tomorrow. Would that suit you?' Cathy nodded. 'Good, then go and enjoy your Christmas. I shall want to hear all about it when I see you again.'

Once outside in the coach, Cathy waved from the window until it pulled out of sight and Margaret slowly made her way back to the drawing room where her mother and Saffie were waiting for her.

Margaret went to stand in front of the fire until she turned to Saffie with tears in her eyes. 'I feel it's time I gave you an explanation,' she said quietly. 'I have felt since the first time you mentioned Cathy to me that you suspected I had a connection to Catherine and I have. But it's not what you think. You see . . . I am not Cathy's mother.'

Apart from a gasp from Saffie and the crackling of the logs on the fire, the room was suddenly silent.

Chapter Forty-Three

Margaret walked to the elegant, gilt-legged chaise longue that stood in the deep bay window and sinking down onto it she stared out at the fast-falling snow.

'Go on, my dear, I know what you have to say will come as a shock to her but I think it's time she knew the truth,' Mrs Spencer-Hughes urged, and with a heartfelt sigh Margaret turned back to face them.

'Very well. I suppose for you to understand I should start at the beginning.' She licked her dry lips and after another glance at her mother went on, 'As you have probably heard, I fell in love when I was very young with someone my father felt was totally unsuitable for me. He was a working-class man and my father had high hopes that I would marry into money.' Her eyes grew soft as her memory went back in time. 'My father threatened to disinherit me if I continued my relationship with Robert, but I loved him with all my heart and couldn't leave him. Eventually it became clear that my father meant every word he said and he would never accept him, so we did the only thing we thought we could do to be together – we ran away, eloped. We were married soon after in a little church in Norfolk where we rented a cottage and Robert took any work he could find. We were as poor as church mice but we were so happy.

'But then Robert was killed in an accident on the farm he was working on and I felt as if I wanted to die too. I had no one to turn to, no one to support me, so I wrote to your grandfather and asked him for help, Saffie. He was such a lovely, kind man and I'd known him since I was a little girl. He rented me a small cottage in Ledbury and made sure that I had enough money to get by, although he wasn't a particularly wealthy man himself. I earned some myself by taking in washing and ironing and I got by, but I knew without Robert my life would never be the same again. And then one day your grandfather came to see me and he was distraught. I'm sorry to have to tell you this, Saffie, but your grandmother is Catherine's mother.'

Saffie's eyes stretched wide with shock and she plonked heavily down onto the nearest chair as she tried to absorb what Margaret had said.

'It seems he had found out that your grandmother had had an affair and had found out that she was with child,' she said softly. 'She had been trying to get rid of it by any means she could. She had even visited a rather dubious character on the outskirts of town who is well known for helping women in that situation, but nothing had worked, so he told her that when it was born, he would bring it up as his own. But your grandmother wasn't prepared to keep the child and went off on an extended holiday to the coast. She contacted your grandfather again when Catherine had been born and told him in no uncertain terms that she would not return home unless he agreed to get rid of the baby. That was when your grandfather came to see me. He asked if I would take Cathy in and foster her, the father of the child had offered to pay me a wage if I agreed and so Cathy was brought to me.'

'So . . . who is Cathy's father?' Saffie asked in a shaky voice and again Margaret glanced at her mother.

'Her father is Marcus's father.'

There was another stunned silence, but Margaret had started the story and now she was keen to finish it; there had been too many secrets and lies and it was time for the truth to be told.

'All was well until I became ill and that was when Cathy's father had her admitted to Hatter's Hall until I was well enough to care for her again. Although he paid, the money always went through your grandfather in an effort to keep the secret. Then he died too and the hall would no longer keep Cathy without being paid. That was when Marcus brought her back to your grandmother's house. The rest you know: your grandmother was so distraught that it caused her to have a breakdown. She hated the poor child and blamed her for everything when in truth she only had herself to blame.

'The problem was that as the years passed, I came to look upon Cathy as my own. From the time she could talk it seemed the most natural thing in the world for her to call me Mama. After all, I was the nearest thing she'd had to a mother. I'm *so* sorry, Saffie. I realise this must have come as a terrible shock to you and I've no doubt it will be to Marcus too.' Tears were trickling down her cheeks, but Saffie brushed aside her apology.

'It isn't your fault,' she told her. 'You only did as you were asked and loved and cared for Cathy. But what will happen now? I know that Minnie adores the child and it would break her heart to lose her.'

Margaret spread her hands helplessly. 'I don't know. Mother and I have spoken of this, and although she isn't

404

mine by birth, I would gladly adopt her. If that is possible, Mother has agreed to accept her as her granddaughter.'

'Well, if you don't remarry, the chances are I will never have any grandchildren,' Mrs Spencer-Hughes pointed out. 'Cathy is the nearest I might ever get to having one. And I must say I do find her adorable. It would be lovely to have a child in the house again. Why don't we have some time to think of it for now and get Christmas over with? The last thing we want to do is hurt Minnie. She's been so good to the child.'

As Saffie sat there the pieces of the puzzle finally fell into place – the way her grandmother had reacted when Cathy was brought home from Hatter's Hall. She must have been terrified that the truth would come out because then her reputation would be gone forever, and she had taken her fear out on Cathy.

Both women rose, they could see that Saffie had a lot to take in, and so they quietly left the room to give her time to come to terms with what she had heard.

Christmas dinner was a quiet affair following the revelations of that morning and delicious as it was, Saffie ate little. It began with a pâté and tiny squares of toast followed by an enormous roast goose, Cook's home-made stuffing and a selection of vegetables, all served with crispy roast potatoes and parsnips covered in thick creamy gravy. An enormous Christmas pudding followed and hot mince pies, but again Saffie had no appetite for them and was glad when the meal was over and she could retire to her room for a while.

The snow continued to fall and by late afternoon the world outside her bedroom looked as if it had been painted white and coated with shattered diamonds. It was then that

Saffie realised she should go and see if Mrs Spencer-Hughes or Margaret wanted anything. After all, she reasoned, that was what she was paid for. But as she reached the foot of the stairs there was a knock on the front door and when the parlour maid answered it, Saffie was shocked to see Marcus enter.

'Marcus, we weren't expecting to see you today.'

'I wasn't intending to come but Mathilda is fast asleep so I thought I'd take the opportunity to pop up and bring you all your gifts. I can't stay long though. The snow is getting deep in places and I don't want the roads to get impassable else you'll have me all over Christmas.'

'The mistress and Miss Margaret are in the drawing room,' Saffie informed him as the maid took his coat and hat. The snow on them instantly dropped to the floor and began to form puddles as it melted. 'Do go in to them, I'm sure they'll be pleased to see you.'

Saffie's heart began to thump again. No doubt Margaret would tell him that he had a half-sister he had never known about, and he would be as shocked as Saffie had been. Suddenly she didn't want to be there when he made the discovery. It would be hard for him to find that his father had been unfaithful to his mother and she couldn't bear to see his pain, so as he set off towards the drawing room, she quietly retreated up the stairs and left them to it.

He had long since gone when she ventured down again and Mrs Spencer-Hughes eyed her worriedly. 'Are you all right, my dear? You look awfully pale.' Then before Saffie could answer she went on, 'We spoke to Marcus about the situation and just as you were, he was shocked. I think what you both need now is time to come to terms with everything.'

'I'd like to go and see Minnie in the morning, with your permission. I think she should be informed of what you want to do.'

Mrs Spencer-Hughes sighed. 'Of course you must go and tell her, my dear. We owe her that much at least and we will never forget how much she has done for Cathy. But the final decision isn't made yet. I pointed out to Margaret that really Cathy should be the one to decide where she wants to live. I realise she has formed a close attachment to Minnie and Davey now, and it just might be that she decides she doesn't want to leave them. Do please tell Minnie that. We are prepared to stand by whatever decision the child makes, because all we want is what is best for her.'

'Very well, ma'am.' Saffie thought that was very fair but she still dreaded having to explain the truth to Minnie. She was sure she would be as shocked as she had been to discover that Saffie's grandmother was in fact the child's mother!

She tossed and turned that night, dreading the day ahead, but as it happened her plans to visit Minnie went out of the window when there was a loud hammering on the door very early the next morning.

Saffie had just swung her feet out of bed when Bossy appeared, clad in a long voluminous nightgown and holding an oil lamp.

'Saffie, Mr Berrin'ton is downstairs. He's really upset an' he says please will yer come down straightaway.' Her face was chalk white and Saffie could see that something must be seriously amiss.

Saffie yanked her robe on and followed Bossy downstairs to find Marcus pacing the hall.

'Marcus, what is it?' She was clinging to the banister as she tried to prevent herself from tripping over her long nightclothes.

'I've just ridden to ask the doctor to come, Mathilda's taken a turn for the worse,' he gulped. 'And on the way back I thought you might like to come and see her.'

'Of course I would.' Saffie's heart was pounding as she looked into his stricken face. Mathilda really must be very poorly indeed. 'Just give me two minutes to throw some clothes on and I'll be with you.'

She was back downstairs within minutes. 'Explain to Mrs Spencer-Hughes what has happened in the morning, would you please, Bossy? And tell her I'll be home as soon as I can.'

'Yes, miss.' Bossy held the lamp high to light them down the steps to where Marcus's small barouche was parked. It had started to snow again and within seconds Saffie's teeth were chattering, partly with fear at what she might find when they reached Marcus's house and partly from cold.

'I-I should apologise, getting you out of bed at this unearthly hour.' Marcus was urging the horse to go far faster than the slippery roads warranted and Saffie held on to the side of the barouche for dear life. 'I don't know why I did really. I suppose I'm afraid and I just wanted a friend to be there with us.'

'It's quite all right.' Saffie kept her eyes trained straight ahead as the barouche slithered from side to side, wondering how anything that looked so pretty could be so treacherous.

Thankfully they reached the house safely and as they pulled into the stable yard Marcus threw the reins to the young groom, telling him, 'Make sure she has a good rub down and throw a blanket over her, would you?' He then grasped Saffie's arm and half carried her across the yard and in through the kitchen door. There was no time for standing on ceremony; he wanted to be back with his wife. A maid was in the kitchen filling the kettle at the sink and he told her, 'The doctor should be here any minute now, Dolly. Will you show him straight up to the mistress's room?'

Seconds later he was back in Mathilda's room with Saffie close behind him. The nurse was bending over Mathilda, who was lying frighteningly still on the bed, but she stood aside as Marcus rushed forward to take his wife's hand. Her breathing was laboured and as Marcus stared at the nurse, she sadly shook her head.

Tears began to trickle down Saffie's cheeks as she saw the raw pain in his eyes and she wondered briefly if anyone would ever love her as much as he clearly loved his wife. But she dismissed the thought. It didn't matter because she had been forced to admit to herself that she loved Marcus and she knew that if she couldn't have him, she would never marry anyone else. She was doomed to become an old maid.

She stood back, feeling strangely in the way, and soon after the doctor arrived, huffing and puffing after rushing up the stairs. Marcus stood aside while the doctor quickly examined his patient and then he shook his head.

'I'm sorry,' he said gravely. 'But I fear the end is near now.'

Saffie felt as if she was once again caught in the grip of a nightmare. There had been so many deaths, so much heartbreak in her short life that she suddenly had the urge to run far away where she knew no one, but she knew she must stay. Marcus regarded her as a friend and he would need her strength soon.

Mathilda passed away without regaining consciousness just as the birds began their dawn chorus outside. Her passing was surprisingly peaceful. One moment the sound of her rasping breathing was echoing around the room and the next there was only silence save for the birdsong outside. As Marcus sobbed, his head on his wife's still chest, Saffie quietly crossed to open the window so that Mathilda's soul might fly free.

'Rest in peace, my dear sweet friend, heaven has gained an angel today,' she whispered as her tears fell unchecked. She had made Mathilda a solemn promise that she would care for Marcus in his hour of grief and now she intended to do just that.

Chapter Forty-Four

Throughout the next month Saffie was kept busy at the school and she was grateful of the fact. Marcus had shown great dignity at Mathilda's funeral and Saffie knew his wife would have been proud of him. He started to call at Mrs Spencer-Hughes's most evenings to talk through the next day's lessons with her, even though Saffie would have been quite capable of planning them herself. She suspected that he was glad to just get out of his house, which he said felt horribly empty, but as January drew to a close, he decided that it was time to return to his teaching and Saffie was able to resume her job as a full-time maid to Mrs Spencer-Hughes and Margaret.

The conversation with Cathy, where they would ask her where she would like to live, had been delayed because of Mathilda's passing, but now Mrs Spencer-Hughes thought it was time and so one cold February afternoon Marcus drove Minnie and Cathy to Lakeside House. Margaret had seen the child on a regular basis and Saffie had been touched to see the bond between them.

Cathy bounced into the drawing room where Mrs Spencer-Hughes and Margaret were waiting for her and as always, she flung her arms about Margaret's waist.

'We did sums at school today, Mama, and I got ten out of ten!' Cathy's face was alight as she bragged of her achievement and Margaret smiled as she tenderly stroked the hair from her forehead.

'You're a very clever girl,' she praised. 'But . . . the thing is, darling, I asked you and Minnie to come here today for a reason. You see, now that I am much better, I would be able to care for you again. But . . . and it's a very *big* but . . . only if that is what you want. I know you love Minnie and so if you decide that you would rather stay with her, I would quite understand.'

Cathy's little face instantly became solemn as she stared from Margaret to Minnie.

'Before you make your decision, I think I should tell you that my mama and I have decided to go and stay in our London town house, perhaps for a very long time,' she went on gently. 'There has been so much sadness here recently and we both feel that it would do us good to have a complete change.'

'*London!*' Cathy's eyes grew rounder. She had seen pictures in books of Buckingham Palace and the River Thames and couldn't imagine how marvellous it would be to actually visit them and see them in real life. 'But if I came with you what would happen about school?' she asked innocently.

'That would all depend entirely on what you wanted,' Margaret told her patiently. 'You would be given a choice. I could either employ a tutor to come in and teach you at home or I could arrange for you to go to a school there.'

Throughout the conversation, Minnie had stood silently by and now Margaret asked her, 'How do you feel about this, Minnie?'

'I want what's best fer Cathy.' Minnie managed a weak smile. 'An' I reckon I know which way she'll choose. I know she's fond o' me, Davey an' Sylvie, but a blind man on a gallopin' donkey can see the love atween you two every time you're together.'

'Will you be sad if I decide to go with Mama?' Cathy stared at her anxiously and Minnie gently stroked her hair.

'Not really, pet. I was only ever supposed to look after yer till we could get yer mama better an' now she is . . . An' it ain't as if I ain't never gonna see yer again, is it now? Yer bound to come back 'ere to visit so if yer want to be wi' yer mama then that's fine by me.'

'Oh, I *do* love you, Minnie. Thank you for all you've done for me. You've been so kind!' Cathy threw her arms about her and gave her a hug. 'But if you're sure you don't mind . . .'

'You go to yer mama wi' my blessin, pet.' Minnie nudged her towards Margaret as she blinked back her tears. 'An' now I'd best get back to feed that 'ungry lot. Yer know what they're like if I'm late wi' the dinner. Bye fer now, pet.'

She left the room hastily with Saffie close behind her and once the door had closed Saffie told her, 'I was so proud of you in there. You've been so brave. It must have been very hard for you. I know how much you've come to care for that little girl.'

'Aye, I 'ave. I'll not deny it. But yer know, I've 'ad time to come to terms wi' it an' I've still got Sylvie an' this little one to look forward to, ain't I?' She patted the mound of her stomach. 'But what's this about London? Are you goin' wi' 'em?'

Saffie shook her head. 'It's the first I've heard about it.' She chewed on her lip. 'But I'm not too keen on the idea because . . .'

'It would mean leavin' Marcus.'

Saffie blushed as Minnie smiled. 'I know yer now,' she said quietly. 'An' I guessed you 'ad feelin's fer 'im some time ago.'

Shamefaced Saffie hung her head.

'Now don't go lookin' like that.' Minnie squeezed her hand. 'It's nowt to be ashamed of. Love strikes where it will an' there's nowt we can do about it. An' don't get worryin' about where you'll go. I've allus been a big believer that when one door shuts another one opens.'

She pecked Saffie on the cheek and set off for home and as Saffie watched her walk away she thought what a remarkable woman she was.

From that moment on the atmosphere in the house changed. Suddenly the rooms rang with a child's laughter and Saffie had never seen her mistress or Miss Margaret, for that matter, look so happy.

'But what will you do, dear, if you don't come to London with us?' Mrs Spencer-Hughes fretted as Saffie was dressing her hair one morning. Saffie had given her decision shortly after Minnie had left.

'Oh, don't get worrying about me. Something will turn up.'

'Hm, just so long as you know I would be delighted should you change your mind.'

Saffie smiled at her in the mirror then set about packing yet another trunk that her mistress was taking with her. Everything was happening so fast that she could hardly take it all in. She hadn't even had a chance to ask around about another position but she wasn't overly worried. Mrs Spencer-Hughes had already told her that she could stay there for as long as she liked once they left and failing that

414

she could always take Minnie up on her offer of staying at the cottage.

The family were planning to catch the train to London on Friday, which was now only three days away, and sometimes Saffie wondered how they were going to do it. There was already a tower of luggage ready to be forwarded, which made Saffie suspect that Mrs Spencer-Hughes would be in no hurry to come back – if she ever did, that was. She supposed she couldn't blame her. Mr Spencer-Hughes had ruled her with a rod of iron but now she could choose her friends and come and go as she pleased, and although she was still grieving for Georgina, already she was blossoming. Margaret was too and she and Cathy were almost insep-arable. They were clearly very fond of each other and Saffie hoped that they would now have the happy ever after they both deserved. Admittedly there were still times when she had a chance to reflect and she struggled to believe that Cathy was truly the child of her own grandmother, but she was slowly coming to terms with it and felt that being with Margaret would be the best for her.

Now all she had to worry about was what she was to do, but that problem was solved the following day when Marcus visited. He had lost a lot of weight since Mathilda had died and his face was gaunt, his eyes haunted.

It was Bossy who answered the door to him before com-ing to find Saffie to tell her, 'Mr Berrin'ton is here to see yer, Saffie. I showed 'im into the drawin' room.

'To see me?' Saffie frowned. She was busy packing yet more of Mrs Spencer-Hughes's undergarments but she stopped to cross to the mirror to check her reflection. 'Can you tell him I'll be down directly please, Bossy?'

She quickly straightened the skirt of her pale grey gown and tucked some strands of her raven-black hair back into the chignon on the back of her head, then slowly she went down to see her visitor.

He was sitting with Mrs Spencer-Hughes in the drawing room and Saffie saw at a glance that her mistress looked concerned.

'Ah, Saffie.' She held her hand out towards her and beckoned her to come closer. 'Marcus has a problem and thinks you may be able to solve it for him, but I have to say, after hearing what he suggests, I'm not so sure that it would be such a good idea for you.'

'Oh!' Saffie was intrigued as she sat down opposite them both and folded her hands neatly in her lap.

Marcus cleared his throat and after casting an anxious glance at Mrs Spencer-Hughes he coughed nervously and began, 'Unfortunately, my new housekeeper, Mrs Jeeves, has received bad news. Her brother, who is a widower and her only remaining relative, has taken seriously ill and has suggested to Mrs Jeeves that she might come and live with him in Brighton to take care of him. Mrs Jeeves has asked if she might leave as soon as possible, which will leave me without a housekeeper and I thought . . . Well, I thought it might solve a problem for both of us if you were willing to take on the role. I shall need a new housekeeper and if you are sure that you don't want to go to London you will need a new post.'

Mrs Spencer-Hughes interrupted at this point. 'The problem I can see is, Saffie, that so soon after dear Mathilda's passing and because of your age, this may cause gossip. You know what people can be like.'

'I can assure you everything would be as it should be,' Marcus said quickly. 'Saffie would have her own room on another floor to mine.'

'I have no doubt that she would, but as I said . . . people may talk.'

'So let them,' Saffie said defiantly with a lift of her chin and a flash of her eyes. 'My mother always used to say while people were talking about us, they were leaving some other poor devil alone.'

'Then if you feel you could handle it, by all means accept the post,' Mrs Spencer-Hughes answered and suddenly it was decided and Saffie was left wondering what life may have in store for her next.

Bright and early on Friday morning, Saffie said a tearful goodbye to Mrs Spencer-Hughes, Margaret and Cathy, and once they had left for the train station, she made her way back to her room to begin her own packing. Marcus would be calling to collect her in the coach later that afternoon when school was finished for the weekend, and she would be moving into his home to begin her new post. She was now feeling extremely nervous about it. After giving it some thought, she had realised that she had no idea what being a housekeeper actually entailed apart from what she had seen of Mrs Beasley, but Marcus had been confident that she would handle it well when she had expressed her concerns. And so now all that remained was to give it a try. Although she would miss her employer and Bossy, she wasn't entirely sorry to be leaving Lakeside House. The staff had warmed to her slightly over the past months, but hand on heart she couldn't really say that she had been truly happy there and so she hoped that the next phase of her life would be better.

The gossip that Mrs Spencer-Hughes had feared began before she had even left the house when, later that afternoon, she went downstairs to say goodbye to everyone. The cook was standing at the deep stone sink with her back to her when Saffie entered the kitchen and when she heard what she was saying to the parlour maid her words cut like a knife.

'I can't believe Mr Berrington would be so daft as to employ a lowly boatie like her, and so soon after his lovely wife's passing an' all.' The woman hitched her enormous breasts up as her head wagged with disgust. 'Poor Mrs Berrington must be turnin' in her grave, the poor lass. I mean it's obvious what he wants her for, and it ain't housekeeping I'd bet me last penny. A young pretty face to warm his bed more like!'

The parlour maid suddenly spotted Saffie standing there and as colour flamed into her cheeks the cook's head slowly turned and she sniffed disdainfully. 'Don't they allus say eavesdroppers hear no good of themselves?'

'I *wasn't* eavesdropping,' Saffie answered in an ominously low voice. 'In actual fact I was coming to say goodbye to you all because despite what you all think of me, I was taught good manners. And I can assure you I will be going to Mr Berrington's *purely* as a housekeeper! I have *never* warmed anyone's bed yet and nor do I intend to.' She then nodded towards the rest of the staff present and with what dignity she could muster, she turned and sailed from the kitchen with her head held high.

It wasn't until she reached the sanctuary of her room that the tears that had been threatening to choke her erupted and rained down her cheeks. Now she had no doubts whatsoever that they would all have a field day tearing her reputation to shreds once she had moved into Marcus's home.

His face flashed into her mind and she took a deep breath. *Let them do their worst*, she thought. She knew that she would never be anything more than a paid help to him, but so long as she could be close to him, and keep her promise to Mathilda, that would be enough.

Chapter Forty-Five

December, 1875

'Why, that looks beautiful, Saffie,' Marcus said approvingly when he arrived home from the school one cold and frosty afternoon. Saffie was just putting the finishing touches to the tree she had been decorating in the parlour and she blushed with pleasure at his praise.

Over the years she had worked for him they had become easy in each other's company and she had proved her worth. Not only did she keep his home running like clockwork but each evening they would sit together after he had dined and she would help him to set out the lessons for school the next day. The year before he had developed a bad case of influenza and had been confined to bed for over a week, but Saffie had taken it all in her stride and after leaving the maid with strict instructions on how to care for him, she had once again run the school until he was well enough to return.

'You really are a woman of many talents,' he praised. Then becoming more serious he said quietly, 'I'm just concerned about your lack of a social life. You're still a very young woman and you should get out and about more. You rarely venture out apart from to go and see Minnie and Davey.'

'I'm quite content, thank you,' she answered demurely as she fastened the last of the tiny candles to a branch. She stood back to survey her efforts and smiled. 'And yes, you're right, the tree does look lovely, even if I do say so myself.'

He chuckled. 'And how are Minnie and the new baby? Have you seen them today?'

'Yes, I popped over this morning but I needn't have bothered. Davey has everything in hand, and Sylvie and little Gertie are over the moon with their new baby brother.'

'Wonderful. It's been quite an eventful year for you hasn't it, one way and another?'

'Yes, I suppose it has.'

In July, Lucy had joined a convent as a postulant as she had decided some time before that this was her calling, and in November Ginny had married one of the boys who lived on the boats, whom they had known since childhood. Granny Doyle was still going strong and Saffie had joked that she would live to be a hundred, which she certainly seemed capable of doing. A letter from Archie earlier in the year had informed her that he had married Miriam, the rancher's daughter, so she had written back and wished him well, although she wondered now if she would ever see him again. Elsie and Bernie were now the proud parents of two little boys and Elsie loved her life as a policeman's wife. The only sad news that year had been when Bernie had informed her that her father had passed away in prison from a severe case of lung fever. She had come to terms with it now and was looking to the future again.

Saffie was now twenty-four years old and sometimes she felt sad to know that she was destined to be a spinster, but that was preferable to being apart from Marcus, so all in all she was happy with her lot, although often it was very difficult to hide her feelings for him. Just as

Mrs Spencer-Hughes had predicted, the gossips had had a field day when she had first moved in with Marcus, but slowly, they had found someone else to gossip about and now the fact that Marcus had a young housekeeper was old news and people left them alone.

Bossy still called to see her sometimes on her day off and the last time she had told her that Mrs Spencer-Hughes had instructed the solicitor to put Lakeside House on the market and that she was going to be a maid for her in London once the house was sold. It seemed that Mrs Spencer-Hughes had met a very nice gentleman and she was now engaged to be married. He was a politician and so following their marriage she would be going to live with him in his home in Mayfair while Margaret and Cathy would continue to live in the town house. Saffie was pleased for them. They all deserved to be happy. Her grandmother was still being cared for by Mrs Jenkins, and surprisingly they seemed to get along well together, although as yet, she had still refused to see Saffie.

But now Christmas was looming once again and as always Saffie was determined to make it as good as she could for Marcus. He had given both the cook and the maid Christmas Eve, Christmas Day and Boxing Day off to spend with their families, so it would be just the two of them and she was looking forward to it. Normally Saffie ate in the kitchen with the rest of the staff to observe the proprieties but because there would be no one else there, Marcus had asked her to join him in the dining room.

On the morning of Christmas Eve, Saffie popped out to see Minnie and Davey to deliver the gifts she had bought for them and the children, and as always, she received a royal welcome.

Minnie was sitting at the side of a blazing fire feeding little Alfie and she looked the picture of contentment.

'Oh, he's *so* adorable,' Saffie crooned as she leaned over and stared at him enviously.

Minnie chuckled. 'He certainly is, though me an' Davey are still gettin' over the shock of havin' another baby. We thought we were blessed to have our Gertie so this one 'ere is just like the icin' on the cake. Davey is tickled pink to 'ave a son, not that he don't adore the girls, o' course.'

'You've been very lucky,' Saffie sighed, and, serious now, Minnie raised her eyebrows.

'Yer know, pet,' she said tentatively. 'You're a lovely young woman an' you could 'ave all o' this if . . .'

'If I left Marcus, you mean?' Saffie smiled sadly as she stroked Alfie's downy hair. 'There's no chance of that happening, although I have to admit I'm envious of you.'

'And how is Marcus?'

'Actually, he's seemed a lot more settled lately.' Saffie took the baby from Minnie and put him across her shoulder to wind him as Minnie fastened her blouse. 'I think he's come to terms with Mathilda's passing now.'

There was no more time for conversation then as Sylvie and Gertie descended on her, demanding she play with them and the next hour passed pleasantly until she said, 'Well, as much as I'm enjoying myself, I'm afraid I shall have to get back now. I'm responsible for cooking the Christmas dinner this year as Marcus has given Cook the day off and I've a million things to do.'

As Saffie made her way home, the first flakes of snow began to fall, making the shiny red berries on the holly in the hedges stand out in sharp contrast. The rest of the day was spent preparing the evening meal as well as the Christmas dinner and just for good measure she baked a tray of mince pies. She doubted they'd be anywhere near as good as the ones Cook made but she knew how much Marcus loved them.

'Why don't we eat in here this evening?' Marcus suggested when the evening meal was almost ready and he joined her in the kitchen. 'There's only you and me here so there's no need to stand on ceremony and it's so cosy in here. I can lay the table if you like.'

Outside the snow was still falling fast and the world had turned white, giving everything a magical appearance.

'Well . . . if you're quite sure you don't mind eating in the kitchen,' Saffie answered uncertainly.

As promised Marcus laid the table and they sat down to eat together. Saffie felt strange; anyone glancing through the window might have taken them for a couple and she wished it were so but knew that it could never be. Marcus still loved Mathilda and she doubted that would ever change.

After the simple meal of cottage pie, potatoes and vegetables she served him with apple pie and custard and when it was done, he sat back and patted his stomach contentedly, noticing how the flickering firelight turned her hair to molten ebony.

'That was delicious,' he praised and she blushed as she rose to clear the dirty pots from the table.

'Let me help,' he offered, but she shook her head.

'No, you go and read the newspaper and have a glass of port. This is my job and it's Christmas Eve.'

He chuckled. 'It's Christmas Eve for you too,' he pointed out in a gentle voice as feelings he had not felt since Mathilda's death surged through him. Why hadn't he ever noticed before how pretty she was? he wondered. 'And as for it being your job . . . well, all I can say is I don't know how I would have got through the last few years without you. You've been my rock and have done far more for me than you should have.'

'Nonsense.' Saffie avoided his eyes as she carried the dirty pots to the sink.

She wasn't aware that he'd come up behind her until he gently laid his hand on her arm. She went rigid, hardly able to breathe – she had waited for his touch for so long.

Seeing her reaction, he stepped back, his face aflame. 'I . . . I'm *so* sorry.' He was clearly distraught as he ran his hands through his hair distractedly. 'I shouldn't have done that . . . I really am so sorry. I didn't mean to embarrass you.'

Suddenly, Saffie could take it no longer. Keeping her back to him, her chin dropped to her chest and she leaned on the sink, unable to hold back the tears that had sprung to her eyes.

'Saffie, *please* . . . forgive me. I honestly didn't mean to insult you.'

'Y-you didn't.' She gulped, staring down at the dirty water in the sink, unable look at him, because if she did, he would surely see what she felt for him shining there. 'It's just I-I . . .' And then, unable to say another word, she fled from the room.

She didn't venture downstairs again until she was sure Marcus had gone to bed, and she was shocked to find the kitchen neat and tidy as a new pin. Marcus had washed and dried the pots and had even put them away, though some of them were in the wrong place.

She was putting coal on the fire the next morning when he appeared holding a small gift-wrapped package. 'Merry Christmas, Saffie. I, er . . . got you a little something.'

'Oh!' She quickly wiped her hands on her apron before crossing to take it from him and when she opened it, she found a small heart-shaped locket on a slender gold chain.

'I can always take it back and exchange it for something else if you don't like it,' he muttered self-consciously, but she quickly shook her head, her delight shining in her face.

'Oh no . . . no. I mean . . . I love it,' she told him breathlessly. 'Thank you. Would you do it up for me?'

She handed it to him and turning she lifted her sheet of hair to expose her neck.

Marcus broke out in a sweat. 'I'll, er . . . just be a minute.' He was suddenly all fingers and thumbs but eventually he managed it and she raced to the mirror to admire it before snatching a gift for him from beneath the tree.

'It's not much, I'm afraid.'

He opened the parcel to reveal a fine pair of leather gloves and a soft cashmere scarf. 'They'll be just right for this weather,' he told her as he nodded towards the window with a wide smile. 'But now how about I cook breakfast for you. I can't promise it will be up to much – Mathilda always said I could burn water – but seeing as you're going to be cooking the Christmas dinner, it's the least I can do.'

They entered the kitchen side by side and Marcus managed to fry them some sausages and eggs, which were just about edible. But then Saffie shooed him away. She wanted the dinner to be just right, so she set to.

Later that morning she set the table in the dining room with the finest china and crystal glasses on a snow-white tablecloth. A candelabra took pride of place in the centre, surrounded by bowls of holly that Saffie had picked from

426

the garden, and by the time the meal was served they were both easy with each other again.

Marcus began to carve the goose, which was far too big for just the two of them, while Saffie served the crispy roast potatoes and sage and onion stuffing, along with a variety of vegetables. When they were seated Marcus poured them both a glass of wine and held his up in a toast to her.

'To you, my dear. I truly don't know what I would have done without you and I want you to know I appreciate everything you've done for me. Cheers.'

'Cheers!' They clinked glasses and started to eat and the mood was light and cheerful for the first time in a very long while. Following the dinner Saffie served up a delicious pudding, which the cook had had soaking in brandy for months, and Marcus managed a second helping before groaning as he held his stomach and laughed.

'Oh goodness. I fear I've made an awful pig of myself. I don't think I shall eat again for months. Now come into the parlour and we'll have a game of chess. The washing up can wait till later and I'll help you with it. It is Christmas Day after all, and you deserve a rest too.'

The afternoon passed pleasantly as they played cards and chess and by teatime Saffie was in a mellow mood as she thought of Christmases past spent with her family. They could never come again and yet she wasn't unhappy to be where she was.

The snow was inches deep by that time and there was nothing to be seen but a white winter wonderland as she drew the curtains late that afternoon. She had loved every second she had spent with Marcus all to herself and wished it could go on forever, but she was aware that after the next day everything would be back to normal. Cook and the maid would return, Marcus would go back to schooling and she would resume her role as the housekeeper.

She was staring into the fire musingly when he suddenly interrupted her thoughts to say, 'A penny for them.'

'What? Oh . . .' She smiled. 'I was just thinking how nice it's been . . . just the two of us.' There, it was finally said and she didn't regret it.

He stared at her thoughtfully for a moment before saying softly, 'I think so too.'

As their eyes locked, Saffie felt as if she was drowning. And then suddenly he blurted out, 'I have to tell you, Saffie . . . I find you very attractive.'

Her heart started to beat faster as he moved closer and took her hands. 'I've felt like this for some time now, which I know is wrong. After all, I am so much older than you. You're twenty-four and I'm fourteen years your senior.'

'Age is just a number,' she said quietly as she continued to stare at him and before she knew what was happening his mouth gently came down on hers and every part of her body started to tingle, as if she was suddenly coming awake after a very long sleep.

But then once more, he suddenly put her abruptly from him and started to apologise. 'I'm sorry . . . I don't know what has come over me.'

'Neither do I . . . but whatever it is, I like it.'

He stared at her as if he could hardly believe what she was saying but for Saffie there could be no going back now. 'I've loved you for so long,' she told him gently.

'You *have*?' He looked shocked – amazed. 'And I have feelings for you,' he admitted. 'But the thing is . . . I loved

428

my wife and I don't know if I could ever love anyone else enough to marry them. What I'm saying is, it wouldn't be fair on you if anything was to happen between us. You are a beautiful young woman. You could have any young man you wanted, whereas I can't promise that I'd ever wed you.'

She smiled; a gentle smile that touched his heart.

'It wouldn't matter if you never did. My mother and father were never legally married, were they? The boat people don't worry about formalities like that. It would be enough for me just to be close to you and to know that you cared for me.'

'But you would lose your reputation should it ever become common knowledge,' he pointed out.

Another shrug from Saffie. 'So? As my mother always said, "Sticks and stones may break my bones but words can never hurt me."'

She was in his arms again and all was right with the world as he kissed her once more before soundlessly leading her by the hand towards the staircase.

Inside her heart was singing as she fingered the delicate gold locket. She was finally where she wanted to be and if this was all she could ever have of him, it would be more than enough.

Epilogue

Notice in local newspaper, Nuneaton, March 1881

The marriage of Miss Sapphire Doyle, spinster of this parish, and Mr Marcus Walter Berrington, has taken place in the parish of Coton at Chilvers Coton Parish Church. Mr Berrington is well regarded, and responsible for setting up and funding the highly successful free school in the town, and Miss Doyle is known for starting up the soup kitchen and raising funds for the workhouse as well as teaching with her husband at the free school. The wedding was attended by the couple's friends and family members, and their two daughters, four-year-old Mathilda and two-year-old Olivia, acted as flower girls. Following the couple's wedding, the family went on an extended holiday to the Isle of Wight where Mrs Berrington gave birth to a son, William Reuben Berrington.

Acknowledgements

As always, a massive thank you to my 'Rosie Team' at Bonnier Books UK! Each and every one of you always goes the extra mile to help make each book as good as it can be. Kate Parkin, Sarah Bauer, my editor, Katie Meegan, Eleanor Stammeijer and Gillian Holmes, my brilliant copy editor. There are too many of you to mention but you all know who you are and I want you to know I appreciate every single one of you.

Never forgetting my amazing agent Sheila Crowley at Curtis Brown who helped to put me on the path to where I am today. I couldn't have done it without you.

And of course, a huge thank you to my family and my long-suffering hubby who spends endless hours alone while I am locked away with my fur babies and my imaginary characters in my office without a word of complaint! You're my rock.

Last but never least, a big thank you to all my lovely readers. Your reviews and messages always make my day and make every single second I spend writing worthwhile. Please keep them coming.

Welcome to the world of Rosie Goodwin!

Keep reading for more from Rosie Goodwin, to discover
a recipe that features in this novel and to find out
more about Rosie Goodwin's next book . . .

We'd also like to welcome you to Memory Lane,
a place to discuss the very best saga stories from
authors you know and love with other readers,
plus get recommendations for new books we think
you'll enjoy. Read on and join our club!

www.MemoryLane.Club

f www.facebook.com/groups/memorylanebookgroup

Hello everyone,

I do hope this finds you all well and enjoying the better weather. I'm delighted to share *A Lesson Learned* with you all and do hope you'll enjoy it. In this one we meet the lovely Sapphire, or Saffy as she prefers to be known. Sadly, this is the last of my Precious Stones series and I've enjoyed writing it so much that I'm almost sorry to see it come to an end. Each of my characters were so real to me and I came to love them all as I hope you will.

In this one we get to cruise the canals of Warwickshire. I had great fun writing it as I researched how the boat people lived back in time. Their lives were so incredibly hard and yet overall, it appears they accepted their way of life and were content. Our lovely Sapphire was no different although deep down she always dreamed of becoming a teacher. It made me think back to my own school days. I have to admit I was appalling at maths when I was at school but I always excelled at English and my dream was to become a journalist. I just loved inventing stories which I would tell to my school friends during breaks and lunchtime and I was forever scribbling. I can remember walking to school in thick fogs when my imagination would take over as stories formed in my mind. I think I spent most of my time in the school library when I wasn't in a class and can't even remember a time when I didn't love reading anything and everything I could get my hands on. I still do!

My love for writing continued after I left school and my children were weaned on stories that I wrote for them but after getting married and starting my own family and then fostering dozens of children besides, it was purely a hobby. I didn't become published until 2004 after my husband urged me to write a book and I am now writing my forty-third novel!

Somewhere along the way my dream of becoming a journalist changed to becoming an author, although I never dreamed I would manage it. Recently my publishers had a count-up of the books they have sold and I was delighted (and shocked) to find that the number had gone from one million, which I thought was wonderful, to over four million, so thank you all so much for your support! You all really have made a dream come true and I can promise there are lots more books to come.

The next one, which will be out later in the year, is to be called *The Lost Girl*. This one is a ghost story and I hope you'll like it. As always, I'd like to urge any of you who haven't already, to join The Memory Lane Book Club on Facebook. It's a great club where you'll be kept up to date with what myself and the other memory lane authors are up to, and also there are some great prizes to be won. And thanks once again for all your lovely reviews and messages. I really enjoy reading them so please keep them coming.

So now it's back to work for me and all that's left is to wish you all a very happy summer. I hope you all get to have some lovely holidays and I'll speak to you all again very soon. Take care.

With love,
Rosie xxx

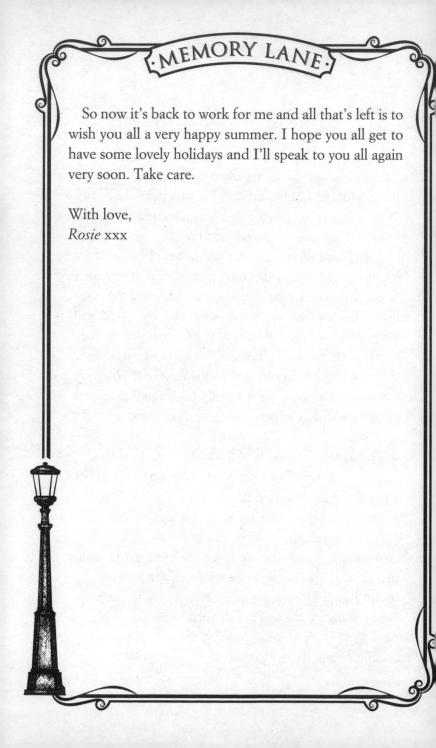

Saffie's Beef Stew

This cheap and hearty meal is a common dinner for Saffie's family on *The Blue Sapphire*. Saffie manages to make a few extra pennies for her family by selling stew to their neighbours.

Saffie would have cooked this on the stove, but you can also make this in a slow cooker or stew it in the oven if you prefer.

Serves 4

You will need:

1kg stewing beef, chopped into chunks
2l water
500ml beer or ale
2 onions, peeled and diced
2 carrots, peeled and diced
1 turnip or sweet potato, peeled and diced
1 large potato, peeled and diced
1 piece of celery, finely chopped
Salt and pepper, to taste
1 tbsp butter, to thicken
1 tbsp flour, to thicken

·MEMORY LANE·

Method:

1. Wash, chop and prepare the vegetables. Chop the beef into small chunks.
2. Put the beef, beer and water in a large, lidded saucepan and simmer for 5 minutes, then carefully skim off any fat.
3. Add the vegetables and a sprinkle of salt and pepper.
4. Cover, then stew gently on a very low heat for 3–4 hours, or until everything is soft and tender.
5. Add the flour and butter to thicken.
6. Serve with thick bread or dumplings.
7. Enjoy!

Turn over for a sneak peek at Rosie's next novel

The Lost Girl

1875

With their father missing and their mother suddenly
passing, Esme and Gabriel are forced to track down
their estranged grandfather in Lincolnshire. Cold and
unwelcoming, he is reluctant to take them in, but aware
of his standing as the village vicar, he knows must protect
his reputation, and allow the children to stay with him.

Esme's relief at finding refuge soon turns to despair
when Gabriel is sent to boarding school, leaving her
alone in their grandfather's unhappy home. But the
house isn't as empty as it first appeared and Esme, with
her unusual gift of being able to see spirits, begins to
encounter the ghosts of young women in the abandoned
rooms and dark corridors of the rectory. The women are
trapped between this world and the next, seeking help
from Esme and leaving her with a mystery to solve if she
is to stand a chance of establishing a peaceful, happy life.

**Can Esme lay the ghosts to rest to save herself and
find the life she deserves?**

Chapter One

Nottingham, November 1875

'Is there any sign of your dadda, Gabriel?' the woman lying on the bed muttered feverishly.

The young boy beside her mopped her forehead and shook his head sadly. 'Not yet, Mammy, but he's sure to be back soon.'

She sighed. He had been telling her the same thing for weeks. In the meantime, they had been surviving on the scraps of food Gabriel could buy with the little he earned doing any jobs he could find. But now all hope of her husband ever returning was fast fading, and Constance knew that she was too.

The old vardo she lay in had been the only home either Gabriel or his younger sister Esmeralda had ever known, but since Django, their father, had left some months ago, hoping to trade in their old horse for a slightly younger one, they'd had had no way of moving it. Instead they had been forced to remain on a piece of common on the outskirts of Nottingham. When Django had left, the gold hoop in his ear glittering in the sunshine and a gaudy neckerchief tied beneath his chin, he had promised to return as soon as he could, but there had been no sign of him and Constance feared for his safety. There was no way he would have left them otherwise.

Added to her worry about her beloved man, Constance now also feared what was to become of her children when she passed. Her cough had worsened as the winter had progressed until she had been forced to take to her bed. Now she could barely raise her head from the pillow and she sensed that her end was near. At first, she had managed to hide the blood she coughed up from the children, but it had become impossible to do so, and her heart broke at the fear she could see in their eyes.

'D-don't be frightened, my loves,' she said breathlessly. 'We shall be fine.'

Esmeralda blinked back tears. At thirteen years old she was dainty and petite with big blue eyes and hair the colour of spun silver, much like her mother's, whilst Gabriel, at fifteen, looked like his gypsy father, with hair as black as coal and grey eyes.

'B-but how can we be all right, Mammy?' Esmeralda, affectionately known as Esme, whimpered. 'We've only a few pennies left in the jug an' there's barely any coal for the stove.'

'Don't get worrying about that,' Gabriel said with a confidence he was far from feeling. 'I'm bound to find some odd jobs soon, an' I can go an' collect some logs for the stove from the woods, so we won't freeze. An' I can go an' snare some rabbits, so we won't starve either, I promise you.'

Since his father had left, he had proudly taken on the role of the man of the house but now he felt that he was letting his sister and his mother down dismally.

Even so, Esme brightened instantly. She idolised her big brother and believed every word he said. Unlike her, he was tall for his age so he looked older than his years, but it broke Constance's heart to see him have to shoulder the responsibility for them when he was still just a boy

Gabriel turned and passed the small tin bowl of water to Esme telling her, 'Come on, lass, you come an' sponge Mammy's head an' I'll go an' get those logs now. Then tonight we can warm up that bit o' stew that's left from yesterday, an' wi' the stove goin' we'll be as snug as a bug in a rug.'

The vardo was a lovely place to live in the summer months when Esme and Gabriel would often sleep out-side beneath it, but they all knew that should they ever not be able to feed the stove, they would all freeze to death in the winter.

'But I reckon it's startin' to snow,' Esme told him anx-iously as she glanced towards the tiny window.

Gabriel laughed as he shrugged into his warm jersey. 'So what? A bit o' snow never hurt anyone.' He grinned at her then disappeared out of the door as Esme turned her attention back to her mother.

Very soon Constance slipped into an uneasy doze and Esme climbed onto the bed and joined her. When Constance woke some minutes later, Esme was fast asleep and gently snoring. Snuggling into the warm little body, Constance let her mind slip back in time to when she had first met Django, the love of her life.

Her first sight of him had come one evening as she walked home from church with her father, who was the vicar of St Thomas's Church on the east coast. The vardo had been parked close to the rectory where she lived with her father and his housekeeper, and as they passed, Django had smiled and given her a cheeky wink. Her heart was instantly lost to him and she had blushed prettily. Unfortunately, the smile was not missed by her strict father and it earned her a severe beating when they got home. But that was nothing new – she was used to it and it did nothing to erase the thought of the handsome stranger's sunny smile.

During the following weeks, Constance had slipped out to meet Django every chance she got until one evening she had arrived home to find her father waiting for her with his belt in his hand and a murderous expression on his face.

'You *devil's spawn*,' he'd growled. 'Do you deny that you have been to see that . . . that gypsy *scum*?'

For the first time in her life Constance stared back at him rebelliously. 'Yes, I have as it happens, Father. Though he is far from scum. Django works hard every chance he gets!'

With a roar her father had set about her and by the time the housekeeper came running after hearing her screams, Constance's back was livid with angry bloody wheals.

'Stop it, sir! You'll kill her!'

Breathless, he'd stood back to stare down at his daughter then he'd thrown down the bloodied belt and stormed from the room leaving the old housekeeper to kneel beside the girl.

'I-I'm going . . . this very night, Nellie,' Constance had whispered through swollen lips. 'If I don't, he'll kill me.'

The woman had nodded in understanding, tears sliding down her cheeks.

A few hours later, when her father was in bed and she was able to stand again, Constance had packed her bag and left to begin her new life with Django, and she had never returned. Despite the fact that they had little in the way of material things they had been deliriously happy. Wherever they were Django could turn his hand to any job that needed doing and when the children came along, he had been devoted to his family, and Constance knew that he would never have deserted them voluntarily. Something must have happened to him. But now her most pressing concerns were for her children. What would happen to them when she passed over? Where would they go?

Sometime later, Gabriel returned with a full sack of logs and as he fed them into the stove and the temperature in the little vardo rose, Esme warmed up the stew and divided it into three dishes.

'My loves . . .' Constance gasped as fear gripped her. 'I-if anything should happen to me you must look in my special tin . . . Inside you will find the address of someone who will help you – your grandfather.' The children would never know what it cost her to tell them to go to him, but she was terrified at the thought of what might become of them. She could only pray that the passage of time might have softened the man who had made her life a living hell. Because what other option did she have? It was either send them to him or the workhouse and she couldn't bear the thought of them being incarcerated in that God-forsaken place.

'Don't talk like that, Mammy,' Gabriel answered with a catch in his voice. 'You'll be well again soon. You'll see, when we get the winter over with, you'll feel better.'

Constance wished with all her heart that what he was saying could be true but deep down she knew it wouldn't be and looking towards them she gasped, 'I love you . . .'

'We love you too,' the children answered in unison as she fell into a deep sleep.

Esme and Gabriel exchanged a worried glance then Esme placed her mother's stew on the top of the stove to keep warm while she and her brother ate theirs.

It was over an hour later when the two children became concerned about how quiet she was. Usually, even when she was asleep, they could hear her laboured breathing but now there was nothing but silence. Suddenly the sound of an owl twit-twooing in the treetops outside reached them and a cold finger traced its way up Esme's spine as she looked fearfully at her brother. Her father had always told them that an owl's cry was the harbinger of death.

'Mammy!' Esme nervously approached her mother and tentatively shook her arm. When there was no response she stared at her brother in panic. 'I-I can't wake her, Gab!'

He hurried to her side and he too gently called out to her and squeezed her hand. When there was still no response, he stood up and said fearfully, 'Fetch me a mirror, Esme.'

She was back in seconds and she watched in horror as he held the mirror in front of his mother's lips before saying brokenly, 'I-I'm afraid she's gone, Esme.'

'*No, no* she can't have!' Esme shook her head in denial, and yet deep down, as young as she was, she knew that he was telling the truth. The gentle, affectionate mother they had both loved was dead, and in her place was an empty shell.

·MEMORY LANE·

The next hour passed in a blur as they clung together seeking comfort from each other, but eventually Esme asked, 'What shall we do now, Gabriel?'

Gabriel took a deep breath and noisily blew his nose, then sitting up he took control. 'First of all, we must open the door to set her spirit free.'

Esme silently opened the little door and they shivered as the cold air rushed in until Gabriel nodded at her to close it again.

'Now fetch Mammy's private tin,' he said quietly. 'She told me that our grandfather's address was in there, and he would help us.'

Constance's precious biscuit tin was the only possession she had owned that they had never been allowed access to, but now they had her permission to look inside it. Gabriel gently removed the lid to find a number of letters tied with a red ribbon addressed to their father.

'These must be what Mammy wrote to Dadda before they were married,' Esme whispered reverently. 'Though why she bothered I don't know. Dadda could neither read nor write.'

'I suppose she would have read them to him,' Gabriel answered as he delved beneath them. And there he found another two letters, but this time they were addressed to Reverend Septimus Silver, The Rectory, Crook Bank, Theddlethorpe, Lincolnshire. Gabriel knew that this was a long way away, at least eighty miles, he assumed.

'This must be our grandfather,' Gabriel said. The only thing their mother had ever told them about him was that he was a vicar, but she had always refused to speak of him or her childhood if questioned. 'I wonder why she never posted them? And I wonder if we have a grandmother?' Gabriel mused. He could never remember one being mentioned.

Esme was still silently sobbing and Gabriel placed his arm about her. It was up to him now to care for his sister and his mind was working overtime. Beneath the letters were a few precious pennies that Constance had always kept as an emergency fund, but they wouldn't get them far.

'Is there enough there to pay for a funeral?' Esme asked in a small voice.

Gabriel shook his head. 'We'll set fire to the vardo with Mammy inside it and do it the way our dadda would have wanted us to,' he said decisively. 'And then we're going to set off to find our grandfather. He won't turn us away in the dead of winter, surely? But tonight, we'll try to get some rest, eh?' He gently pulled the thin blanket across his mammy's beloved face and he and Esme cuddled together for the last night in their home, such as it was.

Early the next morning they stood and gazed about their little dwelling. Gip, the small mongrel who had been their constant companion and who was older than either of them, pressed into Gabriel's side as his young master absently stroked his long silky ears. The children took in the pretty flowered curtains that their mother had stitched to hang at the tiny window, and the horse brasses that were polished to a mirror-like shine. Constance had always taken such a pride in them and it hurt them both to know they would never hear her singing gaily as she cleaned them again.

'Come on, lass.' Gabriel's' voice was choked as they each placed a final kiss on their mother's face. 'There's no sense in delayin'; it's time we was on our way.'

Esme stepped out into the biting cold as Gabriel sprinkled the last of the paraffin they used to light the lamps about the gaily painted vardo. He then joined his sister outside and struck a match and watched, tears pouring down their cheeks, as their childhood home disappeared behind a wall of fire.

'Goodbye, Mammy,' Esme whispered as the flames licked into the leaden sky. And then she saw it: a white shape floating from the roof and disappearing up into the grey clouds.

From as far back as she could remember Esme had been able to see spirits. Her mother had called it a gift. Her grandmother Griselda had had it too, although she had died when Esme was still quite young.

Then Gabriel took her hand and, squeezing it gently, they turned and, with Gip at their heels, began their long journey to find the grandfather they had never met.

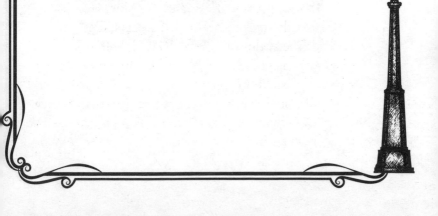

· MEMORY LANE ·

The Days of the Week Collection

Have you read Rosie's collection of novels inspired by the 'Days of the week' Victorian rhyme?

  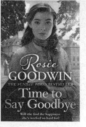

Available now

The Precious Stones Collection

If you liked Saffie's story, get to know
Opal, Pearl, Ruby, Emerald and Amber in
the rest of the Precious Stones series.

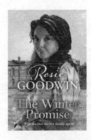  

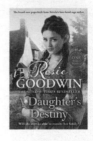  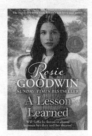

Available now